Sleeping Dogs

Also by Tony Vanderwarker

Writing With The Master

Forthcoming

Ads For God

Say Something Funny

Sleeping Dogs

Tony Vanderwarker

AuthorsPress Publishing
Charlottesville, VA

Published by

AuthorsPress Publishing, LLC
Charlottesville, VA

Printed in the United States of America
Cover design, Heidbreder / Seedhouse
Text and cover, Mayapriya Long, Bookwrights.com

ISBN 978-1-940857-03-9

To John, my mentor and muse

[Acknowledgments]

When I pitched the idea for *Sleeping Dogs* to John in 2004, he immediately went for it. Eight years later, he's kept the faith and it has been his constant support that has kept me going and enabled me to realize this novel. Along the way, he's prodded me to jack up the quality of the dialogue, cut mercilessly to keep the story spare and engaging and flesh out the middle without padding or wandering off-plot. For the experience and invaluable counsel, I am indebted to him.

No writer can gut through the challenges, hurdles and inevitable pits of quicksand involved in creating a novel without a best friend, shoulder to cry on and whipping boy. Being married to a writer is a special curse I wouldn't wish on anyone. But my dear wife Anne has persevered twenty years of enduring the highs and lows without losing her equanimity, patience or sense of humor. I couldn't have done it without her.

And to my guys, Joe, Bruce, Bob, Tom and Dan, always there when I needed them to provide both cold splashes of reality and heartfelt encouragement.

1

[In flight over Massachusetts, August 14, 1958]

Anyone would say it was too nice a day for bad things to happen. Bright sun, blue sky, puffy clouds. Routine mission—if anything was ever routine piloting a B-52 on its way to a rendezvous over Russia.

"Climbing to ten thousand feet," Risstup answers the controller.

"Roger, climbing to ten thousand," he hears. Risstup liked to explain to friends it was more like driving an eighteen-wheeler than flying a plane. Over fifty yards long, three stories high and capable of lugging thirty-five tons of nukes through the skies, the B-52 was a beast. Risstup loved to regale his buddies with his flyboy stories, always finishing up with, "And you know what its nickname is?"

A dramatic pause and then, "Buff—B-U-F-F—and that stands for big, ugly, fat..."

Not missing a beat, his friends immediately chorused out the answer and Risstup reveled in the chortling and manly grabass that followed.

Always amazed him that the damn thing got off the ground in the first place, up until the last feet of runway the huge wheel trucks lumbered on, weighing the plane down like ten-foot-tall wet boots, until finally in the last few seconds when there was precious little runway left the wings bulled the wheels into the air.

Risstup sits silently next to the pilot as the Connecticut countryside floods by two miles below. Even though Horton's a chatterbox, there wasn't enough small talk on the planet to fill up twenty-two hours of flying time. A blueblood know-it-all born with a silver spoon in his mouth, Horton was an okay pilot but to hear him tell it, he should have won the Distinguished Flying Cross years ago. His kick-off topic was always a bunch of sports babble followed by his latest sexual exploits. Risstup had been showered by the same blather at least twenty times. Just as they're passing over Long Island, Horton starts to air his gums.

"So tell me, Major, whaddya think the Giants' chances are?"

"I've got my fingers crossed, sir. The way Conerly's passing and Gifford and Webster have been running I'd say their chances look pretty damn good."

"They've led us down the primrose path before..."

"Tell me about it." Prudish by nature and desperately wanting to avoid the inevitable blow-by-blow about the last covey of dames Horton's bedded, Risstup flicks on his radar to check the weather.

"Wind from the east at twenty-four knots," they'd heard from the briefer at the pre-flight, followed by the alarming, "Possible thunderstorms around coastal areas, some may be severe."

With a max ceiling of fifty thousand feet, Risstup's confident they can cruise over practically anything. But since they fly the pants off these babies to keep the Russkis scared shitless that we'll annihilate them, lurking in the back of pilots' minds is the nightmare of structural fatigue.

B-52s have been known to fall apart in mid-air, one weld out of thousands giving way, or a single rivet popping and a string of others following, huge gashes renting the skin and instantly making the plane unflyable. Pilots didn't talk about it because the prospect was unpredictable, like cancer or a sudden stroke. But they thought about it. Particularly since they were carrying live nukes on board. So when it came to pushing the plane too far, it paid to be cautious.

Even though he's seen everything in his thirteen years in the Air Force, what he next sees on the screen gives Risstup the willies. Barreling along at six hundred mph, they're heading into a squall line that's building before his eyes. Seemingly up out of nowhere, the radar image oozes like green slime across the screen.

Risstup shakes his head and grumbles.

"What's the matter?"

Risstup runs his finger around the outlines of the storm, a noose that's quickly tightening around them.

Never at a loss for words, this time "Shit" is all Horton can come up with.

Tilting his mike up, he tells the crew, "Boys, looks like piss-your-pants weather coming up, gonna be a wild ride for a while here. See you all on the other side."

Just then all hell breaks loose. Like someone flicked the lights off, the sky goes from gray to black and the B-52 starts to rock'n roll.

"Let's get this puppy up," Horton shouts, hooking his arms on either side of the stick and straining to lever it back. But the damn plane is slamming into air pockets that fling it down so fast all Horton's efforts are futile, the altimeter spins crazily, the pitching and yawing creating all kinds of ominous sounds Risstup's never heard before, pieces of metal not liking each other, animal-like groaning punctuated with screaming shrieks as the fuselage comes close to its breaking point.

It's only three in the afternoon but it seems like midnight with lightning crackling around, bolts exploding like they're in the very center of a Fourth of July fireworks display. Horton's screaming, trying to raise Westover on the radio but there's no talking in this pandemonium. The plane's taking a real shellacking, like a crazy roller coaster ride going up, up, up and then getting punched back down, both pilots rag-dolled around. Horton walloped so hard there's blood dripping down his chin, Risstup guesses from chomping on his tongue.

No secret to either pilot that unless the storm lets up, this baby isn't making it. The instruments pop and sizzle, fried by the lightning. They're not even flying the plane anymore, the storm's taken over. Only a matter of time, Risstup's thinking, either we break through the weather or she comes apart at the seams.

Standing orders are to jettison the nukes over deep water in case of an accident. But the instruments are useless, the radar screen black, no knowing where they are now. He screams for orders about the weapons. Of course Horton can't hear.

More crashing and cracking, then a tremendous roar, a lion two inches from your ear. Like the aircraft had taken a huge punch to the belly and the plane begins a slow lean into a right bank like the wing's ripped off. Then a screaming sound, turning into a deafening whistle. *Part of the fuselage is gone and that's the ball game,* Risstup thinks, jerking the lever to jettison, feeling the lurch as four tons of nuke departs the plane.

Just before everything goes black.

2

[NEW BRUNSWICK, NEW JERSEY, MONDAY AFTERNOON, OCTOBER 23, 2002]

He set a perfect trap for her. But he was the one who ended up falling into it. Which is what he intended all along.

"I just want to talk, that's all," the coed with the spare tire and four hundred dollar shoes said to him.

"I told you, I don't have time." He was almost double-timing across the quad and she was falling behind, he could hear her panting. This was the fifth time he'd stonewalled her in the past two weeks. Sooner or later she'd catch his drift.

"C'mon, I'll buy you coffee?" she pleaded over his shoulder. Except for a few hayseeds who'd go out with anyone, she's having no luck finding a date for the sorority party. And she wanted desperately to prove she could bag a boy.

"I don't drink coffee."

"How about a smoothie, then?"

"No, thank you, but no."

"I've seen you working out over at Werblin."

"What?" Her comment stopped him. He was sure he was off everyone's radar but why was she bringing his workouts up?

"Actually, maybe I would like a latte..." he said, turning toward her and amping up his brightest smile.

His beaming face made her spine tingle. "There's a Starbucks in the student center and I'm buying."

"My name's Mehran," he said, "Mehran Zarif."

"I know," she said, "I know everything about you. Your nickname's Denny, you're from Iran, you study engineering, you're a big swimmer and there's one more thing," she said, trying like hell to act coy so it didn't come across as a bald come-on, which of course it was.

"What's that?'

"You're cute as hell."

"Stop," he said, "I'm not going there, okay?" And Mehran put enough edge into his voice so she'd get the message.

She blushed. She'd never been good at coming on to guys and now she'd been caught again. *But he was so cute and his skin was to die for. Mocha colored, just like the latte she carried over to the table where he was sitting.*

"Thanks," Mehran said as she set the coffee down in front of him and joined him at the table.

"No problema," Melanie said, trying to conjure up the smile she'd practiced a million times in front of a mirror. Despite the thousands her parents had spent on her face, it was still a mess from her bouts with adolescence.

"Funny, but I've never seen you at Werblin." He needed to poke around the edges just to make sure she wasn't onto something.

"I don't go over there half enough, doctor says I need to do an hour a day but I can't stand it."

"It's the only way I can get through my studies."

"But isn't your country mostly desert?"

"Ever heard of the Persian Gulf or the Caspian Sea? Half of Iran is surrounded by water. I've been swimming since I was this high," he said, holding his hand just below the table.

"Ooops, my bad."

"So I swim to how do you say it, reduce the edge?" He knew what the expression was, just wanted to act like a language-impaired foreign student.

"Take the edge off, I think you mean," she corrected him, hiking up her skirt just a touch above her knee to show off her legs, which were nice. At least she had a few assets, nothing like her sorority sisters who were all size 6 blonde goddesses with perfect figures, deep tans and little turned-up noses their daddies bought for them.

"Look, I'm sorry, but I really must go," Mehran said, quickly standing, shooting a quick glance down at her exposed knee and frowning ever so slightly so she'd get the idea it wasn't where he wanted to go. "Thank you so much for the coffee."

"Bye, Denny," she said, almost wanting to pull her skirt back down but figuring, *what the hell, I've blown it anyway. He's probably Muslim and thinks I should be wearing one of those black towels over my head.*

As much as she tried to run into him on campus, she only caught him once or twice out of the corner of her eye and only one time was she even able to get the slightest wave out of him. So she gave up on Denny, the Iranian swimmer and engineering student, went to the sorority party by herself and kept herself gratified with Internet porn and her little pink machine with the amazing fingers.

So she was shocked when she opened her email two weeks later and saw the message from Mehran Zarif with the attachment. And she almost fell off her chair when she opened the picture of the beautifully muscled young man standing poolside wearing a wide smile on his face and a Spandex swimsuit that left little to the imagination. *So he's huge or he's hard,* Melanie thought to herself. *Either way I can't wait to get my hands on him.*

3

[University of Virginia, Charlottesville, Virginia, the Monday before Thanksgiving]

Odd, Collyer thinks as he crosses the campus, *how your heart can bring you back even though your head's not in it.* It was ten years since he'd been on Grounds but as he walks down the well-worn path, bits and pieces of memories from the past elbow their way into his brain. Bonfires blazing up and down the long, grassy courtyard as the ragtag pep band played the school's fight song and the team carried him into the victory celebration on their shoulders.

He pauses halfway across the Lawn, stopping to look up at the arching trees for a few moments, then lets his eyes wander along the portico toward the magnificent Rotunda at the far end.

The celebration lasted well into the morning with some diehard fans blearily greeting the dawn. Collyer's apartment was wall to wall with his frat buddies and teammates lying around on sleeping bags and blankets, great heaps of beer bottles accumulating in the corners, everyone determined to continue savoring the incredible victory. Howie finally had to curl up in a closet and pull the door shut to get some sleep.

He was the most unlikely hero and his kick was a miraculous fluke. But having had only a handful of victories in the past ten years, to the students at the University of Virginia this win was as sweet as they come. And they all knew they had one member of the team, Howie Collyer, to thank for it.

Virginia football fans quickly forgot the field goals Howie had missed that fall. As dependable and consistent as he was his first three seasons, in his senior year he choked, twice failing to bail the team out of a loss, and talk around campus was that the coach was seriously considering shifting a backup quarterback who had kicked in high school to replace him. So the pressure was on as Howie loped out onto the field that day, snapping his chinstrap, listening to the roar of the crowd and praying his right foot would come through for him.

Howie didn't disappoint.

As the crowd went silent, the ball caromed off the inside of the left upright and milliseconds later, while thirty-seven thousand fans held their collective breath, some say a puff of wind, some the hand of God, but some force partial to the Virginia Cavaliers intervened to nudge the ball slightly east so it dropped like a stone into the end zone, winning the game for UVa, salvaging the team's season with a win over a nationally ranked opponent and earning Howie an immediate and permanent place in UVa athletic lore.

His amazing kick was memorialized with the nickname bestowed on him by a sportswriter for the local rag, *The Boot*, a handle that has stuck to Howie throughout the almost four decades since his graduation. Howie never took his achievement that seriously for he knew that if the pigskin had tumbled one inch the other way, he would have been no more than another face in a yellowing team picture on the walls of Mem Gym. And he realized his kick paled in comparison to the achievements of other Virginia football greats and would have been a minor footnote had it not been the one bright spot in an otherwise abysmal season.

Howie's ability to laugh at his good fortune and to put his achievement in perspective enabled everyone who met him to share in the extraordinary event and somehow over time added to the kick's luster.

"With Lady Luck smiling on you the way she was on me that day, anyone could have made that kick," Howie was fond of saying. And since it was close to the truth, Howie greased the skids of a successful career with his feat, had more than a few free drinks slid his way and in his younger years found the kick to be an easy conversation starter with any young thing who happened to know a thing or two about UVa football.

"You aren't The Boot, are you?" a chick meeting Howie for the first time would exclaim, and Howie's "aw shucks" manner, boyish mop of auburn hair, bright green eyes and ingratiating manner would soon have the tantalized woman falling all over him.

The last thing Howard Collyer wants to do a couple days before Thanksgiving is lecture a bunch of students halfway out the door for the holiday about lost H-bombs. But Drummond's an old friend and he'd committed months ago. Heading down the columned walkway, he sees a delightful-looking young lady standing at the end waiting as he approaches. Howie has to squint to make sure his vision isn't playing tricks on him. Drummond told him he would have a student waiting to guide him through the maze of corridors to the classroom. *With any luck,* Howie's hoping, *this lovely thing is my escort.*

"Hi—Mr. Collyer?" Tall, blond and marvelously constructed, the Virginia coed wears a white button-down and the shortest kilt Howie has ever seen, leaving his imagination little to fill in. Not only is her skin perfect but the top two buttons of her blouse are undone. Howie wonders if she can tell he's about to start drooling. Hand outstretched, gracious smile, she radiates the kind of fresh beauty matched with a blooming sexuality that makes older men curse their age. Howie nods as he shakes her hand, all the while struggling to maintain eye contact.

"Hi, I'm Bridget, Bridget Heard. Welcome to the University of Virginia. We are honored to have you lecturing to us, Mr. Collyer," she says as she half turns and scoots sideways, leading Howie through a doorway and down a corridor. Her legs are tanned and perfect, the hem of her mini-kilt swishes and swings tantalizingly, and Howie brings himself to say the only words he can think of at this point in time.

Clearing his throat to keep his voice from breaking, he asks, "So what year are you, Bridget?"

Bridget whirls around, flashing Howie a radiant smile. Again Howie fights to keep his gaze from dropping to the gaping placket of her blouse that's inviting his eyes in. Song lyrics run through his mind, something about what makes a grown man cry.

"I'm a third year, a junior," Bridget says in a Deep South drawl that comes out as *june-yeah.* "I'm so excited to hear what you have to say because I don't have the slightest idea of what I want to do when I graduate. But I've been thinking of government so like I said, I'm really interested in seeing your presentation. And if it's as good as I think it will be, it might just help me make up my mind, which would be a big help to me at this point in time." As cute as she is, she's cursed with the undergrad yap disease, prattling on incessantly about whatever. Fortunately, Bridget stops at a doorway, stands aside for Howie and motions him inside.

Peeking over her shoulder at the hall full of students, Howie's kicking himself for accepting Drummond's invitation. Lecturing to civic groups and garden clubs was cutting butter compared to a roomful of distracted twentysomethings. In addition, Thanksgiving break is right around the corner and if they are anything like Howie was back then, he knows the students are already smelling the barn.

Drummond saunters up, looking tweedy as ever, an invisible fog of pipe tobacco hovering around him, "Boot, good to see you," he says in a low voice, wanting to acknowledge their personal relationship while keeping his students from overhearing a tenured professor stoop to using a nickname originating from a crass sporting event.

"Class, I'd like to introduce Howard Collyer." A few of the students nod, many look like they've just tumbled out of bed, their eyes at half mast even thought it's almost eleven in the morning. Some wear earbuds, their skinny white cords snaking down their chests like strands of spaghetti. All are splayed helter-skelter in their seats, arms and legs scattered every which way, as if it's an imposition to sit up straight. Howie knows he's going to have to work hard to earn his honorarium—two seats in the president's box for the Florida State game.

"Give me a few minutes to set up, Henry." Howie leans down and begins to unpack his audio-visual materials.

"Can I be of any help, Mr. Collyer?" Bridget offers.

"Sure," Howie says, handing her his laptop, "usually goes together pretty easy."

"I'll see if I can set the stage for you, Howie," Drummond says. "How long before you'll be ready?"

"Two, two and a half minutes if we're lucky," Howie says as he opens his case and slides out the projector.

Drummond turns to the class. "While Mr. Collyer is setting up, let me roughly sketch the frame for the picture that he will draw for us."

He winds up and goes into a brief overview of the Cold War as Howie and Bridget fuss with the tangle of cables, an octopus of rubber and jangling metal connectors. Fortunately, Bridget is a technological wizard, keeps her lip zipped and makes short work of it, connecting Howie's laptop and helping him set up the projector on a nearby table so that in no time his Windows desktop flashes up on the screen.

"You're good to go, Mr. Collyer," Bridget says, giving him another radiant smile. Howie has to fight the temptation to say, "Call me Howie," instead he limits himself to a quick, "Thanks very much, Bridget," as he takes his place. He clips through the few setup slides to get to his starting point.

"So without further ado, I'd like to introduce you to Mr. Howard Collyer, a veteran Pentagon weapons specialist and our guest lecturer for Poli Sci 123."

"Thank you for having me, Professor Drummond. And thanks to my friend Bridget here who helped me get all my equipment together." Howie has saved a special smile for her.

Howie pauses to straighten up and furrow his brows, drops his voice a register, leans forward and delivers a shot across the bow of his sleepy audience.

"I'm going to take you back to a dark time in this nation's history and show you things that are shocking and horrifying. But I hope you will put your revulsion and anguish to work. Because since our generation has turned its back on the problem, your generation has to step up. For your own sake. And for the good of the entire world."

Howard Collyer taps the keyboard, flashing the first slide on the screen above his head. In the eighteen months since he was forced out of the Pentagon, he has culled the slides intended for a military audience, only keeping those that play for civilians. The garden club ladies always gasp out loud at the destruction of Hiroshima and Nagasaki. Most of the students are still snoozing though Howie sees some stirring here and there, a few sitting up, starting to pay attention.

The facial disfigurations of the men and women wandering helplessly through the smoking ruins of the Japanese city widen their eyes. Horrible scarring, lacerated and mutilated bodies, charred limbs and always somewhere in the picture the haunting face of a dazed child. Howie moves rapidly through the Army Medical Corps closeups as he recites the statistics of the destruction. Forty-five thousand Japanese men, women and children incinerated in the first few seconds. Thousands more so permanently affected by the radiation that their lives were no longer worth living.

In the twenty lectures he has given since he left the Pentagon, Howie has seen the power of his presentation. He's watched the garden clubbers' eyes tear up and the Rotarians quietly shake their heads. This audience is still half asleep but he begins to see students nudging each other, pointing at the slides projected over their heads. Born forty years after the cataclysmic events, though they might have read about Hiroshima and Nagasaki in history books, never has the raw truth of the devastation and the shocking human toll been so graphically presented to them.

Howie pauses to let his message sink in. Bridget is sitting in the first row, off to the side of the lectern. Her hand is clasped over her mouth and her eyes are reddening. She looks like she's ready to pop someone in the nose.

He continues paging through his presentation, through the slides of Little Boy, the clumsy-looking, brutish black bomb that wreaked the devastation on Hiroshima, and the photos of the early generation of nukes, some sleek and skinny, others bulbous, ungainly green and brown barrels resting on steel and wood gantries, looking more like medieval siege cannons than weapons capable of obliterating an entire city, vaporizing millions and irradiating hundreds of thousands more. Howie talks about the absurdly suicidal Cold War policy of Mutually Assured Destruction—its acronym, MAD, accurately characterizing a policy of each side having enough nuclear weapons to wipe the other off the face of the earth.

Indignation spreads across the faces in his audience. Even the students who were half in dreamland when he started are now wide awake, a number of them busily jotting down notes. Howie brings up a list of the atomic bombs produced in the United States alone. Over seventy thousand nuclear weapons during the past fifty years, many with hundreds of times the force of the Hiroshima bomb.

Now Howie gets to the good part.

After showing slides of B-52 bombers, their crews shoehorned into cramped cockpits and wearing skin-tight high altitude pressure suits covered with tubes and endless rows of lacing making them look like early Russian cosmonauts, he launches into the animated portion of his lecture.

"Imagine how these B-52 crew members felt flying toward targets in Russia, their planes loaded with nuclear weapons, each one capable of causing infinitely more death and destruction than the bombs we dropped on Japan."

His audience is sitting forward. In a couple more minutes, he'll have steam pouring out of their ears.

Howie keystrokes the introduction to Operation Chrome Dome. His video shows a swarm of B-52s taking off from bases all over the country, their flight patterns crisscrossing the country. Soon the map of the U.S. is streaked with yellow lines showing as many as a hundred and fifty B-52s flying round the clock—thousands of missions being flown every week—each lurking around close to the Russian border with at least one nuke in its bomb bay, some two, many three and four. The pilots waiting for the orders to set course for Kiev, Moscow or Vladivostok.

"But fortunately the call never comes," Howie continues. "So the bombers turn around, refuel over Spain and fly back over the pond."

Bridget's hand shoots up in the air. "Were all these bombs armed?" she asks, her voice anxious and concerned.

"Good question—and the answer is *yes*. They had to be because at that time they were our only defense against a Russian attack. Having planes in the air at all times with primed nukes guaranteed we would be able to immediately strike back if Russia launched missiles. Early on, the bombs had crude fuses that would explode on impact. So think of these B-52s as loaded guns, cocked and ready to fire."

"So they were flying armed nuclear weapons over the United States?"

Howie smiles. She couldn't have given him a more perfect setup.

"These airborne alert missions went on for a good ten years, Bridget. From 1958 to '68. And that's not the worst of it."

The girl is half out of her seat she's so angry. Howie sees the opportunity and skips forward, keystroking the command to run the video. Soon the sky is swarming with the gigantic bombers, all armed and streaming toward Russia, zooming out over the audience with their eight Pratt and Whitney jet engines roaring, the students sitting spellbound as the thundering racket echoes around the hall.

"B-52s took off from these bases around the country," Howie says, dialing down the volume as green dots flash on the screen showing the scores of Air Force bases where B-52s were assigned. "All of this activity was highly classified. The Air Force called the flights *training missions* and never admitted that armed nuclear weapons were carried on the planes."

A second student in the back of the lecture hall picks up on the direction Howie's going and wildly waves his hand, blurting out his question before Howie can acknowledge him.

"If there were that many planes in the air at all times as you show, weren't there accidents? Couldn't one or two of these planes have gone down somewhere with nukes on board?"

"I'm glad you asked." Howie clicks a key. Four red flares suddenly flower on the green southern coast of Spain. "On January 17, 1966, a B-52 collided with a tanker aircraft while refueling and both planes plummeted to the ground near Palomares, Spain, with four nuclear weapons aboard."

"We nuked an ally?" the student in the back pipes up.

"Yes, two of the bombs exploded," Howie answers. "Not completely, but the TNT in the other two detonated on impact and scattered radioactivity all over the Spanish landscape, which they are still retrieving today." Howie keystrokes again. "And then two years later, another B-52 crash landed on the polar ice near our Air Force base in Greenland and the explosions melted through the icecap releasing radioactive materials into the ocean."

Another student has become involved, a thin girl with glasses and a pageboy sitting in the front row near Bridget. "How come no one knows about these incidents? Why hasn't more been made of it?"

"I'll get to that. But there's more. A bomber with a nuke aboard crashed in North Africa." Howie's video zooms into the Moroccan base to show the burning aircraft. "One of our planes disappeared somewhere over the Mediterranean with two bombs aboard. We dropped two off the coast of British Columbia and had a scary accident in England where a plane went off the runway and crashed into a storage building housing three nukes and came within a hair's breadth of detonating them."

The students are chattering to each other, connecting the dots, recognizing the nerve-wracking implications. The student sitting next to Bridget sneers, "British Columbia is close enough. I certainly hope they didn't drop any in this country."

Howie winds up, his tone of voice restrained but ominous. "I wish they hadn't."

"You're not going to tell us there are nuclear weapons lying around the United States?" Bridget is perched on the edge of her chair.

"Unfortunately, yes. A bomber came apart in mid-air and we dropped a couple of nukes on a farm in North Carolina. Here's another jettisoned into the swamps off the coast of Georgia after a mid-air crash, two more discharged into the Atlantic somewhere off New Jersey after another aircraft mishap."

His audience cannot believe what they are seeing. Eyes wide and mouths dropped open, the students stare mesmerized at the screen. Howie touches a key and looks over his shoulder at the simulation of a bomb plunging into rural farmland. "This nuke came too close for comfort—at least for a farm family in North Carolina. Accidentally dropped from a B-47, the TNT in the nuke blew a crater seventy feet wide and thirty feet deep, destroying the house and injuring six family members."

"How come all this was never made public?" Bridget asks, on her feet with her hands planted on her hips. "Why didn't someone tell us about this?"

"As I said, the Air Force claims these were training missions with no armed nukes aboard. And you have to remember there was no Internet back then, no CNN—only three networks with the news tightly controlled by the Pentagon. And we were at the height of the Cold War. People were building fallout shelters in their backyards, the Russian nuclear menace was on everyone's mind."

Not bothering to raise his hand, the student in the back row jumps up. "They have certainly recovered all these bombs?" he asks.

"Unfortunately—no."

"Bombs are still out there?"

"Yes."

"How many?"

"Eleven—at last count."

Howie brings up a slide. "Here are the eleven unrecovered nuclear weapons reputable sources believe are scattered around the United States. Could be one as close to you guys as the Chesapeake."

Howie hears gasps from his audience. "If you think I'm kidding, go on the Net and search for yourself, check out my website—sleeping-dogs.us."

The room is dead quiet.

"This is where I need your help. No one in Washington will pay attention to this problem. It happened on someone else's watch almost a half century ago. Many of the generals and admirals in the Pentagon were in diapers when these accidents happened. That's why I call my website *sleeping dogs*. That's the Pentagon's approach, let sleeping dogs lie. I tried for ten years to get them to pay attention to the threat. And didn't do my career any favors as a result."

"Your job was affected by blowing the whistle on these lost nukes?"

"Let's just say they got tired of listening to Howie Collyer and they made me an offer I couldn't refuse. The Pentagon's version of forced retirement."

A young man sitting in the middle of the audience who looks out of place in his pressed white shirt and thin black tie, his hair cropped short, raises his hand, stands and introduces himself, "Mr. Collyer, I'm Martin McFarlane."

"Yes, Martin." Howie had noticed the student scowling and shaking his head, right off the bat Howie chalked him up as a wiseass troublemaker.

"With all due respect, I'd like to point out that these weapons are fifty years old. Maybe they are duds, or buried so far down in the mud they don't pose a threat. I can't believe our government would allow a potential calamity such as you describe to imperil us like that."

"You know, Martin, I had the same reaction. Our government, as you put it, wouldn't put the nation in danger like that. Plus I was working at the Pentagon, I knew a lot of these people, they were my friends. I liked and trusted them. But the more I dug into it, the more I ran into denial and double talk. And over time, I began to get the feeling that no one, particularly at higher levels, wanted to deal with the subject. That's when I decided that they were taking a *let sleeping dogs lie* approach.

And let me ask you a question. If they don't think the bombs are a threat and are better off left alone, why did they spend six months and millions of dollars trying to find the one off Georgia before giving up?"

Howie reaches into his bag for the DVD that's his killshot, the piece of film that inevitably silences those who want to think the government couldn't possibly allow nuclear weapons to lie around on American soil. He slips the DVD into his laptop as McFarlane protests, "Still, sir, I cannot help but think you are exaggerating the threat."

"Okay, but let me run this video of a United States Senate committee meeting on August 3, 1992, and then tell me if I'm exaggerating," Howie says. It's one thing for him to talk about the missing nukes, it's another to have a U.S. senator discussing the problem on film.

"This is Senator J. Bennett Johnston from Louisiana speaking." Howie rolls the grainy color tape of the sixty-year-old Democratic Senator, thin hair graying on the sides, his long face with its pointy chin dipping down to speak into a microphone in a Senate hearing room: "We have been very, very lucky in this country," Senator Johnston says.

The video shows Johnston holding up a report. "I have here a description of thirty-two different nuclear weapons accidents—thirty-two. It makes absolutely fascinating and hair-raising reading to realize how close to absolute disaster we came. There was an accident in Palomares, Spain, where you had the weapon that hit the ground, there was a detonation of the high explosive, it spread plutonium over a very large area. Luckily, it was a rural area. But it spread plutonium over a large area. In Thule, Greenland, the same thing happened. In Alaska, the same thing happened. Perhaps the most hair-raising of all was the accident in North Carolina where a B-52 broke up in flight. Two nuclear weapons were released. One the parachute deployed and was recovered, and the other, the nuclear weapon went down and hit the ground. When the Air Force experts rushed to the North Carolina farm to examine the weapon after the accident, they found that only a single switch prevented the 24 megaton bomb from detonating and spreading fire and destruction over a large area."

"This is public testimony from the United States Senate," Howie continues. "The report goes on to substantiate eleven bombs are still out there. How many more are a switch away from detonating and setting off a nuclear holocaust right here in the United States? Read the report yourself. I have a handout with websites you can go to. And the more you dig into this, the worse it gets. A few of these lost nukes from the early years have primitive fuses. Who knows what could set them off? A fishing boat's trawling net? A hurricane? Or maybe a terrorist finds the one in the Chesapeake, detonates it and obliterates our capital and half of Maryland and Virginia in the process?"

McFarlane raises his chin and snorts. "Excuse me, Mr. Collyer, but all this is pure conjecture and, I believe, a good deal of fabrication on your part."

"Is it, Martin? Or is that what the Pentagon would like you to believe?"

"But these weapons are fifty years old. How could they possibly pose a threat?"

"Fifty years old, yes, but packed with radioactive plutonium, tritium, uranium, beryllium and four hundred pounds of TNT—are they harmless? Something we shouldn't worry about? That is a bet, Martin, that this country cannot afford to take."

McFarlane puffs himself up into a haughty posture and snorts, "In this post 9/11 world, where we are threatened from every side we have to believe in our government—not in half-baked conspiracy theories."

A chorus of hisses and boos rises from his classmates.

"Martin," Howie continues, "if you want to talk about conspiracies, I can give you evidence that there is a secret operation at the Pentagon to suppress information about these unrecovered nukes."

"That's just pure rubbish, Mr. Collyer," McFarlane retorts as jeering and catcalls echo around the room.

"You're certainly welcome to your point of view, Martin. But it's obvious a number of your classmates do not share it."

Drummond stands up to intervene. "I think we've had a fair and full discussion and I don't see the point in debating this further. Please sit down, Mr. McFarlane. Thank you, Howard, that was a provocative and fascinating lecture that I'm sure will have all of us thinking for some time about the threats you have outlined for us."

Howie gets a hearty round of appreciative applause from the students, except for McFarlane, who grumpily collapses into his seat. The rest of the students flock around Howie as he starts to pack up, eagerly taking his handouts and complimenting him on his lecture.

Howie smiles and shakes hands, basking in the flattery.

"Thank you, Mr. Collyer," one student who Howie noticed was sound asleep when he began his lecture gushes, "I'm going to write my congressman and tell him we have to do something about these nukes."

"Great job, Mr. Collyer, thank you for coming."

"I'm glad you're blowing the whistle on the Pentagon, they deserve it."

Howie nods and smiles for fifteen minutes, keeping up a running banter with the fired-up students.

"Thank you, thank you, thank you very much."

"Glad you enjoyed it."

Though he revels in the attention, Howie knows that like the Rotarians and the garden club ladies, once the students return to their routines his cause will take a backseat in their minds. In a few days, the energized and engaged students will be busy stuffing their mouths with mom's turkey. Maybe they will bring up Howie's talk at the dinner table, maybe not. But Howie is accustomed to being dismissed and ignored, as he likes to joke, "I'm much too bullheaded to take it personally."

"Thanks, Boot," Drummond says as he helps Howie load his gear into the backseat of his car. "I think you woke a few of my students up."

"I hope so. Maybe someday one of them will be inclined to do something about it. Take care, Henry. Thanks for having me."

"I'll send you those FSU tickets. Should be a good game."

"You bet. Look forward to seeing you there."

Drummond and Collyer shake hands and BS a bit before Collyer says goodbye, heading around to the driver's side while the professor waves at his old friend and turns back down the path toward the Corner.

Just as Howie leans down to climb in, he hears someone calling his name. Looking back over the top of his car toward the Rotunda, he sees Bridget running down the hill toward him, waving frantically.

"Mr. Collyer, Mr. Collyer!"

Howie smiles. He finds himself wondering whether she is going to ask for an internship. Maybe she wants to volunteer to work with him? He can imagine introducing Bridget to his wife. The eye roll his wife Sylvie would give him would be world-class. Maybe she wants to have lunch with him and discuss the issue? Howie's imagination is running away with him.

"Mr. Collyer," Bridget pants, half out of breath, her face flushed and her chest heaving. Howie can't wait to hear what she has in mind. She pauses a moment to catch her breath.

"I'm glad I caught you."

Howie smiles thinking of the hours they could spend together in his office over the garage. Obviously computer savvy, Bridget could help him update his website, chase down the hundreds of leads sitting in his *To Do* box. The possibilities were endless—and heady.

She rummages around in the pocket of her skirt. Pulling out a short computer cable, she dangles it out to Howie. "You forgot this, Mr. Collyer," she says.

"Oh, yeah, thanks," Collyer says, staring at the foot-long length of cable, hoping he's hiding his disappointment.

"Good talk you gave, sorry about that guy McFarlane. He's always like that."

"No problem. Appreciate your help, Bridget."

"Keep it up—your lectures I mean. I think you're really onto something with this lost bombs thing. I think you should stay with it until somebody listens—at least that's my opinion," Bridget says, flashing a self-conscious smile and shrugging her shoulders. She turns and gives him a girlish back and forth wave as she bounces up the path toward the Lawn. "Bye, Mr. Collyer, thanks for visiting us."

Howie allows himself one last look before he gets into his car and heads home.

4

[Veterans Administration Hospital, Pittsburgh, Wednesday]

"So how we doing today, Major?" she asks, bending over the shriveled form.

For three and a half months, though assigned to another ward, Sharon Thorsen often took a shortcut through 3. He first caught her eye by raising his hand each morning as she walked down the row of beds, giving her a feeble wave and a faint smile. Soon she found herself making it a part of her routine, first waving back, then occasionally pausing to chat with the former Air Force major, and not long afterward visiting with him on a daily basis.

Looking into his eyes it was obvious not many lights were on, yet since her initial visit her nurse's instinct told her someone was home. Brought in off the street a couple years ago, he used to rant and rave about all kinds of stuff before they crammed him full of meds. Senile dementia was the diagnosis and everyone dismissed him as crazy old loon. Now tucked away in a chemical Never Never Land, he came across to Sharon not as demented but as disoriented, frail, lonely and craving company.

Her curiosity about his past had taken her down to the records room in the sub-basement. Sharon always thought the lack of files on him was odd, but she chalked it up to sloppy record keeping, not the first time the massive VA bureaucracy had misplaced something. All that remains in his folder is his last name, not even his first name, plus barebones information—the date he was admitted, rank and serial number, date of birth and a series of yearly diagnoses confirming his dementia and prescriptions for sedatives to control his anxiety.

Random comments he'd made convinced her he shouldn't be written off as a vegetable. Plus, the more time she spent with him, she realized how much he reminded her of her father. His eyes particularly, the same steely gray cast her dad's had. As well as a mannerism, a rolling wave of his hand as if he was physically trying to continue a thought. Just like her dad.

It had been almost seven years since the phone call in the middle of the night and it had occurred to her that spending time with the major was like being with her father. Pop psychology probably, but after chatting him up she always came out of the ward with a big smile on her face.

So when Sharon had the time, she would make a point of sitting down next to him and chitchatting about the local high school football team, her bowling score or the weather forecast for western Pennsylvania, all the while peppering him with questions, hoping another phrase or word would pop out of his mouth.

She'd asked him if he'd ever played any sports and when he said, "Football," she practically fell off the bed. He said the word cautiously, almost a question. But who cared? At least one light was on.

"In college or in high school?" she quizzed him. She was a football brat, her dad had been a coach so she understood the ins and outs of every position, even the fight songs of every major team by heart. As her dad had told her countless times, "If you aren't going to play football, you're going to know every darn thing about it."

"I bet you were a scatback, Major Risstup, one of those speedy little guys who runs circles around everyone. Or a wideout, I can see you running patterns, turning, your eyes guiding the ball into your hands, then tucking it under your arm, turning on the afterburners and going all the way."

Every morning she'd return to the subject, poking and prodding his memory, coming at him from every possible angle. She brought a football in, borrowed a helmet from her dad's former equipment room, but it wasn't until the day she thought to ask him about his school mascot that Sharon rang the bell for a second time.

"So was it an eagle, bulldog, gamecock? How about Spartans, wolverines, maybe tigers?" Sharon asked him. It was a Tuesday, almost three weeks ago. She remembered it well. Without hesitation, the major looked her straight in the eye and answered clearly and distinctly, "Bears."

"Way to go, Major, way to go," she said, leaning down to give him a quick peck on the cheek. "Golden Bears—like at Cal? Or did you play for the real Bears—the pros, the Chicago Bears?"

No answer. His face was a blank slate.

"C'mon, Major Risstup!"

Still nothing.

Then she had a crazy idea. She knew she had the worst voice, even her mother begged her to mouth hymns in church. Leaning down so her lips were five inches from his ear, she hummed "Big C," the California fight song, watching carefully for a reaction. She couldn't believe it when he shook his head, slowly but distinctly, he was telling her *no.*

Next she tried the tune the Chicago Bears had made famous. Again he moved his head back and forth. She was about to give up when she had one more thought.

The Bruins, the UCLA Bruins. She searched her memory for the words. They came to her after a couple seconds, "Sons of Westwood." She knew there was no point in trying to stay on key, she always sounded like an out-of-tune kazoo, but she made up for it with gusto, *Da, da, da, dum, dah—da, da, da, dee da!*

Risstup nodded, the tiniest smile sneaking across his face. *Was he a Bruin? Had he grown up in California?* Now she had a whole new angle to work. The old man in Ward 3 had made her day.

Ever since that moment, Sharon's convinced that Risstup is intent on telling her something crucial. His eyebrows slant down and his forehead bunches up as if he's struggling to find the words. Often he wedges an arm under his body and raises himself up, lifting a finger as if to get her attention. But that's as far as it goes.

Two days ago, she talked the supervising nurse in the ward into backing down Risstup's dose, making the case it wasn't good for his heart. Not tipping her hand, she was hoping that bringing him out of his drugged state might help him reveal what was on his mind.

Since spending Thanksgiving at a girlfriend's house has become an annual ritual, Sharon made a special point of stopping in the day before to visit. She stands by the major's bed, a wide smile spread across her face, trying to get him enthused about the upcoming holiday. "So, Major Risstup, I bet you can't wait to have some of that delicious turkey they're cooking up downstairs. Can't you just smell it? Stuffing, mashed potatoes, cranberry jelly—it'll be a feast, won't it?" she says, taking his bony hand in hers.

Sharon pauses, looking down at him for a response. When she sees a slight grin, she says, "Oh, I know you are just licking your chops, Major. But you're going to have to wait one more day for Thanksgiving."

She neatens up the collar of his gown so he looks more comfortable, "Me, I'm going over to one of my girlfriend's houses for dinner. We're a bunch of old maids but we mix up a batch of mimosas, fire up a big bird and have a good old time. We even get a little rowdy, sometimes put on some records." She leans down and confides to him, "And promise you won't tell? Sometimes we dance. It's silly, I know, but we do have a good time."

She looks into his eyes as she always does, hoping that she'll detect a glimmer of response. From the increasing softness in his expression and the slight widening of his mouth, she keeps up a steady patter sensing she might be getting through. "My girlfriend lives in the country. It's real quiet out there except for the dang roosters. The stupid things wake you up at an ungodly hour. You ought to hear them. They make a horrible racket."

She stops suddenly. He has that same look on his face.

Though she's noted in her last two visits that he seems to be slightly more lucid, his eyes clearer and his vision more focused, Sharon Thorsen is not prepared for what happens next.

Risstup suddenly fumbles for her hand, his fingers searching around in the bedclothes. Finding it, he grips tightly and turns his head to look up at her, a look close to panic in his eyes. She watches in amazement as the eighty-some-year-old man's lips part and he says, slowly and haltingly, his head straining up off the pillow, "You have to help me..."

Sharon immediately ducks her head down close to his mouth and whispers into his ear, "I beg your pardon, Major, help you with what?"

"You have to help me…"

"Yes, Major."

"Bomb..."

"Come again?"

"The bomb. Help me find it."

Sharon looks at him quizzically, "A bomb? What bomb, Major?" Her first reaction is to smile and shake her head, since what she's hearing makes no sense. But Risstup seems so disconcerted she has to take him seriously.

"I don't understand. Where is this bomb?"

"Lost, I lost it, lost it from my plane."

"When? How?"

He shakes his head, frowns, grimaces, memory is on the blink. He looks pained, his features contorting as if he is desperately trying to dredge up the information but is getting only a busy signal. His hand slips out of hers and his head sinks back on the pillow.

"That's okay, Major," she says, patting him on the arm. "Don't you worry yourself about it, we'll try again sometime. You just relax now." Sharon stands beside his bed looking down at him. *What is this lost bomb business?* She's wondering as she finds her eyes wandering over to the security camera overlooking the ward. It slowly pans across the room, its convex lens reflecting the ward in bug-eye miniature. As she stares at it, Sharon swears the camera stops. She can hear the electronic buzz of the lens zooming in on her. She has an urge to reach up and fix her hair.

Am I losing it? She looks away from the camera. Then looks back. It has resumed its slow tracking back and forth across the rows of beds.

I've got to get a grip. She promptly clears her mind of the thought that someone may be watching, deciding her imagination is playing tricks on her.

After a couple minutes, the major's eyelids slowly drift together and Thorsen backs away from his bed, saying softly, "I'll come see you first thing Friday morning, Major Risstup. Now you have a wonderful Thanksgiving, you hear?" Resisting the impulse to look back over her shoulder at the camera, she quickly flings open the swinging doors into the hallway, glancing at her watch and deciding, *I'm going to punch out an hour early, I have some work to do.*

First thing Sharon does when she gets home is to change out of her uniform, throw on jeans and a tee and slip into comfy shoes. Postponing dinner, she pulls out her chair and sits down at her computer. Clicking on the space bar, she waits impatiently for the lame old thing to awaken.

After she left Risstup in his ward, she stopped and wrote down the words he had whispered to her. *You have to help me find the bomb.* And, *I lost it from my plane.* While at work, she kept turning to the page where she had jotted down what he had said, reading and rereading her notes, trying to understand what he was straining to tell her.

Clicking through to the search engine, she types in the words *lost bombs* and taps the search button.

When Google asks, *Do you mean lost H-bombs?* She clicks *yes* and watches wide-eyed as the information pours down the page. Halfway through the list is a website called *Sleepingdogs.us.*

In forty-five minutes, reading everything on the site and checking through its listed links, Sharon now knows more than she needs.

Sorting through what she's learned, she goes to the refrigerator and peers inside. What she sees tells her it's sandwich night. Getting out the fixings, she tracks back over the new information. Eleven nuclear weapons lost during the ten years from '58 to '68. Dropped all over the country from British Columbia to North Carolina. Sharon rapidly does the arithmetic. Risstup would have been in his thirties during the time H-bomb armed B-52s were flying missions.

Standing at the counter, she pauses with the knife plunged halfway into the mayonnaise.

"Damn, it's possible," she says out loud. "He could have been a pilot on one of those things."

Then her good sense prevails. *I'm getting buggy. It's not possible, totally farfetched.* The website and the other sites suggest a conspiracy on the part of the Pentagon to cover up the lost nukes. Then the image of the security camera focusing on her pops into her mind. *Could someone have been watching me?*

She pulls herself together. *I'm normally so sensible and practical, what the hell's going on with me?*

Then she thinks of the major lying helplessly in his bed in Ward 3 and decides—*If anything happened to him I'd feel guilty for the rest of my life.*

Without giving it another thought, she reaches for the telephone and briskly dials a number.

"Hello Sharon, what's up?" her host for Thanksgiving dinner answers.

"Hey, listen, I've got to run into work to check on something. So I'll be a little late, okay?" She listens to Lucy prattle on about dinner getting cold, then cuts her off: "I'll be there, okay? Gotta run, bye." She sets the phone down in the cradle carefully. In the back of her mind is a growing concern about the wizened old man in Ward 3. *Does he really have some secret he's kept hidden all these years? And could someone want to keep him from revealing it? Jesus, how spooky is that?*

Sharon prints out the contents of the *sleepingdogs* website. In the upper corner of the first page is a photograph of the webmaster with his address and phone number, a good-looking fifty-something guy who lives down in Charlottesville. She checks the clock at the top of the screen. *It's too late to call*, deciding to wait until she checks on Risstup in the morning.

After all, in a couple hours it will be Thanksgiving. Her pragmatic nature kicks in. *And it's silly to get all worked up about something that could turn out to be nothing at all.*

5

[New Brunswick, New Jersey, the day before Thanksgiving]

When he sees the curly-haired, dark-skinned student swim his first lap, the coach thinks he's died and gone to heaven.

A couple hours after practice ended in the Werblin Rec Center, the team now high-tailing it for home and turkey day, Johanson is sitting up in the stands finishing up practice notes with no reason to notice the well-muscled young man lowering himself into the pool. But the combination of his unique stroke and kick immediately catches his eye.

It was the most unorthodox style he had ever seen, to say the least, as if the tail of a porpoise had been grafted onto a windmill, his legs double-dolphining in perfect unison to propel his body forward at an incredible speed while his arms churned through the water, accelerating to a pace that Johanson can't believe until he takes out his stopwatch. While his stroke is half crawl, half butterfly and would have been illegal in competition, his times easily rival NCAA records for either event. Adapting his stroke would affect his time but even so Johanson expects the swimmer could have a huge impact on the program.

After finishing his workout, the coach saunters up as the swimmer's toweling off at the end of the pool. He's with a chubby girl wearing a Rutgers sweatshirt over her suit.

As Johanson approaches he says, "Excuse me, but can I ask you where you learned to swim like that?"

"Been swimming since I was a kid."

"Where? If you don't mind me asking."

"Why are you so interested, if you don't mind *me* asking?" the swimmer says.

"Your stroke, I've never seen anything like it. Are you a student here?"

"And you are?" his voice giving the coach the cold shoulder.

Flashing a smile, Johanson extends his hand. "Miles Johanson, assistant coach of the Rutgers swimming team."

"Yeah, hi," the kid says, not impressed.

"And you are?" the coach says, turning to his friend.

"Melanie," she's taking the frosty approach too, not even taking Johanson's hand.

"I'd like to talk to you about trying out for the team," he said, ambling along the pool deck with them. "I think you could start swimming competitively for us in a very short time."

"Thanks, but that does not have interest for me."

"Would you just sit down and meet with our head coach?"

"I'm sorry, I am very loaded down with studies."

"We have a number of dean's list students on the team. They all get their work done."

The student's voice took on a hard edge. "Thank you, I appreciate your interest. But not something I want to do, you understand?"

"Would you consider talking to the head coach—just talking?" Johanson was almost jogging alongside him now.

"I think I've been clear, now, really, we need to go."

Johanson stands watching the two walk down the deck wondering if he had come on too strong. *Or was the kid shy? Maybe he has immigration problems? Or just insecure about his English? And what's with the girlfriend, he's a finely tuned machine and she's a load.*

The coach is not giving up easily. He checks around, finds out his name, talks to his advisor, fellow students. The faculty advisor informs him that Mehran Zarif is a brainy Iranian studying engineering who goes by the nickname Denny and keeps a low profile on campus. Every time Johanson runs into him at the Rec Center, he tries to talk Denny into trying out. But he's never able to get more than two sentences out before he says thank you, always says thank you, smiles, shakes his head and walks away.

Johanson tries having the head coach engage him. No luck. Zarif is polite but has no interest in meeting and stops returning the coach's calls. It soon becomes abundantly clear that the last thing on Denny Zarif's mind is swimming for Rutgers.

Though he gives up trying to talk to him, over the following weeks, the coach can't help remarking on Zarif's activities at the aquatic center. Three days a week and once on weekends, Zarif comes in either at midday during free swim or after varsity practice. Sometimes the girlfriend's with him, sometimes not. When she is, she always seems more interested in playing video games than jumping in and getting some exercise.

The coach's curiosity is piqued by his workout. Starting with an inflated exercise ball, the kid does an incredible series of exercises, a hundred pushups with his feet on the ball, followed by bridges, calf raises, back flies and ab extensions. Then with dumbbells, he went through a series of step-ups on the stands, then wall squats—two exercises having little to do with the muscles used in swimming events. Again, multiple series of each, fifty reps apiece.

When he slips into the pool, he's a machine. Swimming a couple thousand meters a day, many under water. He's ripping along, arms churning, when all of a sudden his head ducks under and his body goes arrow-straight as his powerful double-dolphin kick takes over. His lung capacity is astounding; swimming two hundred meters under the surface in four fifty-meter laps easy as pie. He pops up at the wall, takes a breath and plunges for another two hundred.

When Zarif slides a twenty-pound weight into the diving pool and jumps in to retrieve it, Johansen finally figures out what he's training for and why he has no interest in swimming for Rutgers.

When Zarif wasn't around, the coach tried it. No piece of cake. Busted his lungs bringing it up from the bottom. So why in the world would he bring a barbell plate up fifty times in a row?

It can only be recovering sunken treasure. And all the exercises he's doing make sense for getting in and out of boats, off swim platforms, all that stuff.

Obviously the kid's in training for one of those treasure-hunting expeditions, Johanson's thinking, a company secures the rights to dive a wreck and recover the loot and has to keep it secret until their mission is completed so competitors won't discover the location and raid it in the middle of the night.

That explains why he's acting so standoffish. Must have connections with an international diving outfit and with big money involved, gold coins, bullion, gems—you keep your mouth shut.

One thing for sure about these foreign students is they can act so strange.

6

[Charlottesville, late Thanksgiving afternoon]

"Did I tell you I had a little chat with Drummond when I was at the university?"

"How's my favorite professor doing?" Sylvie asks her husband as she chops a row of carrots on her cutting board. Though Sylvie makes elaborate preparations for Thanksgiving, with their kids and grandchildren joining them, it always turns out to be much more of a production than she anticipates.

"Seems fine, hasn't changed a bit."

"And they liked your presentation? Wait—take out the trash before you answer," Sylvie says, shoving the bulging can toward him with her knee. "The kids will be here in a half an hour and I'm already behind. And besides, you completely ducked the question I asked you a half hour ago. I asked—didn't think you'd talked enough about your lost bombs at our picnic in September?"

Howie stops at the door and turns to her. "Donald's always seemed fascinated with my project," he says, knowing he is sounding defensive.

"You know your children think the world of you, but lost nuclear weapons aren't a subject for the dinner table."

Sylvie Collyer wonders if she isn't being too hard on Howie until she sees he's already wrestling the garbage can out the door. Though his colleagues at the Pentagon often laughed behind his back about his preoccupation, Sylvie has always taken it seriously. To her, there are enough unanswered questions about lost nukes to warrant concern. And the reluctance of the Pentagon brass to deal with the subject creates at least suspicion of a cover-up.

No question Howie's obsession with unrecovered nuclear weapons cut short his career, though no one at the Pentagon would ever own up to it. Once a Pentagon favorite in constant demand for his graphic magic, he soon became a pariah. Too strident, self-righteous and unwilling to listen to reason, his former colleagues sealed him off, avoiding his nods and glances in the hallways.

The handwriting was on the wall—the Pentagon had had it up to here with Howie Collyer. Someone planted classified documents in his desk drawer and reported the infraction. Three times and he was effectively framed and labeled as a security risk. Early retirement was the only option.

Though his pension was measly, Sylvie got lucky with a local dot-com venture, making a bundle before it went belly up. The tiny farm they had bought outside of Charlottesville made for a perfect retirement retreat. With their nest egg, his pension and their Social Security, they have plenty of money to live comfortably, do some traveling and write a few checks to the kids. And they are still young enough to enjoy life around Charlottesville, football games, concerts, lectures and some scrappy doubles games. Howie is playing golf again in a regular foursome and his game is showing signs of the brilliance he'd displayed on the links when he was younger and had a seven handicap.

Sylvie wants him to move on and put all the Pentagon stuff behind him, lost bombs included. *Let bygones be bygones* is one of her favorite sayings.

"Raccoons are at it again," Howie says as he comes back in with the empty can.

"You live in the country, you put up with critters," Sylvie says. "Now you go tidy up your office so Grace will have someplace to put her things."

Howie's christened the space over the garage his "War Room" and every square inch, every nook and cranny is chockablock with maps, charts, photographs and newspaper articles. Each of the eleven lost nukes has its own separate section with a title card above it: "The Jersey Bombs," "St. Lawrence River Bomb," "New Mexico Bomb." Each card notes the date the weapons were lost, the aircraft that carried it, the type of device and the location where the aircraft crashed or the bomb was jettisoned.

Howie stops at the door when Sylvie calls to him, "Before you leave, I need some advice. I'm thinking of making either turnips or rutabagas—which one?" Sylvie stands behind the counter holding up a beige vegetable in one hand, a round brown wax-coated one in the other.

"That's like asking whether I prefer lethal injection or a firing squad."

"Not funny..."

"Okay, I'll take lethal injection," Howie says, pointing at the rutabaga. "Just make sure you add a ton of butter. I can stomach anything as long as it has enough butter in it."

"I'm sorry you feel that way about my rutabaga, I think it's a great recipe," Sylvie says, acting miffed.

"Don't take it personally," Howie says as he walks around the kitchen island to the sink where his wife is standing. In her mid-fifties, Sylvie prides herself on being still attractive, holding back the aging effects of graying hair and gravity with exercise, a careful diet and regular trips to her hairdresser. Howie puts his arms around her waist and gives her a kiss on the neck.

"I'll put in a pound of butter as long as you promise not to talk about lost bombs."

"No lost bombs, it's a deal."

Howie manages to finish cleaning up just as the first load of guests pulls into the driveway. He stands at the window watching Bridey and Donald's minivan circle the drive before hurrying downstairs to greet them.

"Happy Thanksgiving!" Howie's daughter-in-law squeals as she bursts through the door. An elementary school teacher who had ambitions of being an actress, Bridey cradles her latest production, a Rubenesque baby girl with rosy cheeks and a curly wisp of blonde hair dangling down her forehead. Jasmine is Bridey's third, the other two come bounding in the door behind her followed by their father, Donald—Howie's oldest, thirty-four and a philosophy professor at a local community college.

"Hey, everybody! Happy Thanksgiving," Howie says, heading for the mob flocking in the door. Howie high-fives and low-fives Jock and Richie, one four, the other six, as they race into the kitchen. Both are irrepressible hellions, much to their grandfather's delight. They jump and leap over Howie like a couple puppies, squealing and squawking while Howie hoists them up, swinging them in whirling orbits to the consternation of their mother and grandmother.

"Put the boys down before you hurt them," Sylvie chides as she watches her two grandsons circling through the air.

Bridey holds Jasmine up for her grandmother.

"She gets more beautiful every time I see her," Sylvie says, taking the baby in her arms. "Honestly, I bet this child could make a fortune modeling."

With both grandsons hanging off his legs, Howie struggles over to Donald like he's running a three-legged race and throws his arms around him.

"Good to see you, Dad," Donald says. Howie and Donald couldn't have been further apart. An affable ex-jock who could charm the pants off the stiffest flag officers in the Pentagon, Howie's son Donald is an academic who acts like he is carrying the weight of the world. Plus he's slim and anemic-looking with a permanent case of bedhead and no interest in his appearance. The family speculates that Donald looks and acts the way he does since his father had, in their words, *taken up all the air in the room*, when Donald was growing up. But Donald's made his own mark, his last book was briefly talked about as a Pulitzer contender and with his wife Bridey, he has turned out three beautiful kids.

"Jeez, boy, you're practically wasting away," Howie says, clasping his son by his shoulders. "Bridey, you've got to get some meat on this boy's bones quick."

"My weight is within normal parameters," Donald asserts, pulling away from his father.

"Feel like a stick to me, boy," Howie says. But when Sylvie shoots him a warning sneer Howie promptly relents. "To each his own, I guess. So—everybody up for a big Thanksgiving dinner? We have a solid gold turkey this year, damn thing cost me an arm and a leg."

"Howie, it's free range."

"Free range, you bet. Know what free range means? Farmers don't have to spend a cent feeding it. But we've got to pay through the nose to eat it—now what kind of deal is that?"

"Here comes Grace!" Sylvie hoots, taking advantage of her daughter's arrival to change the subject.

Grace is the only member of the family who can keep up with Howie. A divorce lawyer in Raleigh, she is tough as nails, quick-witted, has a million stories and keeps her mouth in the gutter, as much to shock as to keep people off guard. Sylvie has a deal with Grace not to use the *eff* or *ess* words at family gatherings. Even so, every time Aunt Grace visits, Bridey and Donald's boys go back to school with a new stock of cusswords.

"Jesus Christ, whole damn clan's here!" Grace bellows as she comes in the door. Her shirtsleeves are rolled up to display a nasty-looking lump on her forearm. Though she has her mother's pretty face, from somewhere in the family's genetic history, Grace inherited the body of a fireplug. Having gone to college in Canada and fallen in love with hockey, Grace started a female league in Raleigh and loves to show off her bumps and bruises. She drives a pickup with big wheels and goes to every Nascar race she can fit into her busy schedule. Her dates are truck drivers and mechanics, for the longest time she went with a professional rodeo cowboy. Sylvie can only shake her head whenever she contemplates her daughter. So curious that Grace had been the one to adopt her father's outgoing manner instead of Donald. Even more remarkable was that she had taken Howie's irrepressibility out the window and is able to set her father back on his heels on a regular basis.

"Hey, Daddy, how the hell are you?" Grace says, slapping Howie on the back and planting a fat kiss on his cheek. "Getting a little porky around the middle here, got to watch those pounds," Grace says, grabbing her father's waist with both hands and wheeling him side to side.

"So whatcha been up to, Daddy? Found any lost bombs lately?"

Sylvie quickly interjects, "We're not going to talk about it this Thanksgiving, so let's drop it. Grace, what have you been up to?"

"Whoops, no lost bomb talk. Okay, I'll tell you about my latest divorce case. First, I'll need a drink."

"I think we can take care of that," Howie says. "Anyone else?"

"I bought a nice chardonnay to go with the turkey, there are a couple bottles in the fridge," Sylvie volunteers. While Howie opens the wine, Bridey surveys the dishes her mother-in-law has lined up on the counter.

"I hope you won't mind if I pass on the rutabaga, Sylvie, the stuff makes me gag," Bridey says.

"Try a little taste, I put loads of butter in it."

"You could put whipped cream in it and I'd still barf."

"Okay, you get a pass on the rutabaga."

"That's a relief."

"Okay, everyone, dinner is ready," Sylvie says, wiping her hands and taking off her apron. "Let's all line up. Howie, you pour the wine, and Grace, you tell us that story you've been threatening us with."

Howie hustles around filling glasses while Grace starts on the details of the divorce that has been the talk of Raleigh for the last three months, keeping them spellbound with her story, her ribald, jocular delivery even coaxing a smile out of Donald.

Howie surveys his family grouped around the kitchen island as they listen to Grace's tale, everyone smiling and full of good feeling—the way he always hoped their holidays would turn out. Howie picks up his glass and raises it in the air.

"To the Collyer family, to our continued health and happiness! I'm delighted to have you all here. Happy Thanksgiving, everybody!" Feeling he's on the verge of tearing up, he snatches a napkin off the counter.

"Hear, hear!" Bridey, Grace and Donald chorus, hoisting their glasses in return.

"Okay, everyone. Dinner's ready, c'mon and get your plates," Sylvie calls. The family packs in around the island, each taking a plate as they line up.

The grating ring of the telephone interrupts the clinking of china and glasses. Howie sneers at the beeping phone. "Who could possibly be calling on Thanksgiving Day?"

"I bet it's a telemarketer. You ought to get yourself on that no-telemarketing list the government's got, Howie," Bridey says. "Donald and I did and we haven't had a telemarketer call for three months."

Howie puts down his plate and walks over to the wall phone. He grabs the receiver and answers gruffly, "Hello."

Listening for a moment, he quickly responds, "Look, I'm sorry but we're just sitting down to Thanksgiving dinner."

Howie pauses, then says, "I beg your pardon, could you go over that again?" Sylvie watches as her husband's expression goes from peeved to perturbed. Is it a call from the nursing home about his parents?

"Hang on a minute. Let me move to another phone," he puts the call on hold. "You guys go ahead and start, I'll make this as quick as possible," Howie promises as he hustles down the hall.

"You heard your father, let's go ahead and eat," Sylvie says, handing Bridey a plate and waving her hand to indicate she should start serving herself.

"Won't be the first time in this house a holiday dinner's been interrupted," Grace says as she helps herself to the creamed onions.

"Or the last, I'm sure," Donald adds.

"Wonder who would call Howie on Thanksgiving?" Bridey asks.

"Maybe someone found a lost bomb digging in their backyard?" Donald cracks, chortling at his dig at his dad.

"Not funny, now eat your dinner," Sylvie says, trying to smile but knowing inside that her son's joke might have more than a ring of truth to it.

"I thought I cooked a wonderful dinner. Too bad you couldn't enjoy it," Sylvie says as she throws back the covers and climbs into bed. She's miffed he took the call during dinnertime and sat staring off into space throughout the meal. "You didn't fool the children either, they knew what the damn call was about."

"The woman was beside herself," Howie says, pecking away at the computer perched on his lap.

"Cripes sakes, Howie, it's Thanksgiving and you had no business being all absorbed in some business at a VA hospital. Your mind was a thousand miles away."

"I'm going up there tomorrow."

"You're what?" Sylvie whirls around to face him.

"In the morning I'm driving up."

"We had plans to take Grace to see your mom and dad tomorrow."

"You two go. Grace'll understand."

"Howie, this is nuts."

"One of the nurse's patients is trying to tell her something. Two days ago, she backed down his sedatives hoping it would make him more lucid, but when she went into the hospital this morning, she found that someone had upped back to the original level. And she has no idea who."

"What in the world does this have to do with you?"

"The patient's telling her something about a lost bomb."

"Oh, Howie, don't tell me—"

"Look, if it smells funny, I'll back off."

"It already stinks to high heaven—lost bombs, someone messing with a patient's prescription. Why don't you just give Winn a call and let him handle it for you?" Winston Straub was Howie's college roommate, went on to become a spy on the Soviets and then a top level CIA staffer. Straub prides himself on being in the know about everything. Great friends for the past thirty years, Howie and Winn are practically brothers.

"I will call Winn. But I promised this nurse I'd come up."

Sylvie reaches up and turns off the light. She knows when her influence ends and her husband's stubborn streak begins.

"I wish you wouldn't."

Howie doesn't answer.

"Then promise me you'll be careful," she says, lightly patting him on the leg.

"I promise," Howie says, in as honest a tone as he can muster, fully aware caution won't do him a bit of good if he steps into a world of shit.

7

[VA Hospital, Pittsburgh, Friday morning]

Sharon Thorsen breathes a sigh of relief when she pulls into her assigned space. Priding herself on being a safe driver, she hadn't noticed the car pulling out and narrowly missed sideswiping it. The driver leaned on his horn, made an obscene gesture and yelled something Sharon knew wasn't complimentary. She crawled the rest of the way.

She's a wreck and she knows it. All the girls at Thanksgiving dinner remarked on how distracted and out of sorts she seemed. And then she'd slept fitfully. At first troubled by the mysterious change in Risstup's dosage, then tossing and turning the worrying about whether she did the right thing in calling Howard Collyer.

She checks her watch. Collyer would be arriving in two hours. *What if the change on Risstup's chart was a mistake? Could it have been a legitimate change with a reasonable explanation? Was it nuts to even imagine someone would want to shut Risstup up?*

Collyer didn't think so. But as understanding and helpful as he was on the phone, who's to say this Howie Collyer isn't a wild-eyed kook? A total stranger who she'd spent five minutes talking to, he could turn out to be a complete fruitcake.

Sharon climbs out of her Subaru, locks it and strides across the parking lot toward the side entrance, trying to look as determined and purposeful as possible. As if creating the illusion that she is in control will compensate for her rising panic. Frightened for the poor old man who's tormented by a haunting memory from his past, yet at the same time knowing she might be getting in over her head.

In her uniform she attracts no attention, even though it is her day off. She walks down the hallway and takes the elevator to the third floor. Pushing open the swinging door, she strides down the row of beds. At first relieved to see the familiar form lying in his assigned bed, she's alarmed when no gaunt hand lifts from the mattress, no smile spreads across his face.

Her hand darts for his wrist, her fingers expertly locating the artery. His pulse is weak. Grabbing his chart, she shuffles through the pages to find the most recent entries.

What she sees scrawled on the last sheet of paper chills her to the bone.

Howie Collyer was out of bed and sipping his first cup of coffee at five-thirty and on the road a half hour later. Six hours and twenty minutes is what his nav system told him. But it doesn't know how fast Howie can go when he's motivated. A pleasant fall morning, the temperature is higher than normal for just after Thanksgiving. Fifty-eight degrees and sunny.

He thinks back over the call during Thanksgiving dinner. Someone's manipulating the patient's prescription. When the nurse reduced his dose, he began to talk about the lost bombs. Yesterday the dose was mysteriously raised back up to the original level. *Was the pilot beginning to come out of some kind of amnesia and they drugged him up again so he wouldn't reveal any more?*

Howie distracts himself with a book on tape he started on his last trip. A Mafia potboiler with blood and guts, tough talk and dime-a-dozen gangster molls with plunging necklines and six-inch stilettos. By the time the hero's bumped off all the bad guys, Howie's well into Pennsylvania. He catches the last of *Car Talk* on NPR.

As the two funnymen mechanics are signing off, Howie's phone chirps. He checks the window, doesn't recognize the number but the call is from a Pittsburgh area code.

"Mr. Collyer?" The voice on the other end is female and frantic. "Mr. Collyer? It's Sharon Thorsen. Now I'm convinced there's someone behind this."

"Why do you say that?" Collyer wonders whether he should pull over. Even though he has a hands-free, going seventy-five on a highway crowded with trucks doesn't make it easy to concentrate. "Hang on a minute," he says to her, flicking his turn signal and changing lanes, slowing and pulling off into the breakdown lane.

"Okay, go on."

The nurse continues, her voice increasingly shaky, "There's an order on his chart to up his dose again—this time to a scary level. His heart won't be able to tolerate it, I'm certain."

Howie stops the car and turns off the engine.

"Where are you now?"

"About to jump out of my skin. They seem to know everything I'm doing."

Collyer checks the screen on his direction finder. "I'm less than two hours away. Can you hang on?"

"I'm not sure. I'm worried to death."

"Can you take his chart?"

"I guess."

"They can't shoot him up if they don't have the chart, right?"

"True."

"Okay, so grab the chart, stick it under your arm and get the hell out. Can you do that?"

"I guess."

"Head for someplace where we can meet. Don't take your car, somewhere you can walk."

"How about Starbucks?"

"What's the address?"

Sharon Thorsen stammers for a couple moments.

"I need the address."

"I'm sorry, Forbes and Atwood."

"Forbes and Atwood. How will I recognize you?"

"Look for a nurse."

"What if there's more than one? Give me something else."

"Some people say I look like Angelica Huston."

"Sorry, but I don't know who she is."

"Okay—tall, long brown hair, sort of a narrow face."

"That'll do. I'll see you in an hour and fifty, give or take a few."

"Please hurry."

"As soon as I can I'll be there, now get the hell out of there," Collyer says, hanging up and keying in the new destination, feeling the tension tightening up his shoulders as he pulls out onto the Turnpike. He swivels his neck to try to loosen them up. Howie knows Sylvie would kill him if she knew what he was getting into. *But what else am I supposed to do? I can't turn around and go home. Not with the trouble the nurse is in.*

Howie quietly laughs. *Who's kidding who?* He was hooked the minute the VA nurse told him she was caring for an Air Force pilot who was talking about a lost bomb. For all he knows, the pilot might hold the key to the weapon dropped off the New Jersey coast. For years he's heard rumors about the Jersey bomb, scuttlebutt around the Building that it wasn't jettisoned out over the Atlantic. People clam up quickly whenever he's raised the subject, *what does that tell you*?

Howie checks his rearview and steps on the accelerator as he pulls out into the passing lane, taking the Accord up to eighty while keeping an eye out for cops. Last night, after talking with the nurse, Howie knew he might be heading up a blind alley. *The old man could have a screw loose, or the nurse might be misreading the situation.*

But now everything's changed.

He takes it up to eighty, the hairs on his neck standing up, adrenalin's making his heart hammer.

Someone has prescribed a fatal dose. That means a raw nerve's been hit. And he has a good idea it's somewhere in the massive five-sided building called the Pentagon.

8

[ZTA house, Rutgers University, Friday afternoon]

They start the party early as it's for the kids who, for whatever reason—divorce, parents on a cruise—don't go home for Thanksgiving or those who come back early to spare themselves the family scene. And even though school is officially closed, it's always a blowout.

"Denny, Denny," the girls shriek as they shimmy up to him, bumping and grinding against him to the hip-hop blasting out of the DJ's speakers, their blonde manes flowing, their skirts tight and short, all suntanned legs and bouncing bosoms as they fondle his cheeks and glide their hands over his arms. Mehran's the sorority's own boy-toy and as much as it rattles Melanie, he plays it for all it's worth.

While they get sillier and drunker on the lipstick-colored cocktails from the bar, Mehran paces himself with a beer and flashes his winning smile back at them, doing his best to keep up with his girlfriend's frantic dancing. Neither blonde nor a size 6, Melanie knows she was last in the looks line, but the size of her dad's wallet adequately compensates. He carts Melanie's sorority sisters around in his jets and gives them fat discounts at his ritzy stores in Manhattan. So they put up with their pudgy sister with the bad skin and she lets them put their hands all over Mehran.

Though Melanie did draw a line when one of her sisters tried to lure him upstairs at an event two weeks ago.

"C'mon up and see my new flat screen, Denny," Kristen, who was draped all over him, cooed in his ear.

Before Mehran was two steps up the stairs, Melanie was in her face. Grabbing Mehran's hand, what starts as a tugging match soon becomes a raging catfight, Mehran standing on the stairs with Kristen, the blonde goddess, pulling on his right and chubby Melanie hanging on for dear life to the other. Both girls drunk out of their skulls and raging mad.

"Denny's gonna be my fuckbuddy," the blonde named Kristen slurred, swatting at Melanie while she planted a slobbery kiss on Mehran's cheek.

"Fuck you, he's *mine*," Melanie blurted, yanking on Mehran's arm.

"Fat pig!" Kristen snarled, tossing the dregs in her cup at her, half the purple drink splashing down Melanie's front, wetting her neck and staining her blouse.

"Stupid whore," Melanie raised her leg and kicked out but lost her balance and started to stumble. Mehran caught her in his arms before she tumbled. Regaining her equilibrium, she threw her arms around her boyfriend and shouted triumphantly at Kristen, "Tough shit to you, bitch."

"Girls, girls, girls, that's enough, c'mon, let's go back to partying!" Mehran shouted, leading Melanie away from the stairs, through the crowd of revelers now hooting, whistling, clapping him on the back like he'd just come out of the ring after scoring a knockout. Of course, Melanie's on cloud nine having faced down one of the blonde princesses who tried to take away her boyfriend. Pretty soon they're back to drinking and dancing.

This party's just like all the others, but he acts like he's having the time of his life, grateful to be accepted as another foreign engineering student and to have a girlfriend with rich parents. She pulls out her credit card whenever he needs equipment or wants to go diving at the quarry south of town.

It's just another hour and a half of partying. Then the same routine, he'll help Melanie stumble back across campus, get her up the stairs and pour her in bed. Usually she tries to come on to him but seldom gets past fumbling with his fly before she passes out. Sex is mandatory in the morning but that's after he's had a chance to get a full night's work done with no one looking over his shoulder. Engineering is the perfect cover since everyone knows those students are glued to their computer screens 24-7.

That night, he goes through the same ritual with Melanie. Except halfway across the quad she leans over and pukes her guts out, then gets all blubbery and guilty about being drunk and begs Mehran not to think less of her.

Finally getting her into bed, he turns off the light, walks to the closet, turns on his computer and shuts the door behind him. Peeling through dummy websites set up for cover, it's been three years, three long years, but is he maybe getting the news he's been waiting for? His heart drumming in his chest, he makes sure he translates the coded message correctly. No question about it, something's going on. Can't tell for sure, but it's a definite indication.

He sits back in his chair, one thought crowding out all the others.

His target's on the move, could he be tracking a lost bomb?

9

[Pittsburgh, Friday afternoon]

Peeking through the window, she's easy to spot, forget about the Angelica Huston business, she's the only person in hospital garb. For downtown Pittsburgh, Howie expected the area to be bustling with business people and Pitt students ordering up their afternoon caffeine fix to get them through to dinnertime, but the place is empty. He remembers it's the day after Thanksgiving, everyone's bound to be on break.

He strolls down the block, keeping an eye on the coffee shop. Then crosses the street, carefully surveying left and right. After ten minutes, he takes out his phone. It's risky, but he has no choice.

"Leave Starbucks and take a right, walk two blocks and take a left," he says when she answers, Then repeats himself, "A right, two blocks and then a left," and hangs up before she can get a word out.

Seconds later, the door opens. Sharon Thorsen is in her late thirties or early forties. Looking frazzled as he expected, her hair mussed and face flushed, attractive but offbeat—not classically pretty. Tall and trim, with a longish pageboy, she scurries down the block, peeking over her shoulder more than Howie would have liked.

He crosses to her side when she reaches the second intersection. Though he knows Pittsburgh well, he's never been in this neighborhood. Down the street, he spots a short order place, the kind with coffee and sweet buns in the morning, burgers and fries the rest of the day. He flips open his cell and touches the redial button. "See that luncheonette up ahead? I'll meet you in there. Find a booth in the back and order coffee."

He waits fifteen minutes. The traffic on the street is light, he doesn't see the same car twice, he checks the pedestrians' faces carefully, one woman walks by him a second time, but she's obviously lost. It's safe.

He pushes open the door and takes a quick look around. She's in a booth halfway down. The place smells like every other hole-in-the-wall eatery, grease mixed with coffee. As he approaches, she gives him a cautious nod.

"Thank you so much for coming, I'm at my wit's end," she says, her gaze shifting nervously around the diner as if she expects someone to suddenly burst in the door.

"Where's your coffee?" Howie asks, pointing at the table.

She shrugs, her hands flutter up, "I forgot, sorry."

"If you don't have something you stick out like a sore thumb. What can I get you?"

"Small coffee, one Equal, if you don't mind."

Howie walks to the counter and places his order. He looks back at her. She has sparkling blue eyes, auburn hair and a nice figure but is clearly distraught, fidgeting with her purse, her eyes regularly darting to the front door.

"I'm glad you called," Howie says as he sets the coffee down in front of her. Sticky bun for himself.

"Are we safe here?" Her voice falters.

"Depends…" Howie didn't want to tell her that if someone intercepted her earlier phone call both of them soon would be identified. *Have they tapped his phone? Did they know he was in Pittsburgh with Thorsen?* No way to know.

"Let's just assume we're a couple steps ahead of them," Howie adds.

"Who's *them*?'

"It's a long story," Howie says, checking his watch as he takes a sip of his coffee.

"I have time, I think," she says, the faintest grin drifting across her face. She's prettier when she smiles.

"We shouldn't spend hours in here so I'll make it quick. There's a group in the Pentagon. Funded by billions in under-the-table funds, it has no published budget, no assigned staff, no offices, no name, no discernible presence whatsoever. It's called a 'black program' and it's invisible—until you run into it."

"I don't mean to sound naïve, but how can they operate in secret? Aren't there congressional committees to oversee stuff like that?"

"Exactly why they exist, to get all the dirty business done without anyone asking questions. And I mean *anyone.*"

"Even the Secretary of Defense?"

"Even the president. This program most likely was initiated during the early days of the Cold War—seven presidents ago. Eisenhower or Nixon might have originally signed off on it but during successive administrations, it's secreted itself under so many layers of deception and disinformation that now it has no more than a shadowy presence in the Pentagon."

"So what kind of dirty business?"

"Supposedly Vector Eleven is—"

She interrupts him, "Vector Eleven—wait a minute, you said black programs don't have names."

"You have to understand how this stuff works. There are always a million rumors flying around the Pentagon and the buzz about this group is that it's called 'Vector Eleven.' It's all hearsay but the word is part of their mission is to keep all the mishaps in the nuclear weapons projects as well as in the entire nuclear program—all our Chernobyls, if you will—under wraps so they can keep getting billions to produce more."

"We've had disasters like Chernobyl?"

"Three Mile Island was a hair's breadth away from a catastrophe and there have been close calls with nuclear materials that would curl your hair. For sixty years we've been cranking out spent fuel rods from nuclear power plants and high-level radioactive garbage from weapons production. But we haven't had any safe place to stash the stuff. They've spent billions on a massive underground storage facility in Nevada but it's hung up in politics and red tape."

"Yucca Flats—I've read about that."

"Right. In the meantime, this crap's piling up at over a hundred sites all over the country faster than they can find room for it. Every week there's some kind of fire or spill. They keep a really tight lid on it and when anyone starts poking around, alarms go off big-time."

"That's what happened with Risstup?"

"That's anyone's guess. Compared to the threat posed by the mountains of nuclear trash, these lost bombs are just a blip on their radar. Still they don't like the subject brought up. Which only makes me more suspicious. When I was at the Pentagon, I got too close for comfort so they framed me and forced me out. I was lucky. These people play for keeps. With their billions, they can buy off almost anyone. To achieve their ends they've ruined reputations, wrecked marriages and ratted on people to the IRS."

"Nice bunch."

Howie takes a bite of his bun. "You bet. And every once in a while when they are backed up against the wall, you'll see the gloves come off. Nothing's ever been pinned on them of course, but once in a while freak accidents occur. I don't know whether you caught it on the news some time ago, but a prominent nuclear scientist who threatened to go public with news of severe radioactive contamination on a facility outside of Denver ended up with his car T-boned by a propane truck. All they found of him was a few pieces of denture material. Two years ago, a high-level Energy Department employee accidentally blew his head off cleaning a shotgun the day before he was supposed to testify about leaky storage casks before a congressional committee."

"So you think it was these same people who raised the dose?"

"Maybe getting too risky with you nosing around?"

"I can't believe someone can order a murder like they're ordering a sandwich."

"No one person does it. It's all impersonal and institutional. An order is passed down the chain of command. General at the top orders the next guy, he orders the next, it gets passed along from level to level, getting more and more impersonal each time it changes hands. By the time it gets to the bottom, the order to increase the dose on a VA patient has no more import than an order to gas up a tank."

Howie sees Sharon's face redden, veins on her neck are standing out. She looks off over his shoulder. Howie's seen his wife with the same expression on her face, a blank stare while her emotions boil over inside. Sylvie will either burst into tears or go into a slow burn.

Sharon Thorsen chooses the latter. Lowering her brows and furrowing her forehead, she says in a low, almost grim tone, "They'll pull the plug on Major Risstup over my dead body." She looks up at Howie—resolute, her eyes flashing, "We have to get him out of there."

"I'm glad you came to that conclusion."

"You knew that the minute I called you."

"I didn't come up to go to a Steelers game."

Sharon looks off into space. Then down at her cup of coffee. She hasn't taken a sip. Waits a beat and says, "Let me think."

Howie gets up from the booth, "While you're thinking, let's get my car. We've been in here too long already." He wraps the bun in a napkin, thinking he might need it later.

The walk to Howie's Accord takes two minutes.

"You didn't bring yours, right?"

"I left it in the lot like you told me."

"Good girl." He opens the door for her and goes around to the driver's side, gets in and turns the key. "Which way's the hospital?"

"Take a left," she points, sliding into the seat beside him. "Fortunately, it's the day after Thanksgiving so no one will be minding the store."

Howie swings out of the parking space, heads down the street and turns at the intersection.

"I figure I can act like I'm taking him down for tests. Just put him in a chair and wheel him out of the ward. Once I'm out, I'll be okay. And if I wait until the shift change I'm hoping no one will notice. Make sense?" she asks.

"Sounds like a plan," he nods and smiles.

She had no idea what to expect of Howard Collyer. Yet there doesn't seem to be anything flaky about him, he's earnest and strong-willed, seems like a straight shooter. And for a fifty-something guy, he's also cute. Reminds her of a younger Sam What's His Name, the actor on *Law and Order*, but taller. Heavy eyebrows, long nose, thin face, aristocratic-looking. Still has a thick head of hair, great green eyes, a few added pounds around the middle, but the most important—he seems openhearted, kind and clearly concerned about her patient.

"I think I can pull it off. The place is like a morgue at night. I can walk into the ward and wheel him out like I'm taking him down for an x-ray or something. What's the worst that can happen? A guard stops me? I can handle those dudes."

"They most likely won't be expecting anyone to take him out of there. Even if someone is watching, you'll have the element of surprise."

"But sooner or later they're going to wake up and find out Risstup's gone."

"We'll be far away by then."

Sharon's attention drifts over to him. He can tell she's trying to piece together their next steps.

"This is your way of letting me know we're going to be away for a while."

Howie shrugs. "Your guess is as good as mine. First we have to protect your patient. Then find out what he knows. And decide what to do about it."

"You're not telling me we're going to end up on a search for a damn H-bomb?"

Howie shrugs.

"I'm not sure I'm up for that."

Howie turns to look at her. He hasn't wanted to think about what they'll do if the major provides information they can act on. What if he gives them the location of a lost nuke? How would three people go up against Vector Eleven with all its resources? If he has trouble dealing with the thought, he can only imagine what Sharon is thinking.

"Look, we're just going to have to make this up as we go along."

"Okay, I can deal with that, I think."

"I have to ask you, do you have family or friends, anyone who will miss you?"

Sharon shakes her head. "What family I have left is far away. In Hawaii, mostly. I don't even have a cat. My friends might get concerned but they know I work crazy hours and sometimes go for days without talking to them. I don't mean to sound like a sad sack, that's just the way it is. How about you?"

"Wife, two grown children. I'll have to make some arrangements."

Sharon points out the front window, "Pull up here and stop. The hospital is down the block and to the left. I'll hoof it from here."

"You have your cell, right?"

"Yup, so I'm going to go in there and act busy until the shift change. When I get him out, I'll call. I'll draw you a map to show you where to meet me."

"Call me only once. Let's not make it easy for them. And use some code when you've got the pilot, say *The Condor is landing* or something like that."

"Pretty corny, can't you do better than that?"

Howie smiles. He watches as she sketches the map. Spunky and smart. Howie can only imagine what he could have ended up with—a bubble-headed young nurse or a frosty old maid—instead he has someone who can keep up. "Why don't you just say *The package is ready*?"

"Much better." Thorsen hands him her drawing of the hospital grounds. "So I guess I should face up to the fact that the days of being a regular old VA nurse are over."

"It's play-it-by ear time. Who the hell knows what'll happen?" What he hasn't told her is that if they succeed in getting the pilot out of the VA hospital, they will only have a few days—three, four, five maybe. Too many people will be looking for them. But if the Pentagon is slow to react, they might have more time. Howie knows they're going to need it.

She opens the car door, swings her legs out. Turns back. She's got something on her mind. Scowling, her body tensed and her expression indignant, she huffs, "What the hell I'd like to know is how can they think they can get away with crap like this in the United States of America?"

"Damn good question." Someday Howie would find time to tell her that people would stop at nothing when billions of dollars worth of defense contracts, the future of the nuclear weapons program and the careers of thousands of people in the Pentagon and the defense establishment are threatened.

Chitchat is over, Sharon checks her wristwatch. "Okay, I'm off," she says. "Make sure your cell's on. The shift change isn't until nine so I'll be at least two hours."

Then Thorsen makes a gesture that surprises Howie. Through the open door she extends her hand back to him.

"Wish me luck," she says. Howie leans over to join her in a handshake.

"You'll do fine," he says.

"I know," Sharon smiles breezily at him and quietly shuts the door. She walks off down the darkened street, as nonchalant as if she's off to run an errand.

As he watches Thorsen disappear around the corner, Howie reminds himself to give Sylvie a call. She would be expecting to hear from him by now. He hasn't the slightest idea what he's going to tell her but he owes her some kind of explanation. And he needs to contact Winn Straub. Without a contact on the inside, Howie knows they don't stand a chance.

He turns around and heads back the way he came with an eye out for someplace with an Internet connection.

Two lattes and two hours later, Howie is sitting in his second Internet café chatting with a Carnegie Mellon grad student who sat down next to him and started pecking away at a laptop, putting the finishing touches on his dissertation. Knowing enough physics to carry on a conversation, Howie's able to kill time making small talk about the grad student's paper.

When he puts his computer to sleep and folds the case shut, Howie jumps at the opportunity, "I couldn't borrow your machine for a minute, could I?"

"For what?"

"I need to send a couple emails. Mine's in the shop."

The grad student rolls his eyes, he's hesitant.

"I'll delete them when I finish, no skin off your butt. It'll just be a couple minutes."

"I guess…" he says, reluctantly sliding his computer across the table to Howie.

"Thanks, appreciate it."

Using an alias, Howie opens an account at Hotmail. Then he composes a draft to Sylvie.

> Sylvie, You must not be alarmed if you do not hear from me. Things have developed up here that necessitate me staying away for a few days, maybe as long as a week. I'll keep in touch via email. For some reason my cell phone is on the fritz again.

Howie rereads the email, tosses it and starts over. He needs to act breezier, less concerned.

> Hi Honey. Everything's fine up here. No problems. But I might have to be up here a few more days doing some research. And my cell's on the fritz again so I'll stay in touch by email. Talk to you soon. Love you, Howie

Five minutes later, he receives an email telling him his Hotmail account is active. He sends off his revised email to Sylvie. Then composes a second to Winn Straub. Two years ago when Howie left the Pentagon, Winn gave him a secure email address, confiding in his former college roommate, "If the Pentagon ever tries to pull any funny stuff, use this email address to contact me and I'll get them to call off the dogs."

I'm going to need your help, Winn, he types. Winn Straub was a bookworm at UVa, an honors econ major who relished being the roommate of a varsity football player. And after Howie's famous kick, for years he's loved boasting that he was The Boot's roommate at college. Straub has a job at CIA that's so secret even his wife isn't sure what he does. Back in his heyday, he was stationed overseas—Eastern Europe in the height of the Cold War. Winn confided in him once over drinks, "If I could tell you just a couple things I did over there, I'd have your hair standing on end inside of two minutes."

Now assigned to the Pentagon, he acts like just another high-level bureaucrat. But Howie has always assumed that Winn Straub is a major player—the CIA's watchdog at the Pentagon maybe? Straub would never own up to it of course. But the fact that Winn can hand out secure email addresses attests to his roommate's stature at the Agency.

Howie pauses as he composes the email, he isn't sure how much he should tell him. He decides he'll keep most of the details to himself in this first email, only letting him know he might need assistance in the next few days.

Having sent and deleted them, he logs off and hands the laptop back to the grad student. "Thanks, appreciate it," Howie says.

For a moment he wonders if he shouldn't make an offer for the machine. After one last cell call, they should stop using the phones as they are too easy to trace. Howie knows the Internet will be their only option, poaching on hotspots at airports, libraries, colleges or roaming around suburban neighborhoods—until they pick up a signal and piggyback on some unsuspecting family's Wi-Fi connection. Even if the analysts and codebreakers at the Defense Intelligence Agency or the National Security Agency could locate them on one wireless setup, as long as they keep hopping from one to another, Howie is guessing they can stay a step ahead.

About to make the grad student an offer that he can't refuse, Howie realizes he needs to conserve his cash. Going to an ATM would be sending a telegram to Vector Eleven. Before he left, he grabbed all the money from his secret stash in the locked drawer inside his war room, but fifteen hundred bucks can only hold up so long. From this point, he knows he has to start thinking like a damn spy, every action examined for its potential ramifications down the line.

Howie checks his watch. He wonders how Thorsen is doing—two hours and counting since she left for the VA hospital. Time to head for the hospital. Thanking the grad student again, he sets out across the parking lot for his car.

Two rights and a left later, the ten-story tan brick government building comes into view. He pulls up and parks in front of the building, turning off the engine and dousing his lights. Surrounded by a sea of parking lots, the building has its night security illumination on, pinpoints of crisp blue against a dark sky. The neighborhood is quiet. Bordering the campus of the University of Pittsburgh, the streets around the hospital are deserted except for a few parked cars.

Sharon stays out of sight up until the shift change, changing her uniform and assembling a bag of drugs and medications that the major would need. At nine, she calmly pushes an empty wheelchair into the darkened ward. Leaning down beside him, she shakes his shoulder and whispers, "Wake up, Major Risstup, we're going for a ride."

His eyes snap open, filling with alarm as they race around the unlit room.

"It's okay, Major Risstup," Sharon reassures him, patting him on the arm. "We're just going downstairs."

"I don't understand, I don't understand," he repeats, sitting up in bed and looking around helplessly. "Who are you? Why are you doing this?"

"It will be okay, you have to trust me."

"Leave me alone, I need to sleep," he protests, pushing her hands away. *I can't have any more of this business,* she thinks.

Around the ward, her colleagues jokingly call her *The Sharpshooter,* as her aim with a needle is uncanny and she can find veins where others only strike muscle and bone.

She quickly flips Risstup over, lifts his gown, slips out her needle and deftly jabs it into the only square inch of flesh on his butt. She has two more hypodermics prepared. But one should do the trick. As she monitors his pulse waiting for him to go under, she keeps glancing up at the camera mounted on the wall praying no one is watching her. When Risstup slips into dreamland, she loads his limp body into the wheelchair and rolls him out.

Letting the door to Ward 3 slowly shush shut behind her, she checks one way down the dark hallway and then the other. Quickly pushing the chair, she makes a right and then a left, speeding toward the elevator bank. One more corner to go.

Hearing footsteps echoing off the bare walls, heading in her direction, she comes to a dead stop. Backing the chair out of the light, she stands motionless in the shadows.

At the far end of the hall, a figure rounds the corner and stops. *It's a guy*, she's sure but it's too dark to see who it is. The footsteps begin again, he's walking toward her. In the dim blue glow of the security lights, she can tell he's not in uniform. A big guy in a suit, burly. She's never seen him before. *Who is he and why is he here?*

His flashlight suddenly clicks on, its beam flitting around the inky corridor. Sharon flattens her back against the wall, hoping the beam of light doesn't catch her.

She's holding her breath, back pressed to the wall, hoping the dose she gave Risstup keeps him under. The last thing she needs is for him to wake up now. The shaft of light creeps down the corridor, passes them, then stops.

The footsteps get louder. *He's coming closer.*

All of a sudden the flashlight glints on the chrome wheelchair, then a second later spills all over her. Sharon blinks in the sharp light.

"Mind telling me what you're doing, ma'am?" He walks up to her, the light from his flashlight playing on her and the old man in the wheelchair. He is wearing an ill-fitting, off-the-rack suit. Young, short haircut, muscular-looking.

"Just taking my patient down to Imaging," trying to sound casual but sweating bullets. "He's having issues and I need to check an x-ray."

"Imaging isn't open, you know that."

Sharon thinks fast and holds up her car keys, "I have a key."

The guard focuses his flashlight on her raised hand. Her heart is pounding. The car keys don't fool him. He steps forward, "You're going to have to come with me, ma'am." His tone of voice quiet but threatening, "Give me the wheelchair," he says, elbowing his way in front of her and taking the handles of the chair. His body bumps against her, solid as a rock.

"We're going to take Major Risstup back to his ward and then you and I are going downstairs," he tells her, his voice all business.

Oh shit, he knows the major's name, he must have been watching.

As he starts to wheel the chair away, in a flash Sharon reaches into her pocket, slips the plastic tip off the hypodermic, whips it out and jabs the needle deep into his carotid. Before he can react, a double-dose of the powerful sedative is surging through his body. Leaving the syringe dangling, Sharon scoots back and watches the drug do its work.

Motionless, frozen, he begins to wobble. Lifting his arm to pull out the needle, his knees go to jelly and he does a slow-mo header onto the linoleum, skull and bones clattering on the floor like a bunch of muffled drumsticks.

Sharon grabs the wheelchair and races off down the corridor, rounding the far corner, grabbing the handle of a fire alarm and jerking it off the wall.

A wailing siren shatters the tranquility outside. Lights snap on all around the building, flooding the area in a greenish-yellow glow. Howie grabs his cell off the seat, focusing on it, waiting for the call.

C'mon, Sharon, call, fucking call me, c'mon.

More lights flick on. A second siren sounds, a shrill series of blasts pulsating in waves out from the building. Howie stares at his phone screen, his eyes begging it to light up.

Where the hell is she?

The first ring isn't finished before he's punched *TALK.*

"The package is ready—at the loading dock in back," Sharon says.

He tosses the cell on the seat and guns the engine, tires screeching as he wheels through the parking lot in front of the hospital with his lights off, holding the napkin with directions over the steering wheel to guide him to the loading dock. *No point in trying to be quiet with all this ruckus going on, just stay out of sight as much as possible.* Pulling around the back, he stays out of the streetlights arching over the center of the lot.

A third siren goes off. Howie's ears are burning. *So much for the patients' sleep for this night*, he thinks, craning his neck searching for the loading dock.

He sees a figure rushing out from the shadows of the building, racing across the lot toward him at a dead run steering a wheelchair.

It's Sharon. Changed clothes, now she's wearing green scrubs and cap, her hair tumbling out as she sprints in his direction. He accelerates toward her, jams on the brakes and throws open the side door as she pulls alongside.

Sharon's at the rear door of the Honda, steering the chair in close, a bent over form slumped down in the seat. Howie pops the trunk, then hops out and hustles around to the passenger's side.

"I'll get him in the car, you stow the chair," he says, flinging open the rear door and leaning down to scoop Risstup up. He's surprisingly light, Howie thinks as he jockeys the out-for-the-count patient into the back seat. *Guy can't weigh over a hundred pounds soaking wet.* Sharon collapses the chair in a few quick motions and slides it into the trunk, slamming the door and hurrying around to hop in.

Howie jumps into the driver's seat, Sharon pulls her door shut. Howie slams the Honda into gear and tromps on the accelerator. He hears shouts from the loading dock. If they have cameras outside, they could ID the car. *We'll have to find a new one or steal some plates.*

"Head out that way," Thorsen says, pointing at a playing field bordering the parking lot as she slams the door.

"Where?"

"Over there, across the grass, hurry the hell up."

Howie jumps the curb and steps on the gas, squinting to see the way as he steers the Honda off across the turf, its wheels spinning, rear fishtailing around seeking traction on the soft ground.

"There's a blocking sled up ahead," Sharon says, poking Howie in the shoulder to indicate the direction. Howie doesn't see the long low football machine until he's almost upon it. She grabs the wheel and suddenly wrenches the Honda left, leaving the obstacle behind them. Howie keeps the pedal to the floor. He hears more sirens.

"You'll come up this hill and see the road, make a right," she shouts. He guns the car up the hill, seeing the street ahead just in time. The Honda bottoms out, crashing against the curb. He spins the wheel hard to slide sideways into a ditch, then steps on it to pull the car out. The Accord jumps up on the pavement. He straightens out, following the road.

"Now you can slow down," Thorsen says, pulling off her cap and letting out a sigh of relief. "We're okay."

"Are you sure? What about the sirens?"

She interrupts, "That was me. I pulled a bunch of alarms to keep them occupied. They won't have a clue until they do a head count. It'll be a good hour before they find out. Just act like we're a couple heading home from dinner with gramps in the back seat."

"How is he?" Howie asks, nodding in their passenger's direction.

"We're lucky we got him out of there when we did. He wouldn't have made it through the night."

"Good work," Howie says.

"I had a little run-in back there, someone tried to stop me."

"How did you handle it?"

"Told him it was time to go beddy-bye."

When Howie's expression turns quizzical, she takes the remaining syringe out of her pocket, holds it up and adds, "I shot him full of enough sedative to stop a train."

"So would you mind putting that away?" Howie nods at the hypodermic. "Needles make me nervous."

Sharon tucks the syringe back in her pocket as she looks down at her wrinkled scrubs, "I'm going to need some clothes, can't wear these for too long."

"We're not going to find anyplace tonight. I've got an extra pair of jeans and a UVa sweatshirt you can wear in the meantime."

"On second thought, maybe I'll stay with the scrubs. So you're a Cavalier?"

Howie is about to reveal his class when his vanity gets the better of him. He nods instead.

"Bet you were a jock."

Howie smiles. "What makes you think that?"

"The way you carry yourself, got jock written all over. What sport?"

"Football—place kicker."

"Any good?"

"I got off a few nice ones in my day. You a fan?"

"My dad was a coach for years. I grew up on gridirons. So where are you taking us?" Sharon asks.

"We need to look for a parking lot. We need to borrow some plates in case they caught us with a surveillance camera."

"Then where?"

"Any place we can find a computer. Got any ideas?"

"As a matter of fact..." Thorsen says, pointing at a sign for Pittsburgh International. "Turn right up here, we'll head for the airport. We'll get the plates off a car in the parking lot. Then I'll dig up a computer for us."

Right off the bat he's impressed by her resolve and ingenuity. Plates and a laptop, two birds with one stone. *I can't wait to see how she pulls this one off.*

For an hour and a half Collyer has been fighting to stay awake. Only two cars have parked on his floor, both close to the elevator. He's on the far side, his Accord hidden behind a low wall, new plates front and back swiped from a car out of range of the security cameras. No point in stealing plates if someone catches it on tape. The next thing he did was locate another way out of the parking garage. The gate was up at an unmarked employee exit, he was in luck.

Risstup hasn't moved a muscle since Sharon's been inside. Howie stared into the old man's wizened face for a long time. *What secrets does he have hidden away? Which bomb does he know about? Could it be the Jersey bomb? And will we ever get the information out of him?*

He had to admit Sharon's idea was damn good. At first he thought she was off her rocker when she told him to head for the Pittsburgh airport, that's the first place they'd check for us, he told her.

"We're not going anywhere," she explained. "We're going to lift a laptop from some road warrior. With no connection to either of us it'll be untraceable."

She was right but they would still have to stay on their toes. In the last five years, the National Security Agency has been fine-tuning its surveillance procedures and capabilities to catch terrorists. NSA deliberately leaked one story to improve its image inside the Beltway and for a week it was the talk of Washington. A cutting-edge software program had pulled up the email addresses of all the senders of emails containing the term "quartersawn mahogany" and promptly labeled them suspicious since mahogany doesn't grow in Lebanon, Sudan or Libya. Four hours later, security forces were kicking down doors in three countries.

Howie's startled by a loud thump. Then another. He peers out. Sharon's leaning down, gesturing at him to unlock the door. Howie clicks the button. Sharon jumps in beside him, pulls out a gray laptop and slides it across the seat to him, "Dude, you got a Dell!" she says proudly.

"Good work," Howie says, realizing that's the second time he's said that to her in less than three hours. He opens the laptop. "How did you get it?"

"Borrowed it from a friend. It's got a wireless card, Bluetooth, it's loaded."

"What took you so long?"

"Guys don't just hand over their laptops, you have to put some english on it."

"What kind of english?"

"Nothing racy, I can assure you. These guys get a few drinks in them and they all want to take you for a test drive. It's like being back in high school."

"Don't you have to cozy up to them a bit?"

Thorsen gives him a look that immediately tells Howie he shouldn't have gone there.

"Sorry," he says.

"What kind of a girl do you think I am?" Sharon asks, acting affronted.

"Damn clever one, I'd say. How did you get it away from him?"

"He was like a little kid with his new Dell. Practically begged me to try it out. When he had to go to the men's room I pretended I was in the middle of a long email to my mother and I told him, 'Go, I'll take good care of it for you.'"

"You sure did that."

"Laptops get lifted every ten seconds in airports. Read a story about it recently, that's what gave me the idea. It's no big deal to him, the guy will have his company FedEx another PC tomorrow—cost of doing business these days." Sharon twists around to check the back seat. "How's our patient?"

"Haven't heard a peep."

"He should be out for a while more. But we'd better find someplace and get him settled in. If he comes to in the backseat of a car with two strangers, it might be too much for him to handle."

"First we need to put some miles between ourselves and Pittsburgh."

Howie starts the Accord and pulls out of the space, heading in a different direction.

"We didn't come in this way," Sharon says.

"I found another way out. We're not taking any chances. As long as we have Risstup they will be looking for us. Make you nervous?" he asks.

"I'd be lying if I told you no."

"My friend Winn Straub will help us out, my roommate back in UVa days. He's a top guy at CIA. There's not a lot of love lost between him and the Pentagon."

"Why's that?"

"Inside the Beltway politics. CIA and the Pentagon have been at loggerheads over who should control intelligence—civilian or military—for years. And the recent reorganization of the entire setup has everyone on edge."

"What's going on?"

"Turf battles. A lot of money and control at stake. Every agency is back on their heels except the Pentagon. Right now they hold the high card."

"Because of Iraq?'

"Iraq, Afghanistan, the war on terror. But the whole picture is much more complicated." He doesn't take it any further, there will be time for that. Working at high levels at the Pentagon, Howie had been in the thick of the political intrigue swirling around the agencies involved with national security. Now he understands from talking to former colleagues the hurly-burly has been jacked up to new levels. Howie has said many times how relieved he is that he's out of it. *Or is he suddenly back in again?*

Sharon looks over her shoulder at Risstup. "I'm sure glad we got him out of there. The poor thing."

"They must have parked him there years ago."

"And forgotten about him until I woke him up."

"I tell you, it's the break I've been waiting for." As soon as the words are out of his mouth, Howie is wishing he could take them back. The temperature in the front seat is soaring. Sharon Thorsen slowly turns and gives him a cutting look. Howie's seen it before. On the faces of colleagues at the Pentagon, on Winn Straub's face, even on the faces of his wife and daughter. The look that says he's gone one step over the line and turned into a sanctimonious whistleblower. One of his closest friends at the Pentagon made the most cutting remark, it still rings in his ears, "You're so goddamn self-righteous about this lost bombs thing, Collyer, makes me want to puke."

Sharon swings her head away, staring out the window at the passing landscape. Howie knows what's coming.

She turns back to face him, her eyes firing indignation. "So this is not about saving someone's life, it's all about Howie Collyer's quest for lost bombs."

He's already backpedaling, "I didn't intend it to come out that way."

"But that's what you meant. We've got a little bit of the Crusader Rabbit thing going on with these lost bombs, don't we, Mr. Collyer?"

Howie winces. He's heard the word *crusade* used before but Sharon has found a cutting new context.

"Your website reeks of it. Recover the nukes and make the world safe for humanity. Look, Mr. Collyer, I'll play along with your little game. But my priority is Major Risstup—his well-being. And I'm not going to put up with you grilling him 24-7 about lost bombs. Get this message loud and clear: the minute I see an opportunity to get the major to a safe place then you can count me out of your little adventure."

Howie keeps his attention on the road. There not much he can say that won't sound lame. He's hoping she's the kind of person who'll back down after blowing off some steam.

"You've made your position clear."

"You bet your ass on that," she says, with a final huff.

The roadway flies by under the hood of Howie's Accord until

Sharon breaks the silence, "By the way, I need some stuff—toiletries, makeup."

"The first chance we get. Anything else?"

Sharon shakes her head, and then shoots him a quick look that seems a bit conciliatory, as if the storm has passed.

"So what do you do when you're not playing nurse?" Howie asks.

"See friends, read and watch football every chance I get."

"Don't say?"

"I told you—my dad was a high school coach. Won the state championship three years in a row."

"What's he doing now?"

"Both my parents were both killed seven years ago in an accident."

"I'm sorry."

"They named the field after him, Thorsen Field."

"Must make you proud."

"I go to all the games, sit in the VIP section, it's nice."

"I hope you don't have a game this weekend."

"Season's over. Just as well, crappy team this year. Rebuilding time. So how many points did you kick?"

"Came close to breaking eighty, but the big deal was I got the winning field goal in our last game against a nationally ranked team."

"No kidding?"

"People still talk about it."

"Not much else to talk about in those early years of Virginia football."

"The program's getting hot now."

"Tell me about it. New coach, new stadium."

Sharon stops, looks out the window and then turns back to Howie. "Hey, I was a little harsh back there, the Crusader Rabbit business was out of line."

"Not a problem. It's not something I take personally," Howie says, lying through his teeth.

"I do appreciate your help, everything you've done, coming up here, helping me get him out of there—I want you to know that."

She's relieved to have staked out her turf in no uncertain terms. Now he knows she won't hesitate to step on his toes or even pull the rug the minute she feels he is taking advantage of her patient. She curls her legs up on the seat and crosses her arms.

Alone in a car fleeing from some shadowy Pentagon force in the middle of the night with a man she's known for barely five hours, she's determined to make it clear she's ready for anything. But the last thing she wants him to know is that she's scared to death.

The two unlikely allies silently stare out the window at the dark walls of trees rushing by on either side of them, a few patchy clouds in the sky overhead, only an occasional vehicle overtaking them.

Both know their first sparring match now was played to a draw. But Howie Collyer and Sharon Thorsen also know there will be more to come. For both have realized that each is stubborn as the day is long.

10

[Georgetown, early Saturday morning]

Rubbing his eyes, Winn Straub wobbles into the kitchen in his bathrobe and slippers to find the lights blazing. His wife must have fallen asleep in front of the TV and forgotten to turn them off. He clicks the switch and flips open the top of the coffeemaker. Following his morning ritual, he opens the cabinet, takes out a paper filter and fits it into the top, carefully spoons grounds into the filter, then touches the space bar on his laptop that's sitting alongside. As he fills the pot with water, the computer's hard drive whirs and the screen blinks to life.

Straub is accustomed to getting up at five. It's before noon in most European capitals and the end of the day in the Far East, a good time to check to see if any new crises are brewing. As he's putting the pot together, he pauses when he notices a flagged email.

"Jesus H. Christ," Straub says out loud, leaning toward the screen when he sees the name. Starting the coffeemaker, he opens the email. It has been six months since he's heard from his college roommate.

Winn hoped that retirement would mellow Howie, but as he reads the message, he knows Howie's back to his old tricks.

> Winn, I'm onto something that could turn out to be big. Won't know for a while but I'm going to see where it takes me. But I might step on some toes along the way and need your help.

Not that Howie's cause wasn't worthy of concern, Straub has recognized for years that unrecovered nuclear weapons was a Cold War loose end the Pentagon had swept under the rug. And in the wake of 9/11, to anyone aware of the bombs' existence, the thought of terrorists fishing a nuke out of the water and detonating it was distressing. Yet conventional wisdom put the threat of terrorists using stolen or black market nuclear materials or devices way above the probability of attempting to recover one of the missing weapons. As far as Straub knew, there wasn't a single contingency plan covering lost nukes in any federal agency. Buried in mud or half-covered with coral in unknown or highly classified locations, they were off everyone's radar. The only danger lost nukes posed was in his college roommate's mind.

Straub pours himself a cup of coffee and carries the laptop over to the island. He begins typing,

> Howie, I hope you're not messing around with some sensitive Pentagon program. I suggest you get your butt back to Charlottesville and bury your nose in a good book, play some golf, take that nice wife of yours out to dinner and keep yourself out of trouble. Best, Winn

Straub rereads his email. He knows Howie has never paid any attention to advice—even from an old friend. So he types in the link to a more secure email server that only Straub and the agents under his control have access to. For the time being, it will give Howie added cover.

He takes a sip of coffee, listening to the first plane of the day roaring down its glidepath into Reagan. Back in his heyday, he skulked around Eastern European cities, Budapest and Bucharest, Sofia and Vienna, and developed a reputation as a master schemer who took deceit and deception to new levels.

He puts down his cup. Out in the garden, a robin that forgot to head south perches on the edge of the birdbath.

As much as he tries to chase the thought from his mind, it keeps returning, popping back up, and to Straub's surprise, gaining plausibility and attracting his interest each time it presents itself. If Howie is poking around in the dark recesses where the Pentagon's secrets are hidden, leaving him out there might pay off. *Maybe he'll provoke the Pentagon into doing something rash—making some bonehead move I can capitalize on.* And the risks could be minimized if the circle of people who know what Howie's up to can be kept tight. The one thing he can count on is that the intelligence community shares information about as freely as they share budgets. Even within individual agencies, secrecy is paramount and information is so jealously guarded that one hand often has no idea of what the other's doing. If he can stay behind the scenes, giving Howie cover and feeding him information, the upside could be huge.

Dicey game, using his college roommate as a decoy for the Pentagon—but to Straub, dicey was the only game in town.

☢ ☢ ☢

An hour later, a hundred miles south in Charlottesville, Sylvie and her daughter Grace are sitting in the kitchen over their third cup of coffee. Since her husband left for Pittsburgh, Sylvie has been a wreck. Yesterday they visited his parents in the nursing home on the other side of town. Grace thought it would be a good distraction. But the visit only added to her mother's anxiety.

"I thought they looked well," Sylvie frowns to Grace as they rehash the visit to the life care facility. "But they both seemed upset Howie didn't visit."

"You're the one who's upset, Mother."

"I have a sixth sense about these kind of things."

"Look, Dad's a big boy and even though he goes off half-cocked sometimes, his head is on straight enough to keep himself out of trouble," Grace says.

"He could have called," Sylvie repeats for the umpteenth time. "He didn't call all yesterday and he always does when he's away. I'm worried that those people from the Pentagon are after him."

"That's cuckoo, Mother. *Those people from the Pentagon*—do you know how nuts that sounds?"

"If Howie's after some bomb it isn't."

"Wait a minute here, let's not let our imagination run away with our good sense. We don't really know if there are any lost bombs. The whole thing could be a figment of his imagination. We've always said that. And second, this whole conspiracy deal at the Pentagon, that's totally wacky if you ask me."

"I just wish he hadn't gone up there."

"He's been gone for thirty-six hours, you know how he loses track of time." Grace has an idea. "Did you look at your email? Maybe he sent you an email."

"I've checked it five times already."

"When did you do it last?"

"I don't know, two hours ago."

"It's worth looking again," Grace mumbles, walking over to the computer at the home office Sylvie has set up for herself on one wall of the living room.

"If you'd heard what your father told me about that phone call he got during dinner, you wouldn't think I'm crazy."

"All that stuff about a pilot hidden away in a VA hospital starting to blab about a lost bomb is just too far out for me. Aha! I told you, here's an email from The Boot himself. Sent an hour ago."

Sylvie trips over a chair leg rushing to the computer. "What does it say? Is he okay?"

"You read it..."

Sylvie peers over her daughter's shoulder as she reads the email, "You're right," she says. "He does sound okay. So his cell is on the fritz, I guess that's why he's emailing. He's been having trouble with it for a while."

"See? I told you. There it is in black and white. Now don't you feel stupid having gotten yourself all worked up? Dad's fine. His phone's fried, that's all. It says right here, 'Everything's fine...' and he might have to be up there a few more days. So what's the big deal?"

Sylvie stands at the computer reading the email for the third time. "I guess he is all right. He's probably just preoccupied with something. You know how he can go off on a tangent."

"Tell me about it," Grace says, rolling her eyes.

No point in alarming Grace, but Sylvie Collyer is certain something is amiss. Sure, he sounds fine. But there's some other reason he's emailing. *If his phone wasn't working, he could have used a pay phone.* And Sylvie has sent enough emails to notice that there's no sending address, as if the email magically came from out of the ether. She wonders if Winn Straub is involved. Has he given Howie some kind of cover? On one hand she's relieved, on the other she's scared to death. *It isn't good to mess with them.*

Them. As overdramatic as it sounds, Sylvie Collyer knows they exist. Ghost programs run by the faceless and nameless operating by unpublished rules to achieve unknown ends. A woman she played tennis with whose husband worked at the Pentagon. He made a stink about something that made all the papers. And all of a sudden the family moved away. Up and vanished. Happened every once in a while. Mysterious car accidents. Hunting mishaps. Always talk about large amounts of money. Stories suggesting sinister forces lurking behind veils of secrecy invisibly acting in the name of national security.

"Mother, is something the matter? You look like you've seen a ghost."

"Worse," Sylvie says.

"But Dad sounds great. I don't see what you're fretting about."

Sylvie fakes a smile. "Grace, you know me, I'm just a worrier at heart."

11

[Pentagon, Saturday morning]

That morning, Wishnap is thrilled to see a message come in with a routing code he doesn't recognize. Special codes are kept in a looseleaf notebook stored in the safe in the large file room off the chief of staff's office, which means he can spend some time chatting up the chief's bevy of secretaries. Hours cooped up in a cubicle staring at a screen leave him craving human contact.

Sent from a Veterans Administration hospital in Pittsburgh, Pennsylvania, the email is directed to Vector Eleven. He guesses Vector Eleven is a Special Access Program requiring special security clearance. SAP or black program participants are never directly identified and their agendas are classified Polo Step, a level above Top Secret—the addresses on incoming mail are the only indications of their existence. Even the addresses themselves are Polo Step. Vector Eleven would have a seven, eight or nine digit routing designation in the notebook, which, when he punched it in, would electronically sort the message directly to those individuals in Vector Eleven without revealing their names.

In his three months of duty in the Pentagon, he has been surprised at the number of black programs, many with ominous-sounding names—Orange Talon, Rising Blade, Domino Twist—names that tantalize with implications of mysterious and sinister activities but ultimately leave the guesser stymied.

Wishnap had hoped a senior staff assignment in Washington would burnish his resume. But after three months, he's already itching to get back into the field. After 9/11 the Pentagon is a 24-7 operation, the place works around the clock. Wishnap finds himself working weekends and since the Pentagon is largely staffed with officers—the building is literally crawling with colonels—being at the bottom of the pecking order effectively reduced him to a pencil pusher with a high security clearance.

To add insult to injury, sitting at a computer terminal receiving information and routing it to the proper channels is clerical work. The Army didn't hand out Purple Hearts for carpal tunnel syndrome. Sure he works in a SCIF, called a "skiff" around the Pentagon, a Secure Compartmented Information Facility, and he has a top secret security clearance, but all the impressive keypads on the doors, armed guards at the entrance and Secure Telephone Units on the desks can't make up for the fact that he is a glorified clerk.

Commuting from his tiny apartment in Fairfax with the hordes of other Pentagon workers, he stands in slug lines waiting for a ride-share then is packed in like a sardine for the half-hour ride to the massive structure known as the Building or the Squirrel Cage—since from an aerial perspective that's exactly what it looks like—the nerve center of the American military machine.

The chief of staff's office is a five-minute walk down the D ring into the walkway to E. As a young officer, the sweep of the five-ring, five-spoked Pentagon with its endless corridors, colorful displays of maps and insignia and flag officers loaded with stars around every corner used to be impressive. Now used to it, it feels more like Wishnap's old township high school back in Illinois, characterless and institutional, one corridor the same as every other, long stripes of overhead fluorescents reflecting in the gleaming floors, everything polished within an inch of its life.

A slender and attractive secretary named Gretchen, high heels, hair pulled back, is standing at the water cooler reading *Vogue.* The chief likes his secretaries trim and athletic, and each day his staff starts with a 5:30 workout at the POAC, the Pentagon athletic club. She's an up and comer, rumor has it she's slated for a slot at the White House.

"Are you slumming, Colonel?" Gretchen asks as he pauses on his way to the safe. "Don't see you often in this area."

Wishnap holds up the envelope containing the document, "Got a Polo Step communication and I need a routing code."

"Polo Step, huh? How does it feel to be in the inner circle?"

"I'm afraid I'm just a messenger."

"You know what they say about messengers," she winks.

Their conversation is interrupted by a flurry of activity. The chief of staff, General Nerstand, is on the move and it isn't healthy for the career of an aspiring Army officer to be seen standing around the water cooler gossiping with one of the general's shapely young secretaries.

"See you, Gretchen," Wishnap says, scurrying off in the direction of the file room before the flying wedge of brownnosers surrounding the senior officer in the United States Army sweeps through the area.

Opening the safe, he takes out the codebook, "Vector Eleven," he wonders as his index finger pages down the sheet in the notebook and settles on the organization. "Wonder what in the hell Vector Eleven does?"

Lieutenant General Greg Watt is pissed, really pissed. It's Saturday and he's sitting at his desk in the Pentagon instead of in the VIP box at Byrd Stadium watching the Terps play Clemson. Plus, the situation in Pittsburgh has gone from bad to worse. Wednesday, Watt was alerted that a nurse at the VA hospital was sniffing around a patient, a man Vector Eleven had arranged to be committed three years ago. For some reason, she had altered his meds.

Watt scanned the man's file and knew he had to act. Yesterday, he'd ordered the patient's former dosage reinstated, but the damage had been done. The nurse had become more suspicious. So the order went out to raise the dose and eliminate the problem.

Too late, dammit all to hell, Watt snorts, slamming the email down on his desk.

Watt's heavily lidded eyes were the first to see the email to Vector Eleven from Pittsburgh. At 2135 hours, a VA nurse, Sharon Thorsen, abducted Risstup from the hospital, escaping by drugging a member of the security detail. The only thing Watt can figure out is that she must have seen the reinstatement order and was trying to protect him. *But why? Out of the goodness of her heart? Or does she have another agenda—maybe one backed by CIA or another agency hoping to dig up some dirt on the Defense Department?*

Watt checks his watch. Almost 1600 hours. In a few minutes, the video from the security cameras will be transmitted.

Turning the key to activate his secure phone, Watt grumbles to the lieutenant outside his office, "Any news from the VA hospital?"

"They were finishing encoding it a few minutes ago, sir," his aide tells him. "It should be coming in any moment."

"I'll keep an eye out," Watt says.

Watt sets the phone back in its cradle and flicks the key to the OFF position. Communication within Vector Eleven is always on a secure phone, called a STU, or *stew* in Pentagon parlance, even routine calls like the call Watt just made to his aide in the outside office.

Kicking his feet up on the windowsill, the general stretches back in his chair. Out his office windows, Watt can see a fair number of cars in South Parking. Recently retrofitted with bombproof glass, the panes are now an inch thick and tinted a greenish yellow that bleaches out the color from the surrounding landscape so it looks like you're peering through dime store sunglasses. The lot is half full, at least he isn't the only one working on a Saturday.

His stew buzzes.

"Watt," he answers.

"Sir, the video from the VA hospital was just downloaded," his aide informs him. "It should be up on your screen."

"Join me, Williams. I'd like your read on this."

Watt opens the file. He leans forward in his chair looking at the black-and-white footage from a security camera. Overlooks the intersection of two corridors, ceiling fixtures pool light in evenly spaced dots down the empty hallways.

Williams walks into Watt's office, the general motions him over to his PC.

"Get our contact at the VA hospital on the line while we watch the video."

"Yes, sir." Lieutenant Williams walks over to the stew and turns the key, punches in a number and puts the receiver up to his ear.

"Give me Bigelow...this is Lieutenant Williams at the Pentagon calling," Williams says into the stew. "Bigelow, please hang on while we review the tape in case General Watt has any questions." Normally his boss is a cool character, but Williams notices that the events of the last two days are beginning to take their toll. Watt has even more of that Khrushchev demeanor that people around the Pentagon have remarked about if only because of his stocky build, doughface and closely cropped white hair. Now he's looking even older and more rotund, an obvious contrast to most of the officers at his rank who are ramrod slender and buff to the extreme.

Williams' eyes shift over to the computer. On the screen a female nurse in scrubs comes into view pushing a wheelchair down the corridor. Her head's bent down, she checks back over her shoulder.

"How do you pause this damn thing?" Watts grumbles as he clicks buttons on his screen.

Williams puts down the phone and finds the pause button for his boss.

"We're going to have to get some video technicians in on this—you can't tell who in the hell these people are."

"Wait a minute, let me check," Williams says, picking up the stew. "Bigelow, we are at the place on the tape which you indicated. What can you tell us?"

"Yes, we can see the wheelchair and the nurse. Who are they?"

"I see," Williams responds to the voice on the other end of the phone, and then turning to Watt, says, "The patient's name is Risstup and the nurse is a VA employee named Sharon Thorsen. Apparently she shot our security guy full of sedative then took off with Risstup."

How in the hell can this be happening? Watt asks himself. He knows full well who the patient is. The nurse is still a big question. "Ask him what's the story with this nurse?"

Lieutenant Williams pauses. Then rephrases his boss's question, "Why would you think a nurse would kidnap a mentally ill patient from your hospital the day after Thanksgiving?"

Williams snaps into the phone, "Maybe you would prefer to use another word, Bigelow, but from our vantage point, it sure looks like a kidnapping."

He waits for a reaction, then says, "Okay, we'll do that. He says we should look at the part with the car."

Williams taps on the screen to fast forward the tape. In the scene, the nurse dashes across the lot toward a car parked in the shadows, the wheelchair zipping along in front of her.

"It's a car, but it's too dark to tell what make or whether someone's in it. Could be another person involved," Watt says, his frustration level rising. "Ask him if he has any theories why a nurse would abduct our man."

Williams asks the question, and then shakes his head at Bigelow's response. Holding his hand over the receiver, Williams says, "He says he's only been on the ward for a month. Anything else you'd like to ask, sir?"

Watt scowls at his aide. Williams gets the message and ends the call.

Watt drums his fingers on his desk. *Whoever is behind this operation is one jump ahead. Obviously an inside job, the nurse had kidnapped him but did she have an accomplice? And if she did, who the hell is it?*

General Watt knows he will be called on the carpet. Everyone will be looking to him for the answers. As Critical Material Officer, Pentagonese for the job of riding herd on all the spent nuclear materials—military and civilian—stashed all over the country, Watt is the Pentagon's atomic janitor, responsible for storing and safekeeping all the nuclear trash discarded over the past sixty years. Hundreds of thousands of barrels of radioactive waste stacked ten high at the Savannah River Plant, spent plutonium pits and nuclear fuel rods in storage casks all over the country, hundreds of acres of contaminated soil at Rocky Flats, Colorado, and radioactive buildings in Dayton, Ohio. Every week brought him a new headache, some spill off a truck or leakage from a rusting tank, radiation mysteriously emitting from a safe room or a fire at some facility in Norfolk or New London threatening to release radiation.

In addition to dealing with the atomic garbage, he has the chore of keeping an eye on the lost nuclear weapons. Except for an enterprising journalist occasionally sticking his nose into the subject, the unrecovered nukes have stayed out of sight and out of mind.

Now a nurse in a VA hospital has to stir the pot. Watt has twenty-four hours, he figures, to find out where in the hell the missing patient is. *If ever the label "loose cannon" was applicable, this was it.*

He looks up at Williams. "Find out everything you know about Thorsen and Risstup—down to their shoe sizes and whether they like their eggs over easy or sunny side up. In the meantime, get me everything in the building concerning Risstup. And I want to know every number called out of that hospital for the last two weeks."

"I have Risstup's file on my desk, sir, I'll have the call log within the hour."

Thankfully, Williams is always two moves ahead of him. Normally, someone higher up the chain of command would snag a promising young officer like Williams. Yet once the doors of Vector Eleven opened for you, they closed behind you just as abruptly. A few officers had made the unwise decision to opt out of Vector Eleven—only to find themselves permanently posted to the military mission in Khartoum, or banished to a missile range in the Utah desert. Williams willingly accepted the tradeoff—a commitment to a career in Vector Eleven to guarantee he would stay at the center of the action and avoid a merry-go-round of low-profile assignments.

The file on Risstup is in two parts. His service records up to the time he was presumed lost and a second section that began three years ago with his admission to the VA hospital. The assumption on the military's part had been that the crew went down with the B-52. The last words about the six were written on granite gravestones in Arlington National Cemetery—*Missing in Action*—their cases closed until three years ago when the Pentagon began receiving crank calls from some character in Pittsburgh. When Watt picked up on the story, alarms went off and he acted fast.

The caller claimed to be a survivor of the crash. Was warning anyone who would listen about an H-bomb jettisoned before his plane went down. Insisted it was recoverable but couldn't give a coherent reason why. "His memory kept going in and out on him," the crack team Watt sent out to assess the situation reported, "flickering on and off like a light bulb on its last legs."

The caller could barely remember his name, had lived hand to mouth for years, often homeless. No family but was well known in shelters, soup kitchens and police stations, having been picked up for vagrancy numerous times. The team's report noted that before they had him hosed down and cleaned up they could barely stand to be in the same room. Their conclusion was that he was probably the missing Air Force major but he did not pose a threat. After years on the streets, his health was a question mark. Doctors called in said the only issue was which of his organs would give out first. His arteries were shot, heart weak—who knows how many minor strokes he'd had—it wasn't a matter of *if* but of *when*.

Watt's people recommended that the former pilot be treated with respect. Committed to the senility ward of a local VA hospital under his own name and left to live out his remaining days in peace and in a stupor, a daily cocktail of sedatives insuring he didn't make any more crank calls to anyone.

While he had reservations about the course of action, Watt was under the gun on a number of projects and signed off. Within a week, the man was diagnosed to have advanced senile dementia and committed to the Pittsburgh VA hospital. Watt was guaranteed that people were going to keep an eye on him and was assured that for all practical purposes Risstup might as well have disappeared off the face of the earth.

Hard to get good help these days, he sardonically observes. *If they'd taken care of him back then, I wouldn't be in this mess.* But Watt knows that as easy as it was to blame his crew, he had taken his eye off the ball, if only for a second. And that he would be the one to pay.

He quickly scans the first part of Risstup's file. The officer's last assignment was in 1958 to the 57th Air Division, 99th Bomber Wing, 348th Bomber Squadron at Westover Air Force Base, near Worcester, Massachusetts. Co-pilot on a B-52D, Risstup flew multiple airborne alert missions during the time he was at Westover.

On the next series of documents he opens up Watt has to note his security classification number and sign his name. Marked SCI/SAP, SCI refers to Sensitive Compartmented Information and SAP to Special Access Programs. The Polo Step designation is the final hurdle. Even the SecDef's eyes aren't cleared. Only Vector Eleven members have access.

The file has not been opened in a while—from the color and feel of the paper Watt guesses for years. Mishaps with nuclear weapons were carefully concealed from congressional watchdog committees and prying investigative journalists.

Though never admitted publicly, it was common knowledge around the Pentagon that squadrons of B-52s and B-47s carrying armed nuclear weapons flew around the clock for ten years. Flying three routes, over the Arctic, the U.K., and over Spain, thousands of SAC bombers went to failsafe points two-thirds of the way toward Russian targets before turning back to base.

Watt loves to tell the story of the B-52 landing in Moscow on the first friendly visit back in the 1970s. A Russian official greeting the huge plane welcomed the pilot by saying, "Welcome to Moscow. This must be your first visit here."

The pilot smiled and responded, "Oh, no, we've flown to Russia many times before."

Halfway through the SAP document, Watt finds what he's looking for. He speedily reviews the information. His concerns are confirmed.

The language used is pure bureaucratese, but the story could have come out of Hollywood. He immediately recalls the details. It was August, thunderstorm and northeaster time on the East Coast—August 14, 1958—if his memory serves him right. Watt checks. It does.

He reads on. Risstup's plane flew into a nasty weather pattern not long after takeoff. Westover lost radar contact with the plane early in the flight. Metal fatigue and equipment breakdown was the price paid for keeping so many of America's B-52s in the air at all times. The airborne alert missions lasted over twenty-four hours and covered over ten thousand miles, again and again the aircraft went out, for weeks, months and years. Not surprising there were stories of B-52s coming apart in mid-flight.

Watt pours over the map, tracing the plane's route with the tip of his pencil. The flight path is a straight line from just east of Westover south to a location over central New Jersey. At the point radio contact was lost, the flight path turns into a dotted line.

Watt leans back in his chair, exhaling heavily. Right now is when he needs a cigarette. He pops a Tums instead. *A goddamn dotted line means they lost contact and don't have the vaguest idea how much longer the aircraft stayed in the air. Who knows where the aircraft went down? It could be over the ocean—or anywhere in the mid-Atlantic for that matter.*

The comment in the file by the commanding officer at Westover at the time is maddening. "All B-52 crews were given orders to jettison nuclear weapons over water if circumstances deemed it necessary. In all probability the crew followed orders and jettisoned the Mk-15 weapon, serial number 47332, over the Atlantic Ocean."

"*In all probability*—damn!" Watt mutters and pounds his desk. The base commander didn't even know exactly where the aircraft went down—how could he report the weapon was dropped in the drink?

What they used to get away with in those days, Watt grumbles. He remembers the story of a hydrogen bomb that was dropped on a farmhouse in North Carolina sometime in the late '50s or early '60s. Fortunately it was out in the sticks and the Air Force hustled out to the site and sealed it off. The family was given immediate medical treatment, they patched up the mom, dad and the kids, set the family up in a new house and bought their silence with a fat check, recovered one of the nukes near the surface, left the other buried, put a chain-link fence around the site, established an easement preventing digging and simply walked away. It was over and done with. Now it would be another story.

If a nuclear weapon were jettisoned from a plane today, CNN would have instant around-the-clock coverage with correspondents all over the world fanning it into major news. There would be a congressional committee immediately formed to investigate, politicians would swarm all over the mishap, the administration would be on the warpath and heads would roll in every ring of the Pentagon.

Not much worries Greg Watt. But the thought of an ex-Air Force pilot on the loose who knows where a nuke was dropped was like a live grenade rolling under his desk.

What had been ancient history, stale information from Cold War days that was supposed to have fallen through the cracks, suddenly gets moved up to the front burner. The blanket of secrecy Vector Eleven had thrown over the nukes lost during the Cold War could be compromised. The implications were clear. Everyone up the line would take the heat—but because he hadn't taken care of business Watt would get the shaft.

"Excuse me, sir, I have the phone logs," Williams said, poking his head through the half-opened door.

"Let's see what you have."

"Nothing from the VA hospital in the last two weeks. I've had three men combing through them for the last hour. But the nurse's cell phone record has one call that leapt out at me."

"Smart of you to get her log," Watt says.

Williams briskly shuffles through to the seventh page. His finger stops at a line. "Right here. The nurse made a call on her cell to a number in Charlottesville, Virginia."

Watt looks up at Williams. "So?"

"That number belongs to Howard Collyer."

Watt has to struggle to keep his jaw from dropping. "Holy fucking shit," is the only phrase he can come up with. "Not *the* Howie Collyer?"

"The same. I double-checked. He retired from the Building and moved to Charlottesville over a year ago—deemed a security risk—if you remember."

"How could I forget?" Though Watt has never met Collyer, as a diehard ACC football fan, he's well aware of the story of Howie Collyer and his freak field goal as well as with his fixation on lost nukes. Watt drops his head into his hands. *If Collyer's involved in this...* Watt doesn't finish the thought. His alimentary canal burbles disagreeably.

Watt picks up his stew and dials a number. He barks into the phone, "Prepare a flying squad to head down to Charlottesville immediately. I want to know everything that's going on in Collyer's house. And if Howard Collyer, a nurse named Sharon Thorsen and a VA patient named Risstup are anywhere around there, I want them detained. Code Five authority. Call me when you have something."

Two more calls and Vector Eleven is on full alert—its intricately woven web extends into all corners of the Pentagon and every agency having to do with national security. If the president knew of Vector Eleven's influence, he'd be envious. With operatives in the Defense Intelligence Agency, the National Security Agency and all the intelligence branches of the armed services, not to mention Vector Eleven's own Special Ops unit based at Fort Belvoir, finding Howard Collyer should be a walk in the park.

One more loose end Watt is determined to take care of. Collyer has a close friend at CIA, guy who was a top spook in the '70s in Eastern Europe. Watt searches his memory for the man's name. *Straub, Winston Straub. Yes.* Just in case he's tempted to give his buddy a hand, someone's going to warn Straub it's something he'd better not stick his nose into.

Watt is fairly confident that by the end of the day he'll have the situation contained. The last thing he wants is to stand up in front of a hostile audience of Vector Eleven members and field questions about Howard Collyer and a lost nuke.

But for some reason, as Watt looks out at the cars leaving South Parking, their headlights already on at four-thirty in the afternoon, his intuition tells him the search for Collyer might not be quite as easy as he's hoping it will be.

He sets the stew receiver back in its cradle, thinking, *This feels like one of those damn times where we just sit back and wait for the other shoe to drop.*

12

[Rutgers campus, Saturday morning]

Mehran quietly slides out from under the covers, stands, stretches and looks down at Melanie, who's sound asleep, snoring lightly. He checks the clock. *1:15. Just what I planned.* Quietly climbing into his sweats, he tiptoes into his tiny study, closes the door, turns on his computer and logs onto the Net. One of the windows looking out on the quad is open slightly, a draft of chilly air sneaking into the room. *Good, that will keep me alert.*

He types in the first address, clicks on a link leading him to the second, then taps a button that takes him to the third: *Jeffri'sGarden.com.* The website comes up on Mehran's screen, the photos of the flowerbeds appear, then the photograph of the smiling woman holding her clippers and basket of freshly cut flowers. With her welcoming smile Jeffri Adams could be a red-haired Martha Stewart hosting a site dedicated to the cultivation of flowers, their care, planting, all the details involved in creating a bountiful and beautiful garden.

While the Americans have the latest satellites and the most cutting-edge technology, millions of powerful computers, giant radomes positioned all over the world to track satellites and instantly relay information, his cell's operation on the other hand is homespun, almost rudimentary—basic codes, off-the-shelf electronics, commonplace computers—all neatly tucked in under the radar of the Americans.

The American intelligence geniuses and their thousands of analysts and experts would never suspect that the pleasant-looking middle-aged lady with the straw sunhat and gardening website is actually the cover for Mehran's cell and the other cells assigned to the mission.

Mehran only knows his own codes: anything involved with dahlias. He has never been told what the other plants on the site might mean to other cells—chrysanthemums, orchids or daylilies. Maybe they are decoys, Mehran guesses, distracting context for the thousands of cryptographers and analysts sitting in cubicles at the National Security Agency in Fort Meade listening to telephone calls and downloading emails and information on websites.

When someone posts a message on the site to visiting gardeners in Zone 5, a coded message is instantly conveyed to the slim Rutgers engineering student.

Mehran sits forward in his chair reading the post. *Dahlia lovers know that despite the wonderful weather we are having, it is time to locate your dahlias and set aside some time to dig them up. Leaving them in the ground over the winter, even in Zones 5, 6, 7 and 8, will expose them to more cold and frost than most dahlias are able to handle.*

Mehran's eyes widen as the post continues. *I heard from Cindy in Virginia that she got a call from her friend in Pennsylvania telling her that there might be dahlias she had overlooked. Cindy is going to double-check with her friend. Remember, gardeners, every dahlia bulb you carefully store over the winter will rebloom in the spring.*

Mehran cannot believe what he is reading. *Cindy in Virginia* is the code designation for his assignment, the person named Howard Collyer, the man with the website. He checks the time on the post: 1:03 PM. He bends over the screen and carefully interprets the coded message: *Someone in Pennsylvania called to alert Cindy*, means Collyer has been notified of some information about a lost bomb.

In his training in Jakarta, Mehran had been drilled on the code words and phrases so thoroughly they have become a second language to him. Mehran and his cell members could sit in a restaurant and practice conversations in dahlia speak. Each part of the dahlia—bloom, petals, tuber and stem—is assigned to a component of an H-bomb. And each of the twelve groups of dahlias—singles, mignons, duplexes, anemones, etc.—specifically identify bomb models. A mignon stands for a Mk-15, an anemone, a Mk-39. The language is complete and precise yet so veiled and obscure that no one in the restaurant overhearing their conversation would have suspected they were anything but botany grad students. And the master code-breakers in Washington, even if they could unscramble the code words and break down the firewalls to gain access to the site, would inevitably overlook a bunch of dahlia lovers chatting about their favorite perennial.

He continues decoding the post. *Dahlias she might have overlooked* translates to *there could be a bomb that can be located.*

Cindy is going to double check with her friend tells him Collyer will be debriefing someone who might have information about a bomb. He is going up to Pennsylvania to follow up on some information—to find out from some yet unidentified person about a lost nuke.

Mehran knows if Collyer proves to be on the trail of a bomb, the operation will ramp up fast, the money to undertake the operation will flow into the cell member's accounts, the necessary equipment will be delivered, and people will contact him to carry out his assignment.

So far the news is encouraging. The zones mentioned in the post are in Mehran's assigned area—the Middle Atlantic States. That could change, but for now Mehran knows he stands a chance of being the lucky one. He sits back, arms clasped behind his head, reveling in his good fortune.

All of a sudden, Mehran's computer screen blinks and goes dark. He checks his Internet connection, fumbles around in back of his machine to make sure it is plugged in. He is immediately relieved when his screen comes alive again. But he is shocked to see the message spelled out across the screen. *This website is down for repair and redesign. Please check back in three days.*

He restarts his computer, examines the cables again. But when he logs onto the site, the screen comes back with the same message: *down for repair and redesign.* What does that mean? Has the website been discovered? Or did it crash again? Mehran suddenly feels isolated, out on a limb. For three years, Jeffri's Garden has been his refuge, the one place he knew was safe.

He checks the companion site based on American crafts, a backup in case Jeffri's Garden becomes compromised. DownhomeCrafts.com is the address and Mehran's subject is quilting. He opens the quilting section looking for posts. Same message. *This portion of the website is down for repair and redesign. Please check back in three days.* He logs on to sleepingdogs.us. No new posts. At least it is business as usual on Howard Collyer's site.

Mehran has a frightening thought. What would he do if FBI agents showed up at his door? Or would they follow him first? Try to find out who his friends are, who he talks to, would they detain Melanie? Fortunately, he only knows the code names of his fellow cell members—not their locations or responsibilities. If the Americans interrogate him, he could reveal little about the entire operation. Still, he did not want to even entertain the thought. Though he has been trained, put through hours of arduous grilling and intimidation, he fears what he might reveal under duress. He's heard stories about the tortures Americans use on terrorists. He once shared a meal with an interrogation victim. The man's nerves were so shot he could barely manage food to his mouth.

He hears a knock on his door. Mehran turns to look at it, not sure of what to do. Then silence.

Mehran gets up and tiptoes to the door. He leans in close to it and listens.

"Denny Zarif?" At first he does not recognize the voice.

His body relaxes as he hears Melanie say, "If you can't sleep, Denny, I can do something that will help."

13

[Georgetown, Saturday evening]

Buttoning his coat and flipping up his collar, Winn Straub hunches his shoulders to shield himself from the biting wind as he stands on a Georgetown street waiting for Sparky to find the perfect hydrant. Sparky's almost fifteen and Straub has to carry him down the steps of his brownstone to walk him, morning and night. His housekeeper attends to the dog's needs the rest of the day.

For two days after Thanksgiving, it's much too cold for this time of year and now the temperature's threatening to plunge into the low twenties. He's the only one out on the street. If they have any sense, his neighbors are curled up in bed with a book or sitting by a warm fire.

Sparky rejects the first hydrant. Straub tugs his leash in the direction of another. A carload of Georgetown students whizzes by on the way to a local watering hole, the booming hip hop seeping through their rolled-up windows.

"Winn—that you?" he hears a voice call out. He looks across the street. Someone is standing on the curb waving at him.

"It's Steve—Steve Lubell, Winn," the man calls, his voice echoing down the empty street. "What are you doing out on a night like this?"

"At least I have an excuse," he says as Lubell crosses toward him. Straub's professional curiosity kicks in. He immediately questions why Lubell has chosen to stop him. Normally people with sensitive jobs in the intelligence community don't acknowledge each other out of the office. When he thinks about it, Lubell doesn't even live in Georgetown, Straub is sure he lives somewhere in the burbs.

Lubell takes off a glove and extends his hand. "Good to see you, Winn. Nice dog you have there."

Straub looks down at his aging Jack Russell, mangy, swayback, arthritis in his hips—the last word anyone would use to describe him is *nice.* Lamest attempt at small talk Straub's heard in a long time. "This is Sparky. He's a good old guy," he says as he and Lubell shake hands. "Just takes him a while to get the urge going."

Lubell works for DIA, the Defense Intelligence Agency. And Straub has always suspected him of being involved in a black program. He had to have friends in high and dark places. No other reason for the guy to have gone that far, he's a jackoff with nothing but space between his ears. If Straub were to take a stab in the dark, he'd guess Vector Eleven since Lubell had worked at Oak Ridge earlier in his career. And those nuclear guys are tight as ticks. Straub's imagination immediately starts spinning, *Is Lubell a night messenger carrying some warning from Vector Eleven? If Vector Eleven's the group Howie's managed to rile up, he's in more trouble than I thought.*

"So how've you been, Winn?"

"Fine. What brings you to Georgetown on a night like this?"

"Just moved in right down the block. Margie and I separated six months ago."

"I'm sorry."

"She ran off with her physical trainer. Fifty-year itch, I guess. So after thirty years I'm back to batching it again. Live in that apartment building on the corner." There's an awkward pause, then Lubell asks, "Mind if I walk the block with you?"

"Of course not. But when Sparky finds his hydrant, I'm heading home."

"You bet. Say, I've been meaning to ask—whatever happened to your old college roommate—Collyer?"

Lubell is smiling innocently, as if his question is no more than friendly chitchat. But it's clear to Straub that Lubell has something on his mind. Howie Collyer is Lubell's subject of interest. All the talk about the weather and his wife has only been a warm up. Straub can feel his heart start to drum, he's suddenly glad he lost the argument with his doc about the blood pressure pills.

"Why do you ask?"

"I don't know. Guess he came to mind when I was watching a UVa game on TV. I know he retired from the Pentagon, just curious where he ended up."

Straub plays along with him, hoping he can lead him into showing his hand. "Howie's back down in Charlottesville. He and his wife bought a farm outside of town, used it as a weekend place until he retired. Howie plays a lot of golf, putters in the garden, bush hogs his fields, gentleman farmer-type."

"Still searching for lost nukes?"

His question is a fingernail on a blackboard, Straub struggles to keep his voice calm but his words give him away. "What's your point in asking that?"

Aside from his suspicions about Lubell's questions, Winn Straub has never liked Lubell's style. Clumsy, with the grace of an elephant, Lubell is mean-spirited on top of it. Though he's only had one professional encounter with Lubell, it left Winn with a bad taste in his mouth.

"Don't go getting your back up. There are two things that stand out about Howie Collyer—his kick and lost nukes. As far as I'm concerned, both are fair game."

"I think he's put the bombs issue to bed. But I don't know for sure. You'd have to ask him yourself. Give him a ring, he's in the phone book."

"I just might," Lubell says, his voice now sarcastic, almost taunting. Straub wonders if they have intercepted his email to Howie. He's glad he sent Howie the address of another server.

"We had dinner early last spring but I haven't seen him in months."

They walk six more steps before Sparky pauses to anoint a hydrant.

"That's it. You'll have to excuse me, but I'm going in, Steve, too damn cold out here," he says as Sparky drops his leg. His mission finally over, Straub wheels around, jerking Sparky's leash toward home.

"You bet," Lubell says. "Good to see you. And say hello to The Boot for me when you see him next." Lubell pauses and over his shoulder delivers a Parthian shot, "Tell him I'm glad he's staying out of trouble."

Straub knows he doesn't have to answer. He has all he needs to know. Reaching the stairway to his house, he leans down to scoop the dog off the sidewalk.

To Winn Straub, Lubell's message is crystal clear. *Vector Eleven has their eye on Howie. Lubell was tapped to convey it to me. He was obviously watching my house and when I came out with Sparky, he started his little stroll.*

Straub enters the warm front hall, kicking the door shut and setting Sparky down. The dog immediately scampers into a corner, lifts his leg, and before Winn can grab him, pees a steady stream down the hand-printed French wallpaper. A puddle the size of a small saucer collects on the parquet.

Normally he'd be cursing at Sparky but he has other things on his mind. Straub hustles off to the kitchen for a wad of paper towels. Returning, he squats and sponges Sparky's liquid gift off the floor as his mind sorts through the options. If they sent a blundering fool like Lubell out in the middle of the night to send an inept and awkward signal, they are obviously shooting in the dark. Warning me not to help him, hoping they can shut Howie down before he does any more damage.

Straub clicks off the first-floor lights and creeps over to one of the front windows. Sneaking back the drape, he peers up and down the street. Sure enough, there is a tan raincoat standing at each end. One of them is smoking a cigarette, looking like he s playing a part in a John le Carré novel. *They don't have any more idea of where Howie Collyer is than I do. And they're hoping I can lead them to him.*

Straub has sat in his office in the D ring for four years watching the Pentagon capitalize on the CIA's misfortunes. Humiliated by a series of major intelligence failures, the CIA's stock has hit new lows and morale is in the dumps.

And the Pentagon, CIA's main rival in the intelligence game, is not only gloating over the civilian agency's bumbling but rapidly extending its influence, using the war on terror to strengthen its hand internationally and domestically.

Finished mopping up after Sparky, he stands and looks around at the lavishly furnished interior of their brownstone, French antiques, chintz and brocade, yards of gold roping, oriental carpets costing as much as a Mercedes. Years ago, his wife's family made a killing in Alaskan oil rights. No CIA official could afford a house on S Street. Barbara's money made it possible for Straub to have a career as a spook while living a lavish lifestyle. Ten years ago he was one of the best. Now he's regarded as another superannuated Cold Warrior waiting to be put out to pasture, parked in an office in the Pentagon to watch as the military extends its reach and builds dominance in the intelligence community.

But if Howie can flush them out—

Straub stops and smiles as he marvels at his own capacity for duplicity. A career in espionage has taught him to turn every event or situation over and carefully examine the flipside for the unexpected advantage. Good or bad, things are never what they seem. The worst situation can have a silver lining while the best can go belly up and turn sour in a second.

The last thing he wants is any harm to come to Howie. He will go to any end to protect him. But if Howie's going to doggedly continue his quest in disregard of the danger, is there any reason why he shouldn't try to turn it to his own account? As they say at CIA, you can take the spy out of spying, but you can't take spying out of the spy.

"Winn, is that you?" his wife calls from their upstairs bedroom.

"Yes, dear, it's me," Winn responds—*just scheming, double-dealing, deceitful and devious me.*

14

[Lancaster, Pennsylvania, Sunday morning]

With a faded downtown full of boarded-up buildings, Lancaster, Pennsylvania is a once prosperous city in the middle of Amish country. Its centerpiece is a massive eight-story brick factory that cranks out flooring for the thousands of subdivisions sprouting up and down the Eastern Seaboard.

A half mile out of town sits the campus of Franklin & Marshall, a highly regarded liberal arts college bordered by Lancaster's fashionable residential district where many F&M faculty members reside.

As they drove through the college in the middle of the night, Sharon pointed out blocks of stately brick homes illuminated by turn-of-the-century streetlights, bordered with generous plantings and surrounded by neatly manicured lawns.

"I bet every other house in this neighborhood has a Wi-Fi setup. They're all academics and spend all kinds of time on the Internet."

Though Sharon attended Franklin & Marshall, she didn't graduate so Howie thought Lancaster would be a safe spot, at least for a while. And the no-tell motel four blocks off campus that Sharon recommended would be the last place anyone would think of looking.

The lights were blazing at the Nite Owl Motel when they pulled in at three in the morning. Howie struck a deal with the owner, a birdlike septuagenarian lady with a screechy voice and a lit Pall Mall dangling from her lip who padded around in terrycloth slippers and a housecoat, for three adjoining rooms on the ground floor for a hundred bucks. No secret the Nite Owl is a hot sheets motel, threadbare carpets, weeds growing in the courtyard, mangled window blinds and sheets worn so thin you can see your hand through them, but the rooms are clean and the baseboards crank out enough heat to keep the cold at bay. And with a C-store down the block, a short order place around the corner and an easy walk to campus, they can stay out of the car. Though they lifted new plates, he wants to drive it as little as possible. So at least for a day or two, the Nite Owl fills the bill.

Thorsen laid out her plan for Major Risstup on their way over. First she was going to make her patient comfortable.

"You have to remember for a couple years he's been drugged into a near coma. Without being pumped full of sedatives, the world's going to be a scary place to him. So before we can expect him to make any sense we have to wean him off the drugs and let him become familiar with his new surroundings."

"And how long would you expect this is going to take?" Howie's trying to be on his best behavior, knowing the nurse will eat his face if he steps out of line.

"Look, I'm not going to drag it out but we have to give him time."

So Howie spent the day scrambling around the Web looking for any information they might use to jumpstart the major's memory, ordering food from the nearby diner, trading football stories with Sharon and staring at the wallpaper while they waited for Risstup to get his bearings. Which was the last thing Howie wanted to do since he knew it was only a matter of time before Vector Eleven put two and two together. *But Sharon made herself clear. The major would be available when she damn well pleased. And for now, I can't do without her.*

At the crack of dawn Sunday, Howie's back at the diner ordering breakfast. Around the corner from the Nite Owl, the greasy spoon is run by a Lebanese family. The place is bustling, the owner shouting out orders, bacon hissing on the grill, plates clattering, the odor of fryer oil hanging in the air. He puts his order in then walks toward campus. Sharon was right, there is a sea of hot spots in the F&M neighborhood, the connection window of his laptop jumps from hot spot to hot spot like an electronic frog, offering him three, then four different avenues to the Net, a bunch without passwords.

Taking a seat on a bench next to the college library, he smiles as he opens the email from Winn Straub and reads,

> ...so I suggest you get your butt back to Charlottesville and bury your nose in a good book, play some golf, take that nice wife of yours out to dinner. Enjoy life and keep yourself out of trouble.

A little late for that, Winn, Howie thinks. When he notices the new email address Winn recommends he use, Howie immediately substitutes it for the old one.

There's a second email from Straub. Sent late Saturday night, it has more of an edge than the first.

> The Pentagon is all over me like a cheap suit. They sent a stooge out in the middle of the night to tell me they are after you. This is serious business, Howie. If you're off on some cockamamie mission, you better think twice because they are wheeling out the big guns. I think Vector Eleven's after you and you know those guys play for keeps.

Just as he figured. They had to be the ones who gave the order to raise the dose on Risstup and then to jack it up to a fatal level. It was only a matter of time before the alarms would go off at Vector Eleven. As he reads the last sentence of Straub's email, a smile flashes across his face.

> ...but if you're onto something you think I should know about, Howie, let me know what I can do to help.

Only a college roommate would try to scare the piss out of you and then in the next sentence ask you if he can come out and play.

In his response, Howie briefly sketches out the situation without giving many details. He asks Winn to contact Sylvie and make sure she's okay and then gives him a list of programs he needs: Keyhole, Photoshop, his customized versions of X-Plane and Taxiway and he tells Straub where to locate all the special programs he developed in his years at the Pentagon—his grab bag of visuals, tricks, special effects—he knows his whole repertoire is going to have to come into play on the buried memories of the pilot.

"Hi, honey, I'm home," Howie announces as he nudges the door open carrying his laptop and bag of breakfast goodies. Things have lightened up since their testy exchange in the car Friday night.

"If it isn't the Nite Owl Motel room service," Sharon jokes.

"Wait until you see the spread I've got." Twenty bucks bought the place out. Howie has enough scrambled eggs for a Little League team, hash browns, three egg sandwiches, a container of oatmeal and cups of OJ and tomato juice.

"No fruit?"

"In this place, if they can't fry it they don't serve it."

Howie notices Sharon has wheeled Major Risstup's chair into the room. He sits in the corner staring at the television. The volume's off, a *Wheel of Fortune* rerun on.

"Major Risstup, how are you doing today?" Howie leans around the side of his chair, smiling into the major's wrinkled face. No reaction. He glances at Sharon.

She shrugs as if to say, *Look, buddy, I told you it would take a while.*

Howie changes the subject, attacking the food from the eatery around the corner. "C'mon, time for some chow."

Sharon joins him and soon they are both downloading calories. As he shovels scrambled eggs into his mouth, he says, "You're right about the hot spots. There are loads around the campus."

"I was pretty sure there would be."

"Got an email from Winn Straub. He has me on an encrypted server so I can email him freely." Howie knows he has to focus on the good news. What he's learned about Vector Eleven would freak Sharon out.

"What's this encrypted business?"

"It's an Internet site that's buried so deep in codes and passwords no one can get near it unless they know the language. Our emails are secure."

"You certain about that?"

"Winn Straub has worked for CIA for thirty years. Senior guy there, he knows the ins-and-outs of the intelligence business better than anyone."

Sharon stabs a hash brown and pops open her coffee. When she sees milk in it, she realizes it's for Risstup. She'd noticed his coffee on his breakfast tray at the VA hospital was served with milk so she asked Howie to bring him a light coffee.

Risstup is sitting in his wheelchair silently gazing at the curtains.

"Brought you your coffee, Major Risstup," Sharon swings the cup in front of him.

"Thanks, with a little milk?" Risstup says to her casually, as if carrying on a conversation was the most normal thing in the world to him.

The word *yes* is almost out of her mouth before she realizes Risstup is speaking to her for the first time in three weeks. Howie's holding his paper plate, his mouth agape, he can't believe what he just heard.

Sharon manages to keep her cool despite the fact that her heart rate just doubled.

"Yes, Major, with a little milk just like you like it."

"Thank you," he says, taking a sip. His brow wrinkles as he looks around the room. He's taking everything in, eyes sweeping the floors, walls, ceiling and examining her face. After a minute he asks, "Can you tell me where are we?"

"In a motel in Lancaster, Pennsylvania."

"Why here?"

"It's a long story."

He looks up at her, the questions running through his mind contorting his expression, "Don't get me wrong—you seem very nice—but who are you?" Sharon shoots a quick look at Howie, as if to say, *What did I tell you?*

"I'm Sharon Thorsen, your nurse from the hospital. You were in a VA hospital, remember?" She takes the major's hand in hers. Looks at his crooked, shriveled collection of fingers, the skin thin, almost transparent and dappled with age spots.

"I'm not sure."

"That doesn't surprise me."

"I was in a VA hospital?"

"For a number of years, yes."

"Was I sick?"

"The Pentagon put you there to keep you from talking."

"Why would they do that?"

"Because you have information about something they don't want anyone to know."

"I don't understand," he says, his eyes fogging over. "Where are we again?"

"Lancaster, Pennsylvania. In a motel. I went to college here, Major Risstup. At Franklin and Marshall." She's making small talk as she eats, hoping something will stick.

"Franklin and Marshall, I think I've heard of Franklin and Marshall. I went to college—" Risstup's voice trails off.

"You were a Bruin, Major Risstup. You told me you went to UCLA—the fight song, you recognized it back in the hospital, remember?"

Risstup's face is a complete blank.

"Sons of Westwood," she says, then hums the tune.

Howie's wincing at her singing, "I'm not surprised he doesn't recognize it. You sound like a crow with a cough."

Risstup swings a finger in Howie's direction and asks Sharon, "Who's he?"

"Some wiseacre I picked up in Pittsburgh."

Howie steps up and offers a handshake, "I'm Howard Collyer, Major Risstup, good to have you with us." Risstup stares blankly at Howie's outstretched hand.

Howie lets his arm drop to his side. "Guess that's it for today, huh?"

"Look, for someone who's hardly made a peep in the last three months, that was the Gettysburg Address."

"You're the boss. More hash browns?" Howie asks, threatening to ladle another deep fried hockey puck on her plate.

"It's cardiac arrest if I eat any more of that crap," Sharon says, pushing back her plate.

"Good, then you can start on the day's mission," Howie hands over the laptop. "I'll babysit and you take a stroll, glom onto a hot spot and do a search on the name 'Risstup.' Maybe we can uncover some of his relatives. Maybe get really lucky and get a picture from someone. That would sure go a long way toward rebuilding his memory."

"How many Risstups do you think there are in the United States?"

"If he went to UCLA like you say, start in California." Howie gives in to temptation and snatches the last hash brown.

"Okay, I'll do that," she says, an *okay, smart ass, you want to play it that way, here goes* look on her face as she thrusts Risstup's bowl of oatmeal and the spoon at him.

"And you finish feeding the major."

15

[Charlottesville, Sunday morning]

It's a bracing late fall morning in Central Virginia. As she walks to the car the leaves crunch under her feet. Though it's sunny and clear, the breeze is chilly. Her Volvo starts sluggishly. Grace gives it a minute to warm up before putting it in gear and pulling out.

Out for the Sunday paper and coffee, Grace navigates the potholed driveway toward the main road. Pauses before pulling out, checking to her left and right as the road is twisty and has seen nasty accidents over the years. If she had looked more carefully, she might have noticed the mid-sized motor home pulled into a turnoff down the way from her parents' mailbox. Had she seen it, she might not have given it another thought after reading the tall black letters painted on one side, *Environmental Protection Agency, Mobile Air Quality Monitoring Station.*

But the motor home was well concealed, blocked from her view by shrubs, tree trunks and a thicket of bamboo, and Grace, preoccupied with getting back to keep an eye on Sylvie, never saw it.

Even on her return, coming back from the convenience store in the other direction, she's worrying about spilling the coffee as her station wagon jounces up the narrow and rutted gravel drive toward her parents' house so she doesn't peer through the woods toward where the motor home, its roof bristling with satellite dishes and antennas, is parked.

Pulling up in the courtyard, she tucks the paper under her arm and carefully juggles the coffees off the seat, slamming the car door with her hip.

"Got the goodies, Mom, come on down before it gets cold."

Grace's voice can be heard over the three men's headphones as clearly as if she was sitting next to them. As she clumps toward the kitchen her footsteps echo through the house. On the monitor, she can be seen setting the newspaper and cardboard drink carrier down, then opening a microwave.

During the night, while they were out to dinner, five wireless high-resolution cameras no larger than matchboxes were carefully situated in strategic positions around the Collyer residence. Now everything is projected on five plasma screens on one wall of the motor home. Sensitive mini-microphones snaked into air conditioning and dryer vents pick up the faintest sounds, a wireless router was positioned to peek into electronic communication and the phone system was tapped. Everything instantly transmitting to the dishes and antennas mounted on the roof of the motor home.

The Collyer house is now an open book to the three government gumshoes sitting at the consoles. Up and running since dawn, they've been eavesdropping for three hours. So far, they have notified the Pentagon that Collyer's car is missing and that there's no sign of him.

When they hear Collyer's wife say, "I got another email from Howie," their ears perk up. Waving a sheet of paper over her head, she steps into the camera's view wearing a plaid housecoat and slippers.

"Get that email up now, Ed," the man on the right orders, his tone of voice indicating he's the boss. Retired military, still in shape, gray hair cropped to fuzz. The man sitting in the middle, trim and efficient-looking, plastic pen holder in each of his two shirt pockets, enters a code into the keyboard in front of him and the window of the Collyer's desktop flashes across the monitor.

Ed toggles down, selecting and opening Howie's email:

> Sylvie—I'm fine, how are you and Grace? My research is going well up here, shouldn't be away more than a few more days. Will talk to you soon.
>
> Love, Howie

"Where's Collyer sending from? Locate that email's origin," the gray-haired man demands.

"I'm checking, Pete, gimme a quick minute," Ed Grossman says, his fingers a blur flying over the keyboard.

Grace says, "Let me see it," as she takes the printout of Howie's email from her mother.

"How does he sound to you?' Sylvie Collyer asks.

"Okay, I guess. A bit cryptic, if you want to know the truth." Grace finishes reading the email and tosses it on the counter. "I'd like to know what's this *research* he claims he's doing."

At the console, Grossman turns to his boss, "The email came from downtown Pittsburgh."

Pete runs his hand over his fuzz, "Backtrack the location."

"Coming right up."

On the screen, Sylvie Collyer can be seen throwing up her hands. "The whole email thing had me tossing and turning all night. Why doesn't Howie pick up a payphone and call us? That's what any sensible person would do. So that's why I'm so worried. Now I know you think I go overboard when I start talking about the Pentagon..."

"Don't go there again, Mom," Grace warns.

Sylvie Collyer carefully opens the plastic lid and takes a sip of coffee. "I just hope it's something else beside lost bombs. That scares the bejesus out of me."

In the motor home, Pete snaps his fingers three times, anything about lost bombs is what they've been waiting to hear, "Quick, get the Building patched in."

Grossman instantly routes the audio and video to the encrypted, pre-selected address at a classified location in the Pentagon.

General Greg Watt hears the steady, high-pitched beep coming from his computer and promptly touches the button on the screen. Within seconds, the color feed from the kitchen in a rural area of central Virginia appears, as it does on his assistant's screen in the office outside.

"Sir," Watt listens as the team leader explains, "You're looking at the interior of the house. Collyer is definitely after a bomb, his wife just mentioned it. And she seems concerned about the Pentagon's reaction."

She damn well ought to be, Watt thinks.

Pete continues, "Collyer sent an email to his wife yesterday at 1715 hours. We've tracked it to somewhere in downtown Pittsburgh."

"Not good enough, I need it pinpointed," Watt says.

"We're working on it. When we get it, we'll be able to identify the machine and locate the sender."

"I'll stay on the line," Watt tells his team leader. Two minutes go by, then three, then four. Watt knows he has to be patient. Even if he is a general, it is Sunday and harder to get stuff done when everyone's at home munching Cheetos and watching football.

His patience is rewarded when the team leader announces, "General Watt, that email came from an Internet café. We're running a locate on the machine."

Two minutes later, Williams gives a perfunctory knock on his boss' door and barges in. General Watt will appreciate the good news. Fortunately, a high-level VP at the cell phone company was at his desk on a Sunday afternoon. In ten minutes, he'd retrieved the needed information. Nothing like the phrase *in the interest of national security* to get someone's attention.

"Sir, I have the records of their calls. Sharon Thorsen made a call to Howie Collyer at 1135 hours Friday. At 1530 hours Collyer called Thorsen and at 2105 hours he put in a second call to her."

Watt remembers the time code on the surveillance tape, "2105 hours—that was around the time they were taking Risstup out of the hospital."

"That's correct, sir."

"Any other calls?" Watt asks. He knows Collyer's next move will be to communicate by computer since he's aware cell phones are a snap to trace. Though Collyer is a decent computer jock, he'll be no match for the legions of highly trained professionals at the National Security Agency and the Defense Intelligence Agency. It will be David against ten thousand Goliaths. Watt smiles at his analogy. *Corny but no overstatement.*

And when they manage to hunt down the machine used to send the email, the noose will tighten on Howard Collyer.

Watt's attention is drawn to Collyer's wife on the screen. "I wish there was something we could do to find him," she says, setting down her coffee cup and leaning on the kitchen island as if she needs its support. "I don't know how much longer I can just sit around. I'm about to go bonkers."

She hasn't yet told Grace of her suspicions about Winn Straub's involvement. Still trying to decide whether she should give him a ring at the CIA and flat-out accuse Straub of colluding with her husband or demand that he send Howie home and stop this craziness. But she doesn't know Straub that well. *Would I even be able to get past his secretary?* She's decided to give it another day.

"You always said patience was a virtue, Mother."

"Save the lectures, dear," Sylvie counters. "I just hope to God my crazy husband's okay."

Watt turns away from the screen, letting Collyer's wife's remark echo around in his mind as he thinks, *He won't be if I can help it.*

The end game is set. A middle-of-the-night flight on a Pentagon jet to a prearranged hellhole in the Middle East and Risstup, Collyer and the nurse will be out of his way for good. The threat to Vector Eleven eliminated.

He clicks off his computer. Checks his watch. So far he's been on duty almost forty-eight hours straight. So much for the weekend. And his Terps got clobbered by Clemson. No running game, three picks, he was lucky he missed it. Soon he can sleep, eat a thick steak, enjoy a glass of wine with his wife. There will be better days ahead.

His optimism is immediately rewarded as Williams sticks his head in and announces, "Sir, they've tracked the computer Collyer used to send the email to his wife. NSA ran it down for us in a matter of minutes. He also used it to send a second email."

"To who?"

"Blacked out, completely encrypted. And there's no sending address. All we can tell is that Collyer sent out a second email. We don't know what it said or to whom it was addressed."

"Find the machine that sent those emails. If we can get our hands on it, NSA will mine the hard drive and get the goods."

Watt scratches his neck. His wife dropped off a fresh shirt but it hasn't been washed enough and the collar's like sandpaper. The news Williams gave him is equally irritating. He doesn't like the sound of the second email. It's been encoded, evidence Collyer is getting help from someone in the intelligence community. Winston Straub at CIA, Collyer's college roommate, most likely. They are watching him carefully and have warned him to keep his nose out of their business.

The Pentagon's a favorite target these days. Everyone has some beef with the Building. Could be another person at CIA or someone at the FBI, both of those agencies have been taking it on the chin ever since

9/11. Not to mention Homeland Security—any of those outfits would love to see the Pentagon take it in the ear.

Watt clicks on his computer and speaks to the team in the motor home. "Any luck on the machine that sent the email?"

"Yes, sir. It's registered to a grad student at Carnegie Mellon. We'll be paying him a visit."

"Quick, please, we're running out of time."

Matt Simon is scrambling to add the finishing touches to his dissertation that's due in a week. Simon's advisor is a stickler for details so he's absorbed in proofing the first section, making notations in the margins, correcting punctuation and spelling and double-checking his footnotes. There's no reason for him to notice the two men slowly walking through the reading room of the engineering library surveying the faces of the few students still up and studying at this hour.

He only looks up when he hears his name.

"Mr. Simon?"

Simon turns to his left, a man in a plain dark suit pulls up a chair next to him. Buttoned up and buttoned down, very businesslike, too businesslike in contrast to the casually dressed students.

"Yes?"

"We have some questions to ask you." Simon is aware of someone on his right. He swivels to see the man's twin, right out of Central Casting. Short hair, scrubbed and cleanly shaven faces. Cops or FBI agents. Straight from a *Dragnet* rerun. Simon guesses the next thing they'll do is pull out black leather cases and flip them open to show off their sparkling badges.

"Who are you?" he asks.

"Mr. Simon, did you fill out a United States income tax return in 2004?"

"What business is that of yours?" Simon asks, silently saying a prayer and at the same time knowing it will do no good.

"You had income in 2004, Mr. Simon, over fifteen thousand dollars. Yet you did not file a return. That's a crime, Mr. Simon."

Oh shit. His mother had lectured him. His girlfriend said he was crazy. But Simon had taken a calculated risk. The money was for a plum consulting job, paid by personal check, no 1099 issued. He was up against the wall, maxed out on his cards, up to his neck in student loans. He'd had nightmares about this moment. Simon's chest is beading with sweat. He finds his foot nervously tapping the floor.

"If you give us what you need, Mr. Simon, we'll put in a good word for you with the IRS."

"You're not from the IRS?" Simon squeaks, his voice going south on him.

"Let's just say we're from a closely affiliated agency."

"What is it you want?" he asks, pleading more than requesting.

The man on the left points at his laptop, "Bring your computer, let's find a place we can talk."

The three stand in unison. Matt Simon shuts his laptop and tucks it under his arm. The two men give him tight smiles and steer him off toward the stacks. They stay close to him, too close. He's being escorted, but he feels as if he's under arrest. All for a few thousand dollars.

They enter the dimly lit stacks filled with endless rows of metal bookcases reaching to the ceiling, dark concrete floor, place feels gloomy, the air frosty. The door clicks shut behind them. The two men turn to face him. *So this is how it goes down, one minute I'm working on my dissertation, the next I'm being shaken down by two government goons because I failed to report some income on my return.*

From his jacket pocket, one of the Feds pulls out a photograph. It only takes a second for Simon to recognize the middle-aged man who borrowed his laptop. *Are they after him?*

"Mr. Simon, we know this man used your computer yesterday to send two emails from the Bravo Café. Do you know him?"

"Never saw him before. I sat down next to him and I haven't seen him since."

"Did he tell you his name?"

"No, we just talked about my dissertation."

"Why did you let him use your computer?"

"Is that a crime?"

"It very well might be, Mr. Simon."

It doesn't take him long to decide to be cooperative. "Look, he asked to use my PC to send out some emails. It was no big deal to me, I was finished using it so…"

"Did you get a look at them?"

"Deleted them before he handed it back to me. Made a fuss about that, you know, about deleting them."

"And then?"

"I said goodbye, took my computer and left. That was it." Simon feels like he's back on solid ground. He risks a question: "Can you tell me what is going on?"

The two men shake their heads in unison—robots. One looks at the other. There is a bit of unspoken conversation between the two, eyebrows lifting, slight head nods. As if they'd previously agreed on something. The man on Simon's left takes out an envelope and points at Simon's laptop.

"We're going to have to take that."

"Beg your pardon?" Simon tightens his grip on his machine.

"Your computer is now government property—evidence." The man hands Collyer the envelope. "Here is five hundred dollars in compensation."

"But my dissertation is on it."

"I'm sure you've saved it. You're much too smart not to have done that. And too bad if you haven't."

Simon takes the envelope and surrenders his laptop at the same time. Small price to pay for avoiding the IRS. The men turn to leave. One turns back as he swings open the door to the reading room and says, "One more thing, Mr. Simon. Maybe you'd consider using the money to make a down payment on the taxes you owe. I know the IRS would appreciate it."

The two men exit out the door they entered through. It slams shut behind them.

Simon is left standing alone in the gloomy light of the engineering library stacks, feeling both victimized and lucky at the same time.

Greg Watt loosens his tie and leans back in his chair. It has been a productive twenty-four hours. They are filling in the blanks. Overnight his team descended on Collyer's house, discovering he traveled to Pittsburgh in response to the nurse's call. After picking up the scent of a lost nuke, with help from the nurse Collyer kidnapped the pilot. He's emailed his wife and someone else.

Shaking down the grad student was easy, a little IRS cooperation and now the laptop's in their hands. Soon NSA's experts will be deconstructing its hard drive. With any luck, he will discover the identity of Collyer's contact and they will be one step closer to running him down.

But one discovery his team has made is puzzling. Watt doesn't know what to make of it.

Grossman, the flying squad leader, explained it to him over the secure phone connection. "Someone had been tapping Collyer's line before we got to it. We saw the signal on our monitors. Someone was definitely bugging it."

"Who?" Watt snapped.

"Here's the problem. The minute we saw it we ran a backtrace but the bug disappeared, evaporated as if it had never been there in the first place. Has to be a pretty sophisticated setup to sense a second tap and disconnect that fast."

Watt thrummed his fingers on the stack of papers in front of him. *Who the hell else is involved in this?*

"Thing I don't get," Grossman continued, "is why in the hell would anyone want to eavesdrop on a kook like Collyer?"

16

Solo, Indonesia, Monday morning, EST + 12 hours

Abu El-Khadr stumps along the wooden sidewalk just feet from the choking traffic, the metal peg replacing his right foot clunking on the boards. The streets are bustling with vehicles, cars and scooters, trucks and bicycles, a teeming mass of popping and roaring machinery belching smoke and soot into the air mixing with the din of honking horns, irate shouting, music blaring from everywhere, all orchestrating into a deafening cacophony that's amplified by the metal roofs overhead so that the sweltering 105° temperature in the mid-sized Indonesian city seems even more stifling.

In his younger days, he was careless with plastic and paid the price. Now honored with his face on thousands of wanted posters and a five million dollar bounty on his head, he's in the top echelon of the organization and has people to do his dirty work.

The armpits of his dishdasha are stained with sweat, the front garnished with tomato sauce that slid off the slice of double cheese pizza he was enjoying with his new recruit, who though twenty years younger and unencumbered by a peg leg and middle-age pounds, still has to hustle to keep up.

Speaking to Naguib in hushed tones in a Yemeni dialect that none of the Indonesians scarfing down lunch in the restaurant could understand, Abu El-Khadr outlined the task. His message was simple and direct. When Naguib completes this assignment, he has the job. It's both his initiation and a guarantee he will never leave. For once you kill for the organization, it has you by the heart. El-Khadr calls it taking ownership of the position, winking to let the younger man know it's his idea of a joke.

"You will escort Hamil out to lunch on the pretext of getting to know him. Hamil's bladder is weak so he will get up to use the WC. Follow him as if you have to go too," El-Khadr explained. "And when he squats over the hole to do his business, helpless and half-naked with his garment hiked up around his chest, that is when you will put one bullet between his eyes, another in the throat for insurance and as his body crashes backward, a third in the heart for good measure."

Naguib's face went ashen at the directive and he quickly hid his trembling hands under the table. Abu El-Khadr continued with his instructions. "The restaurant owner is one of us. He will take out the garbage for you. Once you have completed the task, you can return to your lunch. If you still have an appetite," El-Khadr joked without cracking a smile.

Abu El-Khadr clomps down the steps and hustles down the narrow alley leading to his headquarters, sending a pack of mangy dogs scurrying for the shadows. Naguib's tagging along after him, still reeling from the task he's facing.

Solo is in the center of Java, its main island, and for three years has been El-Khadr's base of operations. Though the Americans have a major presence in Jakarta, few are seen in Solo. The ones that do visit get their business done in a hurry for it is well known that the city is a terrorist haven, and it is much too easy in the swarm of people for someone to slide a flashing blade into an American's back or roll a grenade under an embassy sedan crawling through traffic.

El-Khadr stops at the battered wooden door of the former auto body shop that has been converted into an offshore call center. The sign over the door reads *Far East Phone Marketing* and though nothing's being sold inside, it provides convenient cover. No one would guess that the banks of computers inside and the staff that comes and goes at all hours would add up to anything more than another offshore call center fielding calls from cranky Americans about their balky computers.

His chunky fingers tap a quick code into the dial pad and he whispers two sentences in Arabic into the speaker.

In the front section of the call center, behind a reinforced steel partition, the middle-aged Egyptian programmer named Hamil jumps as he hears the sharp clap of a door slamming behind him. The tea sloshes in his cup as he swirls around.

Abu El-Khadr stalks in swinging his signature riding crop, his chubby face beet-red. Meek-looking, an accountant by profession, his cherubic face ringed by a thin black beard and framed by granny glasses, his rotund body makes him look like a Middle Eastern Santa Claus. Only his cruel and high-pitched snarl, ominous and animal-like, gives any hint of his ruthless nature. His resume is impressive. He can describe in detail the smoking ruins of the Khobar Towers barracks in Saudi Arabia, the USS *Cole* listing at the dock at Aden with a thirty-foot gash ripped amidships, as well the pile of rubble swarming with rescue workers that was once the American embassy in Dar es Salaam.

Hamil doesn't recognize the stranger shadowing him. Tall and thin, he wears casual clothes, jeans and a T-shirt. He is also Middle Eastern, Hamil guesses, Yemeni or Saudi. The stranger is cool and composed in contrast to El-Khadr, who's as pissed off as Hamil has ever seen him, storming toward him brandishing his crop over his head.

Hamil knows he's in for it. Too much has unraveled over the past two days. And he's going to pay. *He's going to make an example of me for this stranger,* Hamil thinks, cowering under the crop looming high above him.

"You are supposed to be a computer genius and you can't even track an old man, a woman and a retiree? What the hell good are you?" he screeches in Arabic. Hamil ducks as Abu El-Khadr brings his riding crop crashing down on his shoulders. Once, twice, three times. The monitors in the back have been switched on so the entire operation can watch. A lesson no one will forget. He flails the crop down again, grunting dramatically for his audience.

"You are becoming the bane of our existence. You've packed the sites with so much information they crash all the time."

Responsible for coding communication, Hamil is sequestered from the rest of El-Khadr's people who sit in a series of control rooms in the back staring into computers, watching satellite screens and talking on sat phones. Working different shifts and all sworn to silence, Hamil has counted over thirty people staffing El-Khadr's operation. Plus a security detail of eight surly Yemenis dressed in black carrying Kalashnikovs, hand grenades dangling like fruit off their armored vests, who lounge around chewing khat, the narcotic sticks many Yemenis are addicted to, and grooving on their MP3 players to pop music they've downloaded from radio stations in Sanaa, the Yemeni capital. That's close to forty people just in Solo. *Who knows how many operatives he has scattered over the globe helping to carry out his mission?*

Hamil knows there is no point in offering an explanation, the bearded leader would have none of it.

"You've made the communication so complicated, it's no wonder you lost him," El-Khadr continues. "All this nonsense about flowers is a distraction. You spent so much time and energy encoding you let him get out of sight. Track Collyer down. He must be found immediately." He gives Hamil one last crack for emphasis.

Hamil can feel the sting down to his toes. El-Khadr must be under pressure, Hamil guesses. And he's taking it out on him—though his encoding has nothing to do with losing Collyer. They had intercepted the call from the nurse and followed him to Pittsburgh, had them right up to the point when they pulled into the airport parking lot. Three hours later, they realized they'd lost them. Where they went from the Pittsburgh airport was anyone's guess.

"I am putting out queries, it is only a matter of time before we reconnect with Collyer. He will be found, I guarantee."

El-Khadr sneers and stalks off to his private office, the stranger following him, the door slamming behind them.

Hamil gingerly runs his fingers over the welts left on his back by El-Khadr's crop. *I will find Howard Collyer, with the help of Allah, I will,* Hamil thinks. He left his father's prosperous Internet business in Cairo five years ago to join the organization, and now he's involved in a project holding the key to its future. *I will succeed,* Hamil tells himself, *I will not fail. I will not let El-Khadr down.*

It is El-Khadr's life's work and the success of the mission will be his shining moment. As they had turned commercial aircraft into weapons of jihad, this time a neglected bomb would be used to create the ultimate catastrophe. Though it was easy to build a dirty bomb with radioactive materials bought on the black market, importing the materials was the problem. As they had with the planes strategy, the decision was made to find a source inside the United States.

Options were limited. Power plants and nuclear facilities were heavily guarded, the radioactive materials cumbersome and hazardous to even move. Breaking into Los Alamos or Oak Ridge where a large stock of weapons-grade uranium is stored was the best option until a young Iranian engineer dedicated to the cause uncovered an obscure American website.

After two months of research, Mehran Zarif took his astounding discovery up the line. Sitting on the dirt floor of a hut in North Waziristan, he detailed the plan. The decision was made. Los Alamos and Oak Ridge were shelved and all resources were diverted to the new opportunity. The leaders of the movement funneled funds, resources and personnel to the mission.

From their Indonesian base in Solo, Hamil was assigned to coordinate the cells and monitor Collyer, checking his website and watching his every move.

Honored for his brilliant discovery, Mehran Zarif was selected to be point man on one of the cells assigned to the operation. Trained on the Gulf and at their base outside Solo, Zarif is now under cover, waiting for the call.

The Americans left the movement the ultimate destructive gift. A nuclear weapon lay waiting for them somewhere in the U.S. The teams were in place. It was El-Khadr's sole responsibility. Now having lost track of Collyer, it is no surprise he is out of his tree.

Hamil toggles back and forth between Jeffri's Garden and DownhomeCrafts.com. Nothing. No one is responding. Collyer seems to have disappeared

But Hamil knows the trail has gone cold for the Americans as well. It wasn't until Sunday that the Americans had a team tapping Collyer's phone and intercepting his email. They inadvertently stumbled on his bug as well, but Hamil hastily disabled it before the Americans could trace it. They now know Collyer was the driver of the car used to kidnap the pilot. But there is no reason to think that they know where he is hiding any more than Hamil does.

The Americans constantly underestimate Collyer. To them he's a former football star turned whistleblower—a nuisance, a bothersome bug that needs to be swatted down and tossed in the trash.

Hamil knows differently. He's gone to school on Howard Collyer for the past two years. Knows him so well he feels like he could step into his skin and live his life for him. He has respect for his intellect, his determination and his conviction that lost nuclear weapons pose a threat to his country's security. Having hacked into Collyer's computer files, Hamil has read and catalogued every piece of information Collyer has assembled about the eleven lost bombs in the United States. To the Americans, the bombs are ancient history, artifacts of another era, rusting away out of sight and out of mind. To El-Khadr and his mission, the lost bombs are gifts from Allah, ready to be turned against the Great Satan.

Hamil smiles. While the Pentagon ridiculed Collyer and ran him out, to them he is a saint and savior. If Howard Collyer manages to lead them to a nuke, his name will go down in history along with the other martyrs to the cause.

Hamil types into his computer, "Does anyone know Cindy from Virginia's address or phone number? I want to ask her a question about a dahlia I want to dig up."

"I've heard Cindy is on vacation," is the first response he receives.

Hamil mutters a curse in Arabic and shakes his head. He tosses his paper cup in the trash. Patience is one virtue anyone who works in electronic media learns right off the bat. They have put an extensive network of cells and operatives in place, all linked with cutting-edge communication. Someone will find Howard Collyer. It is only a matter of time.

He's still staring at the screen when the door to the private office opens and El-Khadr steps out followed by his mysterious visitor. Distracted by the unfamiliar smile on El-Khadr's face, Hamil doesn't notice the visitor is wearing a tan jacket, a loose-fitting garment hiding the telltale bulge under his left arm. Nor does he pick up on the beads of sweat gathering on the visitor's forehead or the jittery look on his face.

El-Khadr steers the stranger over to Hamil's computer station and says, "Hamil, I'd like you to meet your replacement. This is Naguib."

Hamil does not understand. How could this be happening? He stutters as he stands and shakes Naguib's hand. "My replacement? You said nothing about this. Where are you assigning me?"

El-Khadr beams another uncharacteristic smile as he answers, "We have a glorious new mission for you, Hamil, my friend. Now please join Naguib for lunch and fill him in on your tasks. When you return, I will outline your opportunity."

El-Khadr throws an arm over the two men's shoulders in a fatherly gesture, gathering them to him and escorting them toward the door saying, "I want you to enjoy your lunch together. Get to know each other. And do try the duck curry, my friends."

Hamil is not as alarmed as he should be by the sudden change in El-Khadr's tone of voice. More of a technician than a politician, he's not inclined to see behind appearances, taking things at face value and always confident he can find a fix for every glitch. Now all he feels is a sense of relief that someone else will be shouldering the responsibility of finding Collyer.

As they head out the door into the thick, humid air toward the restaurant, Hamil's horizon is limited to looking forward to a good lunch with a new friend and the glorious new opportunity awaiting him.

Little does he know it will be his last meal and his new opportunity will be in another world.

17

[Georgetown, late Sunday afternoon]

"You're not on that damn computer again, Winn—for god's sake—it's Sunday and you promised you wouldn't work on Sundays," Straub's wife whines.

"I'm not working."

"C'mon, that's a bunch of BS."

When Winn looks up, Barbara Straub can tell she's lost him. She's seen the expression hundreds of times and heard all the explanations that accompany it: *agency business, can't talk about it, national security, classified.*

Barbara's stock response when someone asks her what it's like to be married to a top CIA employee is, "It's like your husband is having an affair. You have to listen to all the lame explanations of why he comes home late, leaves the house at the crack of dawn, why he has to duck out of parties early and misses Christmas dinner, but instead of shacking up with some floozy, my husband's having an affair with a bunch of spooks in Langley."

"I'm going into the library and watch the last half of the Redskins," she huffs, counting on the fact that her husband's devotion to the Skins will speed up whatever he's got his nose buried in.

"I'll be right with you, just give me a minute," Winn answers. Barbara harrumphs for she's been married to him long enough to know his minute is her hour.

Winn Straub reads the email for the third time.

> Winn, Spare me the sermons, please, buddy. There's a former B-52 pilot in a VA hospital who might know something about a lost bomb. The Pentagon has kept him drugged up and locked away in a ward. If we hadn't gotten him out of there, he would be

> dead by now. You would have done the same thing. Now we're under cover. It's best I not tell you where we are. We'll be okay for a day or two and then we'll have to move. Two things. I'm worried about Sylvie. Can you check on her for me and make sure she's okay? Don't tell her what I'm up to, I'm sure she's worried enough as it is. Just reassure her I'm all right. Second, I need a bunch of stuff from you...

He listens to the play-by-play of the game coming from the library. Barbara has turned up the volume. The first thing he did was to arrange for the software Howie needed to be forwarded to him. That was easy. *The second will be harder.* He's sure the Collyer house is being watched. *If they are surveilling my house, chances are they'll be all over Howie's as well.*

"Barbara, can you turn that damn thing down?"

"What, dear?" he hears her shout back. The Redskins score. His wife whoops. He looks down at the email message from his college roommate. For years it seemed Howie was concocting his theories about lost bombs and conspiracies out of thin air. With little hard evidence and a concerted campaign on the Pentagon's part to smear him, everyone had written off his lost bombs. But now he's got his hands on a B-52 pilot who may have some hard information. *No wonder they're doing back flips over at the Pentagon.*

Straub makes sure there's sunlight on the window so no one can see in before he peels back the drape and peeks outside. *No raincoats but I bet they're still out there.*

Conflicted. Straub hates the word as much as he disdains the feeling but he can't help but acknowledge it. He winces at the thought. A conflicted spy is worse than a major league batter who flinches at a knuckleball coming across the plate. Or as a friend who played noseguard for the Redskins once told him, "Once you start to think about getting hit, it's time to quit." Normally he's decisive, recognizing all the shadings involved in a decision but knowing that in this business you have to move fast and take risks or the opportunity is lost. The course of action is clear but with a friend involved all of a sudden it's complicated and ticklish. Will it cause him to hesitate, waffle, stumble—or worse?

Yet if Howie is determined to drag Vector Eleven out from beneath the veil of secrecy they've been operating under for years, expose some of the skeletons they've locked away, he realizes there's little he can do about it. It isn't as if he can talk Howie out of it. So his old friend inadvertently ends up as a stalking horse. Straub had been there before. He'd set up double agents with elaborate stories that led the Russians or East Germans to show their hands and reveal their agendas. Then he hurriedly pulled the agents when things got too hot. His timing had been off only once. Winn had chalked it up to the cost of doing business. But with a friend involved, it's a new game—with unpublished rules and an unfamiliar scoring system.

Straub touches the reply window and types:

> Howie, everything you asked for is on its way. I'm going to try to give you as much cover as I can. How much time do you need? Obviously, the longer you're exposed, the more problematic the situation becomes. And rest assured I will take care of Sylvie. You shouldn't worry about that. Talk to me soon, Best, Winn

The clock over the stove reads 4:32. The Skins score again. Straub makes a decision. Calling Sparky's name as he walks through the living room, he heads for the coat closet. He hasn't felt the effects of adrenaline in over ten years. The rush is nice, a pleasant change from feeling rusty. The raincoats won't follow him if he's walking Sparky, assuming he will return with the dog. His bet is that he can duck into the garage, leave the dog there and escape in his car. He'll be over the Key Bridge before they figure out he's ditched them.

Sticking his head into the library, his topcoat over one arm and Sparky in the other, Howie announces to Barbara, "I'm going out for a while."

"You're missing one hell of a game."

"You can give me an update when I get back. I'll make it as quick as I can."

He doesn't let his wife know he'll be lucky if he returns before dawn.

The water is running so Grace Collyer doesn't hear the tires crunching in the courtyard. She is standing at the kitchen sink doing the dishes when she hears a knock at the front door. She turns off the water and listens. Another series of insistent thumps. *Someone's there.*

"Who's at the door, dear?" she hears her mother call from the living room followed by the patter of bare feet on the floor as she scurries to answer it.

"I'll get it, Mother," Grace says, beating her mother to the door.

The two women crowd the doorway jockeying to see who's on the other side, Grace trying to take charge, Sylvie eager for any information about her husband.

"It's the Raymonds!" Sylvie announces, breathing a sigh of relief that it isn't someone with bad news. Tom and Beth Raymond are neighbors, living on the adjoining farm, not close friends but across-the-fence acquaintances, ready to loan a piece of equipment, share mulch or pitch in to dispose of a downed tree. Roly-poly and friendly to a fault, Beth holds out a glass platter with waxed paper over something inside.

"We made a cake for you," Beth Raymond says, cocking her head sympathetically to one side, as if someone in the Collyer household had died.

Tom Raymond adds, "We heard you're concerned about Howie so we just thought we'd offer a little moral support."

"I hope you don't think we're meddling..." Beth adds.

"Oh, no. Not by any means," Sylvie says, reaching to take the platter. "You're so kind to think of us."

Grace notices Tom Raymond's eyes keep dropping to a small envelope tucked alongside the cake. She's puzzled about how the Raymonds would know Howie is missing. But then news travels fast in the country, everyone loves to gossip.

"Beth wrote a card," Tom explains.

"Don't read it 'til we're gone," Beth apologizes, "I can get pretty sappy."

"This is very sweet of you."

"It's chocolate fudge. Double fudge, my grandmother's recipe."

"I hope you enjoy it," Tom says, dipping the brim of his hunting cap as he turns to leave.

"Thank you, you're so sweet to do this for us," Grace says, backing away from the door. She can't wait to get her hands on the card. There were signals from Tom Raymond, the self-conscious way he glanced down at the card, then back up at Grace. As if he was letting her know there is something unexpected inside.

"Can't you come in?" Sylvie asks.

"We'd love to but my daughter's making dinner, we've got to run."

After a second, then third round of thank-you's, Grace snatches the card off the platter and reads it as Sylvie gives the Raymonds a last gracious wave and closes the door.

Right off the bat Sylvie and Grace know who's behind the card. The directions are detailed and explicit, Winn Straub could not have been clearer. Or more disconcerting. *There's a chance the house is being watched, maybe bugged, so don't say anything,* the card reads. *Act like you're going out for coffee. Head for Starbucks at the mall. Go through the store and out the back as quickly as you can. See you soon.*

They obeyed his instructions to the letter. Clamping down on conversation in the house, they piled into the Volvo and headed for Starbucks. Before the counter people noticed, they hustled through the storeroom and out the back door.

"You girls did great. You both deserve Oscars," Winn Straub says as he pulls away, leaving Sylvie's Volvo and the Starbucks behind. "Sorry for all the spook stuff but I couldn't take the chance that someone was watching."

He'd met the Raymonds from the next farm a couple times at Howie's and knew they were the kind of people who would bake a cake and deliver it to a neighbor in need. A call on his cell as he drove down from D.C. was all it took. He gave the couple the note and a quick coaching, drove to the back door of Starbucks, parked and waited.

Twenty minutes later, Sylvie and Grace snuck out, eyes wide as saucers and both relieved to see Straub sitting in the driver's seat.

Sylvie barely has the door shut before she's asking, "I need to know everything you know about Howie, you've got to tell me."

Straub heads toward I-64, taking a circuitous route to make sure no one is following. He knows he's going to have to be at the top of his game to deal with these two ladies, antsy and anxious, they are a handful.

"He's fine, " he tells her. "But he's worried about you and that's why I'm here." Having driven all the local roads in his student days, Straub knows them like the back of his hand, also knows that headlights stick out like sore thumbs. He checks the rearview—nothing. *They are probably just figuring out the two women ducked them.*

"You positive he's okay?"

"I talk with him every day."

"Can you tell me where is he?"

"Somewhere in Pennsylvania."

"That's a big help."

"Keeping his head down."

"It's those people from the Pentagon who are after him, isn't it?"

"What makes you think that?"

"C'mon, Howie talked about them all the time. Ghost programs, black programs. And the person who called him during Thanksgiving dinner? The nurse? That's all she could talk about—*them*. Can't you just tell him to stop this and come home?"

"I'm doing everything I can to help."

"Sorry, that's not enough."

Straub tries to change the subject. "Let me tell you where I'm taking you. CIA has an installation outside of Williamsburg a couple hours away. It's called Camp Peary."

"I know all about The Farm," Grace says, a smirk in her voice. "It's your top-secret spook training ground with its own airport. You fly rebel leaders and heads of state in there in the middle of the night for meetings that never officially take place. You going to lock us up there?"

"Howie asked me to take care of you."

"Answer my question."

"I think you'll find it more than comfortable."

Sylvie interjects, "What about Donald and Bridey?"

Straub realizes Howie's son and his family slipped his mind. "I'm less worried about them. But I'm assigning security to them just in case." He makes a mental note to do that.

Straub checks in the mirror. Grace is leaning forward in the seat, ready to pounce.

"You're stage managing this whole thing, aren't you, Mr. Straub?" she says. He's heard Grace Collyer is a tiger. In Howie's own words, his daughter is tough as nails and afraid of nothing.

"I don't know why you'd think that, Grace."

Sylvie silently cheers her daughter on.

"C'mon, it's written all over your face. You're isolating us at Peary so you can have free rein."

"I'm only doing what Howie asked." Winn settles his voice and calmly says, "You'll be safe there, it's more secure than Camp David." A few seconds pass, he lets his eyes wander back to the mirror again. Grace slumps down in her seat. For the moment, Straub senses she's backing down.

Grace's next question has none of the edge of her earlier one. "And what about Howie? What are you going to do about him?"

Straub knows he's back in control. "Leave it to me. I'll bring him in as soon as I can."

Sylvie is sniveling, close to tears. "The pilot at the VA hospital knows where a bomb is and Howie's gone after it. That's what's going on, isn't it?"

He glances back at Sylvie. Looks like she hasn't slept in three days. *Isn't easy being married to Howie Collyer,* Straub decides. *Howie plays the whistleblower out to save the world and his wife pays the price.*

But there was never as much on the line. His job, yes—but he was close to retirement anyway. Now they are playing on a new level with much higher stakes. And Sylvie Collyer is too smart not to know the rules have changed.

"I'm afraid so," Straub says.

"And he's not going to stop until he finds it. Or someone stops him."

"Let's try to look on the bright side."

"C'mon, Winn, stop trying to soft soap us. Howie's the one who belongs at The Farm, not us."

Straub knows the only way he'd get Howie to The Farm is in handcuffs. "Believe me, if I could get Howie to give this thing up, that's the first thing I'd do—and it's not like I haven't tried. He's just one stubborn son of a gun, as if you don't know that already."

He glances back at the two women. Though neither one of them are happy with what they are hearing, they realize he's telling the truth.

"What are our chances?" Grace asks, acting every inch the lawyer.

He wants to tell her, *God only knows.* But he thinks better of it. The closer Howie gets to the bomb, the more they will turn up the heat. Short of leaving the pilot on the side of the road, taking a flight to central Africa and secreting himself deep in the jungle with a pygmy tribe, Howie Collyer has no choice but to stay in the game.

"Howie's smart. And as I told you, I'll do everything I can."

"You are not answering my question."

"You're right. I'm not." He looks directly at Grace in the rearview. "And I can't because it's a question for which there is no answer right now. Too much is up in the air. But you know he cares too much about his family to put himself in jeopardy. So I'd try not to worry. The minute I have some news, I'll let you know." Winn grins a sympathetic smile and warms up his eyes, letting the ladies in the back seat see his face in the mirror. It works, he can feel the tension subsiding.

Speeding down the dark interstate toward Williamsburg, cruise control on seventy-five, dry leaves swirling across the asphalt in front of him, he's not wanting to consider the complexities of what he's involved himself in. Even in the darkest days in Eastern Europe, he never felt pulled in so many directions. Messy, very messy. Too many things running through his mind.

Is this Howie's personal crusade and I'm only clearing the path for him?

Am I using Howie to advance the cause of CIA?

Is this my own retribution against the Pentagon?

Am I using my old friend to get back in the game again?

Is it that I'm fifty-five and losing my nerve?

Or all of the above?

Straub tries to clear his head. He wonders if the two women can read his consternation. He is relieved to hear Sylvie pose a question he can answer in absolute candor and with total conviction. A pleasant feeling for a change.

She asks, "What about my cats?"

"The Raymonds are going to take care of them. I arranged for that. It's all set."

"Thank you, Winn," Sylvie says. "I appreciate that, very thoughtful of you."

If you only knew, Straub thinks as he watches a light drizzle begin to fleck the windshield. *If you only knew...*

Georgetown is deserted at this time of night. Crossing the street heading for his house, Straub is tempted to stop and rap hard on the window of the black sedan as if to say, *Wake up boys, I'm back. No point in rubbing it in,* he decides, or in letting them know what time he returned. It won't take long for Vector Eleven to come to the conclusion he is outmaneuvering them and they need to put someone with half a brain on the case. In the meantime, he can have his way with them.

Sparky starts his high-pitched yapping the minute Straub turns the key. He called Barbara to ask her to let Sparky out of the garage. You'd have thought he'd asked her to get a ladder and clean the gutters. The grizzled Jack Russell tears out from the kitchen barking so ferociously he sounds like he's intent on sinking whatever teeth he has left into a choice part of the intruder's anatomy.

So much for sneaking in unnoticed.

"Is that you, Winston?" Barbara calls from upstairs.

"I'll be up in a second, dear," he shouts up to her as he hangs up his coat and hustles into the kitchen wondering if Barbara took Sparky out for his evening walk while deciding not to bother even if she didn't. He is much too tired and still has work to do.

He opens his laptop, pulls a stool up to the counter, opens his email and begins typing:

> Howie, I just got back from taking Sylvie and Grace to Camp Peary. Glad I did because your place in Charlottesville was crawling with Pentagon creeps. They'll be okay at The Farm but they are worried to death. Honestly, if I thought there was any way to pull it off, I would try to bring you in. But after what's happened, I doubt I could guarantee your safety so you're going to have to follow through on whatever you've got going. This is no time to be a hero, Howie, don't try to go it alone. You have to tell me exactly what you are up to so I can figure out how to help you at each step of the way. Talk to me soon. Winn

Starting to reread the email, he decides to just send it and hit the sack, figuring it's the best he can do at two-thirty in the morning.

On the way back from Williamsburg Straub turned the same ground over and over in his mind. For the sake of Sylvie and his family, out of good conscience and just because in weaker moments he likes to think of himself as a good guy, Straub decided he had to take one last crack at convincing Howie to give up.

But common sense prevailed. The truth is that Howie is going to be safer on the outside. Winn couldn't keep him at The Farm forever. Sooner or later the Pentagon would find a way to get to him. Whatever he knows, Howie poses too much of a risk to them. As crazy as it sounds, Howie stands a better chance on his own.

Anticipating an earful from Barbara for having been gone so long, as he climbs the stairs to his bedroom, Straub thinks, *At least I've done my duty—whatever that's worth.*

18

[Front Royal, Virginia, Monday morning]

Sharon sits up in bed suddenly, someone's tapping on her door. She hopes to hell its Howie. Grabbing her jeans, she staggers across the room, doing her best to jump into them as she heads for the door.

"Collyer? Is that you?"

"C'mon, open up." She fumbles with the buttons on the fly as she unlocks the door. It's barely light out.

Howie's facing her. Risstup is parked alongside. He's in a daze.

"What's wrong? You look like you've seen a ghost," Sharon says.

"Worse, I got an email from Winn. We have to get going."

"What did he say?"

"Just get your stuff. I'll be waiting in the car."

At the crack of dawn, the manager of the Nite Owl heard the automobile screech out of the courtyard. Pulling back the curtain, she saw the Accord kicking up gravel as it disappeared around the corner. The clock read 6:08. She could never figure out what was going on with the old goat in the wheelchair, the attractive middle-aged gent and the lady who was at least twenty years younger, but they seemed nice, didn't raise a ruckus and paid in cash. What they were up to was the question. All she knew was that she had seen much worse and that she was never going to share their stay at the Nite Owl with anyone. The two bills the man had slid under her blotter guaranteed her lips would stay permanently zipped.

"You want to slow the hell down, you'll get us killed." Sharon says as they speed out of town. Howie backs off the gas.

"That's better, now tell me what the hell's going on."

"We've been there long enough."

"What got you so freaked out?"

"They're pulling out all the stops to find us."

"Great," Sharon sneers sarcastically, "I'm really glad to hear that. So where are we heading now?"

"You'll see."

"Can't wait. What about the photograph I was supposed to get?"

Howie pats the laptop sitting beside him.

"She sent it?"

"I downloaded it a half hour ago. I don't know how you ever talked a total stranger into sending you a family photograph."

"Just because I'm a nurse doesn't mean my skill set is limited to changing bedpans. Let me see."

"Go for it," Howie says, handing her the computer. "It's the PDF on the desktop."

As she's mousing around, she notices Straub's email. "Mind if I read what Winn sent you?"

Before Howie can stop her, Sharon's halfway through. He can feel her starting to steam up.

"This is just great. Now your CIA buddy is hanging us out to dry."

"You weren't supposed to see that."

"Some guardian angel he is."

Howie stumbles around for something to say. "Look, I know this isn't easy."

Sharon's poking her finger at him, as ticked off as he's ever seen her. "Easy? I tell you what this is—a goddamn suicide mission. You're so obsessed with your damn bombs you've got the whole world after us. I didn't bargain for this kind of crap and neither did Risstup. Any minute I can imagine someone running us off the fricking road and gunning us down."

"Aren't you being a bit melodramatic?"

His comment stops her. She whips around to glare at him, her eyes shooting a blaze of sparks in his direction.

"I beg your goddamn pardon?"

Howie notices Risstup is wide awake in the back seat, his eyes glued on their conversation, head swiveling back and forth like he's watching a tennis match.

"Okay, so just what do you propose we do? Return the major here to the hospital with a note of apology pinned to his chest? Tell them we made a mistake and we'll be good boys and girls if they just forget about the whole thing?"

"Doesn't it bother you that government agents are all over your house? Aren't you worried about your family?"

"How heartless do you think I am? But when we took him out of the VA hospital, we both made a conscious choice. If I remember correctly, it was you who used the phrase *over my dead body.* You told me we had no choice but to get him out of there."

Sharon ducks her head as if to concede he has a point. Turns to stare out the window.

"Winn is saying that we're out on a limb, no question about it. But Winn's telling us at this point there's no other way to play it."

She throws up her hands. The words come out haltingly. "I'm sorry. The email freaked me out. Your friend Straub was my security blanket."

"He still is."

"I sure hope so." She gives him a weak smile. As if she wants a pat on the back.

Howie gives it to her, "Look on the positive side. If there wasn't something significant here, they wouldn't be after us. We've saved the major's life and we're on the verge of discovering the truth behind this lost bomb."

Sharon's nodding. Howie knows her well enough to understand she's moved on. While she can be stubborn and hardheaded, she can also turn on a dime. Change her mind when circumstances warrant, her attitude shifting quickly from moody to matter-of-fact.

"So where are we heading?"

"I booked us into the presidential suite at the Four Seasons."

"Fat chance, five'll get me ten we're headed for another fleabag."

Both sit back and let the dust settle as they head southeast through Pennsylvania with the rising sun pouring in through the driver's side.

Sharon studies the family picture sent to her from a lady named Risstup whom she found through searching genealogy sites on the Web. Took a little talking but she emailed a photograph with the long-lost uncle who had once served in the Air Force.

"I can't wait to show the major this photograph."

"Let's hope it works."

"Hey, Collyer, can I ask you a question? Something's been bugging me about these lost nukes."

"In twenty minutes I can tell you everything you need to know."

"I've been on your website and read through all the links. But there are a bunch of things that don't compute."

"Shoot."

"These nukes, aren't a lot of them over forty years old?"

Howie nods. "But they are H-bombs—not bread. They don't get stale."

"Don't they rust, won't water seep into the explosive charge? And the nuclear materials, uranium, tritium—all those radioactive isotopes, don't they have a half life?"

"Absolutely."

"So is it possible that they are so old they are worn out? The explosives wet, the radioactive materials past their prime?"

"As for the half-life business, without getting technical let me point out that the Pentagon is still stockpiling bombs produced forty years ago. They get outmoded and there's minor disintegration here and there requiring replacement of individual parts but they don't go bad."

Sharon nods. In his rearview, Howie notices Risstup is sitting listening.

"Now the other issue," Howie continues. "Though the hydrogen bomb is extremely sophisticated, it is a simple mechanism. Basically, there's a small atomic bomb—no bigger than a head of lettuce—a miniature version of the bombs that we dropped on Hiroshima and Nagasaki, inside the hydrogen one. The atomic device is set off by a four-hundred-pound charge of TNT. That activates the fission process of the bomb, which creates the pressure and radiation to touch off the second stage—the hydrogen bomb part."

"I'm with you."

"The early weapons were so powerful they had to be dropped by parachute so that the airplane didn't get caught in the mushroom cloud. The Pentagon's term for it was *retarded delivery*. Some of them were designed with shock-absorbing honeycomb noses."

"So they had soft landings."

"Yes."

"What made them explode?"

"On the early ones, simply hitting the ground. Even with parachutes, a four-ton bomb makes a hell of an impact. And these things were built like tanks. I mean, the people who designed these bombs designed them to stay intact until they were detonated."

"Even in water or buried in mud?"

"From all the estimates I've heard, the bomb casings will stand up to salt water for another ten years. When seawater starts seeping in, yes, the TNT will be affected. That's what the Pentagon is counting on. Hoping that they will remain undisturbed for another ten years when they will become degraded and less threatening."

"And in the meantime?"

"No one wants to take the chance of going near one and setting off the four hundred pounds of unstable TNT. A dredge from a salvage tug could bump into a bomb accidentally, a line from a fishing trawler could scrape it against a ledge and create a spark—use your imagination, anything could set the explosives off. And in the early days, some of these H-bombs were armed with nuclear capsules, no failsafe triggering mechanisms at all. They were good to go the minute they were loaded onto the aircraft."

"Couldn't they retrieve the bombs with divers? Divers who are precise and careful?"

"The Pentagon has studied that to death. And what they discovered only underlines the gravity of the situation. The chance that a nuke will break apart during recovery is too great. Can you imagine if we accidentally exploded one of our own bombs? Some diver attaches the cable at the wrong spot? It's murky and he can't see? The cable scrapes against the bomb casing, a spark ignites the TNT? Then all hell breaks loose.

So it's in the Pentagon's interest to leave them alone. If *they* are reluctant to go near the nukes, what does that tell you? They're playing a waiting game, hoping that nothing will disturb them before they disintegrate. And in the meantime they are putting the country at peril. Someone at the Pentagon practically admitted it right to my face. That's why they were so determined to stigmatize me, they knew I understood the dimensions of the risk they're taking."

"What if a terrorist locates them first?"

"Hell to pay, an absolute shitstorm. If a group of bad guys managed to retrieve one of the nukes and set it off or detonate it, you could imagine how catastrophic it would be. Thousands or millions would perish, whole sections of the country permanently evacuated, uninhabitable for centuries, the United States would be totally crippled, never be the same again. Despite the enormity of 9/11, in comparison it would make that look like a blip."

"And you think that's conceivable?"

"Was it ever considered a possibility for terrorists to turn commercial airplanes into guided missiles and bring down entire buildings? Look what happened when we failed to gameplay that option."

"That's scary, scary as hell," Sharon says, shaking her head at the thought.

"You can't dismiss any scenario. The more far-fetched, the more potential it might have. That's what I've been trying to tell people."

"And no one would pay attention?"

"There are some smart people at the Pentagon but as in any big organization, they have their blind spots, all too wrapped up in their own priorities to think outside the box."

"So that's why the major's knowledge is so important." Sharon glances back at Risstup.

"If he really knows where that nuke was dropped, it could break the whole thing open."

"Then what would you do?"

"We'd better find it first, okay?" Howie didn't want to admit he hadn't the slightest idea.

Except for a few tourists heading through on their way to the Blue Ridge Parkway and the Shenandoah Valley as well as a steady stream of trucks heading to the freight depots around town, Front Royal is a backwater, a whistlestop in northern Virginia three hours south of Lancaster. Howie's driven through the town many times but until now has never had reason to stop. Now he's cruising the dark streets looking for a place to stay.

Plenty of options on the main drag, the Relax Inn, Shenandoah, Blue Ridge, but he's looking for something more off the beaten track.

Plus at a national chain like a Motel 6 or Days Inn, someone can easily game the reservation system to sort out three people traveling together. A couple of calls and the motel would be surrounded. The door kicked in and the three hustled off in the middle of the night. It's the kind of mistake Vector Eleven is waiting for him to make.

Off Ross Avenue, the Pine Log Motel looks perfect. In the early morning light, Howie can tell it's not only inconspicuous, but also nicely dilapidated, paint peeling and windows dingy, the signboard announcing *Vacancy* dangling by one hook.

Howie wakes up the owner by holding his finger on the bell as the clumsily handwritten card directs: *Keep on buzzing 'til I show, I'm here and I want your business.* It's signed, *Dede Ferry, Prop.* The owner comes to the door rubbing his eyes, bare torso, pajama bottoms loosely knotted around his hips. Probably forty but years of hard living make Dede Ferry look sixty. Before he opens his mouth, Howie knows he's found his next hideout.

"I'd like three rooms," he says.

The owner has to scratch himself in a couple places before he can respond. "That'll be forty-four-fifty a night per room plus county lodging tax."

"Three rooms, I'll pay upfront for two nights."

Howie gets a once over. "You ain't into drugs, are you?" Ferry asks, wobbling around behind the pine-paneled counter, hitching up his pants as he heads for his reservation book. "Don't take no offense, but there are too damn many meth dealers around these days. Blow themselves to kingdom come and burn the place to the ground before you know it."

"We're just tourists. Traveling through with my dad and daughter. Hope to do a little hiking." He gets a grunt of satisfaction in return.

Howie quickly finds a nearby eatery. Esmerelda's Hot Shoppe is two blocks away, a cuted-up former cottage with Howie's favorite sticky buns the owner bakes herself. With a breakfast and lunch menu and her featured attraction, a gleaming chrome Italian espresso machine, it's just what Howie needs.

The joint is also wired so Howie types out an email to Straub while he sips a latte and waits for his order. Updates Straub on their move and the situation with Risstup, then heads back to the motel with a bag and cup carrier, his laptop tucked under his arm.

In the light of day, the neighborhood looks even more rundown. One car up on blocks in the front yard, a couple crows perched on the Pine Log sign. Across the street is a scabby field overgrown with weeds, well on its way to becoming a dump, littered with discarded appliances, old tires and assorted garbage. Howie's moved his Accord ten blocks away to a street on the other side of town in case someone reports stolen plates. The western part of town looks even seedier, full of industrial buildings and warehouses.

Howie smiles. As the ads say, *Virginia is for lovers—but not this part, this one's for losers.*

"I feel like I should work for Starbucks," Howie says as he pushes open the door to Sharon's room. "All I do is run for coffee."

"At least you're good for something, Collyer."

"How you doing with the photograph?" Howie asks as he unloads the coffees.

"Waiting until you got back."

Standing behind Sharon and Risstup, he opens his cup and takes a sip, looking over their shoulders at the emailed photo. A family gathering, looks like in the early 1950s, everyone is in shirtsleeves, there are wreaths on the columns, a string of lights looped across the lintel over their heads. It's a stock Christmas shot, three generations grouped together on the porch steps, grandparents, parents and children.

"Looks like a flock of Risstups here, Major. Anyone you recognize?" Sharon asks. "I imagine you were in your mid-thirties when this was taken. The woman who sent it thought this might be you. Though she was just a kid, she remembered her uncle being in the Air Force."

Sharon points at the face of the man in the third row. "Take your time, Major Risstup. See if you recognize anyone."

Howie and Sharon nurse their coffees, watching as Risstup's gnarled index finger slowly traces along the first row of faces. He is concentrating, carefully scanning for a familiar face.

Nothing there, his finger creeps up to the second row.

Howie steals a look at Sharon. She's silently pulling for the old guy. He stops at the third person from the left. Pauses. His finger slowly lifts and taps on the face, once, twice, three times. Risstup turns to look at her.

Something in the picture is prompting his memory but not enough to make a connection. Risstup's finger returns to the screen, hovers over a face. Howie sees his eyes light up. He touches the likeness of the man in the third row again.

"That's me…I think that's me, I think it is..." Risstup says, glancing at Sharon first, then toward Howie. His statement is as much a question, his expression contorted like his mind is in high gear.

"Yes! Major Risstup, that's you!" She grabs his hand and thrusts their arms into the air. "Way to go, Major. That's at your Grandma Beverly's house in Arcata. Arcata, California, sometime in the early 1950s."

"Arcata…" Risstup says. He nods and repeats the name of the town on the northern coast of California. "Arcata, I grew up there."

Howie sees Risstup's face relax for the first time, as if the fog is starting to lift.

"Anything more, Major Risstup? Anything you remember about growing up there? Do you remember joining the Air Force?"

Risstup doesn't move a muscle. He looks vacantly out across the room. Two minutes go by. The connection's been lost.

Howie shrugs and says to her, "So much for that. At least he made one link with his past."

"I'm not giving up." She slides her chair closer. "C'mon, Major Risstup. You must have been in the Air Force when this picture was taken. You were on leave. You went home for Christmas. To Arcata."

Without warning the words come tumbling out, "I was lucky to get that leave. Another pilot volunteered to take over..."

"You were a pilot?"

"Yes, I flew...I flew..."

Howie jumps in, "B-52s, you flew B-52s, didn't you, Major Risstup?"

"Yes, B-52s."

"BUFFs, they called them. BUFFs, right, Major Risstup?"

"BUFFs, yes..."

"And what does BUFF stand for?"

"BUFF stands for big—ugly—fat..." Risstup pauses, his face reddens slightly as if he's embarrassed.

But then in a moment that Howie knows he will not soon forget, Risstup cracks an impish smile, looks up at Sharon, and in a voice with a big wink in it, says, "BUFF stands for big—ugly—fat—" and his pause is perfectly timed, "feller."

Sharon cracks up. Howie's chortling to beat the band.

Risstup sits in his chair enjoying his own waggish wit, clearly delighted that his mind is finally open for business.

☢ ☢ ☢

10:04. Monday, Nov. 28—the date/time notation on the email reads. Straub's in his Pentagon office. Out of habit, he stands and walks to the door. Closes and locks it. Not that anyone would be reading over his shoulder but it's a clear signal that he wants to be left alone. He sits back down at the desk and reads the email from Howie.

> Winn: Thanks for taking care of Sylvie and Grace. I got your message loud and clear, we just changed locations. Here's the deal. We think this pilot's life was in danger because he knows something—something about a bomb dropped from his B-52. A nurse from his ward is with me. I'm hoping we can rebuild his memory to find the bomb (if there is one). Time is an issue, but I hope we can work fast enough to get whatever we can get out of the pilot before they find us. I would appreciate any help you can give me but I don't know exactly what to ask for. Maybe you can poke around D.C. and see what you can dig up. And stay in touch. Best, Howie.

"Holy Moses," Straub whistles. He wonders where they are hiding. Curious who the nurse is. What the pilot knows. *Howie, a VA nurse and an old coot—what a combination!* He's also marveling at his college roommate. *Is it his fearlessness and tenacity I should be appreciating? Or his reckless persistence? Is he a hero or someone who can't help himself? It doesn't matter,* Winn decides. *Foolhardy or courageous, the fact is few people would have taken the risk Howie has.* He turns to his keyboard and types:

> Howie, Good to hear from you. Glad to help with Sylvie. I know she's dying to talk with you, I'll try to get that set up. We could have a real opportunity here but I don't want to put you at risk any more than we have to. Keep me up to speed on how you're

> doing with the pilot. I'll start arranging some safe houses just in case. At some point we might have to meet. So I'll get that going also. Let's talk every day. In the meantime, I'm going to start turning over rocks around here and see what I can come up with. Courage, buddy. Best, Winn.

Straub sends the email then opens the door of his office.

"Something I can do for you, Mr. Straub?" his executive assistant asks.

"I'm going out for a minute," Straub answers. "You can reach me on my cell," he says as he walks through the outer office toward the corridor.

For the world's largest low-rise office building, on a Monday after Thanksgiving the corridors are surprisingly empty. Some romantic has set up a skimpy plastic Christmas tree outside a door. Straub turns to walk up the ramp to the next floor. The sections of the Pentagon that have not yet been remodeled have long inclines going from floor to floor. Since steel was scarce in the '40s so instead of building stairs they poured ramps out of concrete. Straub appreciates the exercise. Forty-five minutes a day walking the halls keeps his internist happy and his weight down.

Straub walks briskly around the D ring, nodding to colonels, generals and admirals that he's worked with over the years, only stopping to say hello to the few he is on close terms with. He is coming to a decision about the next step he's going to take, the plan taking shape in his mind. *The odds are long, everything has to work perfectly, but if it does...*

While Straub prides himself on never allowing himself to be mawkish or inane, he can't resist the analogy since the more it plays out in his mind, the more apt it seems. He has to resist grinning. Grinning doesn't go over well in the corridors of the Pentagon. So he has to settle for smiling inside.

There are two ugly stepsisters in the American intelligence apparatus—Straub is scheming—*the Department of Homeland Security and the Central Intelligence Agency.*

And to them, I might just be holding the glass slipper.

19

[Pentagon, Monday afternoon]

Watt has been holed up in his SCIF since Friday—four days of pizza, Egg McMuffins and Chinese from the Pentagon food court. His driver brings him a fresh uniform from home and every morning the general showers and dresses at the POAC. He's going to owe his wife a string of dinners as long as his arm.

Watt's suite is now a nerve center, wires and cables snaking everywhere, the reception area packed with work stations, large screen TVs on the walls, every available surface crowded with secure phones and computers, the place is bustling with activity, normal Pentagon channels bypassed, all outside communication routing directly to him.

All day Sunday and Monday, Lieutenant Williams, the general's aide, directed the teams erecting temporary cubicles in his waiting and conference rooms, running the necessary cables, setting up the computers and monitors so that Watt could run the operation without leaving the security and privacy of his skiff.

Though he has teams on the ground all over the East Coast and his contacts at Fort Meade are combing billions of intercepts searching for clues, so far there's nothing on Thorsen, Risstup or Collyer.

"General Watt, it's General Hatkin on your stew."

Damn, that's the third time he's called, Watt thinks to himself. *It's been four days since the patient disappeared from the VA hospital. If I don't have some news for him soon, he's going to start turning up the heat.*

He picks up the phone, "General Hatkin, what can I do for you, sir?" Watt says as cheerily as possible.

Hatkin's tone of voice is gritty, it has not yet become menacing. "You haven't let me down yet, Greg, but I'm going to have to see some progress soon."

"I can give you an update, sir. We have almost finished setting up our unit in my offices. We're up and running as we speak, sir."

"That's housekeeping, I need answers. Anything further on Collyer?"

"All we have is theories, sir. We suspect that he has not gone far from Pittsburgh. He would first want to interrogate the patient. That has to be his main objective. So he wouldn't want to waste a lot of time traveling."

Hatkin's response is crisp and pointed. "I figured that out two days ago, Greg."

Watt tries to move on. "Yes, sir, as I said, at this point in time we're hypothesizing. I am expecting we will have some hard information soon."

"What gives you that confidence?"

"We're not up against a seasoned group of professionals. This is an elderly VA patient, a nurse and Howie Collyer. Sooner or later they will slip up, use a phone or go to an ATM, something, and we will nail them."

"It can't come soon enough, Watt. Anything on Collyer's buddy over at CIA—Straub?"

"We're watching him, sir."

"That's a no-brainer contact for Collyer. With him on the run, it would make sense to have his college roommate running interference for him."

"So far there's been no contact." Watt knows he's shading the truth. Someone is operating behind the scenes and Straub is the likely suspect since he managed to elude Watt's people around the same time Collyer's wife and daughter disappeared. But Watt has no hard evidence. Only suspicions. *For all I know, they could be holed up in a cabin in West Virginia or hidden away at CIA's spook farm outside Williamsburg.*

"Let me know the minute you hear anything."

"Yes, sir." Watt is relieved to hear the line go dead.

It's his aide at the door, "Excuse me, Sir." Lieutenant Williams doesn't look like he has good news. "They lost Straub again. He left his office a little after two o'clock and ditched our people somewhere in town."

"Christ, Winn Straub's almost sixty. How does he keep giving us the slip? He's no Houdini."

"My contacts at CIA tell some pretty wild stories about him. He was in some sticky situations in the Eastern Bloc in the '60s and '70s. Real cloak-and-dagger stuff. Double agents, poison pills. People getting bumped off all over the place. From what I've heard, it doesn't surprise me that he's avoiding us."

Watt wonders whose team Williams is on. He snaps at him, "Get a new group on him. We're not going to have him roaming around the District pursuing his own agenda."

Watt can feel the heat. *Collyer and his two colleagues under cover somewhere plotting to recover a lost nuke. Winn Straub running around town pulling strings for him. Making who knows what kind of unholy alliances with whom? Plenty of wolves roaming around Washington.*

Watt knows the CIA would love to embarrass the Pentagon. Homeland Security is sinking fast and looking for a life preserver and the FBI would do anything to regain its former stature. Even in the Building it's no secret there are people who would love to smoke out and bring down Vector Eleven.

As Watt runs down the list of potential adversaries, the phrase coined by a journalist wag to describe Washington politics occurs to him: *"If you want a friend in this town, get a dog."*

As he looks out the window at the thousands of cars crammed into South Parking, Watt finds himself yearning for the good old days. When he was a younger officer, there was only one enemy and everything was so much simpler. Fighting the Cold War was a cakewalk compared to terrorists and the multiple threats they presented.

I'll take the Russians any old day.

20

[Washington, Monday afternoon]

Misery loves company in the intelligence business these days, so when Winn Straub put in a call to the boss of Homeland Security and dangled an enticing tidbit, Secretary Jimmick was chomping at the bit.

Tucked away in a tranquil residential area in the historic Northwest part of D.C., the Department of Homeland Security is worlds away from the imposing downtown buildings. Though its gate is fortified and armed guards patrol the entrance, 3801 Nebraska Avenue, known as the Nebraska Avenue Complex or NAC, just across Ward Circle from American University, doesn't look like the headquarters of one of the government's largest agencies with a multi-billion dollar budget and almost two hundred thousand employees.

Straub knows the place well. Before the Navy took it over in the 1940s, it was the Mount Vernon Seminary, a private school for girls his mother-in-law attended sixty-some years ago. On close to forty acres, the NAC looks like a college campus, with red brick buildings, tall oaks and elms arching over the lawns and gravel paths winding between the buildings.

But Straub isn't risking a visit to NAC. He stuffs a ten into the hand of the driver of the third cab he's hailed, walks a block, sits at a bus stop reading a newspaper for ten minutes, then waits on the sidewalk across the street from the NAC gates, the sports section of the *Post* held up to cover his face.

Jimmick is right on time. Folding his paper to make sure Jimmick notices, Straub tucks the bad news about the Redskins under his arm, does a quick about-face and heads down the pathway into the American University campus. He told Jimmick to bring a book, sit down on a bench and read. *Spend five minutes on one bench then move to another. At the appropriate time,* he told Jimmick, *I'll join you.*

He did as he was told. As Winn suspected, the head of a major agency would jump through hoops over the tantalizing hearsay coming over the phone. It took five benches and almost a half hour before Straub was satisfied that Jimmick wasn't being tailed. Picking brown pods off the sleeve of his topcoat from edging too far into a stand of bushes, Straub walks up to the bench and sits down next to the Secretary of Homeland Security.

"Made it through hurricane season pretty well this time, Lucien," Straub says. A series of disastrous hurricanes had forced the resignation of his predecessor.

"I take that as a compliment, Winn."

"Absolutely, I wouldn't have meant it any other way."

"What's up? Why all the hocus pocus? You CIA guys are something else."

"When you hear what I have to tell you, you'll understand. I've got a proposition."

"Since when does the CIA do deals with the Department of Homeland Security?"

"This is off the books, just between the two of us."

Jimmick's new to the Washington scene. Imported from Miami where he was tsar of the city's anti-terrorist operation, he did such an outstanding job he was an easy pick when the DHS job opened up. Five years ago Straub worked with him on a case involving a gang of Chechens who were running guns from Azerbaijan to Central America through Miami. Bad dudes. Shot up a houseful of Salvadorians trying to siphon off profits. Women, children, a real bloodbath. Jimmick never lost his composure, handling the case expertly. Together, they cooperated in shutting down the operation. Though they haven't stayed in close touch, Straub has kept an eye on him.

He holds Jimmick in high regard but he doesn't envy his challenge at DHS. Straub remembered reading a reporter's description of the Department of Homeland Security as an "ineffectual behemoth." Cobbled together from other agencies in the days after 9/11, Homeland Security is a gigantic jumble of disparate operations with a wide array of critical responsibilities—protecting the ports and coastlines, handling natural disasters, running airport security, policing the borders and guarding the president.

"Let's hear it," Jimmick asks.

"I know you're not getting a lot of cooperation from the Pentagon."

Jimmick snorts, "When you're dealing with a eight hundred pound gorilla, you keep your head down and hang on like hell to what you have."

"What if I told you that I've found a soft spot over there? You might even call it an Achilles' heel."

"At the Pentagon?" Jimmick says. salivating at the prospect.

Out of the corner of his eye, Straub sees someone coming down the path. In an instant, he reaches out and places a hand on Jimmick's arm with just enough pressure to convey his message. A tall dude in a parka and baseball cap is walking toward them. Baseball caps always attract Straub's attention. Too studied an attempt at looking casual. The two men watch as he ambles by.

No problem, Straub decides, recognizing his shoes, Nike. *He must be a soccer coach at American, that or lacrosse, designed for either sport.*

When he's passed, Jimmick can't wait to say, "Tell me about it."

When it comes to intelligence, Straub knows Jimmick is chafing at being under the Pentagon's thumb. With little intel capability, Homeland Security is limited to raising a red, yellow or orange flag when the Pentagon gives the alert. The color-coded system has been the butt of jokes inside the Beltway since it was first announced. Jimmick's first move in his new job was to permanently shelve the color-coding.

"Potentially the two of us could team up to pull off a major national security coup."

"And the Pentagon would take the hit?"

"You got it."

"Couldn't happen to a nicer bunch of guys. What's the deal?"

"Let's just say it concerns missing nuclear materials."

Jimmick sits up. "Russian?"

"No—ours."

Jimmick's eyes widen. When he was in Miami he wrote a series of articles for the *Herald* on the threat nuclear materials stored in vulnerable locations posed to our national security.

"You mean nuclear waste, spent fuel rods?"

"That's garden variety, I'm talking the real thing."

"A weapon?"

Straub doesn't have to do more than slightly incline his head to cause Jimmick's mouth to drop open.

"You don't mean it—missing from inventory?"

"Not from our arsenal. An H-bomb on the loose."

"How is that possible?"

"Dropped from a B-52 years ago."

"Jesus, you don't mean it? In the continental U.S.?"

"Yup."

"Where?"

"That's what I'm trying to find out."

"One of those nukes that were never accounted for? That the Pentagon keeps saying present no problem?"

"Precisely."

"Does the Pentagon have any idea of what you're up to? They'd have a shitfit."

"That's why I'm talking to you."

"This could blow up in their face."

"That's why it has to be kept between us. They've already been sniffing around to see what I know."

"So that's the reason for the spy stuff."

"They've been watching me for four days, I feel like I'm back in Belgrade."

"How did you find out about this?"

"I have a connection."

The gears in Jimmick's brain are grinding. "Wait a minute. Does this by any chance have anything to do with that character who stirred things up at the Pentagon a while ago? What's his name?"

"Howard Collyer?"

"Yes, that's it. Resigned a year or so ago?"

"You got it. Collyer was my college roommate."

All Jimmick can do is let out a quiet puff of air from between his tightly pursed lips. Then he asks, "What kind of time frame are we talking about?"

"It could break anytime in the next two to three days. Too loaded to keep quiet much longer."

"So if your old buddy Howie Collyer can put his finger on one of these missing weapons, it will look like the Pentagon hasn't been minding the store."

"Worse than that. If they can't ride herd on the weapons they have, Congress will be reluctant to fund more. That whole program they are trying to push to rebuild our nuclear arsenal will go down in flames. Not to mention exposing the sloppy situation at Savannah, the mess at Rocky Flats, botching the Yucca Mountain project—all that stuff you wrote about."

"Can you give me any idea where it's at?"

Straub shakes his head.

"But you know?"

Straub puts on a poker face. "I have a good idea, okay?"

"I have the Coast Guard under my command. I'm gearing it up for domestic ops and getting some really good people on board." Just as Straub expected, Jimmick is falling all over himself to volunteer his services.

"We might need them."

"I can have them mobilized like that." Jimmick snaps his fingers. "So who else knows about this? Have you clued in Dickson yet?"

Straub shakes his head. Abner Dickson is his boss—the CIA director. A political appointee, he spends more time on the links at Congressional than in his office at Langley, which is fine with CIA staffers since they end run him on most of their business anyway.

"So far, no one's in the loop but you and me. We have to keep it that way for as long as possible."

"What do you want me to do?"

"How secure is your home?"

"It was debugged last week."

"Find anything?"

Jimmick nods.

"Have it searched again. I'll contact you there. We'll go have a drink somewhere."

"In some noisy bar."

"You bet. A Georgetown hangout full of students looking to get lucky."

"But we're the ones who will get lucky."

"It will be a woman who will call you."

Jimmick winces. "Do we have to get into that?"

"People will be less likely to suspect anything. It'll look like you're up to your old tricks again."

Jimmick gives him a begrudging smile, "The anti-terrorism expert who can't keep it in his pants. You're a master, Straub."

"Flattery will get you everywhere." Straub rolls back his cuff to check the time. "I've got to get going, Lucien. I'll be in touch with you soon. Her name will be Susie."

They stand and shake hands.

"Appreciate the opportunity to help, Winn."

Straub wants to say, *Don't thank me, thank Howie Collyer.* But instead he turns, waves, says, "Don't mention it," and heads toward Ward Circle to scare up a cab.

21

[TUESDAY EVENING IN SOLO, INDONESIA, EST + 12 HOURS]

Time is running out for Abu El-Khadr. The message came down from a heavily camouflaged and fortified outpost in the barren, mountainous region of northwest Pakistan. Though the last sentence was incomplete, it left an unmistakable impression.

The English translation was more indicative of his leader's attitude than the Arabic: "If you let this opportunity slip between our fingers—" For three years they have been keeping Collyer under close scrutiny, either waiting for something to break on his website or for him to take the first step. Just when Collyer makes his move, they lose him. The implications are clear. It is imperative that Collyer be found.

Their cells in the U.S. have stayed under cover—he is ninety-nine percent certain the Americans may surmise that they are in the country but they have not a shred of hard evidence, not even leads, only a sneaking suspicion that sleeper cells exist. Now is the time to take risks. Though the American monster is awake, only one eye is open.

El-Khadr has left his office twice to check on Naguib's progress. So far, so good.

In his first assignment, Naguib is understandably nervous. He still shudders when he thinks of the incident in the WC. The panicked look in the man's eyes as he stared up at the gun barrel in Naguib's hand. His body jerking around as the rounds tore into him. Blood splattered on the walls, all the way back to the call center the sound of the shots reverberated in his head.

Though El-Khadr's instructions were vague, he follows their intent to the letter. Come up with a way to locate Collyer without tipping their hand. It can't come across as a wanted poster, El-Khadr stressed.

Instead, he must create a cover story that will motivate his special list of Muslims in the Northeast to be on the lookout.

Naguib discards ten approaches before he comes up with the answer. A homemade flier publicizing the misdeeds of an adulterous husband, deliberately crude, with misspelled words and unsophisticated graphics. Naguib designs it so it looks like a handbill one would see pasted on a neighborhood lamppost—an appeal from a jilted wife about her perfidious husband, his picture at the top with the wife's emotional message below. Except the photo is not of an unfaithful Middle Eastern husband but of a former Pentagon staffer.

Lifting Collyer's picture from his homepage, he gives Collyer a Yemeni name and crafts copy written from the wife's point of view. Laying it on thick, he weaves a tale rivaling any soap opera, The husband dishonored her by having a string of affairs, including her niece and closest friend, then added insult to injury by absconding with her family's treasures, including her grandmother's jewelry and a rare early copy of the Koran. The copy rambles on, finally ending with, *I beg you to notify my brothers if you see this faithless rogue so they can deliver him the punishment he so richly deserves.*

Naguib is putting on a finishing touch, creating a headscarf to set on Collyer's head when El-Khadr stalks out and positions himself behind Naguib. He peers down at his console, adjusting his glasses so he can see the image on the screen. Using his mouse, Naguib moves the kaffiya over onto the picture of Collyer and sets it on his head. Naguib smiles at his handiwork. *It fits perfectly. With his head covered, Collyer looks like he could be from mixed parentage, enough like an Arab so he won't arouse suspicion.*

El-Khadr cracks a thin smile. His new protégé has created a one-page potboiler, a perfect screen for an appeal to Muslim Americans to help them track down Collyer. The woman's outrage screams off the page. Hamil could never have created such a masterpiece, he was a mere technician. Naguib has the scientific knowhow but he complements it with a quality Hamil lacked—imagination.

Naguib's heart races as he waits for El-Khadr's reaction. From over his shoulder, he is relieved to hear El-Khadr saying, "Good work. Send it out as soon as it is finished. The email list is here." El-Khadr takes a flash drive out of his pocket and hands it to him. On it is his Who's

Who of Muslims on the East Coast, carefully culled to include those who, though they would never openly express sympathy for the jihadist cause, have become increasingly radicalized in the years since 9/11.

There are too many stories about people who were yanked out of lines at airport security for wearing a chador or whose houses were raided in the middle of the night because they had an Arabic name. Muslims, increasingly under scrutiny, feel a need to band together. He's used the list twice in the past, once to raise funds for his front organization, again to attract potential mujahideen to his cause. Both times the response was positive. He's hoping the flier will have the same appeal and people will forward it to others, casting an even wider net.

El-Khadr is aware the vast web of American intelligence may intercept it. *But will anyone recognize Collyer? If they do, will they be shrewd enough to suspect who is behind it? Hopefully it will sit in a pile on someone's desk for a few days before any action is taken. Or maybe it will get backed up waiting for translation.* Whatever the outcome, El-Khadr knows he has no choice.

Returning to his office, he checks email. In seconds the flier has zipped around the globe and come full circle. Opening it, he admires his new assistant's work. *This will work.* He gets up and goes over to the rug aligned so it points west. *But I will say a few prayers—just in case.*

Dotty Cubbidge has worked for the National Security Agency for three years. Fresh out of Georgetown's Arab Studies program, she was recruited by NSA to shore up their Arabic translation section. Barricaded behind triple razor-wire fences and thick concrete walls, Cubbidge and her eighteen thousand co-workers at Fort Meade and another twenty around the globe are the eyes and ears of America's intelligence network.

NSA has been scrambling to staff up with enough analysts and translators to keep up with the burgeoning flood of incoming data—guesstimated to be the equivalent of a thousand books a minute. Cubbidge is one of the new recruits they threw money at to come on board. Now she deals with the torrent of incoming information on a daily basis. Sitting in her cubicle seven hours a day monitoring Arabic conversations from around the world, after only a few months on the job Cubbidge readily admits to her close friends that, even with four years of intensive Arabic, a lot of it goes over her head.

Before it became the subject of intense interest and scrutiny over its domestic intelligence activities, so little was known about the National Security Agency that its acronym was jokingly interpreted as: *No Such Agency* or *Never Say Anything.* Headquartered at Fort Meade, Maryland in two multi-storied black glass boxes with its own exit off the Baltimore-Washington Parkway, every day Cubbidge drives past the large sign posted on the shoulder alongside the turnoff that leaves little doubt about the goings-on there: "NSA Employees Only."

Cubbidge likes to boast to her friends that NSA has more math PhDs on staff than any other organization in the world—in addition to cryptographers, analysts and specialists in every conceivable form of communication. And while its budget and operations are classified, public record shows that the thousands of computers whirring night and day at Fort Meade make it the second largest consumer of electricity in Maryland.

Fifteen years ago NSA's main worry was a Russian with his finger on the nuclear trigger. Today it's a lone Islamic extremist with a rocket launcher, a sat phone and a chip on his shoulder.

Journalists have reported that two messages in Arabic intercepted by NSA on September 10, 2001—*tomorrow is zero hour*, and *the match begins tomorrow*—might have provided a clue to the debacle that was to take place the next day if only they had been translated in time. Flagged by computers as originating from al Qaeda and awaiting translation, NSA faced such a backlog of al Qaeda intercepts that Arabic translators were not able to get to the critical messages until two days later.

More than once Cubbidge has found herself griping, "Each day I come across hundreds of names, many of which are foreign enough to start with, but then when they start talking about their uncle who is related to their wife's brother-in-law, I lose track of who's who and my head starts swimming. But every once in a while, I'll be monitoring chatter or reading through emails and I'll see or hear a few phrases or sentences that will scare the living crap out of me."

Early Wednesday morning, Cubbidge is working the graveyard shift to bank some extra vacation days. No one would know it's 3 AM as the lights are blazing and the activity is as intense as it would be in the middle of the day. As they say around NSA, *SIGINT* (signals intelligence, NSA's stock in trade) *keeps no hours.*

It is proving to be just another day at the office when the agency's top-secret software flags the flier of the missing husband posted by his anxious wife and pops it up on Cubbidge's screen. The photo's a man wearing a kaffiya. The copy is from the wife's point of view, ranting about her cheating husband. Cubbidge is about to dismiss it as an oddity when a detail catches her eye.

Something's odd here, she thinks. Quickly zooming into the top of the photograph, she examines the folds of the headscarf. She keeps clicking in until the crown of the man's head fills the screen. Normally one would expect a thin shadow at the point where the headscarf meets the forehead—an indication that the two surfaces are different, one skin, one cloth, the two unconnected, the kaffiya casting a faint outline where it sits folded over the forehead. But there is no shadow. The two surfaces are butted together.

Cubbidge instantly recognizes a Photoshop job. The kaffiya has been electronically cut and pasted onto the man's head with the program used all over the world to adjust, improve and doctor photographs.

But why in the world would someone do that? she asks herself. And then, *I wonder what this guy's going to look like without the headscarf?* Saving the original, she makes a copy, opens Photoshop and erases the headscarf. Then replaces the missing part of his forehead and fills it in with hair.

Sitting back and surveying the result, she decides: *Without the kaffiya, there's no doubt he's Western—British or American, Canadian or Australian. So what's his face doing in an email written in Arabic? And why would someone go to the trouble to put a headscarf on him?*

She sends the flier to the translation section and then, as she has been instructed, Red Codes the message in both versions, original and her edit, and touches the SEND button on her keyboard, zipping it to her supervisor and whoever else in the intelligence community is authorized for Code Red. *Have I intercepted an encoded terrorist communication? And if so, what in the world does the disguised Westerner pictured on the flier have to do with terrorists?*

Fourteen miles away in the Pentagon, Lieutenant Williams notices the Code Red intercept the second it flashes on his screen—two documents arriving from NSA. One a crude flier with a picture of a man in a headscarf. But Williams checks the face again. *Is there something familiar?* When he opens the second document. Williams almost spits out his coffee. There is no mistaking the subject of the photograph or the import of the intercept. *Someone has put Howard Collyer's picture on a poster. And the fucking copy is in Arabic.*

Two seconds later, he hears General Watt bellowing his name. As he scrambles around his desk, he can see others in the skiff also staring at the flier. Officers are standing, grabbing for phones, the photo causing an increasing buzz of conversation around the crowded office. *Why did someone put Collyer's face on a flier and place a turban on his head to make him look Middle Eastern? And the fact that his picture is surrounded by Arabic copy is even more alarming.*

"Williams, get in here," Watt yells from his office. "Did you see what just came in?"

"Yes, sir," Williams says.

Watt has already printed out the email and is holding it up for Williams to see. "How many people receive Code Red?"

"Only us as long as our NSA contact plays by the rules."

"Are you sure? We have to know if this was circulated."

"I'll double check, sir."

"Someone who speaks Arabic is looking for Collyer. And most likely it isn't the Arab-American Friendship Society."

"Even though I can't read a word I think that is the only possible conclusion."

"If some jihadist group knows Collyer's on the track of a nuke, it's a whole new ball game."

Watt recalls the bug at Collyer's house that suddenly went dead. He sits back in his chair, tossing the printout of the flier on his desk with a gravelly snort. *All of a sudden the stakes have gone up big time. Terrorists on the trail of a loose nuke—an unsettling prospect—even though the nukes would be hard to find and retrieve and it's only a crank like Collyer who's involved. It's no longer a matter of saving face, there might be national security implications. How long will we be able to keep this information under wraps before we're forced to act?*

"Could be they've lost him," Williams offers, trying to make the best of the situation. "I bet that's why they put this out. Risky of them to send his picture over the Internet. They must have guessed we would intercept it."

Williams leans farther back in his chair, clasping his hands behind his head. "On the other hand maybe they don't give a damn."

"I'm not sure I understand."

"Think about it. As long as they beat us to the nuke, who cares?"

"That's a ghastly thought."

"Tell me about it."

"I'll get it translated ASAP. Might take them a while but I'll put the pressure on."

Watt watches Williams shut the door behind him then looks over at his stew phone. He wonders how long it will take Hatkin to find out about the terrorist connection to Collyer. Watt bets he has his own sources at NSA so it won't be long before he's on the horn to him. Though the terrorists the FBI has rounded up so far have been a sorry lot—from paintball players in the Virginia woods to a bunch of whack-os in Miami—there's always a chance an authentic sleeper cell is out there.

Watt unwraps a fresh roll of Tums, knowing he's going to need at least one pack to get himself through the day.

22

[Rutgers campus, Wednesday, 7 am]

He can hear Melanie in the other room, TV's blaring, she's singing along with a commercial. His early class on Wednesday is a three-hour lab. Mehran puts the finishing touches on his paper then checks email. There's a new message with an odd attachment.

He gets up, quietly clicks the door shut and sits back down, staring at the document accompanying the email. It's written in the words of a spurned wife reaching out to people in the Islamic community to put the finger on her reprobate husband. He puzzles over it. *Wait a minute,* he thinks, *there's something familiar about the face.* He leans in toward the screen, inspecting the photograph closely. Then he does a classic double take.

I can't believe it. It's Collyer's picture from his website. Why do they risk compromising the mission by publishing Collyer's picture? They've dressed him up in a kaffiya to make him look like an Arab. Or maybe to disguise him? But it's such a clumsy job the Americans will see through it in a second.

From the start they have been warned about the millions of American computers sifting through worldwide communication looking for traces of terrorists. His first thought is his own security. Then he worries about the mission. *Have they lost Collyer and are pulling out all stops to find him?*

Quickly checking Collyer's site, he sees nothing has changed, no updates in the past two weeks. Then he goes on the website sent with the email and is immediately heartened. There is a long string of messages, many posted in the last hour, Mehran guesses over fifty. As he watches them multiply minute by minute, the network answering the appeal for information on the whereabouts of the husband in order to turn him in to her bloodthirsty brothers for the appropriate revenge, he realizes it's a stroke of genius. *Someone in the top command must have deemed it necessary to go public.* He chides himself for being so doubting.

If I didn't believe in the leadership, I wouldn't be devoting my life to the cause. I have to believe they have chosen the right course.

Mehran gets up, unlocks his door and walks out into the living room. Melanie is pouring coffee.

"Is everything all right? I heard you close your door suddenly."

"It is okay," Mehran says, taking the cup of coffee she's holding out to him.

"I was afraid you'd gotten bad news."

"Everything is fine, thanks for being concerned."

Melanie gives him a peck on the cheek. The irony of the scene strikes him.

Here I am in this typical American domestic situation, taking a cup of Maxwell House from my smiling partner who's wearing a terrycloth bathrobe and fuzzy slippers, instant waffles heating in the toaster with Good Morning America *booming from the TV. What could be more typically American?*

Mehran thinks and then adds, *If they only knew.*

Though it's well after midnight in Solo, the early summer air is still thick and steamy. Even the torrential downpour during the day has not cooled things off. A flock of mosquitoes insistently buzzing over his head keeps him company. The ceiling fan is whirring noisily, flapping the papers on his desk. El-Khadr has not slept since they sent the email and he's just nodding off when Naguib sticks his head in.

"The network is coming alive. They are beginning to respond to our communication," he tells El-Khadr. Grabbing his glasses and crop, El-Khadr hustles out toward Naguib's workstation.

Nodding in approval as he looks at the posts flooding into the website, he says to no one in particular, "This is good, good, this is very good."

As the flier circulates, connections are being made instantaneously and multiplying swiftly. As Naguib opens the messages one after another for his boss, they read down the string of posts.

People are shocked and outraged by the woman's tale of woe. The stolen Koran is the last straw. The number quickly mushrooms as more and more people log onto the website, a chain of emails, faxes and telephone calls extending over the East Coast as Muslims keep an eye out for the loathsome husband.

El-Khadr looks at his watch. Though he is tired, he cannot afford sleep. *Either we find Collyer or…* He does not need to finish his thought.

Watt is halfway out the door on his way to shower at the POAC when Williams stops him. Other than napping at his desk and catching a couple hours of shuteye on his sofa, Watt's had no sleep. And he's fed up with food court meals, craving wine and a juicy ribeye, but knowing Hatkin might call any minute, there was no way he could leave his post.

"A woman in Pittsburgh called the cops. We've had an alert out with police departments in counties around the area. Returned from a business trip last night to find her plates missing. Only tags stolen from the airport in the past week so there's a possibility it was Collyer."

"If it was him, that's damn smart." Watt thinks, *Hopefully that's the last good move he'll make.*

"Every police department in a three-state area has the number."

"Alert a team, I want them standing by."

"Already done. I activated it before I came in so we wouldn't lose any time."

"Which one?"

"Alpha Orange—one of our best demolitions people, two snipers, an electronic surveillance group, anything we could need."

"And their orders?"

"First locate the car, then check for Collyer."

Watt shakes his head. Motioning for Williams to come into his office, he closes the door. Williams notices the past five days are taking their toll on his boss. He's looking disheveled, his hair matted and his uniform rumpled, a half-day's stubble flocking his cheeks. But the grim determination in his eyes is unmistakable and his voice is clear and direct. "We can't afford to have Collyer on the loose. He could be leading terrorists to a nuke. If it turns out to be his car, all three of them,

Collyer, Risstup, Thorsen, have to be considered enemy combatants."

In order to crack down on terrorism, the term *enemy combatant* is now employed to any suspect, making anyone so labeled fair game for drastic measures.

"I understand, sir." Williams knows he doesn't have to say another word.

As he closes the door, the bell jingles behind him. Though he knows it isn't smart, he is a sucker for her double-skim lattes. Howie quickly surveys the interior. Esmerelda's Hqt Shoppe is crowded with locals, most retirees, folks in their sixties and seventies scarfing down scrambled eggs and bacon, sausage and pancakes, sipping espressos and mugs of steaming java. Everyone gives him a quick once-over as he crosses the room and then goes back to the food in front of them.

Howie gets in line for coffee. Two people ahead of him, one older guy and a secretary-type in a blouse, skirt and heels. *She's a looker,* Howie thinks, appreciating her butt and shapely legs and praying she's not going to order those concoctions disguised as coffee that take five minutes to make.

"Caramel macchiato, please, with an extra shot," she says. Howie gives the man in front of him a look. They nod knowingly, their eyes groaning in unison.

As he waits at the counter, Howie's gaze drifts through the pass-through. The kitchen is a beehive, people scurrying around, smoke sizzling up from the grill, the sound of plates clanking, metal against china, everything at Esmerelda's moving at warp speed.

The woman takes her drink. Then fishes in her purse. *She's not going to write a check?* Howie rolls his eyes. Another two minutes.

Howie needs to get back to work as Risstup's progress has been encouraging. Sharon has helped fill in his childhood in California. His college experience is coming together and he's starting to tell stories about piloting B-52s. Howie's flight simulation software is ready to go. And as anxious as he is to move forward, he knows you can't patch together a lifetime in two seconds.

Then suddenly, just for an instant, Howie catches the eye of someone in the kitchen, a dishwasher maybe? *Busboy? White outfit, stains on his shirt. Dark hair, could be Middle Eastern, staring at me as he slips through the space behind the pass-through—or is he? And what is his expression saying? Do I know you? Have I seen you before? And what is it that I don't like about you?*

It all goes by in a few fleeting seconds—*I am getting paranoid?*

"Sir? May I help you, sir?" the counter girl's peeved.

"Yes," Howie recovers, "two double skim lattes, please, and one coffee with room for milk." He glances back into the kitchen. The busboy has disappeared. *Maybe he shot me a look because he's looking for a little diversion? Or it was an idle glance, nothing more?*

"That will be six-seventy-five, sir," the girl says, handing Howie a cardboard tray holding the coffees.

Howie forks over the cash and turns to leave. One cup tilts, threatening to tumble. Howie catches it and heads for the door. He knows he's rattled but doesn't know what to do. *Why would a busboy at a dinky cafe in a podunk town single me out? It makes no sense.*

But that doesn't keep Howie from heading back to the motel at a good clip, looking over his shoulder a few times to make sure.

El-Khadr is at the bazaar when his cell phone rings. He told Naguib to call on the cell if there were any news—reluctantly, since an American Predator drone has homed in on a phone's signal too many times and launched a Hellfire missile, instantaneously replacing the person talking with a twenty-foot-wide crater.

He cuts Naguib off when he hears what he needs to know and scurries back to his headquarters as fast as his peg leg will carry him.

Naguib is holding the door open. "The message came in two minutes ago," he tells El-Khadr. "Someone saw him in a small town west of D.C. They know where he's staying, even located his car."

El-Khadr is panting, he waits until the door shuts behind him. "Can we be sure?"

"The person who saw him said he recognized him even without the kaffiya."

"Allah be praised," El Khadr whispers. Crossing the room, El-Khadr pulls up a chair at the workstation next to Naguib. He will type out his orders in Arabic, Naguib will encode them.

El-Khadr has already taken a gamble with the flier, he can't risk any further open communication. As cumbersome as the code is, they must revert to encrypted messages.

His first objective is to pinpoint Collyer, then to throw a protective cordon around him so he can continue his search uninterrupted. He has to expect the Americans are pulling out all the stops. He smiles as he imagines the American intelligence colossus falling all over itself as it scrambles to catch up with Collyer, the finger-pointing, the backpedaling—El-Khadr knows Americans all too well.

El-Khadr wastes no time ordering the cell members based around Camden, New Jersey into action. Three of the five cut their teeth fighting the Russians in Afghanistan, the other two are Saudis, veterans of the Chechen conflict. El-Khadr has used them on other operations in Africa and Yemen. All are young, fast, ruthless, fearless and dedicated to the cause.

They also have mastered American slang and customs. Only one has dark skin, the others wouldn't raise an eyebrow standing in line at McDonald's. One works as a waiter, another's a roofer, a third drives a cab, their names borrowed from high school yearbooks ring true, their identities precise and complete right down to their driver's licenses and Social Security cards.

No one would suspect that they are trained assassins dedicated to the overthrow of the Great Satan, devout jihadists determined to bring destruction to the Far Enemy.

El-Khadr claps Naguib on the shoulder as he reads his translation. He is further impressed with his new lieutenant's work. Fast and flexible, creative and nimble, he is proving to be just the man El-Khadr needs to get his mission back on track.

23

[Washington, Wednesday noon]

Watt is around his desk and out of his office faster than Williams has ever seen the paunchy fifty-eight-year-old general move. "Front Royal?" he asks. "Are you certain it's him?"

"Definitely his car, a 1998 Accord LX with the plates from the airport." Both men are examining the digital photo on Williams' computer screen emailed to them by the Front Royal police.

"Any sign of him?"

"I left that up to us, sir. The less said, the better. No reason why any of the local cops should know who we're looking for or why."

Watt realizes his lack of sleep is showing. "You're right," he says, and changes the subject. "How long before Alpha Orange lands?"

Williams turns his wrist so he can see his watch, "Within minutes. They took off from Belvoir a half hour ago."

The minute the Black Hawk touches down outside of Front Royal, the Alpha Orange team jumps out and double-times toward a waiting SUV. Dressed in casual clothes, chinos, baseball caps and windbreakers, the seven men could easily be mistaken for a group of guys off to a football game were it not for their military-style backpacks and long black suitcases. As they stash their gear in the back and pile into the SUV, only four cows on the far side of the pasture pay any attention.

As soon as the team leader is in the front seat, he has a detailed map open on his lap. Twelve minutes into town. Though he knows it's none of his business, as he sorts through his target's photos—the old coot, an attractive woman in a nurse's uniform and the retired guy named

Collyer—a question keeps running through Captain Perini's mind. *What did these people do to get themselves in such deep shit?*

The second he sees the Honda, Perini's on his secure phone to the Pentagon.

Before Watt can react, Williams reaches for the ringing stew. "I'll get it, sir."

Watt's hand is on the receiver before Williams can grab it. "If it's good news, Williams, I want to be the first to know."

"Captain Perini, sir. We're at the car," Perini says over the secure line as they pull up alongside the Accord. "We're going to canvass the area. This is a tiny burg, sir, it shouldn't take us long, only eight or ten motels."

"This is General Watt, Captain Perini. Good start," Watt says into the stew. "You understand you are to use any means necessary. There will be no questions asked."

"Made clear in the briefing. Yes, sir."

"Excellent. Detain them and bring them back to Belvoir for questioning."

"Yes, sir."

"One more thing—"

"Sir?"

"The car, the Honda, I don't want to hear about Collyer escaping in it," Watt tells the team leader.

"Yes, sir."

Perini signs off and snaps his secure phone shut.

They made it down from Camden to Front Royal in record time, staying just over the speed limit to make sure some overzealous cop looking to make his monthly quota didn't pull them over. No one in the cab talked as they took the Beltway around Baltimore, then skirted D.C. and headed west toward the small town in the Virginia countryside.

Wearing stained and torn work clothes and needing shaves, the five look like the migrant workers who flock into the area every fall to pick vegetables. No one in Front Royal would suspect that their yellow Checker, scratched, dented and in need of a paint job, carries enough munitions and weapons to equip a platoon and that under their coveralls and parkas the men are armed to the teeth. The coded communication they had received gave them the information they needed.

Although his car was parked on the other side of town, they were to go directly to the coffee shop. The busboy had seen Collyer heading in the direction of a small motel two blocks away.

Parking down the street, three of the men establish a perimeter around their cab, widening out to secure the immediate area. Odeh and Ahmed head toward the motel, hands in pockets, ambling down the street casually.

Tacked to the jamb of the motel office door is a small handwritten sign with the name of the motel owner. Odeh knocks on the door. No answer. He bangs harder. The door creaks open and one suspicious eye appears in the slit.

"What do you want?" Dede Ferry asks, peering warily out at the two foreigners—one with nappy hair you couldn't comb with a rake, the other the color of a pecan.

"We're looking for a room."

"Ain't got none," he snaps.

"We'll pay in cash, upfront for a week," Odeh says, flashing a handful of Benjamins at the beady-eyed face staring through the crack. Dede Ferry's pupils bulge at the sight. He opens the door a bit to look the two over.

"One of you come in, the other stays outside," he says, swinging the door partially open. Before he can react, Odeh is all over him, whirling Ferry around and hammerlocking his left arm up behind his back. Running him across the room, he slams him against the front desk, pinning his head down and jamming a Glock into his temple. Ahmed's right behind him, closing the door and moving quickly to check the rest of the office.

Odeh flips Ferry on his back and clamps two hands on his neck, his sharpened thumbnails hovering over his Adam's apple, ready to give him an instant tracheotomy. "Where are they? The three, what room are they in?"

"Seven, eight and nine, five rooms down," Ferry rasps.

"Are they in there now?" Odeh starts to apply pressure, his thumbs compacting Ferry's windpipe.

"Chances are, don't go out much," now Ferry is gurgling.

"Are they in there?" Odeh repeats, his fingers compressing the cartilage so much crackling noises are heard.

"Yes—"

Odeh eases up. "Do you have a fire alarm?"

Ferry shakes his head, "Just smoke detectors."

Odeh mutters in Arabic to his partner. Ferry's eyes bug out when he sees the other man heading toward him, sliding the gleaming blade of a knife and a roll of duct tape out of his parka.

While his team quickly fans out down the main drag, the Alpha Orange demo man carefully wires Collyer's Honda, setting the pressure-sensitive fuse so that only a dramatic change in weight would trip it, insuring that a bird perching on the antenna or a car kissing its bumper would not set it off.

The SUV keeps up with the team as they check every motel along the strip, constantly updating Perini by radio.

"No sign of them at the Shenandoah, sir." Perini crosses off the motel on his map.

"Good, go to the next one. Hurry it up."

He glances at his watch. Seven minutes. Four more motels. Perini wonders if he shouldn't have started on the other side of town. But it made sense to begin the search where Collyer had left his car. Would he think to leave his car in a separate location? Perini isn't going to take a chance. He keys his radio to talk to the SUV driver, "Take two men and head over to the other side of town. Start searching from that direction just in case."

Dede Ferry looks like a mummy with the duct tape wound around him. Lying helpless on the floor behind the front desk with his hands and feet wrapped tightly, a slit left for his eyes and a narrower one for his nostrils, Ferry's barely able to inhale but lucky to be alive.

As Odeh and Ahmed make their way through the tall grass behind the motel, Odeh counts the windows until he finds room number 8. One peek is all it takes. Collyer is sitting at a computer, back to the window, the woman standing alongside, the old man on Collyer's left. He knows he needs to move fast. His people with the cab had spread out to check for cops. What his partner Ally had discovered was worse.

The motel is cheaply built, wood frame up on concrete piers, open crawlspace underneath. Ahmad went to bring the jerry cans from the cab and Rahman is stealing a backup vehicle. He checks his watch. Ally had seen men going from motel to motel. The blue windbreakers and the wraparound sunglasses were a dead giveaway. Right off the bat, they knew they weren't selling Girl Scout cookies. Odeh and his people aren't the only ones looking for Collyer.

Ahmed hustles up with the two cans and they quickly douse the ground under the joists, making sure gas splashes on the wood. With the dregs, Odeh dribbles a line though the dry grass down the hill. He checks with Ally, Rahman and Abdullah. Everything is set but there is no time to waste. The black Suburban is now five blocks away. Crouching, Odeh strikes a match and holds it against the glistening grass. The gasoline ignites with a dull pop and the flame snakes up the hill toward the motel.

Dede Ferry is the first to smell smoke winding up through the floorboards, wafting up in thin wisps. Soon he feels the heat, his left side is broiling. Trussed up in duct tape, flames crackling beneath him, *barbeque* is the first word that pops into the motel owner's mind.

Sharon's head quickly snaps to the side as she cocks an ear. "Did you hear that?" she asks.

"What?' Howie answers, eyes glued to the computer screen. Risstup's sitting at his side, staring at the simulated B-52 cockpit on Howie's laptop.

"It was a *whomp*, a dull thud."

"You're hearing things."

"Now I smell smoke. Can't you smell it?"

"Now you're smelling things."

"Holy shit, look!" Sharon screeches as she points to the wall of flames licking up outside the window.

"You get the major out, I'll grab whatever I can," Howie shouts.

"C'mon, Major," Sharon says, steering his wheelchair toward the door. Howie quickly changes his mind when he sees the raging fire outside. *On second thought, I'm not grabbing anything.* Picking up his laptop, he hurries out the door after her. It's not until they get to the street before they turn around. The motel's ablaze, flames leaping twenty and thirty feet into the air, windows popping and shattering in the searing heat, the fire tearing through the structure.

"That was meant for us?" Sharon asks.

Before Howie can answer, five sharp cracks ring out, followed by three more.

Sharon instinctively ducks, "What the hell was that?"

Howie knows exactly what it was—multiple discharges of a large-bore weapon, maybe more than one, but he doesn't want to freak Sharon out. "Whatever it was, we're getting out of here."

"Which way's your car?"

"Forget about it." Howie knows if someone's shooting up Front Royal, there's no time to retrieve the Honda. Just as he's trying to figure out what to do, he sees a taxi turn the corner.

"Are we in luck?" Howie says, raising his arm to flag it down. Sharon sees the yellow cab coming down the street, veering over to the curb in their direction. "C'mon, hop in," he says, opening the door and quickly breaking down the wheelchair.

"Head out of town," Howie says as the doors slam and the driver puts the cab in gear. Howie scans the streets around the motel as they head out of town. Everywhere sirens are wailing. His mind is reeling. He needs to talk with Straub.

The cabbie asks, "Any direction you want, sir? North, east, south or west, take your pick." The driver's looking in his rearview mirror, scanning the mismatched threesome in his backseat. Howie can tell he's trying to decode the relationship.

He knows they need a bigger city, more anonymity. Not D.C.—that would be walking into the thick of it. Baltimore will provide them some cover. He knows the town like the back of his hand.

"Baltimore, head toward Baltimore," he tells the driver.

"Is a hundred miles to Baltimore. Rush hour there. Much traffic. Very much fare, sir."

"I said Baltimore, please," Howie says. "And make it fast."

"Very well, sir, your money," the driver slaps down the flag and steps on it.

24

[Solo, Indonesia, early Thursday morning, EST + 12]

He's dripping sweat. To keep the moisture from playing havoc with his machine he keeps sponging off his keyboard. The mosquitoes are everywhere and the fans are whirring like they're going to take off. He's been scanning the posts for hours, knowing he's losing his edge but also aware that El-Khadr could come storming out of his office at any minute.

Three Red Bulls and four cups of strong tea later, he's still seen nothing from the team in Northern Virginia.

After five minutes, an email jumps into his inbox. Naguib's face brightens as he catches a glimpse of the message. Blinking the perspiration out of his eyes, he reads the email aloud, *Cindy has joined us to help dig up the dahlias.*

He jumps up, shouting the good news toward El-Khadr's office. "They have him!" Naguib is astounded at what their network has accomplished—directed from the other side of the globe, a sleeper cell has snatched Collyer out from under the Americans' eyes.

El-Khadr comes out of his office yawning and blinking, smoothing out his wrinkled dishdasha, his crop snugged under his arm.

"They found him," he turns and announces to his boss. "They found Collyer. He is in a cab heading east."

"They are following him?"

"Even better."

"I don't understand."

"We are driving."

For the first time in two days, as the two stand in front of the screen hurriedly scanning the emails, El-Khadr relaxes enough to muster a faint smile. Allah has favored them. The bet El-Khadr had placed on his special list had paid off. Within ten hours, Collyer was spotted in the tiny northern Virginia town. The cell was dispatched to protect Collyer at any cost. And they have done more than he could have imagined—not only have they safeguarded him, they have him in custody.

El-Khadr dispenses a rare compliment, "You have done well, Naguib," then orders, "activate the next phase—alert Mehran."

She'd never seen him so rattled. Storming out of his study, he demanded she drive him down to Philly. Melanie did her best to stall so she could finish an assignment but he wouldn't take no for an answer, insisting they had to leave immediately.

An hour plus from New Brunswick to Philadelphia. Denny said little, seemed preoccupied.

In a seedy area, he surprises her by suddenly motioning to the intersection ahead, "Stop here," he orders. As she pulls over, he opens the door and hops out.

"Are you sure you're going to be okay? It's pretty scary around here," she says, peering out at the gritty industrial area on the outskirts of Philadelphia.

He stands holding the door, "You should have seen where I grew up. I'll call when I'm finished. If you're not busy maybe you can drive down and pick me up."

"Give me some idea when you think it will be."

"I'll have to call you," Denny's backpedaling away from the car, eager to get on his way.

"Be careful," Melanie says, pulling the door shut. *He can act so strange at times,* she thinks. *Does things that don't make any sense. And what in the world is he doing in an area like this?* Rundown, winos slumping in doorways, dive bars and porn shops, razed buildings, it's a part of Philly she'd prefer not to see again. She puts the car in gear and accelerates, watching Mehran shrink in her rearview.

He waves back at her, hustles down the street two blocks and stops, waiting until her Range Rover disappears around the corner. He carefully checks one direction and then another. Though his destination is only five blocks away, his predetermined course takes him a half hour to complete. *Go down two blocks. Stop. Take a right, go to the fourth intersection, cut through an alley.* He's rehearsed the route more times than he can remember. Nothing is left to chance, every possible precaution taken to keep the destination secret.

He thinks back two hours. The post appeared to be routine: *Be reminded that care and experience gained in digging up dahlias for the winter will pay dividends in the spring. Consult experienced gardeners to make sure you are prepared and have the proper tools and supplies to store your dahlias over the winter so they will blossom next season*—an ordinary message to his cell to stay alert and maintain the training regimen.

But when he read the last sentence his heart started pounding: *By the way, Cindy in Virginia is back caring for her dahlias.*

Collyer has been found! For all its clumsy amateurishness, the notice must have worked. Mehran's instructions are precise. The next phase has been activated. One step closer to fulfilling his destiny, he has a chance to go down in history as a martyr for his heroic feat.

He completes the steps taking him to his destination. Though he's never been to the building, he's viewed it a hundred times in satellite images and digital photos—brick four-story, faceless and unremarkable, another of the hundreds of commercial buildings in this area of Philly.

Seeing his destination at the end of the block, he pulls his collar up and hustles down the street. Fortunately the traffic is light, no one to notice him.

Passing under the security camera mounted above the entrance, Mehran mounts the steps leading to the door and presses the bell. *No answer.* He pushes the button again. *Wait, what's that?* He hears a car pulling up behind him, rolling slowly to the curb and stopping, its engine idling. He freezes, doesn't dare to turn and look.

Slowly reaching out, he presses the button a third time. He can feel the presence of the car, its motor rumbling in the still air. Holds the button down for four, then five seconds. No answer.

The car door opens, the sound of footsteps, *clack, clack, clack,* on the frozen sidewalk, coming closer. Despite the cold, bands of sweat bead up on his forehead. *This is not in the plan. No one told me anything about a car.*

"Excuse me, sir?" he hears from over his shoulder. He feels light-headed all of a sudden, his heart tomtoming in his chest. Slowly turning, he sees a man in a suit and topcoat standing at the bottom of the steps. Hands in his coat pockets. He does not look Arabic. *Is he a detective? FBI? Does he have a gun? Should I take off running? What has gone wrong?*

"What are you doing here?" the man asks. His tone is factual but there is an undercurrent of menace, as if a wrong answer could be fatal.

Mehran knows only one response. Looking the man in the eye, he says clearly and assertively, "I am looking for dahlias to plant in the spring."

Without responding, the man glances up at the security camera over Mehran's head and nods. Behind his back, Mehran hears the lock on the door click open.

Scooting through the open door, Mehran doesn't look back. He slams it shut, leaning back against the wall and breathing for the first time. It is pitch black inside.

He hears footsteps, then a voice echoing out of the darkness, "I hope we did not cause you too much alarm."

Lights blink on. A two-story loft space filled with worktables, lathes, drill presses and grinders—it looks like a machine shop but so pristine and shipshape it might as well be an operating room. An older man in gray coveralls approaches, his arms open wide and a broad smile on his face.

"I am Jamal. Please, come and sit with me and enjoy some coffee." Jamal embraces him, his face pressing against Mehran's cheeks one at a time, then leads him to a seating area off to the side of the shop.

"I am glad to see you."

"I have been anticipating this moment."

"Come, let us not waste any time."

Jamal is in his late sixties or early seventies, Mehran guesses. *Salt and pepper hair, meaty face and dark complexion, slightly overweight, most likely Saudi, though he could be Yemeni.* He pours Mehran a cup of coffee and sits down beside him. His English is accomplished, yet laced with the stilted accent and curious diction of someone who has learned the language overseas.

"As you can see," he gestures back at his machine shop, "we have much important work going on here. We had to be certain of your identity."

"I am honored to be with you," Mehran says, gazing around the expansive workshop filled with rows of benches and machinery.

"I give you some of my background before I get into details."

Jamal explains to Mehran that he worked on nuclear weapons in the Y-12 facility at Oak Ridge as well as at Los Alamos. "I was a junior member of the team that engineered many of these early weapons in the late '60s and early '70s before I returned to my country to work on the Saudi nuclear program. These bombs are like old friends to me. I know their strengths, deficiencies and peculiarities intimately. Setting aside modesty for a moment, I would say there are maybe ten others who understand them as well."

"May I ask you a personal question?"

Jamal nods. He has heard much talk about the devoted and talented young Iranian. They were facing the prospect of doing deals with drugged-up Russian gangsters peddling black market uranium out of their backseats until the young engineering student turned up the prospect of an H-bomb lying in America's backyard and came up with the strategy, a plan of stunning simplicity. Having infiltrated an American university, he is like the bomb he will detonate, secreted under the mud of American culture ready to be turned against the enemy.

"Why did you leave the Saudi program to join us?"

Jamal pauses. "It is a long story. I grew up in Jeddah. My family is closely related to his family. He is like a nephew to me. I will do anything for him."

"I am most impressed that you know our leader."

"We have come a long way. It has been a difficult road. We were both children of privileged families, had the best educations and went to the top universities. But though we are from different generations, we were both troubled by our country's direction. Back in 1945, the royal family made a deal with the devil. In return for our oil the U.S. agreed to provide us military protection and turn a blind eye to our internal politics. The family funneled billions to buy off religious leaders. With their support, the royals were able to stifle political opposition while they led lives of unbelievable depravity. You would see them frolicking on the Riviera, their pockets stuffed with billions of American oil dollars, their faces gorged with steak and truffles, necks and fingers dripping with gold and diamonds. They lost all direction, all sense of honor and duty and devotion to Allah. I grew to hate them, their duplicity, their scheming and licentiousness. And when they permitted American troops to be stationed in our country, the cradle of Islam, that was the final insult.

"When our leader started his Afghanistan operation, he made overtures to his favorite uncle. His vision was like a spark striking dry tinder. I was so disgusted with the leadership of my country and their corrupt and sickening relationship with the United States that jihad became the true alternative."

"And now we bring the jihad to America again."

"Yes, now come, Mehran. I will show you what we have designed for you."

Jamal leads Mehran around the shop proudly displaying his machines and explaining their functions.

"I have the equipment to construct anything in here. But what I have made for you is what I am most proud of." He stops at a row of three long, dull-green metal tubes lying in steel and wood gantries. Mehran recognizes them immediately. Each one he has so carefully committed to memory he knows their sizes and shapes as well as the fingers of his own hands.

"Of course you recognize these weapons. Obviously mockups but their dimensions are precise down to the millimeter."

"Yes," Mehran says, putting his hand on the cone of the first bomb in the row, eager to display his knowledge. "This is the Mk-28, a hydrogen bomb yielding seventy kilotons to 1.1 megatons of explosive force." Almost fourteen feet long and two feet in diameter, it is sleek and trim compared to the others. Jamal's workmanship is impeccable down to the tiniest detail, precise welding and stenciled identification. "I am most impressed."

Mehran continues, moving down the line to the next bomb. Though he has only seen it in pictures and diagrams—fat and stubby, a long, finless column—it is immediately recognizable. "And this is the Mk-39," he explains. "Produced in two configurations, three megatons and four. The third is a Mk-15 mod 0, the first lightweight hydrogen bomb, twelve feet long and just under four tons."

"You have done your homework, Mehran. I have replicated these since they were the models carried in SAC bombers during the years in question. We will be prepared for any eventuality and when we ascertain the model you will be dealing with, I will provide you with this."

Jamal reaches up and takes down a spun aluminum ring—in the shape of a life preserver but larger in diameter—from an overhead rack where a row of similar rings hangs.

"My proudest achievement," he says, cradling the object in his hands. Satiny and lustrous, its exterior is rounded while its inner surface is perfectly flat. He carefully slides the ring down over the cone of the Mk-15 until it clicks into place against the bomb's steel skin as he explains, "The same way the Americans used a shaped charge of TNT to activate the atomic primary stage, I have designed a collar to fit the dimensions of each bomb."

Looking around as if someone might be eavesdropping, he leans in and whispers into Mehran's ear, switching from English to Arabic.

As he listens, Mehran is dazzled with Jamal's brilliant breakthrough. Jamal explains how he has designed the rings for maximum effect and precisely engineered them to achieve the objective. In a million years the Americans could never imagine what Jamal has conceived. They think their sleeping dogs can't be awakened. But with Jamal's collar, Mehran will prove them wrong. The collar will replace the TNT trigger so ignition is guaranteed. It's a dazzling piece of engineering.

Jamal stands and returning to English says, "Now, I am sure you have many things to ask. Please do not hesitate."

"What about the safeguard mechanisms on the Mk-28 and 39?"

"I am confident my collars will override the safeties. And as you know, a few early Mk-15s were fitted with a nuclear capsule—an atomic firing pin that begins the reaction. Finding one of those would be like hitting the jackpot since only mere inches stands between the capsule and the atomic core."

"I have long dreamed that the bomb I find will be a Mk-15 fused with a capsule," Mehran says.

"Maybe, if we are lucky." Though he is not about to let Mehran in on his secret, Jamal knows that good fortune may already be working for them. If the man code-named Cindy begins digging up dahlias anywhere on the Middle Atlantic Coast, their dreams will be realized beyond comprehension. For Jamal is one of the few people alive who knows the truth behind the Jersey bomb, and El-Khadr is the only person in the Flowers operation who has even been given a hint. And all he knows is that if Collyer heads toward the Chesapeake, he is to immediately ramp up his activity.

"How much will each collar weigh?"

"A good question, follow me." Jamàl leads him to a tall wooden tank at the far end of the workshop. Twenty feet in diameter, constructed of wood planks ringed with circular steel collars, it is like the air conditioning vats Mehran has noticed on rooftops in Philadelphia.

"This is my immersion tank. I have done tests on the collars in it. An ordinary buoyancy vest will provide the flotation necessary for the collar to be almost weightless in the water. I have tried them myself many times. You will find them easily maneuverable, and with a few hours of practice you should have no problem. We will schedule time in this tank for you to become familiar with each of them." He doesn't tell Mehran he has allotted twenty hours of training beginning tomorrow morning. When Jamal has finished with him, Mehran will be able to collar bombs in the dark.

"I have a question."

Jamal knows Mehran will have many questions.

"Detonation—how is that accomplished?"

"Of course, a critical part of your mission. In your boat you will carry this," Jamal explains, pulling a small remote control unit from a fold in his robe. "It looks like a garage door opener—which it is by the way," Jamal smiles proudly at his ingenuity. "But in it I have installed a powerful radio transmitter tuned to a receiver in the collar. Press the button and the collar will be detonated."

"At any depth?"

"It will transmit deeper than you are capable of diving, my friend," he says, putting his arm around him. Jamal watches the young man's expression carefully, looking for any hesitation, any doubt. For when it comes to the detonation mechanism, some things are better left unsaid.

Mehran's face relaxes, his tone is assured. "That is good," he says.

"Do you have any other questions for me, Mehran?"

There is one burning subject remaining but he is afraid of offending Jamal. Though he has read widely on explosives, he is not an expert. He is delighted when Jamal reads his mind.

"If you are wondering whether the charge will be sufficient to begin the detonation sequence..."

"I am interested in your answer."

Jamal isn't surprised at Mehran's question. If he is going to set off a thermonuclear bomb, he wants to make sure it will be a magnificent event instead of a minor sputter.

"I have done exhaustive studies and simulations. Each collar has the exact charge needed to guarantee detonation. I can assure you, Mehran, you will go to your glory."

25

[Pentagon, late Wednesday afternoon]

"Is this something I should be sitting down for, Williams?" Watt asks when he sees the expression on his aide's face.

"Bad or good news first, sir?" Williams asks.

Watt grimaces, "All of it."

"Things went badly in Front Royal, sir."

"We botched it?"

"Someone got the jump on us. Alpha Orange located the motel where Collyer was staying—or what was left of it."

"What happened?"

"Burned to the ground, owner got charbroiled."

"And Collyer?"

"Somehow he escaped."

"I thought we took care of his car."

"He didn't take it."

"I don't understand."

"It was illegally parked, sir. Someone tried to tow it. They're still picking him out of the trees."

"Do we have any idea where Collyer went?"

"Not at the moment."

"Now he's going to be even more wary."

Watt pops another Tums into his mouth, then reaches for the Pepcid. It's going to be a long day. Someone is two steps ahead of them. *Could whoever put out the flier have beaten us to Collyer?* Now the suspicion that terrorists are looking for Collyer becomes more credible. And if they are after him, they're more sophisticated and resourceful than he thought.

Watt cringes at the thought of his next encounter with Whitey Hatkin. *If the situation unravels any further,* Watt speculates as he fumbles with the stiff plastic armament of the Pepcid package, *will I end up as the fall guy?*

In the diner on the outskirts of Baltimore, Collyer sits in a booth over his second cup of coffee, his open laptop in front of him. His screen reads 5:35. It's dark already. The man at the next table glances up and makes a face. Howie realizes he's been drumming his fingers on the table. He stops, peering out the window at the cab parked outside. The driver's leaning against the front fender smoking another cigarette. Risstup and Sharon are sitting in the backseat chatting, the major's been talking up a blue streak ever since they left Lancaster.

The *Free Internet Access* sign attracted Howie's attention and he had the cabdriver pull into the diner. In a nondescript, dingy area full of used car lots and freight yards, it's been updated with gleaming stainless and glass, modern decor but with a throwback menu. Burgers, eggs and pancakes, fries served with everything.

They've never heard of lattes so he's making do with black coffee lightened with plastic cups of cream.

Howie made sure his email to Straub was direct and to the point. He rereads it as he sits in the booth killing time.

> Winn, Someone burned down the motel we were staying in. There was a bunch of shooting. Needless to say, Sharon is freaked. What I'm trying to figure out is who's behind all this? Vector Eleven or someone else? Or are your people working behind the scenes? Can you give me any idea of what you think is going on? Howie

Then sends the email, takes another sip of coffee, and prays to hell Straub frequently checks his mail.

A few minutes later and sixty miles away, Winn Straub sits with his computer on his lap enjoying his second glass of wine, the warmth of the fire radiating out into the room. Even though the fireplace in the living room of his townhouse is shallow, Straub has discovered if he arranges the logs just so, he can get the fire blazing without filling the house with smoke.

Straub hears his wife calling him to dinner. He wants to look at his email before he sits down to eat.

"I'll be right there, dear. Just give me a few minutes."

He sits up quickly. Howie's email shouts off the screen at him. Straub instantly feels responsible. *I shouldn't have left him out there. I should drive right out and take him down to The Farm.* Then he wonders if he's thinking straight. Maybe it's the wine.

"Dear, could you make me a cup of coffee?" he calls into the kitchen.

"Couldn't we have dinner first? Normal people drink coffee after dinner."

"Instant will be fine. Something just came up with Howie that I need to deal with."

He hears a groan from the kitchen. One quality his wife doesn't lack is a flair for the dramatic.

He composes one email. It sounds sappy. The next sounds cold-hearted.

Barbara brings out a cup of coffee, setting it down crisply so the cup clinks in the saucer, letting her husband know she's serving him under protest.

His mind works through the possibilities. One stands out. There have been recent reports of increased al Qaeda communication. There are so many fingers in the intelligence pie that any uptick in the chatter level immediately surfaces in the rumor mill. CIA's own intelligence connects some of the noise with nuclear materials but that's nothing new. That buzz has been around since the early '90s.

But still—Straub is reminded of the old CIA parable: *Grandma on the roof.* A woman gets a call that her favorite cat fell off the roof and died. Upset, she berates the caller for breaking the news so suddenly. Says she should have delivered the news more gradually, first called to tell her the cat was on the roof, then telephoned some time later to tell her the cat was creeping toward the edge and in a final call let her know the cat had tumbled off and died. Two months later the woman gets another call—grandma is on the roof.

Has Howie awakened a sleeper cell? Howie has often said that terrorists might get their hands on one of our nukes. Have they somehow picked up he's now on a search for one? He decides to give Howie the straight scoop, no speculation, no embellishment, and see where he takes it.

> Howie, Thank God you're okay. I wish I could say we had something to do with it, but we didn't. I don't want to alarm you but there is an increased level of terrorist chatter out there. I don't know if it means anything in terms of what you're doing but it is something we should keep in mind. Relocate and get in touch with me first thing tomorrow. We'll figure out what to do then.
> Winn

Sitting in the diner, Howie is relieved to see Winn's email pop up on his screen. But relief rapidly shifts to dread for what Howie reads makes his eyes widen and his face flush. *Terrorist chatter*—he keeps hearing himself thinking—*terrorist chatter.* Though he has often maintained that terrorists might try to retrieve a lost nuke, he's always considered it more a scare tactic than an actual possibility. He's rattled by the thought that keeps running through his mind—*what if they were attracted to my website and have been watching me? And now I'm leading them to a nuke?*

His attention drifts up from the computer screen to the cabdriver standing outside. All the way to Baltimore he seemed too interested in our conversation. At first Howie thought nothing of it. He's a typical cab driver, the kind you see in every city. Immigrant, maybe Turkish or Lebanese. Darker skinned, curly hair. Family pictures tucked into the visors over his head, wife, kids, little boy missing front teeth holding a plastic bike, a big smile on his face. Just another guy trying to make a living. But when Risstup shifted the conversation to his flight training in California, the driver's eyes seemed riveted on them—until he caught Howie looking at him and quickly averted his eyes. Eerie that he would be so interested. *Could terrorists have spooked us right into their hands?*

As the cab driver lights another cigarette, his eyes fixed on the interior of the restaurant, Howie puts together a plan.

His first job is to get Sharon and Risstup out of the cab. Then see how the driver reacts. *What he does will tell me who he is.* Howie stands, grabs a menu out of the holder, leaves his laptop open in the booth behind him and heads for the door.

He tries to appear nonchalant, sauntering down the set of stairs toward the cab. Opens the car door, leans down and says in a breezy tone to his friends in the backseat, waving the menu at them to get their attention, "Hey, anyone hungry? They've got great burgers and fries in this place." Catching Sharon's eye, he ducks his head a couple times to make sure she gets the message.

"What took you so long? The major and I are starving," she says, playing along, sliding across the seat and climbing out.

"We won't be long," Howie says as he passes the driver, one arm guiding Risstup along, as long as he has some help he's fine without the wheelchair.

The cabbie nods and holds up his cigarette to Howie as if it's no problem to him. "I stay and smoke," he says.

When the three are seated in a booth, Howie says, "Nice place, huh? Some great stuff on the menu, burgers, fries, cheese fries, corn dogs, barbeque."

Seeing through his feigned nonchalance, Sharon leans across toward Howie and whispers, "You want to tell me what the hell's going on?"

"Read this email," Howie swivels his laptop so she can see the screen. As she reads the message from Winn, her expression quickly clouds over.

"It can't be—" Her eyes flick over to the window, back to the laptop. She looks up at Howie, turns her head to look out at the cabbie again. "There's no way—"

"You have to admit it's possible."

"Just because he looks Middle Eastern?"

"It feels like a setup. He was waiting right in front of the motel and he's been too interested in our conversation."

"So what now?"

"Order quickly and act normal."

"How do you eat at a time like this?" Sharon's eyes are flitting around the interior of the restaurant.

"Do what he says, he's the boss," Risstup pipes up.

Sharon darts a cutting look at Risstup.

"That's a first," Howie smiles.

"This is no time for jokes."

A waitress lumbers up to them, her shoes squeaking on the gleaming floor. Round face and a body to go with it, she's well into her sixties, looks like she's worked there for years. Big smile, Howie can tell she's going to be chatty. She swabs their table with a rag as she begins her banter. "You folks just passing through?"

"Just passing through, right," Howie answers, deliberately terse, dreading the prospect of five minutes of small talk.

"Well, you sure came to the right place if I don't say so myself. People come from miles around to eat here. Burgers are good, omelets are excellent, owner smokes the bacon himself. Fries are famous, been written up in all the papers. We even have Internet as I see you discovered," she tips her pencil at his laptop. "Glad you know how to work it, I don't understand the first thing about that computer stuff."

Standing at the edge of her table, order pad flipped open and pencil at the ready, she finally gets down to business, "So, what can I get for you folks?"

"I'll have a bacon burger medium, fries and coffee," Howie says.

"Good choice, and you, ma'am?"

"Scrambled eggs, wheat toast and a Coke, please." Sharon's voice is thin and reedy, almost on the verge of cracking, the way it gets when she's on edge. Howie can tell she's fighting to keep from looking at the driver.

The waitress is eyeballing her, as if she knows something's amiss.

"Cheeseburger, well done," Risstup orders.

Howie catches the waitress as she gathers up their menus and begins to turn toward the kitchen. "Ma'am, can I ask you a question?"

"Certainly, sir."

"Is there a back door?'

She raises an eyebrow, "Anything the matter with the front?"

Howie thinks fast, he nods out the window at the man standing against the cab, "It's a husband/wife thing, kind of touchy—if you know what I mean."

The waitress's eyes are sizing up the situation, switching from the cab to Sharon and back, putting together a plot right out of a scandal rag—abusive husband, battered wife, family members trying to help her escape.

Sharon picks up the tune, putting on a hangdog look and casting her eyes toward the parking lot, "He's not a nice man," she says, shaking her head and lowering her gaze as if she's ashamed of the situation she's in.

Surveying the three, the waitress leans in and whispers sympathetically, "Oh, believe me, I've been there. I'm very sorry. Yes, the door is just past the ladies room, it goes out into the parking lot. Now, let me run get your orders."

The waitress turns slowly, making sure they notice the quick but unmistakable wink of her eye, letting them know she's on their side.

The next fifteen minutes go slowly. Sharon's fretting, Risstup's anxious, his attention flutters back and forth between the cab outside and the booth. Howie's debating how they are going to get out the rear door without being noticed when the waitress arrives with their order.

Swinging the large tray down to rest on the edge of the table, she starts off-loading their plates. Right off the bat Howie notices a folded piece of paper she sets down next to his food, not a check but a note. Unfolding it, he hastily scans the message inside. When you least expect it, someone decides to do a good deed. The woman is a saint.

She stands back and says, "Enjoy your dinner, folks. Anything else I can get for you?" Her eyes drop down to the note, then lift back up to the threesome. She smiles knowingly.

"No, you've been extremely helpful," Howie says.

"Good luck to you."

A half an hour later, the three are on their way to an empty apartment twenty blocks away. A busboy was waiting for them in his car behind the diner. They were out the back door and on their way in a matter of seconds.

Sharon asks to see the note, and Howie hands it over. The waitress's scrawled message reads, "My daughter got caught up in a mess like you're in so I know what you're up against. You look like nice folks so I've arranged for one of our busboys to drive you to an apartment I own not far away. He'll be outside in a blue Camaro. My place doesn't have a lot of furniture but there's bedding in the hall closet so at least you can get some sleep. That should give you time to put some space between you and your husband. Stay there as long as you like. Leave the keys under the mat when you're through. I wish you well, your friend, Louise."

"Thank God for Louise. Somebody up there really is looking out for us," Sharon says, handing the note back to Howie.

"You should get a best supporting actress nomination for the job you did playing the abused wife."

"There's never a dull moment with you, Collyer."

"Pardon my French," Risstup says. "But he's going to be one pissed-off cabdriver—you stiffed him for an eighty buck fare."

"We couldn't take the chance."

"You don't really think he was a bad guy?"

Howie shrugs, "No point in taking chances."

So far there's been no trace of the driver. Either he's still waiting in the cab or he's tearing apart the diner trying to find them. Howie wasn't about to stick around to find out. Just as they were finishing, the cab driver for some reason climbed back into the front seat of his cab and shut the door, his line of sight just below the front windows of the diner.

Howie took advantage of the opportunity. If they couldn't see him, he couldn't see them. Howie threw down a fat tip and hustled Sharon and Risstup out the back door. He followed. Creeping out into the lot where the Camaro was waiting.

Sitting in the front seat next to the busboy, Howie carefully back-tracks through the events at the diner. Something doesn't add up. The cabdriver let us get away too easily, he decides. If terrorists have been watching my website, shadowing us, maybe even setting fire to the motel to flush us into their hands, they aren't a bunch of amateurs who would let us sneak out the back door of a diner.

All of a sudden Howie pieces together the answer. *They want us to think we've eluded them.* They are staying out of sight until we find the nuke, aware that we're not going to knowingly lead them to it.

Sharon suddenly interrupts, "You want to tell us what's bothering you?"

"I'm just thinking," Howie says.

She doesn't fall for it, "That's B.S., your imagination's getting the better of you again. We got away from a cab driver that was acting suspicious—leave it at that. Stop being so damn paranoid. You're driving me bonkers."

The Camaro brakes and makes a turn into the driveway of an apartment building, pulls up and stops. The driver hands Howie a key chain, explaining in broken English that one key is for the front door, the other for the third-floor apartment. Summoning up what's left of his high school Spanish, Howie thanks the busboy and the three hustle inside.

The apartment is tiny, a double bed in one room, a sleeper sofa in the other, a few chairs, small kitchen with the refrigerator door ajar to air it out. While Sharon starts making up beds, Howie stands at the window looking down at the street.

A brisk wind whips through the trees, the neighborhood is dark, two of the four streetlights on the block are out, bunch of parked cars, no noticeable activity but that doesn't mean they aren't out there. Howie realizes he needs to play down the terrorist angle so Sharon and Risstup can get down to business. The first chance he gets he'll email Winn with his concerns. For the time being, he'll keep them to himself.

"You going to stand there staring out the window all night, or are we going to get to work?" Sharon says to him. Howie turns back into the room. She and Risstup sit in chairs, the laptop open on the daybed in front of them.

While Sharon was working with Risstup in Front Royal, Howie spent hours fiddling with the software Straub had sent him, assembling a virtual B-52 cockpit on the screen of his computer. Even though it's a simulation, a two-dimensional reproduction of the cramped upper deck of the B-52 fuselage, Howie's computer wizardry has recreated the experience of sitting in the cockpit of one of the huge bombers.

Okay, it's show time, he thinks to himself as he sets the laptop down in front of them. *Let's see what we can get Risstup to remember.* "Why don't we shift around so I can sit next to the major," he says, motioning to Sharon to change places with him.

"You're the boss," Sharon says. "I found some instant in the kitchen. Anyone for coffee?"

"Good idea. We're going to need it. Let me show you what I've done."

Howie opens his flight simulation program and clicks on the B-52 folder. Working from aircraft cockpit templates, in the center of the console he's laid in a bank of thirty-two gauges that monitor the eight engines. The gauges are arranged in four rows, the throttles ganged below them with small black-and-white TV screens over the two control sticks. Sectioned windows wrap around the front of the flight deck and with the glass canopy overhead they provide a 180° panorama of the surrounding skies. Though the space is cramped, the expansive view out the windows of the blue sky and billowing clouds gives the cockpit the feeling of an observation deck.

He turns the laptop toward Sharon and Risstup so they can see it. Sharon whistles in admiration, "Wow! That's impressive—how did you do that?"

"Magic," Howie says, "plus years of practice."

Risstup isn't saying a word, silently staring down at the simulation, taking in all the details.

"It feels like we're right in the cockpit," Sharon continues. "Talk about tight quarters, how long were these flights?"

"Twenty-four hours and thirty minutes from takeoff to touchdown. Ten thousand miles including two refuelings."

"No frequent flier miles either."

"Not even a bag of peanuts. And if you think the cockpit looks minuscule, you ought to see the bathroom."

"I'll pass on that." Sharon points at the sky backdrop Howie has superimposed, "Look at all the clouds."

"That's just wallpaper. Wait until I drop in the real-time views out the plane's windows."

"You can do that?"

"Give me a few minutes."

Sharon pushes her chair back and heads for the kitchen. "Go ahead while I get the coffee."

"I'll make the clouds fly by so you'll feel like you're actually piloting the plane." Howie's fingers race over the keyboard as he types commands to lay in the aerial views.

She returns with coffee and stands looking over his shoulder.

"Okay, take a peek at this." Howie pushes back from the laptop so Sharon can see. "Look at those cumuli whipping by," he says, tapping a key.

"That's amazing," she says, bending over the screen and looking out at the skies above and the landscape rolling by as if it were thirty-five thousand feet underneath them.

"With a little more work, I should be able to drop in the exact course the major's B-52 flew right up until it ran into trouble. If I have time, I'll create a thunderstorm to simulate the actual conditions."

"Let's give it a try. Major Risstup, you ready?"

Sharon swivels the laptop toward Risstup. "Okay, Major. See if anything feels familiar."

Risstup leans forward and peers at the screen. He slowly lifts his left hand as if he's reaching for the controls.

"You're on the flight deck, Major—"

Risstup nods, pulling his chair closer to the screen.

"At the controls of a B-52."

Risstup is concentrating, his left hand poised over the keyboard.

"Hold on a minute," Howie says. "He's reaching out with his left for the throttle. If he were the pilot he'd be using his right hand."

Risstup glances down and then up at the gang of throttles on the screen, trying to make the connection.

"Were you the co-pilot, Major Risstup?"

Risstup nods. Then says tentatively, "I was the co-pilot. Okay, yes. I was the co-pilot."

"And when you were a co-pilot, where were you based?" Howie asks.

Risstup stares at the screen.

"Were you based at Barksdale Air Force Base, Westover or March?"

"Boy," Sharon says. "You've really gone to school on this."

"Those were the B-52 bases back in the late 1950s when they started flying round-the-clock missions: Barksdale in Louisiana, Westover in western Massachusetts and March in California. Major, can you remember which one?"

Risstup looks startled, then slowly says, "It was Westover, Westover Air Force Base. In Massachusetts, yes."

Howie smiles at Sharon. "Good work, Major."

"And where did your missions take you, where did you fly to?"

Risstup shakes his head.

"He's stopped tracking—"

Risstup quickly corrects her, "I can't tell you because our destinations are classified."

"They *were* classified," Howie tells Risstup. "You're right. But that was forty years ago. It's all out in the open now."

"It's top secret. Everything was top secret. We couldn't say a word about it."

"Not anymore, Major Risstup. The Cold War is over." Howie presses, "You were stationed at Westover Air Force Base. When were you there? Can you tell me the year?"

"Why is the year so important?" Sharon asks.

"During that period there were as many as five or six kinds of bombs in use, all with different characteristics, some more of a threat than others."

Risstup suddenly pushes back from the table and turns to look at Howie and Sharon. "Can I ask you guys a favor?"

Howie notices an expression on Risstup's face he's never seen before, as if he's about to reveal a secret.

"Certainly, Major."

"I do have a name, you know."

Both Sharon and Howie gape at him.

"Mark, my name is Mark, Mark Risstup," he says proudly, his face lighting up at finally being able to remember his name. Every time they'd tried to call him *Mark,* he'd objected, claiming that wasn't his name though he had never been able to come up with a name that connected for him.

Howie and Sharon raise their hands and slap palms, "Mark. That's terrific, Mark Risstup, Major Mark Risstup from Arcata, California, the man who's going to help us get to the bottom of all this. Way to go, Mark."

"Mark—sure is nice to realize that after all these years," Risstup says wistfully.

"Now can you tell us what years you were stationed at Westover, Mark?" Howie asks. "It must have been in the '50s, right?"

"Yes, I think the '50s," Risstup hesitates. Sharon can see his eyes slowly begin to fog over.

She looks at Howie, "Maybe we should drop the time thing and go back to focusing on the B-52. We were making good progress there."

Howie nods, "All right, Mark. You are the co-pilot flying missions out of Westover Air Force Base. Where to?"

"I remember a number of courses," Risstup says as he stares at Howie's improvised cockpit on the screen. "We flew over the Pole to points over the Barents Sea." Risstup glances at Sharon. "Are you sure I'm not going to get in trouble for telling you this?"

"No, it's okay, Mark. It's all declassified now, I promise."

"Then we flew three routes. The polar route, one over Scotland and a southern course over Spain."

"Where were you flying to, Mark?"

"I told you."

"What are you trying to get him to say?" Sharon asks.

"Give me a minute. You'd fly to a *go, no-go line*, correct?"

"Yes, I remember that."

"But you couldn't cross the line without a strike order."

"That's correct, we had to have a strike order."

"And that would direct you to targets in Russia?"

"Yes, to targets in Russia."

Howie turns from the screen to Risstup. "And why would you be flying to Russia? Was it because you were carrying nuclear weapons? Isn't that what the strike order was all about?"

"I think that is secret."

"No, no, no, Mark, forget about this secret business. It's all out in the open now. So you were carrying nuclear weapons?"

Risstup nods.

"You had hydrogen bombs aboard when your B-52 went down, right?"

"I don't remember."

"But didn't your B-52 carry nuclear payloads on every mission?"

"Yes."

"Then you had to be carrying a nuke the day your plane went down."

Risstup looks up at Howie with a slightly quizzical but still empty expression on his face. "All that is very hazy to me, but what you're saying makes sense."

"That's okay, Mark. We'll keep working on it."

"Sorry I'm acting so dim-witted."

"You're doing fine, Mark," Sharon reassures him. "I know this isn't easy."

"I don't want to end up back in that VA hospital."

"That's the last thing any of us want," Howie says.

He swivels the laptop toward him. "Let's try a takeoff and see what comes back to you."

"I'll give it a shot," Risstup says.

"Okay, Major Risstup, we're cleared for takeoff. Full throttle..."

"Full throttle," Risstup repeats, acknowledging the command.

Sharon stands behind the two as the plane speeds down the runway, the landscape flashing by out the windows.

"With forty-eight thousand gallons of fuel in the wings and a total weight of 488,000 pounds," Howie explains, "the B-52 chews up miles of runway in order to gain altitude."

"Actually," Risstup clarifies, "the wings get airborne first and they sort of bully the huge wheel trucks up off the ground."

"We're airborne," Howie says. "Landing gear up, Major."

"Landing gear up," Risstup repeats.

"Give me the course, Major."

No response from Risstup.

"The course, Major Risstup," Howie prompts him again.

Risstup scowls.

"You were doing fine, Mark. You were right there with me."

Risstup throws up his hands. "I know, but I lost it. I'm sorry. I want to help, but after a while everything goes blank. I start to get into it, I can feel the memories coming back up but then they burst like a bubble and I'm back here sitting in front of your computer. Don't get me wrong. It's not your fault."

"Maybe we can try again later," Sharon suggests.

"There is one thing I could suggest," Risstup says.

His comment gets their attention.

"I hated that medicine they gave me at the hospital, but I think it might have had something to do with bringing back my memory. Although it makes me catatonic, I was able to remember things that normally wouldn't come back to me. It might worth a try."

"What medicine is he talking about?" Howie asks.

"Variations of sodium pentothal used for sedation. I don't want to get technical but at lower dosages that don't result in sleep or unconsciousness, disinhibition can occur."

"Disinhibition? Help me, I didn't go to med school."

"Opening up new pathways in the brain."

"Wasn't sodium pentothal called 'truth serum'?"

"That's what they called it in Hollywood."

"What happened to the hypodermic you were waving around a couple nights ago?"

"It was in my bag. I left it in the cab."

"Damn—we've got to find some more."

"Problem is, without a prescription I can't just walk into a pharmacy and buy it. And stealing it is out of the question, those pharmacies are locked up as tight as a drum."

Sharon hesitates for a second, then adds, "On the other hand, maybe there is a way."

26

[The Pentagon, Wednesday night]

"Let me tell General Watt you're here, General Hatkin," Lieutenant Williams says.

But the three-star shoulders past him, saying, "I don't need an introduction, Lieutenant."

Watt hears the door open just in time to lift his head off his desk. Arranging his hair and straightening his tie, he glances at the clock as he stands to greet his visitor. It's 2205. Must have dozed off for a while, he thinks.

"Mind if I join you, Greg?" Hatkin closes the door in Williams' face. Even Hatkin looks a bit dog-eared, rough around the edges, not his usual crisp self. But then they are both pushing sixty and have been burning the candle at both ends. Watt stands to shake hands, pulling down his coat to iron out the wrinkles.

"You should have called, General Hatkin. I would have come down to your office."

"I was passing by and I thought I'd drop in, better we do it here than attract attention at my place," Hatkin says, extending his arm out to Watt. After shaking hands, Hatkin motions to Watt's chair, "Please, have a seat, Greg."

"Can I get you some coffee?"

"No, thanks."

"You got my message about Front Royal?"

"That's why I'm here."

"Every state and federal agency is swarming over the crime scene."

"How long do we have before they figure out Collyer's involved?"

"Depends on what evidence they find and how fast they move."

"Up until now, I could buy the theory that these terrorists are incompetent amateurs. But not any longer. They might have been monitoring Collyer and could have set the motel on fire to spook him into their hands. For the time being we have to operate on the assumption that we're dealing with a group of motivated and highly trained people. For some reason, they think Collyer is onto something—enough to want to keep him alive."

"Somehow they must have gotten the idea he can lead them to a nuke."

"I think we have to assume that. Our Vector Eleven group has their hands full with a Senate subcommittee that's threatening an investigation of procedures at Oak Ridge. That could go south on us fast. I just had a teleconference on the subject. They're all feeling under the gun. So while they're taking care of that matter, let's discuss our options."

"Can I take you through some scenarios my staff has developed?" Watt asks.

"Certainly."

"I'd like to ask you not to draw any conclusions. I'd like you to absorb the information and see where your judgment takes you."

"Of course."

Watt pulls his laptop off the credenza behind him, walks around to the front of his desk and opens the machine in front of Hatkin. Clicking the keyboard, he brings up a map of the East Coast. A series of lines extend out from Westover Air Force Base, changing from solid to dotted at the point of last known radar contact with Risstup's B-52.

"I projected hypothetical flight paths following the three courses SAC bombers took on airborne alert flights, northern, central and southern, and then estimated the course after the aircraft diverted around the storm. I had my people color code depths in areas where the weapon might have been jettisoned. The lightest blue tone shows the shallowest areas. As you can see, there is a considerable amount of blue around the East Coast."

Hatkin points at the laptop screen. "I'll say. Long Island Sound and the Chesapeake Bay in particular."

"That's right. A good part of the Chesapeake is no deeper than a pond."

"So it's conceivable that someone with a workboat or small tug could recover a bomb?"

"If it is a Mk-15 weapon, a small five-ton crane could do the job."

"And then they could transport it into a population center."

"Yes, load it on a truck with a forklift, pull up in midtown Manhattan or in front of the Capitol, use conventional explosives to blow it to bits and you would have a catastrophe of major proportions. Radioactivity scattered for miles."

"One of our own nukes turned into a dirty bomb that contaminates large areas of a major city rendering it uninhabitable for years. That's the theory Collyer's been harping on since day one."

"And what the terrorists could be buying into."

"Exactly. And there is a more troubling possibility. On the outside chance that they have somehow acquired the technology, they could detonate it."

"Explode a nuke in downtown D.C. or Manhattan?"

"Yes. But in both these circumstances, fortunately there are obstacles. First, they'd have to get it out of the water. Then load it on a truck. You'd need a crane to get it out of the water and a barge to handle it. Some of these nukes are fifteen feet long, this isn't something you throw in your trunk.

And of course there's always the issue of radiation leakage. If the bomb's emitting large amounts, the whole group of terrorists would be glowing. They wouldn't last long enough to drive to D.C. On top of that, whoever's intending to detonate the nuke would have to have a sophisticated understanding of the triggering process. While the technology is widely understood, it is still complicated and highly technical. This isn't a case of lighting a match or pushing a button. It would take extensive planning and resources to detonate a hydrogen bomb on land." Watt sees no point in bringing up the nuclear capsules. So few were actually deployed that it's a distraction.

"After 9/11, we have to assume they are capable of anything."

"Still, the challenges of retrieving a nuke intact, even in shallow water, infiltrating it into a city without detection, and finally detonating it as a dirty bomb—or as a nuke—are substantial."

"They only have to get lucky once."

"But they are going to need a lot more than luck. As you know, we've maintained that lying in mud and seawater for almost fifty years will cause substantial degradation of the casing and payload. And there is a real question if you could even get it out of the water in one piece."

He can tell his discussion is having an effect on Hatkin. He is leaning back in his chair across from the laptop, his fingers tented, staring out the office windows.

Watt continues, "And then remember that our records indicate the aircraft made it out over the ocean before breaking apart, so there's a good chance the weapon was dropped over the Continental Shelf. If the nuke is five thousand feet deep, no one's recovering it. It's a total non-event."

"I have only question. At what point are we going to have to sound the alarm? There must be a point where if we don't take it up the line, we risk compromising national security."

"Not until we are absolutely certain the terrorists are about to put their hands on the bomb."

"You think we can afford to wait that long?"

Watt stands, places his hands flat on his desk and leans forward, projecting an air of self-assured confidence for he's aware the window of opportunity he has will quickly slam shut if he doesn't succeed in getting Hatkin to sign on immediately. "Here's why. They are going to have to expose themselves at some point, run some kind of salvage operation and the minute they initiate it they are going to be vulnerable. My recommendation is that we wait until whoever it is—al Qaeda or Collyer—jumps in a boat to go after the nuke. Wherever they are, off the coast or in a bay or river, a Hellfire from an Apache or Black Hawk can easily take them out."

"But that would attract attention."

"Of course it would. The media will be all over it like a pack of wolves. But we sit back and maintain we foiled a terrorist plot and for national security reasons we can't go into details. We wash our hands of the whole damn thing. We get Collyer, take out the terrorists and make the nuke go away—kill three birds with one stone."

"You'd feel comfortable letting it play out that long?"

"We'll find Collyer before then. Or we'll run down the terrorists. But in the meantime, so we're prepared we should get the Navy involved in tracking down every damn boat that so much as shoves off from a dock anywhere on the East Coast."

"That's the Coast Guard's job."

"Coast Guard is now under Homeland Security."

"Damn merry-go-round in this town these days. Jimmick is running the show over there now."

"Right, and he's as likely to help us as hire Michael Brown back. That goes for the whole crew of them, FBI, CIA, DHS. They'd like nothing more than to pin this on us."

"We taking any heat from that mess in Front Royal?"

"Not so far. From what I hear, it was a zoo. Our agents said they recognized CIA and of course the FBI was swarming all over the place. People were sneaking off with evidence, they said it was a real three-ring circus. All kinds of rumors, Mafia, drug hit and, as always, talk of terrorists. Sooner or later, they'll figure out it was Collyer's car. But I bet it will be a while before anyone figures out he's chasing a nuke."

"Anyone else in Washington who's onto the terrorist angle?" Hatkin asks.

"We've suspected Winston Straub. We don't have any evidence but I'd bet he brought Collyer's wife and daughter into Camp Peary, and as I said there are CIA nosing around Front Royal. I wish we knew more about CIA's interest in this Collyer situation, whether Straub has shared it with anyone and if Dickson is involved."

"If Straub has any brains, he'd stay away from the CIA director. Dickson's the closest thing I've seen to an empty suit in years."

"Still, Collyer might be looking for cover, it could be getting cold out there."

"Any leads on him?"

"After what happened in Front Royal, he's got to be one scared puppy. Keeping his head down big time. But he's going to have to come up for air at some point, and when he does, we'll nail him."

Pause. Watt checks his wristwatch, waiting for Hatkin to deliver the verdict.

"Here's where I come out," Hatkin says. "For the time being, we stay on this course. But we can't let things get past the point of no return. We're playing a waiting game here and I'm okay with that. But we can't let it turn into a bad bet. I know you understand the difference."

"Yes, sir." Watt says, struggling to keep his voice firm and steady. Hatkin gives him a quick, steely look and exits without another word.

27

[Georgetown, Thursday morning]

Straub's Thursday starts at 5:25. Winn goes about his familiar morning ritual, turning on the lights, *click*, coffeepot, *click*, computer, *click*. He's dying to check email to see if there's anything from Howie. Trying to decide how best to help him, Straub had been staring at the ceiling most of the night.

As the coffee begins to perk, his eyes focus on the new message appearing on the screen.

> Winn, We're making progress with the pilot. So far we know his plane was carrying a nuke and we hope we can soon pin down where the crew dropped it. Your comment about terrorist chatter got me thinking. Without getting into all the details, I think they might be tracking us. Needless to say, that's disconcerting as hell. I know you'll figure out the best thing for us to do. Howie

Since the beginning Howie has maintained terrorists could go after a lost nuke—now he claims they are. The ultimate self-fulfilling prophecy. He wonders why Howie thinks they are following him but quickly decides it doesn't make any difference. *If Howie is certain terrorists are after him, that's all I need. What to do about it is another question.* The phone rings, its insistent tones interrupting the early morning quiet.

Caller ID tells him it's the last person in the world he wants to talk to. He'd spoken with Sylvie once and dodged two other calls from her. He's praying she isn't calling about the fracas in Front Royal.

"Sylvie, how are you?"

"Lousy, if you want to know the truth." She sounds sarcastic, almost caustic, not a happy camper. "I can't sleep and Grace is apoplectic about being away from her office."

"It won't be long before this is wrapped up, Grace is back in Raleigh and you and Howie are together again."

Her voice drops a register, "Winn, I need you to level with me. It's all over the news that there was a fire and a car bombing in Front Royal. They said it was a Honda, a silver Accord. It was Howie's car, wasn't it?"

"What makes you so sure?"

"C'mon, Winn, I wasn't born yesterday."

He knows he's not getting away with anything less than the truth with her. Straub takes a deep breath. "Howie's okay."

"It *was* his car." Sylvie's gone from sarcasm to indignation.

"He wasn't even near it when it happened."

"Jesus Christ, Winn, that's supposed to make me feel better?"

Straub looks out the window. In the light from inside the house, the branches of the shrubs in the garden glisten. On the other end of the line he can hear Sylvie seething.

"I wish there was something I could do."

"Get him out of there, goddammit, Winn. Get him the hell out of there."

He takes his first sip of coffee. Straub has no idea of how he's going to pull it off but it's the least he can offer. "How about if I get you two together? You can try to talk to him."

"When?"

"You've got to give me some time."

"Time? They're trying to kill him."

"I'll call you tomorrow."

"Can't you make it any sooner?"

"We'll set it up for tomorrow afternoon."

"What if they get to him before that?"

"They won't."

"You can't be sure."

"Let's keep our fingers crossed until then. Bye, Sylvie."

He sets the handset back in the cradle. *No choice but to buy her off, otherwise she'll freak and do something really stupid.* He has thirty-six hours to put the rendezvous together. He runs through the tasks. Set up a safe location somewhere, ferry Sylvie up from The Farm, find Howie and bring him in from wherever he is—all the while keeping Vector Eleven and a cell of terrorists at bay.

It's a forty-minute drive to Langley, reverse commute so the traffic isn't snarled, particularly at this hour of the morning. Exhaust steams up from the tailpipes of the cars in front of him as he speeds up the George Washington Parkway along the east bank of the Potomac. He was able to nail down an early morning meeting with Director Dickson.

Most top-level people at CIA give the director a wide berth, conducting their operations out of sight. Straub on the other hand has stayed on Dickson's good side, knowing someday he might have to cash in his chips. A political appointee from Tulsa, the director is slim with craggy features and Marlboro Man skin that makes him look like he just rode in off the range. Dickson likes to remind people of his cowboy heritage by wearing expensive hand-tooled boots and fringed suits that Straub thought looked more appropriate at a rodeo.

But as corny and hayseed as he seemed, Dickson was no dummy. He'd made a fortune peddling bargain basement car insurance. And though his agency is now at the bottom of the intelligence totem pole, Abner Dickson has something everyone in Washington envies—a personal relationship with the President of the United States. Though they are hardly seen together in Washington, they share a mutual passion—thoroughbred horses—and often ride together at the president's farm in Kentucky or at Dickson's spread in Oklahoma.

"Good to see you. How have you been, Winn?" Dickson asks as he welcomes Straub at the door and ushers him into his cavernous office on the seventh floor of the old headquarters building.

"Fine, Abner, just fine."

As he rounds his massive desk, Straub can see Dickson's eyes dropping to a cheat sheet in front of him. "And your lovely wife, Barbara?" He's met Barbara Straub only once and wouldn't recognize her if the two were alone in the same elevator.

"Barbara's doing very well, thank you."

Dickson wastes no time. "So give me the lowdown on what your buddy Collyer's up to."

"I haven't talked to Howie in months." He's going to make Dickson work for this.

"Look, Winn, I know everyone around here thinks I'm one brick shy of a load when it comes to the intelligence game, but I sure know when someone is giving me the runaround. We had people over in Front

Royal, it was definitely Collyer's car. He's playing some role in this—whatever it is."

Dickson tosses a color glossy across the desk of the two women standing in front of a cabin. Straub instantly recognizes the setting. He's stayed in it many times.

"Plus, you've brought Collyer's wife and daughter in. Know they are at Peary. You know CIA's not permitted to do that."

"C'mon, Abner. Everyone's running domestic ops these days. You're doing it up in Front Royal."

Dickson's not about to argue, tries a different approach. "Level with me, what's going on with Collyer? I know he's been missing since sometime last Friday. Then the motel where he was staying goes up in flames and his car gets blown up. It's all over Washington."

"What are people saying?"

"Collyer ran afoul of someone high up at the Pentagon and that they are out to get him."

"That's old news, Howie ticked off the top brass years ago. I'll tell you what is new though."

"Be my guest," Dickson settles back in his chair and crosses his legs, trying not to look too curious. Straub drags out his answer, turning one way in his chair, then the other. He imagines what it must be like to be the director of the Central Intelligence Agency and not have a clue about what's going on.

He gazes out the window at the gardens below before abruptly turning toward Dickson and announcing, "Howie Collyer might have the goods on a black program at the Pentagon."

"You're kidding me?" Dickson's eyes gleam. In the seesaw world of Washington politics, Straub knows the second the chum's in the water the sharks start to circle.

"It's going to take some time to see how it unfolds. But if Collyer plays it right, he could end up giving the Pentagon a black eye."

"So you brought his family in to give him breathing room."

"Exactly."

"Good move."

"No skin off the Agency's back if we house a couple nice ladies for a week or so."

"Absolutely not." Straub doesn't mention he practically has them under armed guard.

"So how much time before we get some hard info on this?"

"That depends..." Winn shows his palms. "There are a lot of players involved and the ground is constantly shifting." Straub instructed his secretary to call him at 7:15. Like clockwork, his cell phone chirps.

"Excuse, me. Abner." He listens carefully for a minute, says, "Yes, yes. Okay. Thank you," then flips the phone shut and stands. "Abner, would you mind if I excused myself? Something is breaking and I need to get on a secure phone."

"Use mine if you like."

"Thanks, but I better get back to my own office. Sorry to rush out like this." He reaches across the desk to shake Dickson's hand.

"No, please, go take care of whatever it is."

"I'll keep you in the loop on this, Abner," Straub says as he hustles out of Dickson's office.

"I'd appreciate that. And let me know what I can do to help."

"Keep it to yourself that we're hiding the ladies down at Peary," Straub says over his shoulder. "And give me cover if anyone starts sniffing around. I could be ruffling some feathers in the next few days."

"Good as done, Winn."

Straub stops at the door, "One more thing—"

"Name it."

"I need a secure meeting place," Straub looks at his watch. "Pretty quick, say in the next twelve hours. And it has to be local."

"I've got just the place. We set it up for an operation last week and as far as I know it's still standing. Speak to my assistant outside. Tell him you want to go shopping."

Straub thanks Dickson and leaves his office. He recognized his assistant on his way in. Kid that he interviewed a couple years ago when he first came to CIA. Sharp as hell, summa cum laude fresh out of Harvard.

"The Director said I should talk to you about going shopping," Straub says to the tall, gangly young man in the dark suit sitting at one of the desks in Dickson's outer office.

"Certainly, sir. Aren't you Winston Straub? I interviewed with you three years ago when I interned here. Good to see you again, sir," he says, hopping up out of his chair and reaching out to shake Winn's hand, eager smile on his face as if he's honored to again be in the presence of a man who's close to being one of CIA's living legends.

For a moment Straub basks in the respect as the director's assistant solicitously makes the arrangements for him to use the secure location.

Perfect, Winn thinks. *The last place Pentagon agents or terrorists would think of staking out is the women's department of Neiman Marcus.*

28

[Baltimore, Thursday morning]

"If I remember correctly, there's only a slight variation from the human formula. Vets often use it as a pre-surgery sedative," Sharon explained to Howie as they hustled out of the apartment building toward the veterinarian's office her fingers had found in the Yellow Pages.

Ten blocks away, the office of Dr. Vincent Horder, D.V.M. is a modest bungalow at 1315 Juanita Avenue. They waited across the street, keeping an eye on the building, watching a figure moving around inside. A half-hour later, a middle-aged man wearing a suit came out carrying a black leather doctor's bag. He carefully locked the door, taped a sheet of paper to it, turned and hustled off down the street.

As soon as he turned the corner, they were at the door.

Howie reads the note: *Out on house calls. Back at 11:15. Call cell phone if emergency*, followed by a scribbled number. Howie checks his wristwatch, 10:35. Then rings the bell just to make sure. No answer.

"Around back, c'mon," he tells Sharon. There's a chain-link fence with a gate. The backyard is right out of Disneyland. An obvious marketing stunt to attract business, the vet has created a backyard crowded with conifers manicured into shapes of animals. Two dogs, three cats, a pony, even a bear up on its hind legs.

"Can you believe this?" Howie whispers. "It's a mini theme park."

Sharon's all business, heading for the back door with the nail file she found in a drawer in the apartment. He made a pick for her out of it and taught her how to jimmy. The evergreen animals give Howie excellent cover. He ducks down behind a bush clipped into the shape of a German shepherd as he watches Sharon work the lock. Sharon's a quick study. Turning back to Howie and nodding, she sticks the file back in her pocket, slowly creaks the door open and slips inside.

Howie records the time. *So far, so good.* He scans the sides of the bungalow carefully. Then turns and checks the alley. The neighborhood is part residential, the rest commercial, low buildings, empty lots full of weeds, chain-link fences, squalid and forlorn. An angry dog howls in the distance. He can hear a train whistle, the hum of traffic on a nearby interstate, a low chorus of car horns.

He glances at his watch. Sharon has been in the vet's office for just under two minutes. He looks back toward the alley.

C'mon, Sharon. Two and a half minutes. Howie hears a sharp sound, a twig snapping? *Three minutes.* He listens for movement behind him. Checks his watch again. Then he sees the door open, Sharon quietly slides out.

Good girl. She carefully pulls the door shut behind her and makes her way across the yard, an object in her right hand.

She comes up to him with her index finger raised to her lips.

Whispering, sounding tense and anxious, turning back to check over her shoulder, she says, "I got the pills but I saw a reflection in a window. Couldn't be sure but I think someone might have been watching me."

"I heard a noise in the alley too."

"I'm getting the heebie-jeebies."

"Let's take a walk. If anyone's there, we'll find out soon enough what they are up to."

"That's what I'm afraid of."

"If they were going to do us any harm, they've had plenty of chances before now." Howie stands and takes her arm, hustling her down the walkway, through the gate, along the side of the bungalow toward the street. "Just act like nothing's the matter."

"Easy for you to say," Sharon counters.

"At the next block, we'll split up," Howie tells Sharon.

"Do we have to? This place gives me the creeps."

"You take a right and I'll go left. Go to the next block, turn left, walk three blocks north and then hang a left again. We'll meet back on this street. When you catch sight of me, check carefully on both sides to see if anyone is following."

"Can't we just head back to the apartment?"

"Next left, three blocks, and take another left. Get going, see you in five blocks."

Howie heads across the deserted street. Looking back over his shoulder, he can see Sharon hesitatingly stepping off the curb, looking around warily.

Even though it's a commercial area, people have hung Christmas lights in a few of the storefronts. He passes a waving Santa in the front window of a sanitary supply business with a plastic reindeer posed alongside, his red nose merrily blinking, the two figures looking strangely out of place amidst the jumble of pipes and plumbing fixtures.

Glancing back down the block in the direction Sharon's heading, he sees someone quickly step out of a doorway a hundred feet behind her. Still in the shadows. Howie can't see his face. He looks both ways, then turns and briskly starts down the street in her direction. Sharon turns the corner, taking the left as Howie had instructed, disappearing down the next block.

I can't see her anymore, and now he's coming to the corner, Howie thinks, *in a few moments I won't be able to see either one of them.*

Howie breaks into a sprint, racing toward the intersection. Dashing around the corner, he runs into a newspaper box that clatters to the pavement and sends Howie sprawling ass over teakettle.

Hearing the racket, Sharon whirls around. For the first time notices the person coming toward her. Howie's way back on the corner, picking himself up. She lets out a panicked shriek. Howie scrambles to his feet and takes off.

Sharon's whips her head around to look at the man closing on her. Dark, skinny and getting nearer. She screams again, turning to make a mad dash down the street. Not more than fifty feet ahead of him.

Howie's flying now, closing the gap. Can't tell if he's armed. Dashing through the pools of light from the streetlamps overhead, Howie can see he's small, dark haired, but he's fast as hell. *Mugger? Terrorist? Does he want to kill her? Rob her? Rape her?* Now he's twenty feet away from her. He can hear Sharon's terrified panting. Howie knows he won't catch up with him before he reaches her, he's praying she doesn't stop.

Knowing he's running out of options, he pulls up short and screams, clasping his hands together and holding them up as if he had a gun, "Stop or I'll shoot!"

The man comes to an abrupt halt, glances over his shoulder at Howie, decides he doesn't want to take any chances and quickly slinks into an alley, disappearing into the darkness.

Howie runs up to her, "I'm going after him—"

Sharon grabs his shirt and spins him around, "The hell you are, you're staying right here with me." She blurts, shaken and furious at the same time. "That scared the shit out of me."

"I need to find out who's after us."

"You used me as bait. Christ, you're more heartless than your buddy Straub."

Howie gently takes her arm and steers her across the street, "Come on, let's get back to the apartment."

"I'm not going anywhere until you tell me what the hell's going on. Who was that guy?"

"This is a pretty sketchy neighborhood."

"So you tell me to wander off by myself?"

"We have to figure out who they are."

"You figure it out, I'm getting the hell out of here. It was nuts enough when we were playing cat and mouse with a black program at the Defense Department. But if you're thinking some terrorist group is after us, that's it, I quit." She reaches into her pocket, pulls out the pills and slaps the bottle into Howie's hand, "Here, take your damn medicine. Go grill the major yourself."

Sharon turns and stalks off down the street.

"Where do you think you're going?" he calls, hustling after her.

Sharon whirls around and glares, "I've had it, Collyer. I'm heading back to Pittsburgh. This is absolutely whacko to be messing around with terrorists."

"It is scary, I'll grant you that."

"Give me a frigging break! Leading terrorists to a hydrogen bomb, are you out of your mind?"

"Let's talk about it, c'mon," Howie says, chasing her down the street toward the apartment building. She's walking at a brisk pace, he's beginning to breathe hard, barely keeping up. Out of the corner of his eye, he sees a smear of yellow flash through the intersection ahead. *Could that be the cab that brought us here?* Howie asks himself.

"You can talk all you want," she snorts over her shoulder, flinging open the door to the building and stomping into the hallway. "I'm getting out of here."

"Hear me out first," Howie's chasing her up the stairs.

At the second-floor landing she whirls around, as distraught as he's ever seen her. "You can talk until you're blue in the face but this girl is history."

"It never occurred to me they'd pick up on my website."

"C'mon, Collyer, get real. I found it in a matter of minutes. They've probably been watching it ever since you put it up. It was like bears to honey. 'Hey, get your nuclear weapon, get your free hydrogen bomb.'"

"They must have followed me up to Pittsburgh, then tracked us down in Front Royal."

"Right!" jabbing Howie in the chest with her finger. "And when you find out from Mark where they jettisoned the bomb, they'll follow us to it. And the minute they've got their hands on it, we're expendable—chopped liver." Sharon pokes him again. "And then the whole East Coast gets vaporized. Don't you get it, Collyer? This is nuts! That's why I'm getting the hell off this train. And you should too—before something horrible happens."

"Sharon, I'm only worried about where you can go that will be safe. If I thought you'd be okay somewhere, I'd tell you to scram."

"I can take care of myself. I'm a big girl," she says. "This time I'm not buying this crap about being in too deep to quit. I'm going right straight to the cops. And then I'm calling my congressman."

Howie shrugs his shoulders, holds up his hands, "What are you going to tell them—that you're being chased by a bunch of terrorists because you know the location of a lost hydrogen bomb? They'll laugh right in your face. I wouldn't be surprised if they throw you in the loony bin."

For the first time, Sharon Thorsen is at a loss for words. She's fuming, eyes flashing. She turns and starts up the stairs, taking them in twos. Howie hustles after her. At the landing, he pulls up short when he sees her standing at the door to the apartment, hand up to her mouth, eyes wide as dinner plates.

"Did you leave the door open?"

"No. I'm sure I locked it," he answers, rushing up to join her.

"Major Risstup?" she says, slowly nudging the door with her foot. "Are you okay?" On the hallway floor, Howie notices a cigarette butt. *That wasn't there when we left.*

Sharon creeps through the doorway, as if she expects to find a bloody scene, "Oh my God," she gasps, "he's gone."

Howie rushes in after her. No sign of Risstup. He looks around for the wheelchair, then remembers they left it in the cab, checks behind the daybed. Sharon's in shock, little yelps of horror coming from deep in her throat. In the short time they've been out, Howie can't imagine someone could have broken in and kidnapped him.

He reaches for his laptop, lifts the cover. Opens the program he was using earlier. Checks to see when it was last activated, *10:58.* His watch reads 11:03. *Someone's been on my machine. Someone has been here not more than five minutes ago.*

Out of the corner of his eye, Howie notices the bathroom door is shut. His hand is almost on the handle when all of a sudden he hears the toilet flush.

"Major Risstup?"

Silence. Howie grabs Sharon's hand and swings her around behind him, putting his body between her and the bathroom. "Major Risstup? Are you in there?"

Another pause.

"I'll be right out," Howie hears from behind the door. His shoulders relax, bad enough for someone to have been in the apartment. He knows if they had abducted the major, it would have been the end of the game.

As she twists away from him, Sharon snaps, "That's the last time we're leaving him alone."

Risstup peeks out of the bathroom, sees the look on their faces. "Is something wrong?"

"We came back to find the door wide open. We were worried."

"I'm fine. Aside from that cheeseburger I had that didn't agree with me."

"How did the door get open?"

"Didn't one of you leave it that way?"

"How long were you in the bathroom?"

"A while, I guess, stomach was pretty upset. How long have you been gone?"

"No one came in when you were in there?"

"I didn't hear anything."

Howie's figuring out something must have surprised whoever was in the apartment and he took off quickly.

All of a sudden he hears a loud, plaintive half-moan, half-whimper from Sharon. "I can't take this any longer," she says, collapsing on the daybed. "We're not safe here, we're not safe anywhere. Terrorists after us, the Pentagon. No place to go, nothing to wear, on the run all the time. This is just horrible." Sharon jumps up off the bed and turns her back to him, her fists dug into her hips, head slumping forward. "I'm so frustrated and angry," she says in a gruff but shaky voice.

Howie walks over to her, gently puts his hands on her shoulders and slowly turns her so they are face to face.

"Leave me alone," she says, pulling away from him. Risstup's eyes are wide, taking in the back-and-forth.

"C'mon," he says, understanding she's fighting a losing battle with her emotions. They win and with her eyes brimming, she falls against Howie's chest, throwing her arms around him and letting the tears flow.

As Howie hugs Sharon, his mind flashes back to the one-week vacation he and Sylvie took at the beach a year ago. On their return he wondered if someone had been rummaging around his war room. One detail stuck out. The file on the Jersey bomb had been filed backward, the tab facing the wrong way. At the time he paid no attention, thinking he'd misfiled it. But in that file was his work on the locations where the weapon could have been jettisoned. All the calculations, the maps, the drawings of the Mk-15s with the nuclear capsule. *Had these people broken in and copied the information? Or did they even need to? Much of the information is on my website.* He'd naively posted it there, thinking he was doing concerned citizens a favor.

He has a sudden sick feeling in his stomach. *Not only have I been leading them to the nuke, I've told them everything about it. When we took off for the vet's office, they must have slipped into the apartment to check on my progress. They've wormed their way into every nook and cranny of my life. watching and listening to me every minute, from every angle. Waiting patiently for me to take them to the prize.*

Now I'm damned if I lead them to the nuke, and most likely dead if I don't.

Howie can feel Sharon's body starting to relax, her sobbing backing down. He has no other option but to act like a rock. He takes a deep breath. "Feeling any better?" he asks as she pulls away from him, wiping her eyes with the collar of her shirt, nods and slumps down on the daybed, sniffling. “Sorry. I tried but I couldn’t keep it bottled up another second.”

“I tell you what. I think it’s time I emailed Winn and ask him to bring us in.”

“Will he do that?” She looks up at him, her eyes red but her expression brightening.

“I don’t think he has any choice.”

“I hope you’re right.” Her quavering voice tells him she’s at her breaking point. As tough as she’s been, she isn’t going to hold up much longer.

29

[American University campus, Thursday noon]

Straub pulls up his coat collar. A couple of fat pigeons strut around on the ground hoping for handouts. One looks up at him and cocks its head as if Straub had said something. The wind's picked up, it's getting nasty, temperature's plunged ten degrees. Bitter cold, even for the last day in November.

Sitting next to Straub, Jimmick's thumbs are dancing over his BlackBerry. Straub prevailed on his wife to make the call to Jimmick. She bristled but phoned him anyway, muttering something about owing her big-time for having to play his secretary.

Straub had met Jimmick at the rendezvous a half hour later, the words from Howie's email running through his mind. *Howie is convinced they are pursuing him, a group of three terrorists, maybe more. From the tone of his email he sounds rattled and he has reason to be.*

Straub sniffs at Jimmick, "You going to put that damn thing away so we can talk?"

Jimmick doesn't look up, "I get hundreds of emails a day. My assistants cull them but unless I keep up I get buried. So how is he?"

"Boy's got nine lives."

"Close call in Front Royal."

"Tell me about it."

"Scuttlebutt is that Vector Eleven did the car."

"Big surprise."

"But who torched the motel?"

"That's why I called you."

"So you know."

Straub ducks his head a couple times.

Jimmick looks over at him, his thumbs still jitterbugging on the BlackBerry. He changes the subject. "The *Susan* woman who called me, that was your wife, right?"

"Yup."

"I recognized her voice. Keeping it in the family, huh?"

"Have to keep the circle closed, otherwise it'll spin out of our control."

"What's next?"

"Tell me more about the Coast Guard."

"Whatever you need, you've got."

"A search-and-retrieval team?"

"Good as done. So who torched the motel?"

"Someone else is interested in Collyer. It wasn't Vector Eleven, they were blocks away.

"FBI?"

"Worse—terrorists."

"Holy shit." The BlackBerry slips out of his hands and clatters on the bench beside him. Jimmick whirls around to face Winn. The color has gone from his face. Misplaced or stolen nuclear materials are always causes for alarm, and since he first met with Straub, the possibility that terrorists could become involved had crossed his mind. Though he was not at all inclined to deal with the thought. Now he has no choice.

"Are you sure?"

"Howie is. He suspects they've been following him for the last twenty-four hours."

"They're after the bomb."

"They're not on a fucking wine tour, that's for sure."

"How many?"

"Two, three, maybe more."

Jimmick is floored, his forehead creased, eyes clenched shut. *Since 9/11, everyone in the intelligence game has speculated terrorist cells could be operating in the country but no one has had any hard evidence. The assumption was they had attacked us once and would strike again. But where and how? Would they infiltrate along the Mexican border? Come in through Canada? Smuggle a nuke inside a shipping container? Or have they been here all along?*

And in everyone's mind is the nagging question—would we be able to stop them this time?

He nervously shifts on the bench. "So this is a whole new ball game."

"You got that right."

"Who would have ever suspected they would be watching Collyer?"

"Last thing I would have ever thought of and I'm probably his oldest friend."

"When you think about it, it's so obvious. You want a nuke, go find Howie Collyer."

"It's as obvious as hijacking planes and using them as bombs."

"How about the Pentagon, anyone there know?"

"They know someone is trying to keep Howie alive. Maybe they haven't figured out the terrorist angle but I bet they will soon."

"If we mobilize the Coast Guard, this town will be up for grabs."

"It'll have to be totally under cover, a top-secret operation."

"I'll do what I can, but those snoops at NSA and internal affairs creeps see everything. Hell, they know if I move my goddamn car."

"It's a risk we have to take. We have to cover Howie's back."

"If it's anywhere on the East Coast, I have the perfect unit. When's this coming down?"

"Saturday or Sunday, Monday at the latest. Can you move that fast?"

Jimmick cracks a smile. "Brownie doesn't work here anymore."

Straub chuckles.

"Today's Thursday, Friday I'll be ready." Jimmick's thumbs go back to tap dancing—as if his BlackBerry is a pacifier, the ritual pecking proving comforting.

The two men sit watching the pigeons hopping around, looking for a seed or anything edible on the bare ground. A minute passes, another. The wind is whistling through the trees, leaves tumbling across the grass.

Jimmick breaks the silence. "This can't be easy for you, having your best friend on the firing line."

Straub looks across the bench at him. "You know, it's funny but it's easier that it's Howie."

"How's that?"

"Boy's got no choice. He knows he made this bed and he's got to sleep in it."

"But, Jesus, with terrorists involved..." Jimmick pauses to let his comment sink in. Looks down at his BlackBerry, then across at Straub. "You really are sure we shouldn't be getting more people involved?"

Winn knows where Jimmick is heading. *He's worried about his own butt. Anyone who's worked in Washington knows the game. CYA. Cover your ass. If you are going to be a survivor in this town, you have to know how to play it.*

Straub looks out across the park. He knows that his answer will have more effect if he doesn't look directly at Jimmick. "Do that and you're signing Howie Collyer's death warrant. And the two people who are with him. It would be easy to simply take them out. And we'd lose the opportunity to catch the Pentagon red-handed. So our only hope is to let it play out."

"Could be risky as hell. Nuclear weapons, terrorists."

"Lucien—it's risky already."

Straub pauses to let the information sink in. He can tell Jimmick is wishing he were back in Miami chasing Chechens. Which is exactly where Straub wants him. *You're a lot more motivated when your own ass is on the line.*

30

[Everglades Motel, Baltimore, Thursday afternoon]

Leaving the apartment early in the morning, he took cabs in opposite directions for a half an hour, walking ten blocks before hailing another, going through a building lobby to the street on the other side and getting on and off buses until he was certain he wasn't being tailed

They were on the road for a half hour before checking into a motel in downtown Baltimore. They hardly spoke on the ride over. Both are strung out and low on sleep, with side orders of frayed nerves and lousy dispositions.

Everglades Motel, a step above the ones they've been staying in. Only signs of Florida are a bunch of potted plants in the lobby, palm frond motif painted on the wall behind the front desk and a small stuffed alligator on the counter with its front teeth missing. Sharon administered the meds to Risstup and while waiting for them to take effect, Howie went around the corner to find some food. Bagels and cream cheese, enough coffee for six. He knew they were going to need it.

Howie has been circling the room since returning. Going from Risstup to the plate of bagels, peeking out the window, back to Risstup, then to the bagels, every once in a while glancing at his watch.

"Will you stop checking your watch every two seconds? Sit down and read the damn paper or something," Sharon snaps at Collyer as she spreads cream cheese on a bagel.

Howie holds up his hands in mock surrender.

The plastic knife she's using suddenly breaks in half. Sharon grunts and tosses the knife and bagel aside as if they are too much to deal with. She snaps the lid off the coffee and walks over to a dresser set.

She puts her coffee down and leans on the bureau, inspecting herself in the mirror. She knew both of them were starting to look like they're right out of the cast of a horror flick. Howie's gaunt, his two-day growth of stubble making him look five years older. And she's worse, dark circles around her eyes, a hangdog look, her hair is awful. She lifts a hank and lets it drop back down, greasy, lifeless, she would give anything for a perm, even dreamt about it during the ride over. Sharon takes a sip of coffee. Women always look the worse for wear and a series of crummy motels and washing her underwear in the sink hasn't helped. Now she's down to one set of clothes, She knows she looks like a wreck and that only makes her feel worse.

"What do you say we try doubling up the dose?" Howie asks, pointing at Risstup who's parked in his chair dozing peacefully.

"Crissakes, Howie, every damn thing I do you second-guess," she snorts.

Howie winces. "Sorry."

"My fault, I'm in a lousy mood."

"I couldn't tell." Howie cracks a smile.

"My friends always told me I had a sunny disposition."

"That's a lot to ask for under these circumstances."

She takes another gulp of coffee. "Can I ask you a question?"

"Sure."

"This is silly, but do you think we could find any time for me to get a perm?"

"A what?"

"Perm—permanent," she takes a handful of hair and displays it. "My hair looks like crap."

"Is that something we have to do right now?"

"No. Never mind. It's a girl thing. I know I must sound nuts bringing up my hair at a time like this."

"I'm sure we can find a beauty salon somewhere."

"Thanks, appreciate the understanding." Sharon glances at her watch. It's been a half hour since she gave him the tablets. "Okay. The medication should be working by now. Crank up your machine."

The trick was to get the dose right. Too much and Risstup would drift over the edge, too little and his disinhibition level wouldn't drop to the point where he can call up past events from wherever his mind has parked them. Seating the major at Howie's side, she adjusts him so he's in front of the screen. Sharon leans over and peers into Risstup's face. His look is contented, almost dreamy. She checks his pulse. *Perfect, exactly the way I want him.*

"He's as ready as he'll ever be," she tells Howie." Let's give it a try." She shakes Risstup's shoulder gently. His eyes drift open.

"The B-52 went over land before it went out over the ocean?" Howie asks.

Risstup nods.

"And where were you?"

"When I think about it, I saw land as my parachute brought me down."

"You came down on land?"

"I think so. I remember the ground speeding up at me. Like I was hanging there motionless and it was racing up toward me."

"So that must have been the Eastern Shore?"

"I saw the ground flying up into my face, then I don't remember anything."

"You could have hit your head."

"My helmet was torn off during ejection. I remember that. So I must have cracked it pretty good since everything is a blank between then and the time I started getting my memory back."

"That's a helluva story, Mark," Sharon says, patting him on the shoulder.

"I guess it is."

"It's more than a story," Howie says, pushing back his chair. "It's the key to everything."

"How's that?" Sharon asks.

"Get this—the flight was headed south over New Jersey, right? When Major Risstup saw they were over water, he released the nuke. Then he ejected. But he parachuted down on land so the last bit of real estate he could have landed on was the Eastern Shore. And he's already told us he jettisoned the nuke before he ejected. So it has to be somewhere in the Chesapeake."

"In the bay?"

"I'll have to do some calculations but I'd bet the nuke is somewhere in the northern part."

"Near Washington," Sharon says.

"And Baltimore and fifty million people. An expert on nuclear weapons would tell you that if a thermonuclear explosion were detonated underwater, it would create enormous clouds of radioactive vapor. The prevailing winds would carry some of it out to sea, but if the winds were blowing east to west, they could carry radioactivity inland, possibly as far as the Midwest. The underwater tests they did in the Pacific demonstrated the frightening potential of radioactive drift. Hundreds of Marshall Islanders can attest to that."

"We killed people?" Sharon asks.

"Still paying off their descendants, as a matter of fact."

"So what's our next step?"

"Get this to Straub. The news that there is a nuke in the Chesapeake will sure as hell wake some people up."

"So they'll finally do something?"

Howie sweeps up the laptop and heads for the door. "If I were Winn I'd bring us in."

"Howie, if he does, will you do me a favor?"

Howie pauses. Sharon says, "Tell your buddy Straub that if a retiree, a VA nurse and an eighty-four-year-old are the nation's first line of defense to prevent terrorists getting their hands on a nuke, we're in deep shit."

"You bet."

"I'm serious."

"I know." Howie closes the door and heads down the hallway to find a hotspot, thinking, *The woman sure has a way of putting things in perspective.*

31

[Kalorama neighborhood, D.C., early Friday morning]

The phone rings. Lucien Jimmick rolls over and looks at the clock. The green numerals glow 1:53. *At this time of night the news is never good. Take your pick: terrorist attack somewhere in the world, Secret Service calling to tell me there's been a threat on the president, one of my kids drove into a ditch or my mother-in-law's had another heart attack.* He jumps out of bed, fumbling for the receiver on the stew phone.

He hears a dial tone. *Damn, it must be my home phone.* Dropping the stew receiver back in its cradle, he snatches his landline. "Hello?" he grumbles.

"Secretary Jimmick, this is Agent Wirford from your security detail. Sorry to bother you, sir, but you should come downstairs."

"Who is it, dear?" his wife asks groggily from the other side of the bed.

"Nothing, I've got to go down and talk to the guys."

"Is something wrong?" she's sitting up now, blinking her eyes, trying to arrange her hair.

"No problem, they just want to discuss something. Go back to sleep." He shrugs on his bathrobe and steps into his slippers, chasing them one by one across the cold floor until his feet catch up. Pulling the door to his bedroom shut, he heads down the hallway, clicking on lights as he goes. Kalorama is an upscale neighborhood of ambassadors' mansions and D.C. luminaries' residences, with constant police patrols and a low crime rate. Up until recently, he had turned down Secret Service protection thinking it would only complicate his life.

But as he walks down the stairs and takes in the scene, he's glad he changed his mind. The two agents stand in the center of the entrance hall. Between them is an older man dressed in khakis and a parka. He's handcuffed and disheveled, a bruise on his forehead. One of the agents has the barrel of a .45 jammed into his ribcage.

"We found him sneaking across the front yard, stopped him before he got to the front door. We'll take care of him, Mr. Secretary. But first we wanted to see if you recognized him."

Jimmick does a double take. He's never seen him without a suit. He looks older, and roughed up with a nasty scrape on his head, more like a vagrant than a veteran CIA agent.

He takes the stairs in twos, ordering the agents, "Remove his restraints right away. I know him."

"Are you sure, sir?"

"Absolutely. I hope you didn't beat up on him too much."

"We didn't know who he was, Mr. Secretary. We saw him heading toward the house and didn't want to take any chances."

"Yes, thank you. I understand," he says, throwing his arm around Winn Straub's shoulder and leading him into the kitchen. "Are you okay, Winn? Sorry they treated you like that. Can I get you an icepack for that bump?"

"I'll be fine."

"How about a cup of coffee?"

"Great. Sorry to wake you up like this, Lucien, but no one can know we're talking. I didn't even want the record of a call. So I let your security guys find me. They're good, Lucien, they've got eyes in the back of their heads."

"Again, I'm sorry."

"I expected as much. You don't go skulking around the Secretary of Homeland Security's house without expecting some rough treatment."

"I'm glad they didn't shoot you."

"Believe me, I didn't put up much of a fight. I just wanted to talk, not get killed."

Jimmick closes the door behind him and heads for the coffeemaker.

"You're obviously paying me a visit at two in the morning for a reason..."

"Are we okay here?"

"The house was swept again yesterday," Jimmick says as he spoons coffee into the basket, his back to Straub.

"It's breaking fast, Lucien."

"What's the latest?"

"I just got an email. Collyer's located the nuke."

Jimmick whirls around to face Straub. "Where?"

"The worst place you could imagine—the Chesapeake."

"Christ, twenty or thirty miles from D.C."

"It gets more serious. He's confirmed the bomb is an early version of the Mk-15 with a nuclear capsule."

"Meaning?"

"Crude as hell. Never should have gone into service in the first place but we feared the Russians were ahead in the arms race. Later models had safeguards, failsafe mechanisms built in, codes and counter codes that had to be entered before the weapon would be armed. Setting off this model is as easy as turning on your cell phone."

"It could be detonated in the water?"

"We don't know for sure, anything's possible."

"I hope to hell someone else doesn't figure it out first. Does Collyer know the exact spot?"

"Only roughly, he's going to have to do a search. That's where your Coast Guard comes in."

"I'm all set. Who else knows Collyer's got the location?" Jimmick asks, carrying coffee over to the kitchen table and taking a seat across from Straub.

Straub wags his head back and forth. "No one so far. About four hours ago Howie was able to get the pilot to recall where he jettisoned the nuke. I've got him on a secure server. So right now we have the inside track."

"What about the terrorists?"

"We have to assume they are still shadowing him."

"But if Collyer goes out there on the bay and starts towing around metal and radiation-detecting gear, the whole world's going to be watching."

"Maybe, but think about it. If he's the only one who knows where the bomb is, don't you think the interested parties are going to keep their heads down and let him lead them to it?"

"You mean hide in the reeds until he finds it?"

"If I was Vector Eleven or the terrorists, that's what I'd do. All they want is the bomb, neither of them gives a shit about Howie."

"What if he gets caught in the middle?"

"I'm bringing him in today." Straub checks his Timex. "He'll know what he's up against."

"What are the chances he'll back out?" Jimmick chuckles, as if he's suddenly thought better of what he's said. "I guess from what you've told me about Collyer that's a stupid question."

Straub can't resist a literary allusion. Even though he was an econ major, he had taken every literature class he could. "There's a poet, Dryden, I think it was, who once wrote about someone, 'Fate seemed to wind him up.' That's Howie. Back in school he was a mediocre place kicker on a team with one of the worst records in the country. But one Saturday afternoon in the beginning of November, that group of guys stepped up and had a nationally ranked team on the ropes at the end of the fourth quarter. Down by two, with three seconds left, Howie booted one through the uprights from forty yards out to put UVa over the top."

"That's a great story, Winn, but this isn't football, this is hardball."

"Howie can handle it, believe me." Straub narrows his eyes, his voice tells Jimmick he shouldn't pursue this line of questioning any longer,

"Okay, what's our next move?" he asks.

"Let's find out how good your Coast Guard guys are."

32

[Fairhaven, Maryland, western shore of the Chesapeake, Friday, mid-morning]

Hearing vehicles coming down, Charlie Grimes drops what he's doing and heads for the office. On a one-lane gravel road a couple miles out of town, during the winter he sees maybe three cars a day coming past his boatyard, if that.

Standing overlooking the parking lot, Grimes watches as the procession of vehicles swings into the parking area and pulls to a stop. He counts seven. Four Hummers, a pickup truck, a large black van and a trailer towed by a rig that pulls up and parks on the road outside, evidently too large to turn around in the boatyard's lot. He guesses some kind of boat is under the black canvas stretched tight over the trailer, looks to be thirty-foot plus.

Repo people is the first thing that comes to Grimes' mind. His heart sinks. *Maybe they've finally caught up with us. Damn bank's gone and sold my yard without telling me.* Every winter is a struggle to get enough repairs to make ends meet and stay two steps ahead of his creditors.

He watches a group of men clamber out of the vehicles, looking around his boatyard, sizing the place up.

"Shirley, did you miss a mortgage payment?" Grimes yells to his wife who's working in the storeroom behind the office.

"What?" she calls.

"Did you miss making the mortgage?" he shouts at her.

Shirley comes down the corridor wiping grease off her hands with a rag. "Did I what?"

"Miss payments—there's a bunch of strangers out here."

"No, I wrote the check just last week."

"Why do you ask?"

"Take a look," he says, directing her attention to the front window. "Why else would a crew like this show up?"

"There are at least twenty. Don't look too friendly either."

"Let me see what I can do," Charlie says, heading toward the door. Opening it and stepping onto the porch, he yells to them, "Something I can help you fellows with?"

The leader of the group is in his late thirties, dressed in a dark windbreaker and navy cargo pants, a blue baseball cap on his head. He's clean-shaven and pleasant-looking, yet his smile is tight and calculated.

"We'd like to talk to you about an opportunity, Mr. Grimes," he says as he approaches the porch. "May we come in?"

"You're not from the bank?"

The man shakes his head, smiles faintly. "No, Mr. Grimes, we're here to make you an offer."

"I'm not selling out for development or anything like that. I'm just a small boatyard owner trying to keep my head above water. It's my life's work."

Four of the men walk into his office, the rest wait on the porch.

"Where are you boys from?" Grimes asks as an icebreaker.

No one's interested in small talk. "We're interested in leasing your boatyard for a month."

"Sorry, I'm not in the lease business. If you've got a boat that needs fixing, bring it in. But no leasing."

"Charlie, hear the man out," Shirley butts in, stepping forward, a smile on her face and money on her mind. "It might be okay if the price's right."

"We're prepared to offer you thirty thousand dollars to lease your boatyard for a month. In return, you are to vacate the premises within an hour and not come back until the lease is over. That date would be January 2nd. And you are not to say anything about our arrangement."

"Did you say thirty thousand dollars?" Grimes, dumbfounded, knows in a good year they barely manage to net forty.

"We could go to Florida for the entire month," Shirley adds.

"That's correct, Mr. Grimes. Thirty thousand dollars."

"Can I ask what you are going to do with my boatyard?"

"We will leave it as we found it. It's all written up in this contract," the man says, pulling out an envelope and handing it to Grimes.

"How about I take a couple hours reading it and give you a call sometime this afternoon?"

"We're prepared to give you the entire amount in cash upfront if you sign the agreement and leave by 10:30."

Grimes checks the clock on the wall. "That's an hour from now."

"I can pack fast, dear."

Grimes is shaking his head. "I like the idea of the money, don't get me wrong on that. It's just that we have all these boats to repair."

The man in the navy baseball cap pulls out a second envelope. "Here are two round-trip first class plane tickets from Reagan to Miami in your names and a hotel reservation for a month. The flight leaves at 5:30. One of our people will drive you."

Grimes snatches the tickets. "I guess we can pack in an hour," he says, hustling the agreement over to his desk. Fishing a pen out of the drawer, he scrawls his signature on the document and hands it over.

"Thank you, Mr. Grimes. Here is your cash."

Grimes eyes bulge as he sees the fat stack of hundreds coming in his direction.

"I'm going to run and pack, Charlie," Shirley squeals as she hustles down the stairs.

Grimes takes the money and holds out his hand, an incredulous smile breaking across his face, "Thanks, Mr.—"

"You're welcome."

"Sure wish I knew what you're going to do with my boatyard, but now I took the money I guess that's your business, huh?"

"Yes, sir. The car will be waiting for you. Better get going, you don't want to miss your plane."

A half hour later, the husband and wife are tossing their bags into the backseat and climbing into the Hummer for the ride to Reagan. She's wearing a flowered sundress and flip flops, Charlie Grimes in his best pair of Bermudas and a Hawaiian shirt, the two looking like just another two of the millions of snowbirds flocking down to Florida every winter.

"So are you guys CIA or what?" Grimes jokes to the driver as they pull out of the boatyard.

The look the driver gives him when he turns around tells Grimes he had no business asking that question.

His wife is glaring at him for being nosy, her scowling expression immediately telling him that he's stepped in it. "Okay, forget I asked. Never mind, it's not important," Grimes backs down.

Both Mr. and Mrs. Grimes got the message. For the remainder of the trip to the airport you could hear a pin drop.

By the middle of the afternoon, the Grimes' boatyard is transformed from a collection of shabby wooden shanties with rusting roofs littered with a clutter of discarded engines, driveshafts and broken-down boats to a bustling hubbub of activity. A crew of men in blue utility suits readies two boats, a thirty-foot rigid inflatable with an inboard engine and jet drive plus a weather-beaten workboat tied up at the dock.

Commander Thomas Warren, assigned to the Coast Guard station at nearby Little River, Virginia, is the officer in charge. His orders came down from the Secretary of Homeland Security directly. He took the call from Jimmick at four in the morning and has been scrambling ever since. His orders were extensive and explicit: locate a boatyard on the upper Chesapeake, secure it and ready it for a mission. Commander Warren feels like a Vegas high roller—half a million is major money—the first time his pockets have been crammed with that much cash.

Warren knew better than to ask any specifics. Not something you tend to get into with the Secretary of Homeland Security when he wakes you up in the middle of the night. But Warren knew it would not be a run-of-the-mill operation when the secretary instructed him to remove all Coast Guard insignia and identification not only from the boats but also from their uniforms.

A series of questions cycles through his mind as he watches the crew carefully peeling and scraping Coast Guard emblems from the inflatable. *Why is Jimmick flying in cutting-edge metal and radiation detection gear?* Airlifted in from a top-secret facility in California, he spent the time coming up from Little River reading up on the equipment. He understands the latest metal detectors make searching deep, murky water like looking into a bathtub, and the radiation apparatus is capable of sniffing out emissions lower than the levels coming from your dentist's X-ray machine.

What could Jimmick possibly be searching for? And in the Chesapeake of all places?

33

[Tysons Corner, D.C. suburbs, Friday afternoon]

Tysons Galleria is one of D.C.'s tonier malls with ritzy shops like Versace, Coach, Ferragamo, pricey restaurants and a Ritz-Carlton. Dressed to the nines for the holidays, every square foot is embellished with bells, bows, wreaths, angels and elves, thousands of lights twinkling, silver and gold balls glittering, the sparkling and gleaming decorations transforming the vast mall into a magical Christmas wonderland.

"Despite all the glitz, I'm not getting in a festive mood," Howie says as they walk through a courtyard festooned with thousands of red and silver candy canes and endless loops of glimmering metallic rope, mobbed with hordes of frenzied holiday shoppers hustling from store to store making sure they don't miss a bargain in the pre-Christmas sales.

"Tell me about it," Sharon says. "And I'm not exactly dressed for it either." She's wearing the only outfit she has left, jeans and a secondhand sweatshirt she bought at a thrift store in Lancaster and her once gleaming white but now scuffed and stained Danskos that have been on her feet since she left the VA hospital. "Back home, I would have dressed better to take out the garbage."

"Keep your eyes open, maybe we can find you a new outfit."

"Let's find your buddy Straub first. I'm dying to meet this man."

Straub's email gave precise and detailed instructions on leaving the motel and the route they were to take to the shopping center.

Risstup was to remain at the motel, Winn would have someone keeping an eye on him. They were to grab a cab in the neighborhood and wait under the tall archway clustered with silver ornaments that spans the south end of the atrium.

"Don't expect to see him right off the bat," Howie says as they head across the wide, open space.

"What do you mean?"

"If I know Winn, he probably has some elaborate rigmarole to insure we're not being followed." Collyer's eyes are scanning the floors above for the reflection of a binocular, or someone in a suit wearing an earpiece.

"And if we are?" Sharon asks. Howie can tell she's getting anxious.

"Winn's done this a thousand times."

"So what do we do, just wander around the damn mall until we get a signal?"

"Relax, you were the one who was so eager to come in from the cold—remember?"

Howie takes Sharon's arm and brings her to his side as they pull up next to the soaring silver arch. They stand listening to the Christmas carols echoing throughout the mall while they watch the teeming crowds of shoppers dragging along petulant children and lugging shopping bags jammed to the gills with Christmas goodies, the music and chatter of the shoppers punctuated by the persistent dinging of the Salvation Army Santas' tinny bells.

"What does Straub look like?"

"Back in school, we used to call him 'the accountant.' Sylvie claims he's a dead ringer for Karl Malden, remember him?"

"Won an Oscar for *Streetcar Named Desire*."

"Jeez, on top of knowing everything about football, you're a movie expert too."

"So what's his story?"

"His wife's big on the Washington party circuit so she drags him to everything, but he's a pretty average-looking guy, not a flashy dresser, colorful people don't last long at CIA."

"Talk about flashy dresser, take a look at me. I feel so yucky," she says, holding out her sweatshirt to show the collage of spots on it.

"You look fine." Howie knows it's better not to argue with a woman about her appearance so he isn't surprised when she fires back.

"If I feel nasty, Collyer, that's my own damn business. Don't go there, okay? I look like something the cat dragged in and I know it. My hair's a mess, I don't have my makeup..."

"Excuse me, ma'am?" A slim and attractive young woman wearing a green satin cocktail dress interrupts Sharon. Elaborately coiffed and dolled up with enough blusher, mascara and foundation for three women, she's showing a perfect set of teeth as she holds out a fancy spray bottle.

Sharon is immediately flustered. Unnerved by the contrast between her own frumpy outfit and the model's sparkling attire, she's shaking her head before the woman has a chance to launch into her spiel.

"Would you like to sample Chanel's latest eau de toilette, ma'am? It's quite a lovely scent. I think you would enjoy it."

"No, I don't think so."

"Then please take a coupon for a free sample," she holds out a small card. "It's redeemable at our store on the middle level.

"No, thank you," Sharon says, waving her hands in front of the woman, hoping she will evaporate.

"I'll take it for my wife, thank you," Howie says, reaching for the card.

"I hope she enjoys it, sir," the model says, flashing him a hundred-dollar smile and sashaying off.

"Don't you know the old expression—never look a gift horse in the mouth?" Howie says, turning the card over and examining it.

"I never knew you liked women's cologne," Sharon says.

"I just wear it on weekends. C'mon," Howie says, taking Sharon by the arm.

"Where are we going?"

"To get our free sample."

"This is absolutely ridiculous," Sharon fusses as Howie pulls her along through the throngs. Up the escalator to the second floor, it's broken-field running, weaving this way and that through the swarm of shoppers. With his hand tightly gripping Sharon's, Howie feels like he's tugging along a cranky kid as he dodges the oncoming ranks, both of them bumped and jostled by the bargain hunters with their overloaded bags.

"There it is," Howie says, seeing the sign for the Chanel store ahead of them. Inside, he heads for the nearest counter.

"Excuse me," Howie says to a saleswoman, waving his coupon. "I'd like to collect my free sample."

"Certainly, sir," she says, taking the card and handing him a small bottle of eau de toilette along with a handout. "And with it you get a hundred free minutes of cell phone time when you buy a new Cingular phone. The details are in this pamphlet. Cingular is downstairs just on the other side of Saks."

"Thank you," Howie says to her. As he steers Sharon out of the store, he tells her, "A hundred free minutes, let's go check it out."

"I thought men didn't like to shop."

"We're not shopping, we're following Winn's cues."

"A damn scavenger hunt, that's what it is."

"Where's your sense of adventure?"

"Traipsing around a jam-packed mall in clothes I've been wearing for three days is not my idea of a party."

"It will only take a few minutes." He's hoping Winn won't drag it out much longer as Sharon's starting one of her slow burns.

Down the escalator, past Saks, "There it is," Howie points. "C'mon, let's check out the new phones."

"Just what we need," Sharon snorts. "A phone we can't use."

In the Cingular Wireless store, Howie holds the folder up to a salesman and says, "I'd like some information on this offer."

"Yes, sir." As he takes the folder from Howie, his cell phone buzzes. "Excuse me a second," he says as he takes the call. As he's listening, he gives Howie a quick once-over, nods, then hands him the phone.

"I think this is for you, sir," he says as Sharon gawks at him, her mouth dropping open.

Howie lifts the phone to his ear and is relieved to hear Winn's voice on the other end.

"Okay, see you in a couple minutes." Howie hands the phone back and thanks the salesman.

"Don't tell me that was Straub?"

"He said the coast is clear." Hooking Sharon's arm and leading her out of the store, he tells her, "C'mon, we're going shopping for a bridal gown."

Sharon feigns a shocked look. "But we're not even engaged."

Two men in dark suits stand at the entrance. Both have Central Intelligence Agency written all over them. They nod at Howie and Sharon as they hold the door open. Except for a matronly looking saleswoman who gets up from behind a desk to greet them, the bridal salon is empty.

"Welcome to the Neiman Marcus bridal salon. May I help you?" she asks.

"Yes, my fiancée would like to try on some gowns."

"May I ask when you're planning the wedding?"

"In the spring," Howie says. Sharon's rolling her eyes. "It's going to be a May wedding."

"I'm sure it will be beautiful, so let me see what I can do to help you," she says, eyeing Sharon up and down. "You appear to be a size eight, dear."

Bewildered, her head spinning trying to make sense of the situation, Sharon stammers, "Uh, no. You're very kind, I'm more like a ten. Sometimes twelve, it depends."

Sharon whispers, nudging Howie with her elbow. "I'm not trying on any damn dresses."

"Be a good sport, just play along."

"Please come into our fitting room and make yourselves comfortable," she says, ushering them into a smaller fabric-walled space, chandeliers overhead, a couch in the middle and mirrors on three sides.

"Will this be an afternoon or evening wedding?"

"Afternoon," Howie answers. "A beautiful spring afternoon."

Sharon is looking at Howie like he's lost his mind.

"I'll be right out with some things for you to try on. Just give me a minute," she says, closing the door to the salon.

"Howie, what the hell is going on here?"

"We're in Winn's hands, you play by his rules."

"I'm worried. I wish we'd brought Mark along."

"Winn's email specifically instructed us to leave him at the motel, and assured me he'd have people watching him. No way he's going to let anything happen to Risstup."

A door suddenly opens and a man dressed in a tweed carcoat and green felt hat steps out, announcing, "So this is the lucky couple—"

From Howie's description, Sharon recognizes him immediately.

"Winn, good to see you, buddy," Howie says, standing and giving Winn a hug—one of those brief clasps, more a series of quick pats than an embrace, which men do so they don't act too intimate. "I'm glad you brought us in, things were getting hairy out there."

"I can believe it," Winn says. Straub is short, Howie has a good three inches on him. Sharon quickly sees the resemblance to the famous actor and Straub's personable manner immediately puts her at ease.

Noticing Howie's condition, two-day growth, rumpled clothes, he says, "Boy, you could some cleaning up—a little down at the heels, buddy."

"We haven't had much spare time. Winn, I'd like you to meet Sharon Thorsen, my partner in this adventure."

"It's a pleasure to meet you, I've certainly heard a lot about you," Straub says as he shakes Sharon's hand.

"I'm sorry I look such a mess," she apologizes.

"Not to worry, we'll take care of that. Please excuse all this silliness but the bridal salon turns out to be the easiest place to secure in the entire mall."

"Pretty neat treasure hunt you put on for us," Sharon says.

"Wait'll you see what else I have in store. C'mon, follow me," he says as he turns back to the doorway. "We don't have a lot of time. I'll explain later."

"Where are you taking us?" Sharon asks.

Holding the door for Sharon and Howie, he explains, "We've secured an area in one of the store's workrooms. Nothing fancy but it suits our purposes." They follow Winn down a long corridor and around a corner. Winn stops at a door guarded by two twentysomething men with short haircuts and dark suits. They stand stiffly against the wall, both sporting earpieces, the transparent cords spiraling down into their collars. Straub can see the black nylon strap of a holster under one man's coat. As Sharon and Howie walk past them, the men's eyes follow but do not say hello.

"Come on in. Welcome to CIA—Tysons Corner Division," Straub says as he holds the door open for them. It's a nondescript office, a receptionist sitting behind a desk and an attendant in a pink smock standing off to one side. "Young lady, I know the past week's been pretty rough and tumble for you," he says to Sharon. "So while Howie and I catch up on things, I thought you might enjoy a personal makeover, courtesy of Neiman Marcus."

"You know how to get to a girl's heart, Mr. Straub," she says.

"Call me Winn. After what you've been through it's the least we could do."

The lady in pink steps forward. "Please come with me, Ms. Thorsen," she says, motioning to an adjoining hallway.

"See you boys later," Sharon waves goodbye. "And don't go planning anything behind my back."

"Let's sit down in here," Straub says, opening the door to a small conference room off to the side of the receptionist's desk. "Anything I can get you? Soda or water, coffee?"

"No, thanks." Howie sits down at the conference table catty-corner to Straub.

"Sharon Thorsen is one impressive lady."

"You wouldn't believe what she's pulled off in the past week."

"I'm sure. But she's going to have to sit out the next phase."

"You're going to have a fight on your hands."

"She's a nurse, Howie, she can't play in this league."

"What makes you think *I* can?"

"We'll talk about that later. In the meantime, I have a surprise for you."

Howie hears a door open behind him, then a sudden wail of shock and delight from a voice he immediately recognizes.

"Howie!" he turns just as Sylvie rushes into his arms, throwing herself against him, showering kisses all over his face and neck. Howie hardly notices Grace, who saunters in behind Sylvie, head cocked, scowl on her face, looking bent out of shape.

"Are you all right?" Howie can feel Sylvie touching him all over as if she's trying to make sure he's in one piece. "I was beside myself when Winn told me what happened in Front Royal."

Howie darts a glance at Winn, he shrugs his shoulders as if to say, *I couldn't help it.* "I'm going to leave you folks alone for a while. I'll be back," he says, ducking out of the room and quietly pulling the door shut behind him.

"I'm okay, I'm fine."

"You're damn lucky, that's what you are, Daddy," Grace chimes in. Howie knows he's in for a long afternoon.

"This has been the longest week I've ever gone through in my entire life. I couldn't eat, I couldn't sleep, look—" Sylvie says, leaning back from him and hooking her thumb in her waistband, flapping it back and forth. "I've lost six pounds."

"You look great," Howie says, giving her another kiss then taking her hand in his and sitting her down on the sofa next to him. "And Grace, you too."

Sylvie's all over him, arranging his hair, straightening his collar. "Have you been eating? You look like you're wasting away."

"We've been busy."

"Has this nurse been cooking for you, what's her name?"

"Sharon Thorsen. We mostly eat carryout, no time for cooking."

"I'd like to meet her."

"She's getting a makeover right now." Howie tries changing the subject without appearing obvious. "So Winn has been taking good care of you?"

"You've been with her for an entire week. I want to meet her."

Howie can tell Sylvie isn't backing down. "We'll arrange that. So how's life at Camp Peary, Grace?"

"Just dandy—if you enjoy being in prison," Grace snorts. "If it wasn't for a couple hunk CIA agents down there, I would've busted out days ago."

"We've been going bonkers. They won't let us leave our cabin. Neither Grace nor I are very good at being cooped up. Howie."

"I'm sorry, but under the circumstances, it's the best—"

"Bullshit, Daddy. We are virtual prisoners, sentries all around us, no contact with the outside world except for that bogus phone connection Straub gave us where we can only talk to him. Christ, they might as well be pushing our damn food in through a slot."

"What do you hear from Bridey and Donald?"

"Your pal Straub has them under his thumb, they're being watched day and night."

"At least you're all safe."

"Yeah, but you're not. Straub's got you running around looking for lost nukes with the whole world chasing you. People burning down your motel, blowing up your car."

This is the first time Howie's heard anything about his car, but he's not about to start asking questions about it.

"Howie, you've got to stop this craziness. Grace and I have made up our minds. You're coming home with us right now."

He tries to act nonchalant, breezily saying, "I'll be back soon, we still have a few things to take care of."

Grace is going for the jugular. "What the hell is that supposed to mean, *things to take care of*?"

"Just a couple, you know, finishing touches."

"You've found the bomb then—that's all taken care of?" Sylvie fumes.

"More or less—" Howie nods, but not convincingly enough to cool her down.

His wife's eyes sizzle, Howie knows that's not a good sign. Grace has her hands planted on her hips, ready for a fight.

"You haven't, have you? You're still chasing the damn thing!"

"Daddy, when are you going to realize that hunting for lost bombs is not good for your health?"

"Guys, please, in a couple more days it will be over, I promise."

"Howie, I've had it up to here with your promises. You gave me your word you wouldn't go sticking your nose into this mess, then you do. I saw your car right there on TV, blazing away on the national news—how do you think that makes me feel?"

"Three more days is all I ask."

"No! Not one damn day more," Grace declares. "I don't want you coming back in a bag. Can't you understand?"

"That's not going to happen." Howie stands up and slowly turns around to face down his wife and daughter. "Okay, look. Since you two aren't listening to reason, let me outline the situation for you. A ghost program at the Pentagon is trying to run me down because I know something I shouldn't. So it isn't a question of going home or stopping what I'm doing. I don't have any choice but to keep on."

"What do you mean you don't have any choice?"

"Do I have to spell it out for you? Either I follow this thing through or my life isn't worth a damn. I'm sorry but that's the way it is. Now Winn's backing me up on this—"

"Oh, I bet he is."

"We've been in touch every day, he's watching out for me."

"Of course he is, because he's using you. He's dying to unmask this

Pentagon program and he's putting you at risk to do it. Don't you see that?"

"It's more complicated than that."

"And a damn sight more dangerous too."

"Just three more days and I'll pack it up and come home. Monday, okay? Is that too much to ask?" The door opens. Howie looks up.

Sylvie whirls around, it's Winn Straub standing in the doorway. "Speaking of the devil," she says, not making the least attempt to be diplomatic.

"I wish I could give you guys more time, but we've got work to do." Winn is looking down at his watch.

Grace says, "Time to ship the wife back to prison again, huh? Let her have a few minutes with her husband then send her back to solitary."

"I'm sorry. But given the circumstances—"

"Spare us, Howie already gave us that *given the circumstances* crap."

Sylvie is glaring at Straub. "Does your wife have any idea what you're up to?

"No, she doesn't."

"I guess she's the lucky one then. Keep the little lady in the dark so she won't upset the apple cart."

Howie stands up, takes both her hands in his and pleads, "Sylvie, please, it's going to be okay, I just need a little more time."

"And then what?"

"Then we can put all this behind us."

Grace counters, "Don't let him off the hook, Mother. We had an agreement."

Sylvie pauses a minute. Then says, her voice firm and resolute as if she's drawing a line in the sand, "I want to meet the woman—the nurse. I'm not leaving until I do."

"I'll get her," Straub says, hustling back out the door he came in, happy to get out of the line of fire.

When the door clicks shut, Sylvie moans, "Jesus, Howie, why couldn't you have just left this whole thing alone? Why did you have to go and stick your fingers into it again? It makes me so damn angry." She can't hold back the tears, throws her arms around him, blubbering and sobbing. Howie lets her have a good cry, holding her until he hears the door open behind him.

"Excuse me," Winn Straub says. Howie and Sylvie turn to see Winn ushering Sharon Thorsen into the room. Howie hardly recognizes her. Wearing a bright magenta smock, even with her face half-madeup she looks like a new woman, five years younger, smiling, glamorous and radiant.

"You must be Mrs. Collyer, I'm Sharon Thorsen, good to meet you, and you're Howie's daughter, Grace," she says, stepping forward and holding out her arm, shaking hands with both of them. "Please, excuse the way I look. I'm in the midst of a makeover."

Sylvie daubs her eyes with a Kleenex. "I'm afraid I'm not much to look at myself."

"I've heard a lot about you, Mrs. Collyer. All your husband does is talk about you."

Sylvie's eyes brighten, the hint of a smile glints on her face. She waves Sharon's compliment away with her hand. "Don't be silly."

"I mean it."

"I appreciate you looking out for him."

"On the contrary, he's been taking care of me. I'm just along for the ride."

"That's not what Winn says."

"I do my best." Sharon cocks her head and winks at Sylvie. "If you don't mind me telling you, sometimes your husband can get a little pig-headed."

"My Howie—pig-headed?" Sylvie manages to smile for the first time. "You mean the man with lost bombs on the brain?"

"Sometimes he does have a one-track mind."

"So you haven't been able to talk any sense into him either?"

"Once in a while—"

"She's been a big help," Howie adds.

"I want you to know something, Mrs. Collyer. I don't know if it's going to make any difference to you but I have to take responsibility for involving Howie in the first place. Had I not made that call to your husband on Thanksgiving, we wouldn't be facing this."

"I appreciate you saying that."

"I can imagine this is very hard for you and I regret being the cause of it. But I had no choice. It was a life-or-death situation."

"I appreciate that," Sylvie says.

Grace nods, seconding her mother's statement. Now that Sharon has managed to defuse the situation, Howie knows he has to keep his trap shut. They awkwardly look around at each other, no one knowing what to say until Straub interrupts, "Folks, I hate to be the bad guy here but we're running short of time and we've got some unfinished business to take care of, so if you don't mind I'll escort you ladies out so Howie and I can get our work done."

Howie embraces Sylvie, "It's going to be all right," he says into her ear as he gives her a final hug. She separates from him, starting to let go again.

He throws his arms around his daughter and plants a peck on her cheek.

"I'll keep my fingers crossed for you, Daddy," she says, putting her arm around Sylvie and heading toward the door. Howie tries to smile confidently, acting like everything is going to be all right. Even though he knows he's not fooling anyone.

"You be careful," Sylvie says, wagging her finger at him as she disappears out the door accompanied by Straub and Sharon.

"I will," he says.

"You better," Howie hears her call over her shoulder just as the door closes behind her.

"Your Sylvie's a trooper," Straub says, coming back into the room. Howie notices an envelope tucked under his arm.

"Wish you hadn't told her about the car."

"Nothing to be gained by lying. She would have figured it out. Enjoyed meeting Grace. She's a piece of work."

"Broke the mold when she was born. What was that business about my car being blown up?"

"Vector Eleven booby-trapped it, blew a tow truck operator into the next county."

"Damn glad I didn't go back for it. What's in the envelope?"

"We've just identified the terrorists, caught them on film outside."

"I thought I shook them back in Baltimore."

"Hardly. They're sticking to you like glue. My people got some shots of them and ran them against our databases. They're as bad as they come."

"I'm not surprised."

Straub opens the envelope and pulls out a sheaf of photographs, spreading them out on the conference table for Howie to inspect.

"You guys work fast," Howie says, leaning over to look at the photos—telephoto shots of the cab they took over to Tysons, a man standing surveying the cab, another by an entrance to the mall holding packages as if he's waiting for his wife, a third handing out fliers at another entrance, innocuous-looking photographs of men engaged in everyday activities.

"I doubt the names would mean anything to you but they are major players, dedicated mujahideen. Four years ago the three vanished. The feeling around the intelligence community was that they were dead. One killed in a bombing, another was thought to have died in a firefight outside of Kandahar, and Aziz Odeh was supposedly in a group taken out by a Predator in Yemen. I have always maintained that they might have survived, but I was one of the few."

"Now you're proven right."

"They went underground. Waiting for you to lead them to a nuke."

"When I got that call from Sharon at the hospital, they must have gone into action. Could have masterminded that whole mess in Front Royal and followed us to Baltimore."

"That's why you must spearhead this operation. You obviously have their trust."

"Spare me the irony."

"Don't think I haven't thought about it."

"So what's the plan?"

"You're going to locate the nuke."

"What? Cruise around on the Chesapeake Bay until I bump into the damn thing?"

"We have a top-notch Coast Guard outfit to help you conduct the search, they'll give you all the cover you need. I think you'll be impressed. The Secretary of Homeland Security is personally supervising the operation. And I'll be looking over his shoulder."

"And if I find the bomb—what happens then? What's to keep them from blowing me out of the water?"

"Hopefully we'll be able to neutralize the terrorists before that."

Howie's on edge, the words tumble out of his mouth faster than he can make sense of them. "Do you have any idea what their plans are?

Are they going to attempt a water recovery? Retrieve enough materials to make a dirty bomb and transport it to D.C. or New York? Or try to detonate the nuke in the water? We don't even know how many of them there are. There could be three or thirty. So much is up in the damn air."

Straub stays cool and calm. "It's a developing situation, no question about it. They could be set for a deep recovery with tugs and barges, or a simpler operation in shallow water—whatever that means. We won't know until you locate the nuke. Either way, if we don't expose the sleeper cells and deal with them now, who knows what other unrecovered nukes they could go after in the future. So it's now or never—you know that."

"I also know I'm the bait."

"Let's use the term *decoy.*"

"Bait, decoy, what's the difference?"

"I don't need to tell you I've agonized over this. Christ, I've barely slept. But I think we've both understood from the minute you took that phone call from the VA hospital that we had a rare opportunity."

"What about Vector Eleven? How do you think they figure in?"

"We won't know until they play their hand. But I suspect that when they learn that terrorists are involved in an attempt to recover one of their lost nukes, they'll come over to our side in a second. Even though it means blowing their cover, the last thing they'd want is for one of their bombs to be used against this country."

"But again, their involvement makes everything even more chancy."

"I'm not denying that. But I have a trump card I can play if we have to."

"Don't keep it a secret."

"Abner Dickson is going to be down in Tennessee with the president this weekend checking out some expensive horseflesh."

"So if I find the nuke and you can keep the terrorists at bay, you've got an open channel to the president. Dickson can lay the whole thing out for him."

"The Pentagon will take the heat and you'll be a damn hero."

"Plus the CIA's stock will go up immediately. Not to mention Winn Straub going out on a high note. You have to admit you've thought of that."

"Nothing like a little enlightened self-interest. But look at the upside for all of us. If we can turn the situation to our advantage, we can expose Vector Eleven's out-of-control weapons programs and force the president to take a stand. Cut the Pentagon down to size and recover all these lost nukes—everything you've been crusading for all these years."

"It's going to take perfect timing."

Straub nods. "No question, much of this is going to have to be handled on the fly. We're going to have to improvise depending on what al Qaeda does and how Vector Eleven reacts. But I can assure you, the entire resources of the CIA and DHS will be devoted to making this operation work."

"And the entire resources of a black program at the Department of Defense will be devoted to making sure it doesn't. Not to mention a bunch of fanatic terrorists."

Straub sidesteps Howie's statement, looking down at his watch and saying, "We really should get going."

Howie stands, abruptly ending the conversation, "I don't need any more time, Winn. I'm in. Let's go."

Straub extends his hand. Howie takes it. They shake hands firmly. Straub claps him on the back. "Back in your football days, what was the term you used for a perfect kick?"

"You mean *nailing it*?"

Winn gives Howie a last pat on the back, "Yes, *nailing it*. That's what we're going to do, we're going to nail this one, Howie."

"Thanks for the pep talk," Howie responds as he thinks to himself, *Easy for you to say, Winn, buddy, easy for you to say.*

"Now let's get you back outside so our friends don't decide they've lost you. They will think you went out for a little pre-Christmas shopping. In their minds all Americans do is shop anyway. When you pick a cab, make sure the taxi's number ends in double eights. That way you'll know the driver's one of us." Straub pushes a button on the conference room phone and says, "Please send Ms. Thorsen in if she's ready."

Ten seconds later, the door opens and Sharon sashays in, beaming and proudly showing off her stylish new suit. "Not only am I relaxed for the first time in a week," she says, turning and pirouetting in front of them, gushing over her new clothes, "but I feel like I'm starring in some fashion show. Don't you love my suit? And how about these heels?" Sharon admires her new shoes over her shoulder. "Thank you so much, Winn."

"My pleasure," he says. "Compliments of the American taxpayers. They owe you a new outfit at least."

Sharon stops. Her attention pivots from Straub's face to Howie's. "Wait a minute, why are you both looking so stonyfaced? Is there something you need to tell me?"

Straub turns to her, "You've done a great job helping Howie, Sharon. We all appreciate it."

"This is a brushoff?"

"No reason to take it that way."

"You're trying to buy me off with a makeover and a new suit?"

Howie shoots a look at Winn and lifts an eyebrow.

"This is a male thing, huh? No women allowed?"

"We'll take care of you until this is over," Winn says.

"What? Park me down at The Farm while Howie does your dirty work?"

Howie looks at Winn and shrugs, smiling at him as if to say, *I tried to tell you. I knew she wouldn't stand for this.*

"It's just too dangerous, Sharon," Straub says.

She whirls around and leans down so she's right in Straub's face. "And what do you think this past week has been—a picnic? I've been playing nursemaid to an eighty-year-old while dodging people who are trying to blow us up. Then we find the damn bomb's in the Chesapeake and it's threatening the entire Eastern Seaboard and you have the gall to try and buy me off and ship me home!"

Sharon boils over, pulling off her heels and slamming them down on the table in front of Straub. "You can have your damn shoes back! I'll go change back into my clothes and you can have the frigging suit too!"

"I hope you realize this means putting yourself in even more jeopardy," Straub says quietly.

Sharon glares at him. "You're going to use Howie to bait the trap and you expect me to sit on the damn sidelines wringing my hands like some nervous Nellie? C'mon, Mr. Straub, this is the twenty-first century we're living in. I may be a woman, but I'm not a little girl!"

"I just want to make sure you know what you're getting into," Straub says, knowing it's time to back down.

"You're not going to take me out of the game while Howie puts his life on the line."

Howie stands, a smug smile breaking across his face. "I guess that settles that. Unless you have something else to add, Winn."

"I'd say Ms. Thorsen has made her case pretty clear," he says, getting up and opening the door. Still steamed, Sharon snatches her shoes off the table and storms out.

"Before you go," Straub says to Howie. "Let me give you a few things you'll need."

Hustled out the employee entrance of the mall by one of Straub's men, Howie's carrying packages to make it look like they've been on a shopping spree. He checks the number on the cab waiting at the curb. The last two digits are eights so they pile in for the ride back to Baltimore. Howie scans the surrounding area for the three men he saw in the photos. Just before ducking into the backseat of the cab, he isn't certain but he thinks he sees one hovering behind a car in the parking lot. *Or is it just my rampant paranoia?*

"Except for trying to sideline me, Winn seems like a nice guy," Sharon says.

"You sure gave him a piece of your mind," Howie says, pulling the door shut.

"This isn't the way I imagined spending the holidays, but I wasn't going to leave you and the major in the lurch."

"I tried to tell Winn you wouldn't stand for it."

"Probably would have made it neater if there were fewer people involved, a woman in particular. But I wasn't going to back down. Plus I want to see how you get yourself out of this one."

"You're not the only one who's interested in finding out how I pull that off, I'd like to know myself," Howie says.

He picks up the new cell phone that Straub gave him to replace their email communication. Straub explained that it works on a secure radio frequency proprietary to CIA. "Even our best people can't hack into it, and believe me, during shakedown we tried," Winn told him. "It's a failsafe way for us to communicate."

Sharon turns to look out the cab window at the expanse of expressway zipping by. She's surprised at how strongly she reacted to Straub's suggestion that she pull out. *What's infuriating was that Straub thought he could buy me off with a makeover while he and Howie made all the important decisions. Hell, if he'd included me in the discussion and asked me point blank if I wanted to be let off the hook, I might just have said yes.*

"I enjoyed meeting your wife and daughter," Sharon says. "This can't be easy on them."

"I appreciated what you said to them. I think it helped."

"Frankly, I'm surprised Winn brought them up here. It had to be hell to see you for such a short time."

"I think Sylvie wanted to size you up."

"Wives don't like their husbands staying in motels with strange women."

"What did she think you were going to do, seduce me?" Howie says with a wink.

"You know, Collyer, I hate to let you down but that's the last thing that has occurred to me."

"I must admit, Nurse Thorsen, I'm kind of disappointed."

"Don't take it personally. In another place and time, I could fall for you, Collyer. You're smart, you're kind of sexy and you're a sweetheart."

"I'm too old for you."

"Not necessarily," she says, smiling at him cagily. "But don't go getting any ideas. It's not in the cards, okay?"

"Whatever you say, boss."

"I haven't permanently damaged your male ego?"

"Nothing that a few years of therapy won't fix."

"So what's Straub got in mind for us?"

"Sit tight. I expect we'll hear from him soon. In the meantime, Winn wants me to run the calculations on the course Risstup's plane took and see if I can pin down precisely where the bomb was jettisoned."

"Then what are we going to do—rent a boat and go sailing around looking for it?"

"No way. Winn's setting up a substantial Coast Guard operation. Low profile but I bet it will be full bore."

"Do you have any idea of what the Chesapeake Bay's like in December?"

"Is it December already?"

Sharon glances at the face of her watch. "Sure is. Time flies when you're having fun. By the way, I like my new outfit and I appreciated the makeover. Thanks for setting that up for me."

"No problem. You look great."

"That's sweet of you to say."

A few minutes pass, both of them gazing out the windows at the I-95 roadscape whipping by, and then a propos of nothing Sharon turns to him and says, "Collyer, can I tell you something?"

"Go right ahead."

He's seen the look before, he knows a zinger's coming. She doesn't disappoint.

"I'm scared shitless."

"If it makes you feel any better, so am I."

"Then tell me."

"What?"

"Say—*I'm scared shitless*."

"Okay, I'm scared shitless."

"Good."

"Feel better?"

"A lot."

Howie smiles as they make the turnoff toward Baltimore. In a flash, Sharon's head has lolled back against the seat, her eyes are closed, mouth open slightly, she's snoring lightly, the girl's totally zonked out.

As Howie looks over at her he can't help thinking, *Funny what some people find comforting.*

34

[Solo, Indonesia, early Saturday morning, EST +12]

He hasn't slept in days, only allowing himself a half hour catnap on the cot in his office every eight hours. He eats little for fear of falling asleep. His beard itches. He would like to clean up but he cannot afford to be away from his computer. El-Khadr sits at his desk, his eyes fixed on the screen. The last stage of any operation is always demanding. The Arabic phrase to describe it translates to *the time tension has to be welcomed with open arms.*

He remembers back when they launched the planes operation—the endless waiting for the teams to be trained, the thousands of details, hundreds of forged passports, the shipments of money painstakingly disguised to pass through customs undetected. And then after years of work and interminable months of delays, after setting all the players in place, the last twenty days slowly ticked by with no communication from the field until the incredible morning that made all their effort worthwhile.

Three years of meticulous planning have gone into the Flowers project. Dahlia for shallow-water situations, Chrysanthemum for deep water—both are on schedule. The salvage tug and crew are on alert and his cells are scrambling to put the finishing touches on the installations along the Chesapeake. If Allah smiles on his operation and they are fortunate to locate a bomb in shallow water, Mehran Zarif will be set to strike.

Jamal's reported from their facility in Philadelphia that Mehran underwent his first practice session in the tank yesterday, placing the collars on the mock weapons again and again.

In early December visibility is at a minimum. At twenty feet

Mehran will be lucky to see his hand in front of his face. At forty, it will be like swimming through ink. His facemask will be partially blacked-out during the final training, shifting the position of the bomb so that at each attempt, Mehran will confront a new challenge.

Then Jamal will change the bomb model and send Mehran back into the tank again. Fifty, seventy-five, a hundred times, each time clocking him until he is in and out of the water faster and faster.

El-Khadr is pleased. With the pool and tank training, Mehran is a finely tuned machine. Free-diving with his monofin, he can zip to the target in seconds. In deeper water, even with his scuba gear, his unique stroke can take him effortlessly to the bottom. Depending on the depth, El-Khadr is confident Mehran can be in the water and down to the bomb in a remarkably short time. Jamal estimates the longest as two minutes, the shortest thirty seconds.

His strike will be lightning fast. Even if Mehran is right under the eyes of the Americans, he will be able to detonate the bomb before they know what hits them.

And thinking of his final touch, El-Khadr has to smile. Though Mehran is devoted and exhaustively trained and as comfortable in the water as a fish, he is still human. El-Khadr has seen suicide bombers get panicky and detonate their charges prematurely. No matter how dedicated, when your finger is on the button it is easy for the palms to get sweaty and the will to falter. And when drugs are given to calm the nerves, disorientation too easily results.

For Mehran, he has found the perfect solution. Though Jamal has instructed Mehran to climb back into the boat and use the remote to detonate the collar, he will never have the chance. The second Mehran clicks the collar into place around the bomb the circuit inside will be completed and two milliseconds later the Semtex will detonate, simultaneously triggering the four hundred-pound TNT charge and setting off the atomic chain reaction that will begin the hydrogen bomb's fusion process.

In one glorious moment, a towering mushroom of billowing radiation will erupt in the skies over the East Coast, Mehran's atomized body soaring up in its center, sending out a shock wave that will bowl over buildings twenty miles away followed by a searing firestorm that will immolate everything in its path.

Now it is time to wait for the plan to unfold.

He suddenly sits forward and stares at the screen, alarmed by the post that appears on the website. El-Khadr scans it carefully, then reads it again. *How could they lose Collyer like that? At a mall of all places?*

He checks the time. He disappeared inside the shopping center at 1:35 EST—in the middle of the afternoon. But how? Why would he be shopping at a time like this? Then he remembers it is Christmas in the West. Collyer must have succumbed to the buying mania himself.

A new post pops on the screen and El-Khadr breaks into an uncustomary smile as he reads the message. *Cindy is back in the dahlia garden, we eagerly await her digging up her prize dahlias in anticipation of the approaching winter.*

He leans back in his chair. Whatever caused Collyer to go shopping in the mall, he is now back in their sights again.

"Naguib," he calls as he stands and grabs his riding crop off his desk. "Come, let us take a tour and make sure everyone is prepared. I believe the time is approaching."

Naguib is out of his chair before El-Khadr exits his office. Though he knows El-Khadr hasn't had more than a couple hours' sleep in the past day, you couldn't tell from the way he moves. His peg leg taps like a quickening metronome on the concrete floor. Naguib is eager to go inside the operation's control room for the first time. He has only had a chance to peek in, peering around people as they entered and left. Two security guards, hiding their khat sticks and shouldering their Kalashnikovs, shuffle out of his way as El-Khadr elbows past them and stalks up to the entrance. El-Khadr's fingers tap out the code and the door clicks open.

Though the programming Naguib is doing on his side of the wall is state-of-the-art, when he steps through the doorway he's stunned at what he sees.

"A mission control room, just like NASA," El-Khadr says proudly as Naguib stands, taking in the impressive installation. Banks of workstations crowd the large room, two men to a station, each with a desktop computer and its own large plasma screen suspended overhead, satellite pictures of different areas displayed on the monitors, the entire East Coast of the United States arrayed on the walls.

"No matter where Collyer goes, we can track him in real time with instant updates not only from satellite, but from remote cameras we can position anywhere. Unless the bomb was jettisoned over the Continental Shelf in thousands of fcet of water, we will be capable of directing retrieval. And if we are extremely fortunate, a simpler option will present itself to us."

"You mean *Dahlia*?"

El-Khadr nods. Then smiles and says, "Yes, a hundred Hiroshimas in the Chesapeake."

35

[Pentagon, Friday afternoon]

Watt hears a knock on his door. He looks up to see Hatkin striding into his office, crisply closing the door behind him, a man on a mission.

"Good afternoon, sir," Watt says. From the expression on Hatkin's face, it doesn't look like the day's going well. Walking over to a window, Hatkin stands gazing out at the expanse of parked cars, his mind somewhere else.

"Anything I can get for you? Coffee, soft drink?"

Hatkin shakes his head. After a long pause, he says, "The SecDef just called. He wanted to know if I knew anything about the Coast Guard scrambling a unit out of Little River, Virginia."

"The Coast Guard—Jesus. When did they do that?"

"In the middle of the night."

"What did you tell him?"

"I didn't have any choice. I told him the truth—I don't know a damn thing about it."

"That's has to be Jimmick over at DHS. He beefed up that unit recently, brought in a lot of new people. From what I've heard, it's not a bunch of Coasties anymore. Do we know where they went?"

"I made a few calls. Had someone at Naval Intelligence check. He said the entire place was cleared out. Coffee cups sitting around, half-eaten chow, unmade racks. Like they all just scrammed at a moment's notice."

Hatkin loosens his tie and sits down in a chair, returns to staring out through the tinted windows.

"Somehow Jimmick must have an inside track," Watt offers.

"But how? What can he know? Homeland Security has as much intel capacity as the Department of Agriculture."

Watt can tell Hatkin's feeling the heat. With the Coast Guard involved, now the situation is spinning out of control. And with pressure coming down from the top, he's running out of options. The finger's pointing at him. The top brass would take him to task for everything. Rake him over the coals for allowing lost nukes to surface as an issue, lay the blame on him for not informing them earlier of the terrorist threat—they would assume control of the operation and take credit for the outcome. Then they would eat him alive. Bust him down to colonel and retire him to a one-bedroom concrete block bungalow on the outskirts of some military base in the middle of nowhere to live out his days puttering around in the garden and taking orders from his wife.

And there's no point in calling the group together, he has nothing to tell them. They'd see through any tap dancing he tried to do. Better to leave them in the dark. For the first time in his career, Whitey Hatkin is up the creek without a paddle. And Watt knows he's sitting in the same boat, right alongside his boss.

The bigger they are, the harder they fall. As banal as the phrase sounds, both officers know it's dead on unless they find a way to regain control.

"There's always the possibility the Little River business could be something totally unrelated to Collyer," Watt offers, groping for light at the end of the tunnel.

"Of course, but we can't dismiss Collyer until we rule out his involvement for certain. What I don't get is that with all the resources at our disposal how Collyer has avoided us."

"Unless Winston Straub is orchestrating the whole thing."

"But he's just one guy. Even if he has the Agency's support, the CIA has no domestic capability, no operatives in country, no fleet and no aircraft. And what is Straub—fifty-eight, fifty-nine? That boy's ready for shuffleboard, not a high stakes game involving terrorists and hydrogen bombs. I don't care what he did in Eastern Europe. That was twenty years ago. Have you seen him lately?"

"I run into him occasionally."

"Nebbish, if you ask me. Paunchy, out of shape, looks like a real estate agent out in the burbs, wears duffel coats and suede shoes and one of those fuzzy hats with mallard feathers on the side—that kind of thing. Wife's got all the money, big social climber, supposed to be a bitch on wheels. I know Straub's an old buddy of Collyer but the thing doesn't stack up."

Hatkin sits forward in his chair and reaches across Watt's desk for the roll of Tums. "Mind if I have one?"

"Take as many as you like."

Watt watches as Hatkin peels off three tablets from the roll before tossing it back on the desktop.

"I'm going to activate the unit out of Belvoir, Black Hawks and Apaches to do flyovers of the Chesapeake, get an AWACS into the air to keep an eye on things. Then I'm going to check and see what friends we have in the Coast Guard. Maybe somehow we can neutralize whatever Jimmick has going there. And get some Special Ops people poking around. See if anyone's up to anything."

"What are you going to tell them to look for?"

Watt isn't sure if he's ever seen General Hatkin look stymied before. "Damned if I know," he says.

Watt volunteers, "It's grasping at straws, but years ago when I was stationed down in Florida, Jimmick and I handled some operations together. I could visit him, put quarters in and see what comes out. Push him on Little River, poke around about Collyer, bring up the subject of terrorists, watch his body language. It might be worth a try."

Hatkin gets up, snugs up his tie and straightens out his coat as he says with a snicker, "I never thought we'd find ourselves playing up to the Secretary of Homeland Security."

Watt is about to add, *or running around like a chicken with its head cut off on account of Howie Collyer,* but thinks better of it.

"My driver can run you up there," Hatkin volunteers and then edits himself. "On second thought, maybe you'd better take a cab."

Lucien Jimmick knows he's running on fumes. Ten years ago, he would have been fine. Now just inside sixty, if he doesn't get a good night's sleep, he's not worth much the next day. Awakened by Straub at two in the morning, followed by a long series of phone calls with Little Creek and his operation center, he's ragged around the edges.

A shower temporarily revives him. He buttons up a fresh shirt, puts on a tie, grabs his coat and heads down the hall. His wife is waiting at the bottom of the stairs, wearing a robe and a forced smile, a sandwich held out on a plate in front of her.

"It's a fried egg melt, dear, your favorite," she says. Jimmick takes the sandwich as he stuffs his arm into his jacket.

"I wish you'd sit down at the table, Lucien."

"A few bites are all I need."

She runs her hand over the top of his head. "Your hair is still wet."

"It'll dry going over in the car," he says between mouthfuls of his egg on toast. He needs to get into the office where there's a secure stew as soon as possible. Straub could contact him at any minute.

"You know what your doctor said about eating on the run. It would take me only a minute to make some oatmeal. Or what about some fresh fruit? After all, it is seven o'clock in the morning."

"This is fine, thanks." Jimmick hands back the plate with his half-eaten sandwich, gives her a kiss and reaches for his overcoat.

"I know it's against the rules to ask, but can you give me an idea of how long this crisis is going to last?"

"No crisis, dear, it's just typical end-of-the-year stuff. Everybody has a list of things they want to get done before the holidays. There's nothing to worry about."

"Then maybe you can get off early this afternoon and come home and take a nap? Remember, we have the McDormands' wedding tomorrow. You'll want to be rested for that."

Jimmick tries to decide whether he should beg off now or wait until later. He knows it isn't prudent to let anyone know the Secretary of Homeland Security is canceling engagements. *I might even have to show up at the damn wedding*, he thinks, *just to keep things quiet*. Before he took the DHS job, Jimmick kept his wife up to speed about everything he had going at work, sharing the ins and outs of his operations as well the latest in office politics as it made good cover for his extracurricular philandering. Now he has to shut her down on everything since one innocent and inadvertent comment from her can make the cover of *The New York Times* the next morning.

He leans over and plants another kiss on her cheek. "You have a nice day, dear. I'll try to check in sometime during the day."

Cassie Jimmick stands at the door watching her husband double-timing down the walk toward his waiting car, briefcase in one hand, his other fumbling with the twisted collar of his overcoat. She hadn't noticed that his right shoelace is flopping around. Normally a fastidious dresser, her husband's untied shoelace confirms her suspicion—something significant is going down. Standing on the stoop watching as her husband's car pulls away, Cassie Jimmick says a silent prayer that this Washington craziness will soon be over and she will be back in sunny Miami arranging flowers with her garden club buddies.

Sliding into the backseat, Jimmick waves to his wife. She pastes on a cheery smile and waves back. He makes a mental note to send Cassie a dozen roses from the fancy florist in Georgetown.

Marcus, Jimmick's driver, wants to make small talk about the Redskins playoff chances. Jimmick pulls out his BlackBerry and acts like he has important work to do as the car pulls away from the curb.

Marcus isn't taking no for an answer. Looking at his boss in the rearview, he says, "If you ask me, Mr. Secretary, I say you got to point the darn finger at the quarterback situation. Just no way a guy who's close to forty has any business running the darn team—if you know what I mean."

Jimmick notices the laces on one of his shoes. *Damn, how did I miss that? I must be more distracted than I thought.* He's reaching down to tie them when his cell buzzes in his pocket.

"Hello?" Jimmick answers.

"Secretary Jimmick, it's Lewis."

"Good morning, Lewis." Tim Lewis is his scheduler, bright kid he brought up from Miami.

"I received a call this morning from the Pentagon. A man by the name of Watt, General Greg Watt."

"I know him. What does he want?" Down in Florida they teamed up on a few operations. Now he's Mr. Nuclear at the Pentagon, rumored to be involved in ghost programs up to his elbows, anything associated with radioactive materials from warheads to toxic waste spills. Part of the Vector Eleven group that knows where all the nuclear bodies are buried and dedicated to keeping them that way, he's the last person Jimmick would expect to be calling. But then, *maybe not—is Vector Eleven so in the dark about Collyer they are casting around for clues?*

"He wants to set up a meeting."

"Schedule him at the next available opening. I'll be there in a few minutes."

"I'll take care of it. Yes, sir."

Jimmick slaps his cell phone shut. His driver prattles on about the Skins quarterback situation as Jimmick wonders whether the Pentagon has discovered he's activated the Little River unit. News travels fast in this town. *But have they connected the unit to Collyer?* He'll soon find out.

Jimmick waves to the guard at the entrance to the Nebraska Avenue Complex. The sedan pulls up to the main building. The place looks so much like a college campus, Jimmick has often thought he could be mistaken for its dean. As his driver opens the door for him and Jimmick swings his feet to get out, he notices he forgot to tie his shoelace.

"Better tie these, huh, Marcus?" he says as he leans down. "Wouldn't be too good for the Secretary of Homeland Security to trip on his shoelaces going into work, now would it?"

Two hours later, General Greg Watt is in his office. Jimmick is glad to see he isn't the only one in Washington who isn't getting any sleep. Deep circles under his eyes, he's feigning a breezy manner and his uniform is crisp and creased, but nothing's hiding the fact that Watt's frazzled. He's playing it close to the vest, engaging in a bunch of small talk, weather, plans for the holidays, chitchat about mutual acquaintances down in Florida. *This is going to be interesting*, Jimmick thinks. He can't resist a wisecrack.

"What brings you in out of the dark, Greg? I thought you Vector Eleven guys were allergic to light."

Watt lets it pass. Standing and walking to the window and peering out at the grounds, its neatly tended walks and red brick buildings, he shifts the subject closer to home. "I have great respect for what you've done over here, Lucien. You've got this place nicely shaped up."

"We still have a lot of work to do."

"My father worked here during the war breaking Japanese codes, he was a cryptologist with the Navy."

"You don't say?"

"By 1945, there were five thousand people working here cracking codes day and night on crude, early versions of the computer. My father still insists it was the birthplace of the machine." Watt points out the window. "Right in that building over there."

"I didn't know that."

Watt sits back down. "This place has a interesting past. Did you know that before the Navy took it over it was a girls' school?"

"I did—Mount Vernon Seminary."

"Fascinating. I love history. Anyway, let me get down to the purpose of my visit," Watt says, sitting forward in his chair. He looks directly at Jimmick and pounces, "You activated a Coast Guard unit at Little River, Virginia sometime during the night."

"We have routine operations going on all over the country, just like you folks do over at the Pentagon," Jimmick parries.

"There was nothing routine about it. Our people down there said it looked like they were scrambled."

"I'll check on it if you'd like," Jimmick offers, reaching for the phone. "Can I ask why you're so interested in the activity of one of our Coast Guard units?"

"We think it has something to do with Howard Collyer."

This is going to be easy, Jimmick thinks, *Watt is on a major fishing expedition*. "Howard Collyer?"

"You know Collyer abducted a former B-52 pilot from a VA hospital."

"Howard Collyer?" Jimmick asks, adding a questioning tone. "Name sounds familiar. Where do I know him from?"

Watt shows his exasperation. "C'mon, Lucien. Don't play games."

"I beg your pardon?" Jimmick does his best to sound affronted.

"Collyer's chasing down a lost nuke and we have reason to believe a group of terrorists are shadowing him—you're aware of that. We know you are. And it's in our best interests to share information so we can defuse the situation."

Watt is practically begging for help. "Look, if that's true, Greg—and I certainly hope it isn't—it just goes to show how much more equipped and capable you guys are over there at the Pentagon. This is the first time I've heard anything about it."

Watt frowns and looks out the window. Jimmick is playing poker. And right now he's holding the better cards.

"Give me some more detail. Terrorists after this Collyer guy who's chasing down a lost nuke?"

"We can't be sure."

"But if there is a nuke out there, it certainly can't be a threat. I remember one briefing over at your place back when I first started. The nukes were lost—when was it? During the '50s and early '60s?"

Watt nods. Jimmick has him on the run.

"I distinctly remember the presenter saying that they have been degraded to the point they are harmless. That hasn't changed, has it?"

"That is still our position, yes."

Jimmick's toying with Watt now. He's never seen the slideshow, only heard about it secondhand, but that doesn't keep him from using it. "And if I remember correctly—as I said, this was a couple years ago—in the presentation there was a slide illustrated with a bunch of sleeping dogs. A whole pack of them, it was kind of endearing. One of your artists over there must have created it. And the caption was, 'Let Sleeping Dogs Lie.' The gist was that no matter if the lost weapons might be armed or dangerous, there was no point in disturbing them. Real cute picture—they were Dobermans or some breed like that. And they were all asleep in a pile. Am I remembering this correctly?" Jimmick furrows his brow, playing it for all it's worth.

Watt's eyes are jumping around the room, he doesn't know whether Jimmick's putting him on or he's for real. He quickly sidesteps, "So you know nothing about Howard Collyer and your intelligence has told you nothing about terrorists? No noise about al Qaeda?"

Watt's on the ropes. "Where am I supposed to get intel from, Greg, my wife's garden club? Do I have to remind you that the Department of Homeland Security has precious little intel capability? How can we be expected to know things you guys don't?"

Jimmick thinks of a perfect coup de grace. Walking around to stand in front of Watt, he lifts his hands in a gesture of helplessness, turns to him with a pained look on his face and says, "I mean, c'mon, Greg. This isn't the Pentagon with the National Security Agency and Defense Intelligence Agency plus the intelligence agencies of the Army, Navy, Air Force and Marines. This is a former girls' school—remember?"

In the cab returning to the Pentagon, Watt dials Hatkin's secure line.

"What did you find out?"

"Jimmick's in it up to his ears."

"Did he acknowledge scrambling the Coast Guard?"

"He wouldn't admit a damn thing, the bastard played cat and mouse but it was clear he's involved."

"He'll pay. I've found a way to get inside that unit of his."

"How?"

"I'll tell you when you get back to the Building. Let me just say I found out that the commanding officer of Jimmick's Coast Guard unit is a former Navy Seal."

For the first time in a week, a slight smile breaks across Watt's face. Back in Nam, Hatkin commanded a combined force of Army Rangers and Navy Seals. They went through hell together, a band of brothers if there ever was one. And Whitey Hatkin was their revered leader. In the tight circle of Navy Seals, Hatkin walks on water.

36

[New Brunswick, Friday afternoon]

Melanie's pride is wounded. He had no right. Yesterday her mother showed up to take them out to lunch. Called her the day before, said she wanted to meet her boyfriend. Made a reservation at a fancy restaurant, one of the best in Philadelphia. Denny promised her he would join them. Swore he would. She bought him a new Armani outfit to meet her mother, spent five hundred bucks on it. She couldn't wait to flaunt Denny, see the look on her mother's face. Then he didn't show. Worse, he disappeared. Didn't leave a message, wouldn't answer his cell. Her mother made the most of it. Creating a big fuss about the boyfriend who stood her up.

"Does he do this to you often, dear?" She wouldn't let go, bringing it up again and again, goading Melanie until she was on the verge of tears.

"I was looking forward to meeting him, but if he treats you like trash, I'd suggest you reexamine your relationship," her mother said, pausing to savor a bite of her thirty-two dollar sole Veronique and taking a long pull on her chardonnay before serving up another insult. "I'd hoped we'd given you more self-confidence. I'm surprised you let a boy walk all over you like this."

Melanie waited up to midnight for Denny, rehearsing the tongue-lashing she was going to give him. She thinks back over the past three days. Wednesday he insisted she drive him down to Philadelphia. He returned that night. Acted strangely. Wouldn't try on the clothes she bought him. Wasn't interested in sex. But he promised to meet her at the restaurant the next day.

The next morning he wouldn't answer his cell phone. Then he didn't show for lunch and didn't return until early Friday morning and was off again that afternoon. Had he moved out? Left her for good? She went into his room and rummaged around looking for clues as to where he went. As furious as she was, when she went into the bathroom the sight of something in the sink made her flesh crawl. Twenty seconds later, she was calling 911, her fingers trembling so much she could barely dial the number.

"Get me the FBI, please," Melanie Troost said in a quavering voice.

Normally Agent Fewell would have assigned one of her assistants to interview the student. But Fewell was a Rutgers grad herself and even though most terrorist tips turned out to be dead ends there were aspects of the girl's story that merited consideration. How many times had she heard the story about the Saudi convenience store manager who is running a terrorist group out of his 7-11—wild theories about explosives concealed in the storeroom among cases of Dr. Pepper, Lays potato chips and Mars Bars?

Agent Fewell listens patiently to the distraught Rutgers coed with her tale of deceit and mystery. It takes her no more than two minutes to decide her story has less to do with national security than it does with a relationship gone sour.

"So you don't think I'm crazy?"

"I can understand your concern, Miss Troost. And we appreciate it when citizens bring foreign nationals who are acting suspiciously to our attention."

"You don't think there's any terrorist connection? The terrorists in London did the same thing, cut off their beards before they blew up those trains."

"The fact someone shaves is hardly a cause for concern."

"But all the swimming, and you should have seen the weird way he acted in Philly."

Fewell turns up her palms and bunches her shoulders as if she's a long way from being alarmed.

"So you're not going to do anything?"

"What would you suggest?"

"Bring him in, interrogate him—something."

"See this stack of folders?" Fewell points at the corner of her desk. Melanie nods. How could she miss it? It's almost a foot high.

"In that pile are over a hundred and seventy-five leads I need to run down in the next week. Any one of them could take us to a terrorist."

"So explain to me what he's doing spending all this time in Philly."

"Don't take this the wrong way, but maybe you should consider the possibility your boyfriend is seeing someone else? Here's my card," Fewell says, handing it across the desk to Melanie. "Call me if he does anything else that seems suspicious."

Melanie goes into a slow broil. She feels her neck redden and her forehead light up. She doesn't know what's upsetting her more, the woman telling her Denny is cheating on her or that she refuses to believe her. She's insulted and embarrassed.

"There has to be something you can do—" she stammers.

"Look, young lady, I'm not in the business of giving advice, but if this guy's such a problem for you, why don't you just drop him?"

Melanie daubs at her eyes with a handkerchief. She jumps up and holds out her hand. "Thank you for taking the time to see me," she says, barely able to choke out the words. Turning to head out of the office, she feels like she's going to burst into tears if she stays a second longer.

"You have my card, Ms. Troost. You know where to reach me," Melanie hears the woman say. She's writing me off as a jilted lover. Melanie's tempted to whirl around and flip her off. *But that's probably a damn crime,* she thinks as she presses the DOWN button.

She's angry, humiliated, feeling sorry for herself and scared all at the same time. But her next thought makes her heart sink into her stomach.

What if Denny found out I went to the FBI? What if he followed me and is standing out on the street? The elevator opens to the lobby. She creeps through the revolving doors and cautiously steps outside. Looks both ways, and then scurries down the block to where she left her car. Melanie decides she's going to sleep at the sorority house tonight. Hang around with her sisters instead and pray he doesn't come looking for her.

The sight of her Range Rover parked around the corner from the FBI office is reassuring. She pushes the button on the remote as she approaches. The Rover comes to life.

Getting in, her car door hanging open as she tosses her purse on the seat beside her, she pauses, hearing an insistent voice coming from the middle distance, unintelligible but still loud enough to attract her attention. Looking in her rearview, she sees the FBI agent dashing down the sidewalk toward her wildly waving her arms, no coat on, her black flats slapping against the sidewalk.

"Ms. Troost! Ms. Troost! Wait!"

Melanie's first thought is she left something behind in the woman's office. But she's much too keyed up for that.

The agent comes rushing up to her open door. "I'm so glad I caught you," huffing to Melanie as she tries to catch her breath. "Your boyfriend, the man you were talking to me about—"

"Yes," says Melanie, puzzled as to why the woman who had dismissed her minutes ago is now suddenly so interested. "His name is Denny."

"Is there any chance he works out at the Werblin Center?"

"All the time—"

Before Melanie can complete her thought, the woman blurts out, "I just put two and two together. Come back to my office, we need to talk."

Melanie has never flown down the Pennsylvania Turnpike before—doing ninety with a siren screaming over her head, cars in front of the speeding convoy swerving off into the breakdown lanes to get out of the way, the black Suburban's red lights pulsing, reflecting off windows and the rain-stained pavement. Agent Fewell is in the seat beside her, Melanie's new best friend. The special agent in charge of the Newark FBI office is in the front next to the driver, everyone armed with menacing-looking guns. Melanie saw a rack of shotguns in the back of one van, heard someone mention tear gas and sniper rifles. These FBI guys are dead serious.

Turned out that Melanie wasn't the only person at Rutgers who had noticed Mehran Zarif. A varsity swimming coach had called the FBI months ago about his activities at the Werblin Center. The agent who took the call politely informed the coach there wasn't much the Federal Bureau of Investigation could do about a foreign student even if he had a bizarre swimming style and did odd exercises in the diving pool. Angela Fewell heard about the call over the water cooler later that day. All the agents had a good laugh—until earlier this afternoon when Melanie Troost gave Fewell a second perspective on the swimmer.

The Special Agent didn't need more than five minutes quizzing Melanie to decide her missing boyfriend was a threat. Too many curious coincidences that couldn't be overlooked. Racing her down to the underground parking area, the FBI agents jumped into a long line of waiting black SUVs and roared out of the basement heading for New Brunswick, the drivers slapping blinking lights on top of the cars and flicking on sirens.

Fewell leans into her and shouts over the deafening yowl, "Did you ever get a chance to see what was on his computer?" Fewell has a pad balanced on her knee. Before she wouldn't give her the time of day, now she's taking down every word Melanie says. And the guys in the front seat are leaning back to listen in.

Melanie loves being the center of attention and works the opportunity to get back at Mehran for all it's worth. "You have to understand. He always kept his room locked. Except once."

"You checked it then?"

"Of course," Melanie smiles, playing to the crowd.

"And?"

"What you'd expect of an engineering student, technical stuff."

"Anything to do with bombs or explosives?"

"Never could make much of it. I'm an English major, okay?"

Agent Rathon turns his head to ask her, "Did you ever go through his email?"

Melanie nods, "Of course but I couldn't find a thing. Whatever was so important to him on that computer must have been hidden somewhere."

"We'll send it to the lab as soon as we can get our hands on it."

Melanie can't wait to see his face when they arrest him, cuff him and push him down into a squad car. *It will serve him right. All the presents I lavished on him, the money I gave him, the dinners I bought. Turning the bastard in to the FBI is such sweet revenge.*

"We're going to send one team to check the dorm, the rest will head to the Werblin. Anyplace else we should look?"

"At this time of night, he's either at the dorm studying or he's in the pool at the rec center. Unless he's still in Philly."

"Where do you think we have the best chance?" Fewell asks.

"Fifty-fifty. Can I ask what are you going to do to him?"

"Take him in for questioning. There will be a lot of people who'll be very eager to talk to him."

"How long will that take?"

"Why? Is there something you want to say to him?"

Melanie shakes her head. "I don't care if I never see him again."

Fewell looks at the poor little rich girl with the bad complexion wearing a designer outfit that probably costs as much as her car.

"That's good," Fewell tells her, "because chances are you won't."

Hatkin has his bearing back. He's changed into a fresh uniform, the fruit salad arrayed on his chest—five rows of medals and campaign ribbons from his almost forty years of service—glittering in the light coming in over his shoulder. Sitting ramrod straight in his chair, he's tapping a pencil, the beat slow and steady. Watt straightens out his coat, wishing he looked as composed, knowing the strain of the past ten days is showing.

"I remember meeting this Warren character once at a Seal reunion in San Diego," Hatkin recalls. "Impressive, started out as a jarhead but he told me he thought the Marines were a bunch of pussies so he wrangled a transfer to the Seals. Did two tours in Afghanistan, eating bugs, rappelling out of helos and slitting Taliban throats in the middle of the night."

"Think we can turn him?"

"I'm working on it."

"And Jimmick thought he was being so damn smart."

"Guy got under your skin, didn't he?"

Watt realizes his emotions are on parade. Chalk it up to countless hours of lost sleep. "I can't wait to bring the bastard down. Putting these civilians in positions where they have responsibility for national security—it's like giving the inmates keys to the asylum."

The stew on Hatkin's desk rings. He picks it up, "This is General Hatkin." Watt watches as Hatkin carefully takes notes on the call. Even though Hatkin is normally tightly controlled, his face is now an open book—Watt can tell the news is good.

"Excellent," Hatkin says, swiveling in his chair to look out the window. "And thanks, Frank. I owe you one." He hangs up and swings around to face Watt.

"We have an appointment with Commander Warren in two hours. We'll take my bird." Hatkin looks up at the clock. "Meet me back here at 1900 hours."

"Where are we heading?"

"Boatyard on the upper Chesapeake. Jimmick's got Warren running a search operation there. Radiation detection sled, magnetometer, whole nine yards. Collyer and his cast of characters are coming down tomorrow."

"And Warren's with us?"

"He will when we're finished with him. Already having second thoughts, that boy is, about moving to Homeland Security."

"Good. Now we can really give him something to think about."

37

[Everglades Motel, Baltimore, Saturday morning]

Dishes in the sink, empty pizza cartons scattered around, the rooms are a mess but housekeeping is the last thing on Sharon's mind. She's been up ever since 6:30 when Straub called Howie. She dressed in a flash, got the major up and going, and helped him down the corridor to camp out in Howie's room to wait for Winn's next call. The taste of civilization at Tysons Corner left her craving more and right now she wants to put miles between herself and the cruddy motel. Even though she knows things will be a lot more risky down on the bay, the thought of the Coast Guard is reassuring.

Howie's desk is crowded with empty Pepsi cans and discarded pizza crusts, she guesses he's been up half the night.

"Anything happening there?" she asks him.

"Got it narrowed it down some."

"I'm ready for a change of scenery, even if I'm going to freeze my damn butt off out there on the bay. So why don't you give your buddy a call?" She had slept fitfully and was relieved when Howie rang so she didn't have to stare at the ceiling any longer.

"We have to wait," says Howie, leaning over his laptop screen where he's been working to discover most likely trajectories of the bomb after it was dropped.

She checks her wristwatch for the umpteenth time. "I'm itching to get a move on Just give him a ring and see if he's ready."

"You've got to cool your jets, it's Winn's move. He made that clear." During the conversation with Winn earlier that morning, Howie confirmed the nuke must have been dropped into the upper reaches of the Chesapeake Bay. His hunch was right, the Pentagon didn't have the vaguest idea of where the bomb was but given the B-52's course, the spot where they encountered the severe weather and the fact that the major came down on land, there's little likelihood it could have been jettisoned anywhere else. He gave Straub the coordinates of the three most promising areas. Winn was going to transmit the information to the Coast Guard unit and have them map the search.

Sharon wanders into the kitchen, takes the last Pepsi out of the refrigerator and pops it. Leaning against the doorjamb sipping the soda, she asks, "Do you realize it's been a full week since we first met at Starbucks?"

"And you're wishing it will never end."

"I want it to end right, that's for damn sure."

He glances at her. He knows she's been fretting about the search and wonders if she's seconds away from going over the edge again. She has one of those disconcerted expressions that doesn't augur well. "Believe me, it will go like clockwork," he reassures her. "Winn has the whole operation organized."

"I don't know where you get all your optimism, Collyer. Here you're about to be the bait for a group of terrorists and you sound like you're heading off for a day at the beach. "

"They only want the nuke. As soon as we find it, they'll elbow us out of the way."

"Elbow us out of the way? What do you think we're playing here—pickup basketball?"

"Everything will turn out fine."

"You're telling me to shut up, aren't you?"

He chortles, "I know better than to do that." Collyer returns to the course calculations he's running on his computer until five minutes later when Sharon interrupts him again.

"I've been thinking—I bet your wife and I could be friends."

"What made you think of her?"

"I thought the two of us might, you know, hit it off. She seems like a sharp lady."

"Sharp as a tack. If it wasn't for her nose for stocks, I'd be driving a UPS truck right now."

"What did she invest in?"

"Dot com deal down in Charlottesville in the crazy days before the whole thing imploded. A startup Internet retail operation. She rode the stock to the top then got out two days before it tanked."

"Gutsy move—my kind of lady."

"She thinks you are the only sane one in this operation. Said you have a lot of common sense."

"Not enough to keep from getting involved in this mess."

Howie's eyebrows suddenly shoot up. He turns and looks around the motel room. "That's the phone. Where is it?"

"I picked it up. It's in my purse," Sharon says. "Here," she takes out the cell and hands it over.

He listens a moment, then answers, "We can be out of here in two minutes. Let me jot the directions down on the computer. Grimes Boatyard in Fairhaven, okay—"

"Where are we going?" Risstup questions Sharon as they stand in the doorway watching Howie talk on the phone.

"Don't ask me, I just work here."

Howie continues his conversation, "It's 10:15 now and you say it will take us an hour plus to get to the boatyard. We should see you sometime before noon. Right, a cab with the number ending in eights."

He waits, listening carefully, jotting down a couple notes, then says, "Okay, I hear you—mouth shut and eyes open. See you soon, Winn."

"What was that *mouth shut eyes open* business about?"

"I'll tell you after I find the cab," Howie opens the door.

"Are we paid up?"

"I took care of it earlier," Howie says to her as he backs out. "See you in a couple."

A cab with the number 5488 is waiting on the corner. Howie's glad to see a friendly face behind the wheel. But it's clear the cabbie has been instructed to maintain his cover, no chitchat. Howie gives him their destination. He nods and drops the flag. That's the last bit of conversation he has with the cab driver.

"Say goodbye to the Everglades," Howie says as Risstup and Sharon climb into the backseat of the cab.

"Don't care if I never see the place again," Sharon says, looking back at the motel.

Howie hears his phone buzzing, reaches for it expecting Straub to be on the other end. "Hello?" But it's Sylvie instead. She's called him twice since they met at the mall. He listens patiently, nodding, the even-tempered husband placating the anxious wife.

"I told you what we'd be doing, Sylvie. We're heading down to the shore. We'll be working with the Coast Guard down there, everything will be fine."

Howie smiles, making more small talk with her until Sylvie finally runs out of things to say. "I'll say hello to Sharon for you—yes, dear, I promise. I love you too. Goodbye," and he clicks the phone shut.

"Everything fine on the home front?" Sharon asks.

"Sylvie's got more complaints than a homesick kid at camp. Food's lousy, sheets are scratchy and they're sick of watching movies."

"At least they're safe," Sharon says, surprising herself at the wistful tone in her voice.

"You could be safe down there too."

"And miss all this excitement? Are you kidding? What was that last thing Straub said to you on the phone? About keeping your ears open?"

"To follow his directions to the letter and not worry about it."

"He says *not to worry* a lot."

"Winn means it." That's as far as he takes it with Sharon. Straub told him not to tip his hand down in Fairhaven. They need to get a read on the Coast Guard commander. Having spent most of his career in the Navy, Winn wants to make sure he's not tied to the Pentagon. So far Straub's decisions and timing have been perfect, so Howie isn't about to start second-guessing him.

Once out of Baltimore, they make good time. It's Saturday and the weather is blustery so there isn't much traffic. The trip through the flat farmland is uneventful, the two-lane roads running straight through the fallow fields where soybeans, wheat and vegetables sprout during the growing season. Every couple miles, a stretch of woodland opens up to a series of farmhouses. Usually brick, sometimes frame, all neat, clean and prosperous-looking and surrounded by barns and outbuildings.

Howie verifies the directions on his laptop when they get to the quaint harbor-side town of Fairhaven, though he has the definite sense that the cabbie knows where he's going. White houses, nicely tended yards, friendly-looking signs in front of many of the houses with the owners' names inscribed upon them: *Welcome to the Mulvanys, Home of the Decatur Clan.*

Coming around a corner, Howie can see the sign reading **Grimes' Boatyard**, ***Rentals, Winterizing, Storage, Repairs on all makes of inboard and outboard engines, Painting and General Maintenance, Fully Insured***. A black Hummer blocks the entrance. As the cab pulls up, the driver climbs out and slowly approaches, looking them up and down carefully. He's wearing navy blue fatigues, boots, cap on his head, holstered pistol. Even though he is without insignia, Howie assumes he's Coast Guard.

"Mr. Collyer?" the man asks, leaning down to speak into the back window.

"Yes, I'm Collyer," Howie says, opening the door. Sharon helps Risstup out the other side.

A second man gets out of the Hummer, a submachine gun slung over his shoulder.

"I'm meeting Winston Straub," Howie explains.

"Yes, sir," is all the man says. Sharon is impressed. *Straub sure seems to have his act together.* "Come inside, someone will be out to talk with you in a few minutes." He motions toward the entrance.

Some welcoming committee, Sharon decides, *don't even introduce themselves.* The men climb back into the Hummer, doors slam shut.

The three wander through the entrance into the boatyard, Sharon helping Risstup along, Howie checking out the interior. Though he decides not to point it out, Howie doesn't miss the men stationed on the rooftops with rifles, scopes attached. He counts five. Could easily be more around the perimeter he can't see. Howie doesn't know what it will be like out on the Chesapeake, but at least they'll be safe here.

He's been around boatyards since he was a kid. Except for the sentries, this one's typical. Sheds and barns surrounding a wide area crammed with boats in cradles gradually sloping down to a concrete ramp leading into the water. Though the yard is dilapidated and in need of paint, the place has recently been spruced up. Immaculate, all the cradled boats neatly lined up, not a weed or a piece of trash anywhere, none of the discarded parts and machinery you normally see around boatyards. *Shipshape* is the word that occurs to Howie. And it's perfect for this kind of operation. Someone did his homework. Out of the way and off season, there's no one around to get suspicious.

Though it's chilly with a brisk wind blowing in off the bay, after almost two hours on the road, Howie appreciates the chance to stretch his legs.

"You want to wait for us?" he hears. Sharon sounds peevish. Howie realizes he's way ahead.

"Sorry," he says, stopping to let them catch up. Though he still needs someone to lean on, Risstup's walking more confidently. Waiting for the two, Howie's wondering why no one has come out to greet them.

Had he looked back at the building they passed when they came in, he would have seen a slightly parted curtain. Standing at the window of the boatyard office watching the three, Warren decides they are an odd-looking bunch, the former Pentagon employee, the VA nurse and the old pilot shuffling along arm in arm with her. More like a group you'd seeing strolling around the grounds of an old age home than a threat to national security.

But General Hatkin was explicit about the threat they posed. And concerned enough to pay Warren a visit early yesterday evening, choppering down from the Pentagon with his top aide. Not since his Annapolis days has Warren been in the presence of so much brass. General Watt is a two-star, Whitey Hatkin has three and is a walking myth. Fueled by coffee and adrenalin, Warren sat wide-eyed in the boatyard office while the three-star brought him up to speed.

Watt was curious how Hatkin would handle it. Commander Warren was clearly in a bind. Under orders from the top official in his agency, Lucien Jimmick, the Secretary of DHS, he was now being asked to set them aside and take on another mission. As Watt watched the white-haired general expertly weave the web to catch Collyer in a conspiracy to secure nuclear weapons, an expression came to mind—*blood is thicker than water.*

"Secretary Jimmick bought into this?" Warren asked, incredulous that a cabinet secretary like Jimmick could be so easily hoodwinked.

"Swallowed Collyer's whole cockamamie story hook, line and sinker. Jimmick's plotting to discredit the Pentagon by going after the nuke. It's nothing more than a cheap trick to bolster Homeland Security's stock. A self-seeking and foolhardy scheme with troubling implications."

"Is there actually a bomb in the bay?"

Watt's wondered how Hatkin would field Warren's question. He wasn't surprised when Watt turned to him.

"I'll let General Watt answer, he's our expert on unrecovered weapons."

Watt knows it's no time to be getting into gray areas. "Our records indicate the aircraft jettisoned the nuke over the Continental Shelf."

"So, as you said, it's a wild goose chase."

"The chance the bomb is in the Chesapeake is close to zero. But we need you on board to make sure. Any attempt to retrieve a weapon would be disastrous. These bombs must be left undisturbed so they can decompose. Even bringing attention to their existence creates risk."

Watt and Hatkin detailed what they wanted Warren to do. Provided him with a secure cell phone with preprogrammed direct lines to the Pentagon and assured him he would have their complete support.

Commander Warren peers out the window at the threesome standing around the rigid inflatable in the center of the yard. He remembers Hatkin's warning, "Don't be fooled by appearances. They might look like an older man, a young nurse and a senior citizen. But in reality, since they are conspiring to obtain a nuclear weapon, we have to consider them enemy combatants."

Enemy combatants—hardly the phrase that comes to mind, Warren thinks as he watches the three civilians loitering around the boat. He has seen the enemy before, up close and personal. Men with gaunt faces who've been living off the land for months and who would take out a relative if ordered, fearless and savage zealots who will crouch behind a rock without food or water for hours in the blazing sun waiting to get off the perfect shot.

Warren swings opens the door and takes the stairs in twos, thinking, *Let's go see what this crew is all about.*

"You know anything about boats?' Sharon asks Howie as she watches the lean guy in the blue uniform come out of the building and head down toward them.

"I've had a bunch."

"All I know about boats is I get seasick."

"Now you tell me."

Howie reaches up to run his hand over the tight black skin of the inflatable. "This boat is amazing, can handle anything." He pats one of the engines with his hand. "Bet this baby can do forty knots."

"Fifty, actually," Howie hears a voice correcting him. Turning around, he sees a man in his mid-thirties, slim but well-built, striding toward them dressed in the same outfit the men in the Hummer wore, navy baseball cap on his head, a revolver at his waist.

"I'm Commander Warren, I'm your skipper," he says. "Ms. Thorsen, Mr. Collyer, Major Risstup, pleased to meet you," he greets them, extending his hand to Sharon first.

"I see you already know our names."

"You've been the topic of a few conversations recently."

"I was afraid you'd say that," she winks at him.

Sharon likes his smile, he's around her age and cute. Strong jaw, smooth skin, steely eyes, taut body, if he played ball he probably would have been a strong safety. *The kind of guy I always fall for.* She stops herself. *What am I doing flirting at a time like this?*

Howie shakes his hand and gestures over toward the boat, saying, "Wouldn't mind taking a spin in this baby."

Sharon rolls her eyes. "Can't wait," she groans sarcastically.

"That's our backup chase boat, we're going to be spending most of our time in that craft over there," he says, pointing at the thirty-foot fishing boat moored just off the end of the ramp. In contrast with the menacing-looking inflatable, the smaller craft is ordinary, and with chipped paint and stained planking, appearing as if it's seen its best days.

"Looks can be deceiving. I'll give you a tour later. Right now, please join me for a briefing." He motions back over his shoulder toward the main building. "And I have to warn you. Watch what you say inside—we're still in the process of debugging the interior."

As she guides Risstup up the slope, Sharon takes another look at the lithe and athletic-looking man who's in command, musing—*Maybe there will be at least one saving grace in the next few days.*

One by one they file into the main building. Once an office with a counter and desks, the furniture has been pushed back to create a space filled with a row of chairs facing easels with large maps. With all the stuff on the walls, the interior looks more like a situation room than a boatyard office. Warren pulls up an easel holding a map of the Chesapeake Bay with three colored rectangles, one green, the second a lighter green, the third yellow.

These guys work fast, Howie thinks. *I gave Winn that information just a couple hours ago.* But the specific locations of the search areas are baffling. Though he's low on sleep, he remembers the coordinates well enough to know that the rectangles are off by miles. Howie wonders, *Is that a mistake or was it intentional on Straub's part?* But he also remembers Winn's warning to keep his mouth shut.

Using a pointer to outline the three sections, Warren explains, "Our mission is to mount a concerted search in the areas you have identified for us, color-coded by priority. Green first. We will tow detection gear behind the boat I pointed out to you in the yard."

"What kind of gear?"

"The latest, state-of-the-art metal and radiation detectors."

Tracing the outlines with his pointer, Warren continues, "We're going to be starting with the green first. Think of it as mowing the lawn, going back and forth until it's completely covered. Then we'll search again perpendicular to our initial pattern to checkerboard the entire area. If the object is there, we'll find it."

Warren just gave him the opening he was looking for. Though Warren is textbook military, all spit and polish and by the book, Howie's going to find out just how quick he is. "Commander Warren, may I stop you for a second?"

"By all means."

"Just a clarification. You just said, *If the object is there, we'll find it.*"

"Yes, sir."

"So you don't believe there's a bomb?"

Sharon's eyes are bouncing back and forth between the two men. Warren strikes her as slightly irritated, like he's being backed into a corner.

"I didn't say that."

"But the implication was there."

"You are putting words in my mouth."

"I'm only repeating what you said."

"This is semantics, Mr. Collyer."

"Not really, I'm curious about your personal opinion, Commander Warren. Do you really believe our armed forces could have dropped a nuke in the Chesapeake Bay and left it there for almost fifty years?" Sharon's seeing a side of Howie not evident before, confrontational and brusque. As if he's a trial lawyer trying to rattle a witness.

"I believe Secretary Jimmick is sufficiently alarmed about the prospect to have ordered a search of the area."

"But you don't believe it yourself?"

"My personal opinion is not relevant, Mr. Collyer. I am under orders to conduct a search of the designated sections."

Howie has all he needs to know. He looks directly at Warren for a couple more seconds, then waves his hand and says, "Okay, please continue."

38

[Solo, Indonesia, Saturday night, EST+12]

In the cavernous, dimly lit back room of the call center the activity level is intense. The relentless buzz of conversation combined with the steady clicking of computer keys, the hum of the servers, screens and hard drives and the steady shush of air conditioning raises the sound level in the control room to a booming drone.

El-Khadr circulates from station to station, leaning down to glance at the screens and up to check on the plasmas above, overseeing the overall operation while his people monitor all individual aspects—movements of Chrysanthemum cell members, positioning of the salvage tug, getting all the support for Dahlia into place as well as constantly updating Collyer's activity.

Again, coding is becoming the bottleneck. When events are happening rapidly, painstakingly translating each and every message out of flower lingo is a time-consuming drag. As Naguib scrambles to keep up with the torrent of information flying back and forth between the U.S. and Indonesia, he finds himself falling further and further behind. Whether they are tersely worded commands or elaborate explanations, every word and sentence of each email and web posting has to be encrypted into the project's language. Before he became so snowed under he'd never be able to catch up, Naguib begged El-Khadr to give him a hand, despite his boss' position and his poor typing skills.

In ten minutes Naguib's back with a new computer. In a half hour, it's connected and El-Khadr is sitting alongside Naguib's desk helping him handle the incoming traffic.

"How do I tell the network Collyer has taken up a position on the upper Chesapeake Bay?" El-Khadr quizzes, leaning across to consult Naguib.

"Use the vacation terminology," Naguib ad libs. "Tell them Cindy will be on holiday there."

"But I need to let Dahlia and Chrysanthemum know the specific location."

"Here's what you do," Naguib counsels. "Let them know Cindy plans to tour gardens in the Herring Bay area."

"Of course!" El-Khadr quickly follows through on his suggestion. "As long as they know the general area, once we learn it we will be easily able to give them a precise location." El-Khadr's fingers hurriedly hunt and peck through the keys to relay the information updating the website on Collyer's whereabouts. The people assigned to him have tracked Collyer to a boatyard the military has secured on the shore.

But El-Khadr is not concerned. *At some point they will have to begin their search. And though the Americans may suspect Collyer is being watched, they have no idea the Chrysanthemum or Dahlia operation exists. Either one will take them by surprise.*

He glances up at the three-by-five-foot nautical chart on the wall. In pastel tones of pale blue and yellow, it displays detailed soundings of the bay. El-Khadr has thoroughly studied the Chesapeake. In the center sections, the bay is white, indicating deeper water that would require the tug, barge and deep-sea diving crew. A night recovery has been planned and practiced.

But much of the water is light blue, showing shallow depths accessible to an expert diver like Mehran. So El-Khadr has put his money on him, much neater and cleaner. His preparations have been intensive and hurried. Over the past two days, his teams have been scrambling to provision three boathouses along the length of the bay, quickly moving equipment into place. If Collyer commences his search in the Herring Bay area and finds the bomb in shallow water, the northernmost boathouse will be ideally situated. He quickly does the calculations in his head. Once the door is opened, it would take Mehran no longer than ten minutes to reach any spot in the upper part of the bay.

Though he does not believe in Western superstitions, El-Khadr has his fingers crossed. He struggles to keep his composure. *Patience, above all I need to be patient,* he keeps telling himself. *I must not make rash decisions but I cannot let the opportunity slip away.* He quickly comes to a decision. *Though it is prudent to stay with timetables that have been worked out in the past, it is also necessary to stay flexible.* But he is going to test drive his reasoning with Naguib, just to make sure.

"In the event this becomes a Dahlia operation, I am considering activating Mehran," El-Khadr says.

Naguib glances at his boss. He seems resolute. Naguib wishes he would wait but he has learned that El-Khadr does not like to be argued with.

El-Khadr makes his case, "It's over four hours from New Brunswick. He has to go around Philadelphia and through the center of Baltimore. Holiday traffic can be brutal. I have seen it myself. And when he gets into Maryland, the roads along the shore are all narrow, two lanes at best. One accident can result in a three-hour bottleneck. I can't allow Mehran to be caught in traffic."

"At the risk of offending you, I would like to point out that until everything is set it is not prudent to expose him."

"Why shouldn't we at least move him closer?"

"You disrupt his routine. Moving him before the planned time could make people suspicious. His girlfriend, for instance, who knows? It's injecting a factor into the equation we haven't considered."

"But the girlfriend would have no idea where Mehran is headed or what he is about to do. And anyway, before they could react, Mehran will already be in place and his trail will have gone cold. I have made up my mind. He must be there the minute Collyer starts his search."

Naguib shows his palms, "It is your decision."

El-Khadr's hands move to the keyboard. He composes the message carefully and deliberately. From earlier posts, Mehran will know the location. All that is required is the signal to commence the mission. El-Khadr's fingers move slowly over the keys, typing out the message that will change the course of history:

> Meet with Cindy as soon as possible. She has a prize dahlia she wants to dig up.

He sensed something was amiss the minute he set foot on campus. The quad was quiet. No rowdy groups of students stumbling from one pre-Christmas party to another. No carols blaring out windows. He backed into the entryway of a dorm and stood silently.

After forty-five minutes, Mehran's patience paid off. Though dressed like a student, his shoes were a giveaway. Even engineering nerds wouldn't wear gumshoes. And undergrads don't stand around with their hands in their pockets looking like they are waiting for a bus. A half hour later he saw the second one—again too old for a student and too casually dressed for a professor—amble into the quad. Also wearing telltale shoes.

When the man lifted his arm and spoke into his wrist, Mehran knew he was in trouble. Melanie must have ratted on him, or maybe it was the swim coach. *Who cares? I've been trained for every eventuality.*

He moves fast. Staying in the shadows, he quietly slips around the side of the building and heads toward a busy downtown street where he can lose himself in a crowd of shoppers.

His pace quickens, he turns up his collar against the blowing rain. He doesn't need anything from his room. He will go to an ATM and get money. Check his email at an espresso bar that's off campus, find a hotel room somewhere using a fake ID and keep his head down. All he needs now is a hideout, an Internet connection and patience.

It's a ten-minute walk. At the ATM he takes out five hundred, turning his head so the camera can't catch his face. The money will keep him going for the time being. Two blocks down, he stops. Peers in the window of the espresso shop. Only a few people are in the store. Plenty of desktops available.

He peels off a twenty and hands it to the girl behind the register. Skinny, anemic-looking, red hair done in cornrows. Her ears, nose and lips are pierced and a faraway look fogs her eyes. She's stoned. His luck. She won't remember him. He sits down at a machine and logs onto the first website. Locates the link and goes to the second. Clicks on the button concealed in the flowerbed taking him to Jeffri's Garden. Checks over his shoulder and hurriedly types in his password.

A string of posts scrolls out onto the screen. His eyes quickly scan through the decoys until he finds the dahlia posts. Mehran's eyes flare as he opens the first, then a second and a third. His heart is ready to leap out of his chest as he reads: *Meet with Cindy as soon as possible. She has a prize dahlia she wants to dig up.*

It is my time, the words ripple across his brain. *They have chosen me, it is my time.*

Knowing exactly what to do, he quickly commits the information in the three posts to memory.

A voice inside the shop interrupts him. It's the girl at the register. "Would anyone like have a problem, like, if I put on some carols?" she whines. "After all, it is Christmas."

He glances around the store. The other three customers are shrugging their shoulders.

He pushes the strains of "Oh Come, All Ye Faithful" to the back of his mind as he commits the email instructions to memory, one at a time, over and over until he knows them as well as the opening verses of the Koran.

39

[I-95, SOUTH OF THE DISTRICT OF COLUMBIA, SATURDAY EVENING]

Straub is speeding down the Interstate listening to Dvorak in a rented Mercury. Picking a car at random out of a lot reduced the risk that someone has left a gift, a bomb or transponder attached to the undercarriage. Straub knows Vector Eleven will go to any lengths to stop them.

The second he picks up the phone and Jimmick delivers the news, his finger jabs the button to douse the volume. He listens, and then asks—trying not to sound as aggravated as he is—"A terrorist has been in training for three goddamn years right in our own backyard and no one picked up on it?"

"That's what I'm getting from my contact at the FBI," Jimmick answers. "A swimming coach at Rutgers tried to alert them but it wasn't until the student's girlfriend ratted on him that they put two and two together."

"Who else knows about this?"

"It's just getting into the loop. As far as I know, no one in the intelligence community is connecting it with the events in Front Royal, so the Collyer tie-in is still under wraps. As for Vector Eleven, who the hell knows?"

"Has the FBI had any luck finding this character?"

"He never returned to campus but they've got his hard drive in the lab."

"Stay on their good side in case anything turns up on the computer."

"The special agent in charge is my new best buddy."

"Is the girlfriend involved?"

"They don't think so."

"Any point in talking to her?"

"They think she's given them everything. Guy kept her at arm's length for the most part. There is one interesting piece they are running down. A secret location in Philadelphia. The swimmer wouldn't let his girlfriend go near it. Who knows what's there?"

"Let me know the second they find something out. In the meantime, I need to talk to that coach. Can you get him for me?"

"It might take a couple minutes."

"Hurry. Things are going down fast."

Straub punches the END button and tosses his cell on the seat. It's the worst news he could have imagined. The terrorists have taken their planning and preparation to a level he hadn't anticipated. He grabs the phone and speed dials Howie.

"What would you say if I told you that a Iranian student has been practicing in the main pool at Rutgers University?" he asks him. "Swimming laps underwater and bringing up heavy steel plates from the bottom?"

He expects an immediate response. Instead he hears silence.

"Howie? You there? Howie?"

Howie's walking down the steps to the boatyard as he absorbs the information. "I had to go outside," he tells Straub. "I couldn't risk anyone overhearing us. Jesus, Winn, when did you find this out?"

"A couple minutes ago. Hang on, Jimmick is patching in the Rutgers swim coach now. You can hear it from him."

"This is Coach Johanson."

"Yes, Coach. Winston Straub here. I'm from CIA. Need to ask you some questions about this young man that was training in your pool."

"I took notes on him. I can tell you everything you need to know." Johanson is standing by the side of the pool holding his clipboard. With FBI agents swarming all over the place, things have been pretty exciting at the Werblin Center.

"Do you have any idea what he was practicing for?" Straub asks.

"Like I told the FBI, underwater recovery, as best as I can figure—treasure, wrecks, scuba-type stuff—he had all the gear."

"Why do you say *treasure*?"

"What else could he be diving for?"

As pointed as the coach's question is, Howie and Straub both choose to take a pass on responding.

"Tell me about his practicing," Straub asks.

"Never seen anything like it. Kid swam like a shark. Had a double dolphin kick that ripped him through the water. Like I said, never seen anything like it. Plow down the pool with his head up doing a choppy crawl and then he'd suddenly dive down, straighten out his arms and literally fly. I'd sit there watching this shadow zip up and down the pool. I mean, he had an unbelievable lung capacity. Go four laps straight without surfacing. And two weeks ago, he started bringing a monofin to the pool. Know what that is?"

"No idea."

"A single flipper with holes for both feet. Used in free-diving, the sport where people see how far they can swim underwater on one breath of air, how deep they can go, that kind of thing. Get this—with his monofin on I timed him at close to ten miles an hour—now that's flying. From the very first time I saw this kid I was dying to recruit him for the varsity."

"Was he interested?"

"No way. He was antisocial, standoffish. Like he had a chip on his shoulder."

"So he never talked about what he was doing?"

"On the contrary, kid wouldn't say a damn word about anything."

"What about the weights?"

"That's how I decided he had to be after sunken treasure. Why else would he practice bringing barbell plates up from eighteen feet deep?"

"You've been a great help, Coach, appreciate you taking the time to talk with us."

"Hope you can keep him from doing whatever he's trying to do."

"So do we," Winn says, listening as the coach clicks off the line.

Straub pulls over to the slow lane, drops down to fifty-five before he asks Howie, "What do you make of this weight business?"

"Bringing weights up from the bottom doesn't make sense if he's been training to recover a nuke. The bombs weigh as much as five tons, no way he's going to surface something like that. And it's impossible to take a nuke apart in the water and bring it up piecemeal."

Straub remembers the counsel of one of his mentors, a founder of the CIA. *Turn it around and look at the other side,* Alfred Minor used to say, *the reality is often in the mirror.* Every time he had taken his advice to heart, it had paid off. "So flip it around," he challenges Howie. "Maybe he's not bringing the weights up."

"You mean bringing something down?"

"Yeah, like explosives."

"Jesus, I don't know why I didn't think of that—Semtex, C-4, all that plastic stuff is waterproof. It's the explosive of choice for underwater demolition teams."

Straub knows Semtex is also a favorite of terrorists. Used to blow Pan Am 103 out of the sky over Lockerbie, they packed a wad no bigger than a baseball into a cassette recorder. Easily molded into any shape and composed of rubber and plastic, it's perfect for underwater operations. "Blow the bomb to bits in the water—it would make a helluva mess," he tells Howie.

"He'd be like a suicide bomber, take himself out with the nuke."

"No, Howie. Not a suicide *bomber*—suicide *diver*." From the pause on the other end of the line, Straub can tell the phrase has hit Howie right between the eyes.

"*Suicide diver.* That never occurred to me," he finally says. For the first time, Winn detects a tone in his friend's voice he hasn't heard before—not quite fear, but real close.

"I'm sure it hasn't occurred to anyone else either."

"It's scary as shit but it's absolutely brilliant. They get this swimmer who's like a guided missile in the water. He dives down and sticks a C-4 charge on it quick as hell, detonates the damn thing and before we know it we've got a major calamity on our hands."

"Even if it only detonates the TNT, it would send a cloud of radiation into the air. Imagine seeing that on CNN."

"It would be pandemonium."

"And if they got lucky and set off the nuke—"

"Forget about D.C.—it would be a wasteland."

"So this suicide diver is being positioned somewhere waiting for the signal that you've located it."

"Keep in mind he might not be the only one. If the bomb's in deep water, a scuba diver isn't going to do them a damn bit of good. They'd need a salvage operation with divers, a well-equipped boat, the whole nine yards."

"I think we're just seeing the tip of the iceberg. It's obvious we're dealing with a sophisticated organization."

"This suicide diver business scares the crap out of me. You sure we shouldn't get more people involved?"

"I'm concerned we have too many damn people already. DHS, Coast Guard, Pentagon, CIA, FBI. Christ, we're scrambling now to put a lid on the news about the swimmer. The only chance we have of flushing out these terrorists out is to stay on course. The minute we get a horde of Feebies swarming around, or a couple companies of Special Ops people with their helicopters roaring all over the place, the terrorists will go to ground. This is our one chance. Wait, I've got a call from Jimmick. Hang on."

Howie listens as the *HOLD* tone drones in his ear. He wishes he had his file on the Jersey bomb. A number of times he's brought up the possibility that nukes lost during the late '60s could have been armed with a nuclear capsule, but he can't remember if he'd ever sketched the capsule's location on the Mk-15. Was that somewhere in his files? Could they have seen it? His memory is hazy. *Could that be why the terrorists are using a suicide diver? Do they think they can place the charge near the capsule and activate the nuclear reaction underwater? Have I not only led them to the bomb, but also spelled out precisely how to set it off?*

For the first time, the thought runs through Howie's mind, *Maybe Vector Eleven had the right idea all along. Let sleeping dogs lie.*

"Howie, you there?" Winn asks when he comes back on the line.

"Yes, Winn. What's Jimmick got?"

"You sound really jittery."

"It's this suicide diver thing. I never in a million years imagined it would be possible to detonate a nuke under water."

"Don't go there, Howie. Look, we were able to yank the info on the swimmer from the Counterterrorism Center—at least for the time being. So we have some extra room to maneuver. What about Jimmick's Coast Guard guy, that Warren character?"

"Too early to tell, but my first inclination is not to trust him."

"Figured as much. If they didn't own him already Vector Eleven probably turned him. That Seal group is thick as thieves."

"That's why you sent him the bogus set of coordinates. You had doubts from the beginning."

"Howie, it's in the water I drink. I have doubts about everybody and everything."

"So how are we going to handle him?"

"Let me think about it. I'll give you a call in an hour."

"I thought you were coming down."

"Changed my mind, I've decided to go to The Farm. They have a high-resolution satellite link there. The kind they use to fly Predator drones over the Pakistani mountains searching for bin Laden. It's like having a hawk eye in the sky."

Howie wants to ask, *If they're so damn good, why haven't they caught him yet?* "Going to leave me to fend for myself, huh?"

"It'll be like I'm in the boat with you except I'll be able to see everything that's happening in the entire bay. And you've got a secure cell phone. It's our best way to play this. I've got to go, talk to you soon."

Straub hangs up, leaving Howie standing in the middle of the boatyard as he watches a sliver of moon sneak out from behind a bank of clouds, wondering how the hell he ever got himself into this mess.

Mehran waited patiently outside a McDonald's until a customer left her car unlocked. A harried young mother late to pick up dinner for the kids, in such a hurry she even left the driver's door ajar. Before the woman was through the line, Mehran had hotwired the Camry and was slinking out of the lot.

It's dark by the time he pinpoints the boathouse. Hungry, tired, the drive from New Brunswick to the shore took him almost five hours. Through Trenton and Baltimore, skirting around Washington on the Beltway then down the dinky rural routes to his destination. The roads were chockablock with gas-greedy SUVs, riding up and sitting on his tail even though he was doing seventy-five. Mehran was tempted to salute them with his middle finger. But he has a better way to get back at them.

The road to the boathouse was poorly marked. Before he finally located the turnoff, Mehran drove past it three times. Concerned that he had somehow incorrectly memorized the instructions, he's relieved when he sees it.

Like everything else in the operation, the boathouse is a marvel of ingenuity. A quarter mile down a rutted driveway, an attached garage alongside neatly conceals the Camry. The keys where they were supposed to be. He pulls the car inside, closes and locks the door.

A quarter moon illuminates the boathouse. A long, narrow wooden building sitting on pilings with a corrugated roof, its front half juts out over the water with a garage door opening out onto the bay. Mehran kneels down, peeking under the edge of the boathouse. He can see the water shimmering around the pilings but he can't see up into the interior. *Very clever.* A false floor has been constructed so prying eyes would not be able to see what is stored inside. He pats the surface, it gives easily. Made of black canvas, he figures the floor retracts so the boat can be lowered into the water.

Mehran unlocks the side door and flicks the switch. Fluorescent fixtures on the ceiling sputter. The interior walls are tarpapered to keep light from seeping out. An industrial heater works against the water's chill. Plywood sheathing laid on the rafters furnishes him with a small loft-like living space. Climbing up, he finds a copy of the Koran next to a sleeping bag, a cell phone alongside. The loft is stocked with provisions and water. A wireless weather station reads out wind direction, speed, temperature and barometer readings. Food, water, communication, the Koran—Mehran knows he can last for a week in here.

He climbs down the ladder marveling at the gleaming black Donzi suspended over the false floor. A bullet, long, slim and lethal-looking. The craft can ride out the worst weather and outrun anything. Twenty-two feet long, its 500 horses will rocket it up to eighty in seconds.

Climbing up and lowering himself into the cockpit, he looks around the interior. Equipped as planned, everything blacked out, not an inch of chrome anywhere. He turns the key. The indicator lights glow dull red—nothing to attract attention. He checks the backseat, custom racks hold two double tanks, backup regulators stored alongside, his monofin and a second wetsuit for insurance. Next to him on the console is the handheld metal detector—an electronic bloodhound with a nose for ferrous and nonferrous metals. Mehran has used it in the Red Sea to locate objects buried in the murkiest water.

He slides down into the bucket seat, grasping the wheel with his hands as he surveys the array of gauges. He trained for a week on a Donzi in the Persian Gulf, so everything is familiar. Outfitted with a forty-eight mile radar and GPS, there is even a cradle on the dash for his cell phone. From his perch in the captain's chair, he looks around the boathouse. A two-foot walkway runs around the perimeter, ten five-gallon gas cans lined up in a neat row against the wall. They haven't missed a trick.

Sitting at the helm, he mentally runs through the final steps of his mission. Each is etched in his memory as deeply as images of the streets of the village where he grew up.

When he gets the order, he will jump into his wetsuit, flip the switch to roll up the floor, activate the lift lowering the Donzi into the water, turn the key and wait patiently while the engine warms up, the rumbling burble of its exhaust in the water echoing around inside. Pushing the button to raise the door, he will slam the throttle forward and the engines will blast the Donzi out of the opening and propel him across the bay.

That is the first time anyone will see Mehran Zarif. *And if I am lucky, it will also be the last.*

Mehran pauses. *Am I missing something?* He swings his head from side to side, looking around the interior. Then he peers up into the rafters. *There it is,* he thinks as he looks up at the shiny stainless steel collar, *but why only one? How could he have known which model I would be going after? Why would Jamal have equipped me only with a Mk-15 collar?*

But there is no question about it. Hung from the front peak of the boathouse not two feet over his head, a single collar gleams in the bright light. Clearly labeled, the collar has been designed to precisely fit the nose of the Mk-15 mod 0.

My good fortune, Mehran decides, gazing up at the collar, smiling as he thinks, *this is the nuke I have been dreaming about.*

Jimmick bought some domestic tranquility by agreeing to go to the wedding. So his wife doesn't complain when he leans over and plants a goodbye peck on her cheek at three in the morning.

"Where are you going?"

"I have a meeting."

"Liar," she says, rolling over and instantly falling back to sleep.

In fifteen minutes, he's dressed and out of the house. The DHS chopper is picking him up at a secure pad at Dulles so he won't be noticed flying out of the NAC. The call from the special agent in charge of the Newark office got his attention. The location in Philadelphia was a bomb factory, Agent Rathon told him. No doubt about it.

He had put in a quick call to Straub down at Peary.

"Get your ass up there as fast as you can," was Winn's reaction.

It's a forty-minute flight to Philly. An FBI car is at the helipad to meet him. Large fluffy snowflakes are drifting down through the early morning air. Jimmick wishes he'd remembered his overcoat. Fortunately, the agents had enough sense to bring along a Thermos of coffee. He wasn't going to take the time to make any at home and once he was on the road he didn't want to stop. As if there would have been anything open in the middle of the night.

After mutual introductions, Jimmick asks of the agent sitting in the front seat, "Update me on everything."

He swings around to face Jimmick. "We cross-referenced utility bills and tax rolls, first electricity, then water. Looking for anything that stuck out. Kept running the crosses until we came up with a list of probables then hit the street. We got lucky. It was the fifth place we checked. Water bills were off the charts."

"Why's that?"

"You'll see in a minute."

It's a four-story brick building in a rundown commercial area of four- and five-story buildings, warehouses, signs of gentrification with a smattering of upscale residential but not an area where you'd want to be at night. Yellow crime scene tape strung up all over the place. Snow is picking up, dusting the streets in a sheet of white. An agent holds the door for him.

Up a flight of stairs, he finds a group standing in a large, open workroom. Looks to Jimmick like a small manufacturing facility, lathes and drill presses, workbenches, off to the side a tall wooden tank maybe twenty feet in diameter.

Special Agent Rathon is at the center of the four men, giving directions, clearly in command. Rathon had told him to look for a tall guy. At six-six, he's hard to miss.

Jimmick walks up and shakes his hand. "Rathon, good to meet you. Appreciate you keeping me in the loop on this." The minute Jimmick saw the post about the swimmer, he put in a call to the special agent on the case, letting him know he was working on a high priority inter-agency assignment reporting to the heads of CIA and the Department of Homeland Security. Dropping high-profile names had the precise effect Jimmick expected. The minute Rathon discovered the bomb factory, he was on the horn to him.

"My pleasure, Mr. Secretary," the lanky special agent says.

"So this is the secret location the swimmer was sneaking off to?"

"We've lifted two sets of prints, I'd bet one belongs to him. We're running the matches now."

"When was he last here?"

"Could have been as recently as this morning. All kinds of stuff was moved out of here in a hurry. Tenants on both sides heard the commotion. We're checking that out now."

"Any idea of what they were making?"

"Traces of C-4 in nineteen locations, you can tell they tried to remove it but it's all over the place."

"We need to get an expert in here to tell us what this machinery was used for."

"It's almost five in the morning, Mr. Secretary."

"I know what time it is," Jimmick says, looking directly at Rathon to make sure he gets the message.

"We'll get to work on it."

Jimmick's attention is attracted to six wooden gantries, the cross-pieces concave, hollowed out as if they were constructed to hold a cylindrical object. "What do you suppose these were for?" he asks, having already figured out the answer but not wanting to reveal it until he can get a better read on the special agent.

"Some kind of cradle, I'd guess."

"Curious," Jimmick says. He's seen enough photos of nuclear weapon storage depots. Each of these platforms has a different configuration designed to hold a specific model. *They can't be anything else.*

Jimmick walks over and slaps the wooden planking of the immense wooden structure off to the side of the room. "And this tank, you think that's why the water bills were so high?" A hydraulic hoist stands beside the tank. Jimmick imagines the hoist lowering bombs into the water. The picture is becoming clearer. Only one question remains to be answered. What is the connection between the swimmer, the tank and the bombs?

"You see these things on the top of ten-story buildings," Rathon says, looking up at the tank. "This is one hell of a lot of water for a small manufacturing space."

"You've done good work, Rathon."

"Anything else can I do for you, Mr. Secretary?"

"Yes, as soon as you determine what they were making here, I want to know. Same goes for the prints. And the minute your lab extracts anything off the student's hard drive, call me. I don't care what time it is."

Jimmick sets his hand on Rathon's shoulder and steers him off to the side, turns to him and says *sotto voce*, "And I need to let you know that it is in the interest of national security that this entire investigation be kept absolutely confidential." Jimmick scribbles his secure phone number on a card and sticks it in the pocket of Rathon's topcoat.

"The Hoover Building doesn't open for business until nine on Monday. And if you say so, Mr. Secretary, I can drag my feet on filing a report for another couple days."

"Good."

"Just one question, sir."

Jimmick stops at the doorway, "Yes, Rathon."

"I filed the intelligence on the swimmer at the National Counterterrorism Center late this afternoon. But I had someone check and it's not posted any longer."

"The CIA director personally removed that notice. You understand he has the authority."

"Of course, sir." Rathon looks impressed.

Jimmick smiles as he heads down the stairs. *At least Dickson's name carries weight in some circles.*

Heading for the helipad across an accumulating layer of freshly fallen snow, Jimmick decides to go into the office. By the time he's back in town, it will almost be dawn. Doesn't everybody go to work at six on Sunday morning?

As soon as he's in his chopper, Jimmick is on the phone to Straub. His secure line doesn't answer. *Must be busy.*

It's not until they are circling over D.C. that Straub finally answers. "What did you find out?" Straub presses.

"There's C-4 all over the place," Jimmick shouts over the rotor roar. "Good move to send me up there."

"Why do you say that?"

"They had mockups of atomic and hydrogen bombs sitting around."

"Mockups?"

"Bunch of gantries. Dead ringers for the kind Energy and DoD use to store nukes. And there was a large tank with a hoist. I'm guessing they lifted the mockups into the tank for some kind of test."

"Or practice."

"You bet. We're trying to find an engineer to help us figure out what the hell they were making there."

"I bet the swimmer went to this machine shop in Philly to practice putting C-4 on a nuke in the water. What were they making at that shop for this kid to fasten to a bomb?"

"That's the sixty-four dollar question."

"As soon as you can get me an answer."

Peering out the window of his chopper, Jimmick is surprised not to see more lights in the darkened city until he realizes they are swooping low over Rock Creek Park. As they bank in for a landing, he's able to pick out the streetlights of Connecticut Avenue and the steeple of the Washington Cathedral. The lights around the pad suddenly blink on as the helicopter swings down over Ward Circle, the lights brightly illuminating the yellow *X* on the DHS helipad.

"The FBI is on it. But it's Sunday. Don't know how long it will take to find an expert in milling machinery."

"It better be fast. Howie's going to be out on the water in a couple hours."

"I'll keep pressing them."

"If I were you, I'd go back there and turn up the heat myself."

He's about to say, *I'm already back in D.C.,* but thinks better of it.

"I'll take care of it."

"One more thing—your boy Commander Warren?"

"What about him?"

"Howie and I suspect Vector Eleven's turned him."

"That's not possible," Jimmick responds, realizing his reaction sounds hedgy, for he's well aware that in the helter-skelter of Washington politics any kind of intrigue is possible.

40

[Fairhaven, Maryland, Sunday morning]

As they make their way down to the dock through the half-inch of snow, fog curtains the boatyard, obscuring the bay and anything but the outlines of the nearest buildings. Sharon and Howie can barely see five feet ahead, but they can hear the diesel exhaust bubbling in the water mixed with the sound of the voices of the men scurrying around the boat.

Sharon's on her fourth cup of coffee, the caffeine and lack of sleep has made her jumpy, but it was Collyer's pacing around the boatyard talking on his cell in the middle of the night that really unnerved her.

"You want to tell me what the hell you were discussing until one in the morning," she whispers to Howie as she nudges him in the side with her elbow. "C'mon, 'fess up. I watched you trudging around the yard looking like you had the weight of the world on your shoulders."

"Everything's okay."

"Bullshit."

"Ssssh. Sound carries in the fog."

Sharon grabs Howie by the elbow and whirls him around so they are face to face. "C'mon, Collyer," she hisses into his ear, "what the hell's going on?"

Howie points toward the water, shakes his head and lifts his index finger up to his lips.

Sharon pushes, "It's Warren—you and Straub don't trust him. In that meeting yesterday it was written all over your face."

Sharon can read his mind faster than Sylvie. "We're going to watch what we say around him, that's all."

"He's working for the other side, isn't he?"

"Let's go for a boat ride," Howie says, taking her arm firmly and steering her toward the dock.

Sharon's not giving up. "Goddammit, Howie, you've got to level with me."

Fortunately, his cell rings just at that second. He fumbles around for it. "Hang on a minute, it's Winn."

On the cell, "We're just about to get on board now," he says to Straub.

"Let me talk to him," Sharon snatches the phone out of Howie's hand.

"Sharon, how are you?" Straub asks.

He gets an earful. Straub wishes Howie had found a way to leave her on shore.

"I can understand you're upset," Straub tells her. "Let me just say I'm in the master operations center at Camp Peary and I'm watching you on a monitor, big as life," he says, swinging around in his chair to face the ten-foot rear projection screen displaying the satellite image of the Chesapeake feeding down to the array of forty-foot diameter dishes at the CIA installation outside of Williamsburg.

Straub toggles the joystick to zoom in on Herring Bay. "I can see everything you're doing. I'm going to be keeping an eye on you every minute you're out there. And we have people ready to jump into action in case anything happens."

"Not good enough, Winn, I'm not buying that." She's still fuming. Straub shakes his head. *The woman sure doesn't like being left out of the loop.*

"Then how about if we debrief you when you finish your search?" Straub offers.

No dice, she still isn't on board. It's time for hardball. "Look, Sharon. We don't have time to jaw this to death. Unless you want to screw this whole operation up, get your butt on the boat and keep your trap shut. Okay?"

No answer. She's thinking about it. "Time to be on your best behavior, young lady. Take your lead from Howie."

Straub nods and smiles, *She's backed down.* "Good. Now let me talk to him."

"I'm looking at the boat now," Howie says when he gets back on the line. "It's pretty tight quarters in there. I don't know how I'm going to contact you without Warren overhearing."

"It has a cabin, doesn't it?"

"I think so."

"Either go below or send me a text message."

"Of course, why didn't I think of that?"

"The CIA is a full-service wireless provider."

His remark gets a chuckle from Howie. He sounds more composed than he did six hours ago. Straub was on the phone to him half the night. The suicide diver freaked him out and Howie endlessly ran disaster scenarios Straub did his best to bat down.

What if the nuke happens to be in one of those areas? If we stop to check, don't you have to assume the terrorists are watching? Won't they know?

So don't stop, Straub told him.

Just keep going? Act like it's not there?

Right. Get the GPS reading and keep going.

So how do we flush them out?

Let me deal with that.

Should I tell Sharon?

No point in alarming her. I'd leave her on shore if I were you.

You know how far I'll get with that. What if Vector Eleven is watching?

Leave that up to me, okay?

At one in the morning, Howie finally ran out of questions. Said goodnight and turned in. Straub told him he'd call him first thing.

"So I guess we're all set," Howie says.

"Ready as we'll ever be." The red light on Straub's stew is blinking. "A call's coming in, Howie. Gotta go. Good luck out there."

Straub touches the OFF button on his cell and picks up the stew.

"You sitting down?" Jimmick asks. Straub winces, Jimmick can get hokey at times.

"What do you have?"

"They just ID'd the two sets of prints from the bomb factory. As we thought, the first's from the swimmer, the Iranian student."

"The other?"

"A Saudi national who worked in our weapons program—"

"When?"

"Mid-sixties—"

"That's when Mk-15s were being produced."

"Wait until you hear this. His name's Jamal Abdullah, he's a nuclear engineer with a doctorate in physics."

"He'd know the Mk-15 inside and out. For all we know it could be his baby."

"Al-Qaeda found someone familiar with the bomb and had him design some device the suicide diver could attach to it."

"Something filled with C-4."

"Yeah, and at a point where the bomb is most vulnerable."

"We have to find out exactly what they were making in that warehouse."

"The FBI is flying a mechanical engineering guru in from Carnegie Mellon."

"Couldn't we have found someone locally? Howie's out there now," Straub says, looking up at the monitor. The fog's burning off and as he zooms in, he can see the boat chugging out of the harbor into Herring Bay.

"We struck out with two local guys. Scratched their heads for a couple hours but couldn't put it together."

"Where is the Saudi now?"

"Flew yesterday afternoon to London from Philly on his way back to Saudi Arabia."

"The FBI must have just missed him."

"It was close. His flight landed in Jeddah four hours ago."

"*Jeddah*—shit."

"What about it? This Jamal guy grew up there."

"I was afraid you'd say that." Now Straub knows he has no choice but to hedge his bets. "Now it's time to clue Dickson in. It's time for him to play Paul Revere."

"You're changing the plan."

"You're damn right."

"Why?"

"Jeddah's where bin Laden's from," Straub says as he quickly zooms back out so Howie's boat is a speck on the bay, wondering whether Dickson will step up to alerting the president. *And if he does, how will the President of the United States react to the news that there is a fully armed four-megaton hydrogen bomb mere miles from the White House and chances are Osama bin Laden knows more about it than he does?*

Winn Straub isn't the only one watching a sat feed on the boat's progress. From forty miles above, another eye in the sky is following the small boat as it motors out into the bay with three crew members, a captain and two civilians aboard.

Watt and Hatkin have been at the screen since dawn. Just after 0740 they saw the boat sail out of the yard in Fairhaven heading toward the green areas outlined on the chart, pause a half mile offshore to lower the radiation sled and the metal detector, then continue its course toward the first section, its sensitive gear electronically trolling the bottom. Commander Warren had scanned and sent the map to them the minute Jimmick emailed it. The three rectangles tell them all they need to know about Collyer's operation. Limited to discrete areas—a tiny part of the Chesapeake—if the bomb is there, they can easily prevent Collyer from recovering it.

If it isn't, they have nothing to worry about.

"The unit is standing by at Belvoir, sir," Lieutenant Williams reports, leaning in to inform his commanding officer. "Give the order and they will be in the air inside of two minutes." A Special Ops unit is at the ready, three Apache attack helicopters armed with laser-guided Hellfire missiles and .30 caliber machine guns and two Black Hawks each with a squad of commandos aboard.

"Thank you, Lieutenant."

On the screen in front of them, the tiny object crisscrosses the section on the chart, cruising back and forth on parallel courses a hundred yards apart. Hatkin checks his watch. 1152. They've been sitting at the console for four hours. Feeling less pressured with someone on the inside, they had both been able to grab a decent night's sleep for the first time in a week.

The only nagging question is the terrorists. Yet since they haven't had any red flags since last Tuesday when the flier with Collyer's picture appeared and they have never been able to definitively link the terrorists to Front Royal, they had no reason to be overly concerned.

Until last night when a notice was posted on the National Counterterrorism website informing the intelligence community that the FBI was looking for an Iranian student who had a suspicious workout routine at a Rutgers aquatic center.

Neither Watt nor Hatkin knew what to make of the information, but the fact that the report involved scuba training was alarming.

Hatkin ordered Watt to scour his sources at the Hoover Building but everyone he knew was on vacation or hadn't the slightest idea what he was talking about. So he told Watt to keep an eye out in case further information appeared on the NCTC. Four hours later the information vanished from the website.

"The Feebies must have come up empty-handed," Watt conjectured about the disappearance. "They pulled the post because they ran into a dead end." It was common knowledge in the intel community that the FBI was a fish out of water when it came to pursuing terrorists. Accustomed to nabbing criminals after crimes were committed, it wasn't in FBI genes to deal with offenses that hadn't yet occurred.

"I hope that's all it is," Hatkin said. And they tabled the issue for the time being.

So as they sit watching the boat weave its pattern back and forth over the water—with Warren on board and a Special Ops unit at Fort Belvoir ready to strike—for the first time in over a week they feel like they have a leg up. They are cautiously optimistic the crisis will be resolved with Howard Collyer exposed as a fraud.

The door clicks open. Both men look up at the same time. It's Williams and he didn't bother to knock. His expression hikes Watt's heart rate.

"Sir, a message just came in from NSA. You should both take a look."

Watt's fingers instantly open the secure link from the National Security Agency. "Holy shit—" he says in a small voice as he reads the communication, quickly swiveling the screen so Hatkin can see it.

The intercept of an FBI email from the fingerprint ID section at the Hoover Building to the Newark office confirms a match to the sets of prints lifted in Philadelphia and submitted earlier—the first belonging to Mehran Zarif, an Iranian engineering student at Rutgers, the second to Jamal Abdullah, born in Jeddah, Saudi Arabia in 1929. His resume is impressive, nuclear science degrees from universities in the U.S. followed by five years working at Oak Ridge and Los Alamos—1964 to 1969—before returning to work on the Saudi nuclear program.

"That's the same time period they were designing and building the Mk-15 nukes," Watt says.

"And the Iranian kid, the scuba diver, had recent contact with him."

"Let me see what NSA can find out about this Jamal character."

Watt grabs his stew and calls his contact at the National Security Agency. Twenty minutes later, they have the details.

"He landed at Heathrow last night. On a direct flight from Philadelphia. Then he flew on to Jeddah through Bahrain."

"Saudi nuclear engineer from Philadelphia, Iranian foreign student spending hours practicing in a pool—their prints in the same place. It's too hot, I can't sit on this any longer." Hatkin grabs his STU, "I need to speak to the boss," he says to the aide answering the phone in the office of the Secretary of Defense.

After a pause, Hatkin growls, "I don't care if he's in the crapper. I've got to see him immediately."

El-Khadr wishes he'd worn his sneaker, the sandal is giving him blisters as he shuttles back and forth from one room to another monitoring Collyer's progress, all the while keeping Mehran on his toes in the boathouse with new information. This is the most demanding time for Mehran. Though he's had lots of practice, in training they had isolated him for days at a time with nothing but the Koran.

Naguib can sense El-Khadr leaning over his shoulder checking his work. His fingers dart across the keyboard as he composes the message to the young jihadist on whose shoulders the success of their operation rests. "Digging up dahlias takes patience," he types. "Often they are not where you remember you planted them. So gently and carefully digging up the entire area is necessary to find the missing dahlias. Time and forbearance are critical qualities to dahlia seekers. Once your dahlias are secured in a safe place, they will provide you with lasting delight in the upcoming season."

Mehran will quickly understand the meaning of the message. A search for the bomb is underway. Self-control and perseverance are necessary for your success is almost at hand. In Philadelphia, Jamal had seen the posts narrowing down the location of the search so he had time to choose the correct collar and send it to the boathouse. By now Mehran will have walked up to the wall, carefully taken down the Mk-15 collar and placed it in the special rack constructed behind the cockpit. He is now a loaded gun, cocked and ready to fire.

"Perfect, send it to Mehran," El-Khadr instructs, turning and clomping back into the control room.

All eyes are on the master monitor. Arms folded, El-Khadr stands gazing up at the giant plasma screen.

Monitoring Collyer since he sailed out onto the bay, the satellite data from the Saudi media consortium refreshes every fifteen seconds, drawing a clear image of the boat and its wake as the craft crosshatches a section of the bay.

By layering images from different times, they know Collyer is searching a defined area, towing the equipment back and forth in one direction, then again in a perpendicular course so it is completely covered before moving on.

Two hours ago, Collyer's boat shifted to another section and from their progress, they appear to be a third of the way through. Though the boat is tiny on the immense screen, its size doesn't matter. When there is any indication they have found the bomb, a buoy dropped in the water, the boat pausing or doubling back to a location, GPS readings will automatically be recorded.

If weather conditions are right, El-Khadr will order the GPS coordinates relayed to Mehran in his boathouse. Mehran will enter the location into his finder so the autopilot can navigate the Donzi to the exact spot where the bomb lies, give or take four or five feet.

The rest is up to Mehran.

"Let me get this straight," the Secretary of Defense says to General Hatkin as he tosses his sweater onto a side table and starts for his desk. Still sweaty from the squash game, a damp vee darkens his polo. "The Director of Homeland Security scrambled that Coast Guard unit himself?"

Despite the fact that he was called out of a Sunday afternoon match, Secretary Kessel's seen his share of crises so he isn't rattled yet. But Hatkin knows it won't be long.

"Correct, Mr. Secretary, as soon as I found out he was involved I wanted to follow up with you."

"Go right ahead," he says, dropping into his desk chair. Tall, trim and dignified-looking even in his workout garb—once described as looking like John Lindsay in his heyday—Charlie Kessel is the consummate Pentagon insider, with ties to major military suppliers and a million connections on the Hill. Muckraking journalists have been taking potshots at Kessel for years but no one's gotten anything to stick. Of course he's a hero inside the Pentagon since he keeps the funds flowing for all the admirals' and generals' pet projects.

Fortunately he was enjoying a late afternoon match in the POAC when he took Hatkin's call and forgoing a shower, hustled over to his outside office in the E ring and now sits behind a desk that once belonged to General John J. Pershing, a towel draped around his neck, wearing matching Adidas shorts and shirt, listening as Hatkin updates him.

"So someone's trying to fabricate something out of that lost nukes business and pin it on us?" Kessel asks.

"It started out as amateur hour. A flake named Howard Collyer who used to work here abducted a former B-52 pilot we had interned in a VA hospital hoping he might know where his plane dropped a nuke."

"When? Almost forty years ago?"

"Thirty-nine to be exact. But then someone from CIA gets involved and starts helping Collyer, pulling strings for him behind the scenes. That's when we started taking the matter seriously."

"CIA sees the opportunity to pile on, take advantage of the situation to knock us down a couple rungs."

"Exactly. Then we start seeing indications that a terrorist group might be involved."

"Terrorists? Why? I don't get it." Kessel stands and walks to one of the windows, the ends of the towel grasped in his hands.

"They picked up the scent of a lost nuke."

"But the damn things are forty years old, rusting away in the muck somewhere. Anyone who thinks they could take advantage of one of those nukes has his head up his ass." Kessel wheels around and heads for his desk chair, flops down into it and kicks up his feet. "Whitey, if you weren't sitting here in my office on a Sunday afternoon looking white as a sheet, I'd say you've been smoking something."

"Today we received two new pieces of information. An Iranian student doing peculiar swimming exercises at the aquatic center at Rutgers had contact with a former nuclear engineer who worked on the design of that first generation of nukes."

"What are they planning to do—have the Iranian swim down and strap a grenade to it?"

"Who knows? Maybe dive down with some plastic explosive, C-4 or Semtex, and attach it. Some weapons from that time period had an early model detonator that could easily be set off. Yet this is still a wild guess."

"Where do they think this thing is?"

Watt realizes he's going to be tossing a grenade under his boss' desk with his answer, but he has no choice. "They are out on the Chesapeake searching for it as we speak."

Kessel freezes for a second, then his eyes bug out and he blurts, "On the fucking Chesapeake? Thirty miles from the goddamn Capitol and White House?"

"It's only a remote possibility, sir."

"Who's out there?"

"Howard Collyer—"

"The fruitcake who kidnapped the pilot?"

"Yes, sir, but we have one of our people on the boat. The officer in command is a former Seal. I know him personally."

Kessel's irate and unnerved, his emotions now firing on all cylinders. "Are you yanking my chain, Hatkin, or is this serious shit?"

Hatkin gears down, stays cool and collected, his voice conveying quiet confidence, "Once we're certain there isn't a bomb in the bay, and we think in all likelihood there isn't—"

"What makes Collyer so convinced?"

"The outside chance that this pilot may have credible information."

"I don't need to tell you what would happen if this ever got out—nuke in the Chesapeake—terrorists after it. The media would have a field day. And if there really is a weapon out there…Jesus H. Christ…" He doesn't finish his thought. The color is leaving Kessel's face, his eyes scan around anxiously, as if he's looking for a way out.

"Sir, we're in control. If they do find a nuke we'll be the first to know. We'll cordon it off and take care of it. And in the remote possibility that terrorists try to move in, we've got Special Ops forces out of Belvoir standing by. The minute they show we'll blow them out of the water."

Kessel blinks, runs his fingers through his hair and leans back in his chair. Now that the outcome sounds less threatening, his composure's returning.

Hatkin goes on, "And once we're sure the nuke's not down there, if the terrorists don't show we have a plan to draw them out."

"How the hell are you going to do that?"

"Once the search is complete and the commander is positive there's no nuke, he's going to stop the boat. If anyone's watching, we're betting it will be a signal they've located the weapon."

"You think they'll reveal themselves?"

"If they're out there and have their eye on that nuke, they'll mark its location and sooner or later they'll go after it. When they do our Special Ops unit will be waiting for them."

"And if this boat happens to get in the way, our only losses would be the captain and three crew members."

"Plus two civilians."

"Small price to pay."

"Our man on that boat, Commander Warren from the Coast Guard, reports they've almost finished the search and so far there's no bomb and no terrorists. He's sure Collyer isn't playing with a full deck and the whole thing is a hoax."

"How much longer before we know for certain?"

"A half hour, maybe forty-five minutes."

Kessel tents his fingers as his mind starts to freewheel. "You know if everything works out the way we hope, the president could really make some hay with this—preventing a terrorist attack so close to the nation's capital. He'd be a damn hero. Of course, we'd have to play down the lost bombs business."

"It's your prerogative to inform him, sir."

"I just might do that." Kessel checks his watch. "I know he has a state dinner tonight, Air Force One is flying him up from Kentucky later this afternoon. I do like the idea of telling the president his Defense Department has won another battle for him in the war on terror. Watch CIA take it in the ear again. Let me know the minute you've got it contained."

At the exact moment that Charlie Kessel swings his bare legs sideways, puts his sneakered feet up on his coffee table and sits back to savor the major coup DoD is about to pull off, the last person in the world the Secretary of Defense would expect beats him to the punch.

As the sun slowly sinks behind the rolling hills of the president's thoroughbred horse farm outside of Lexington, Abner Dickson and the President of the United States stand leaning on a four-board white fence gazing out at the dazzling vista. Oak Tree Farm has been in the president's family for three generations and now serves as the summer White House. Though the fields have gone brown, the golden glow of the sunset and the flock of purebreds quietly grazing off in the distance combine to create an atmosphere of serenity that contrasts ironically with the conversation.

Expecting to spend the afternoon shooting the breeze with his old friend Dickson, when Abner told him he had a much more critical matter of national security to discuss, the president sent Marine One to ferry Dickson to the farm.

As Dickson was concerned about security, the president suggested they take a walk. Two hundred yards down the drive, the president plants his elbows on the top board and turns to face his old friend.

"What's up, Abner? I don't think I've ever seen you looking so rattled."

"There is a possibility that terrorists might try to detonate a hydrogen bomb in the vicinity of the capital."

For the next ten minutes, except for the one strand of Kentucky bluegrass the president intently chews on, Dickson has his complete attention as he takes him through the events of the past ten days.

President Langan leans over the fence, lifting his foot to rest his boot on the lowest rung as he turns to his CIA director, a vengeful glint in his eyes. "You're telling me that the Department of Defense would endanger the nation's security to protect their programs?"

"They are so consumed with trying to cover up the lost nukes and disparage Collyer they overlooked the real danger."

"What kind of time frame are we talking about here?"

"They are close to completing the search." Dickson glances at his watch. "We'll have a better read within the hour."

"Is there anything more we need to do?"

"Nothing we're not doing already, Mr. President."

"I'm glad you bypassed channels and brought this to me, c'mon up to the house and we'll wait it out there."

After an hour on deck, Sharon went below and tried reading a book. Forty minutes later, she came up looking green and has been topside for most of time they've been out, bundled up against the slight but insistent breeze and drinking so much coffee she found herself having to make regular trips to the cramped space they called *the head*. Sharon joked that it should be called *the hatbox* instead but no one was in a humorous mood.

So biting her tongue as she had promised Straub, she whiled away the time feeding seagulls, gazing out at the horizon and watching Howie and Warren stare each other down when they weren't taking turns checking the readouts. Although the boat smells funky and looks shabby, inside it's crammed with high-tech equipment, radar and GPS screens, computers monitoring the towed magnetometer and sled and more blinking lights and beeping signals than Sharon's seen in operating rooms.

Sharon is on another trip to the head when she runs into Howie coming back up on deck. "This is the last section, isn't it?"

"We're going to go back over it again just to make sure," he tells her as they stand at the foot of the ladder in the narrow and low-ceilinged cabin.

"You discouraged?"

Howie shakes his head.

"Sort of shoots down your theory, doesn't it?"

"Only for the time being."

"What's that supposed to mean?" Sharon hisses. "Are we in for more of this crap? Look, I've been a good girl, kept my mouth shut. But I'm sick and tired of being kept in the dark."

"We won't be out much longer. Winn'll fill you in on everything when we get to shore."

All of a sudden, Sharon feels the boat lurching. She stumbles to keep her balance.

"What the hell's going on?" Howie mutters, reaching up to grab the top rung of the ladder and quickly swinging himself up on deck. Sharon's right behind him, raising her head through the hatch just in time to hear Howie yelling, "What in the shit are you doing? I told you not to stop."

"Engine's overheating, we're bending the needle," Warren shouts. "If we don't shut down we'll blow the engine."

"We have to keep the goddamned boat going, I told you that!" Howie shrieks at him.

A crewmember pops his head up through the cockpit hatch and calls to Warren, "It's the water intake, sir. One of the hoses has sprung a leak."

"We aren't going anywhere, Mr. Collyer," Warren tells Howie. "Without water in the engine we'll burn the damn thing up. You know that."

"Get it fixed as soon as possible, we've got to get this tub moving again." Off in the distance, Howie hears the faint *throp, throp, throp* of helicopter rotors over the horizon. He quickly raises his binoculars and scans the shoreline.

Sharon's right behind him. "What are you looking for?"

Howie doesn't answer. He turns and scrambles back down the ladder, Sharon close on his heels. He's on his cell phone, his back to her. She hears him telling Straub, "Warren stopped the boat. Claims the engine was overheating. Now what?"

Pause.

"Stay cool? Shit, Winn," Howie snorts, "we're sitting ducks out here."

El-Khadr looks up from his computer as he hears commotion from the control area. He hurries in to find the room on its feet, everyone staring up at the plasma screen, pointing and jabbering excitedly. "He stopped, the boat stopped," El-Khadr hears. "Collyer has located the bomb." The room is buzzing, El-Khadr has to raise his voice to be heard.

"Make sure the system has recorded the position," he commands the GPS specialist at the third console. "Double check we have those coordinates." For the past ten hours they have been patiently watching as Collyer searched the bay. This is the first time the boat has so much as slowed down.

He pulls his riding crop out and brings it smartly down on the table three times. He knows he has a split second to make a decision. He can order Naguib to signal Mehran or he can hold back and wait for a more propitious time. The next weather system is still hours away. *Will Mehran stay patient? And what about the Americans? What if they start sharing intelligence? Discover the connection between Jamal and Mehran? They are bumblers but not complete idiots.*

So many factors to be considered. So little time. All eyes in the room are on him as he paces back and forth, flicking his riding crop up and down, slicing and dicing the air around him.

"Straub just saw the boat stop, Mr. President," Dickson says as they stroll up between the white fences lining the lane toward the massive white house at the top of the hill. Jimmick's on the other end of the line, Straub's updating him from the underground operations room at Peary.

"They found the nuke?"

Putting the phone up to his ear again, he listens then shakes his head. "Apparently not, the boat has a mechanical problem."

"Is it possible someone could misinterpret the boat pulling up? Decide that's where the bomb is?" President Langan asks.

"Let me check." Dickson relays the question and waits as Jimmick consults with Straub. As the president and Dickson wait for an answer, the Secret Service detail respectfully hangs back a hundred feet, watching silently, aware something is going down. Casually dressed, the agents are packed into four Gators, behind them a convoy of Suburbans holds the president's top staff, their retinue of aides and as always, the officer carrying the ever-present Football. Marine One sits on the pad off in the field to the left with four armed sentries standing guard, ready to zip the president over to Lexington where Air Force One waits.

So odd to be out on a country lane with the sun an orange wafer hanging over the horizon, Dickson reflects, standing in the pastel light in the middle of the Kentucky horse country, *as we sweat out a severe threat to the country's security.*

Dickson holds his hand over the cell phone receiver as he relays Straub's answer, "So far they haven't seen anything, Mr. President. But they are watching carefully just in case."

"Good," the president says, looking relieved for the first time since Dickson brought him up to speed. He turns and starts up the walkway to the house, "I'm going up to change. But I won't take off until we have a resolution on this situation. C'mon in and make yourself at home, and let me know the minute you have anything."

"Yes, Mr. President."

Dickson stands aside as the contingent of Secret Service agents gun their Gators and roar off up the lane after the president, the Suburbans close behind.

So far, so good, Dickson thinks to himself. He is surprised when he looks down at his hand holding the cell phone. *It's trembling, shaking like a damn leaf.* Funny, he muses, *I didn't think I was that flustered.* But then it's not every day that you deal with the possibility of a hydrogen bomb somewhere on the bottom of the Chesapeake.

Hatkin and Watt are monitoring the two Black Hawks and three Apaches hovering in the lee of Tilghman Island ready to dart in at any sign of a craft heading to the spot where Warren stopped. "Hold off just out of sight," Hatkin radios the helo pilots. "We have to get a fix on them first."

Neither Watt nor Hatkin could bring himself to believe that a cell of terrorists could be lurking on the shoreline waiting to go after the nuke. But they were not taking any chances. Assured that they had come up empty-handed in their search for the nuke, they gave Warren the command to stop the boat. Warren had ordered a crewman to sneak into the engine room and close the water intake. When the needle on the temp gauge shot into the red ten seconds later, Warren shut down the motor and Hatkin ordered the helos airborne.

Each helicopter is relaying real-time color video with panoramic views of the bay onto the bank of screens arrayed in front of Hatkin and Watt. Monitoring their input in addition to the satellite feed and radar surveillance of the area from the AWACS 707 in the sky overhead, the two generals are poised to send in the helos the second a threatening blip appears.

On deck, Howie scans the horizon with his binoculars for anything coming from shore. Then he spins around to focus the glasses on the western coast. Sharon can only guess what's going on, Howie's close to frantic, Warren's rushing around trying to repair the boat. Howie keeps swinging his binocs around the bay, looking for what? *Vector Eleven? Terrorists?* Sharon watches as Warren drops down into a pushup position on the deck, his head hanging into the hatchway, talking with the crewman in the engine room working on the water line.

"That should do it," he says, hopping to his feet, wiping his hands on a rag as he heads for the wheel.

"Get this scow going, c'mon! It's been too damn long already," Howie shouts to him. Warren turns the key and the engine rumbles to life.

"The boat's underway again," Straub tells Dickson on the secure cell. "So far no one's appeared so we might be out of the woods—at least for the time being."

"I'll let the president know, hang on in case he has any questions," Dickson tells him. Straub waits on the line, realizing for the first time that Dickson has involved his close friend.

On the other end of the line he hears the instantly recognizable voice of the President of the United States: "Mr. Straub, this is President Langan. Director Dickson has briefed me on the entire operation. I want to tell you how much I appreciate the fine work you've done over the last ten days."

"Thank you, Mr. President, but it's not over."

"I'm sure you have a few things to tidy up, but at least we're no longer facing the threat of a hydrogen bomb in the Chesapeake Bay."

Don't bet your life on it, is what Straub wants to tell him. But he chooses his words more carefully, "Yes, Mr. President, we're most likely over that hurdle."

"And you can be assured Secretary Kessel's going to hear about this."

"I'm glad to know that," he says. But inside, he's smiling as he thinks, *Right now, you might be talking about giving Kessel an earful, but if I have anything to say about it you're soon going to be asking for his head.*

"No nuke, and so far no terrorists," Hatkin says, sitting back in his chair, clasping his hands behind his neck as he surveys the monitors and the plasma screen overhead.

"Nope, just another quiet Sunday evening on the Chesapeake," Watt adds, folding up the charts Warren had emailed him.

Hatkin orders him, "Radio the helos to sweep the shore for a final check before it gets dark. I'm going to call the SecDef." Hatkin grabs his stew. Kessel gave him a direct line to his E-ring office. The Secretary of Defense picks up without hesitation.

"Mr. Secretary, I'm glad to report that our mission has been successful. As I expected no bombs turned up and there was no sign of terrorist activity. Frankly, I think it's been a false alarm but we're overflying the coast now just to make sure. In a few minutes it will be dark and no one's going to be doing anything out there."

"Good work, General Hatkin. You've done a fine job in a demanding situation."

Hatkin basks in the praise as the SecDef lays it on thick. Going from having his entire program threatened and his career shot down in flames, he's now sitting tall in the saddle as Secretary Kessel tells him of his intent to take the president aside during the upcoming state dinner and tip him off about how DoD has avoided a potential terrorist attack.

"And I'm going mention your name to the president, General Hatkin."

"Thank you, Mr. Secretary."

Hatkin smiles—in his mind is the prospect of another medal or a presidential citation. It hasn't dawned on him that associating his name with this mission could bring a quick and ignominious end to a long and stellar career.

Naguib has never seen El-Khadr so beside himself. One minute he scrambles up to the monitor and stands gazing at it as if he's hoping it will make the decision for him—the next he's rushing back out to Naguib's workstation—in between he's bending over the console scanning the NOAA website with its detailed forecasts of East Coast weather conditions. Three times he began dictating a message to Mehran, each one starting with the GPS coordinates and ending with exhortations to glory. But every time he pulled up short, telling Naguib, "No, no, no, save it, don't send it yet," and hurrying back into the control room.

From the commotion he's hearing, Naguib guesses they saw the boat stop for a few minutes, lots of yelling and speculation, then the room went silent as El-Khadr scurried from station to station trying to make up his mind. Hearing the bedlam from the control room, Naguib instantly knows the boat must be underway again. He figures El-Khadr is torn between whether or not he should activate Mehran. Either way he will send him to his death. The only question is how many people he takes with him.

This time El-Khadr comes stomping out of the control room, hands up in the air, a mixture of frustration and consternation on his face, muttering incomprehensibly in Yemeni. But it's not hard to figure out that El-Khadr has scrubbed the mission.

"We will wait for a better time," he tells him, turning and stomping off toward his office, slamming the door behind him with such force it rattles the windowpanes.

At the same time El-Khadr is sitting in his office fuming at having to abort Mehran's mission, his nuclear weapons expert is relaxing in a comfortable chair a continent away, looking across his terrace at the tiled roofs and tapered minarets of the neighborhood where he grew up, listening to the commercial hubbub going on in the bustling streets three stories below and the bouzouki music coming from his next door neighbor's stereo.

It had been a long flight, three legs, Dulles to Heathrow, on to Bahrain and then to Jeddah. Fourteen hours, no picnic for a man his age but to Jamal Abdullah it stood out as the best flight he had ever taken. It wasn't the first-class food or the shapely Belgian stewardess with the bright smile who attentively helped him convert his seat into a bed so he could get a few winks between London and Saudi Arabia. It was the incredible good fortune that he was able to savor all the way across the Atlantic.

Jamal had indulged in a rare glass of Perrier-Jouet, and when Marie-Noel served the champagne and asked him what he was celebrating, he proudly told the stewardess, "My son has just picked out a ring for his new wife."

Allowing himself a second glass of champagne, Jamal reveled in the extraordinary set of circumstances. It was icing on the cake, the cherry on top of the sundae when El-Khadr had ordered Mehran to the upper Chesapeake. Everything had gone like clockwork. The collar was transferred to the boathouse team with plenty of time to spare, the moving crew broke down the gantries and moved them out, he turned off the lights, locked the door to his workshop and hopped a cab to the airport.

For all he cared the Americans could be tearing the place apart. They could run chemical tests to find explosives, bring in experts to examine his machinery. Even if they concluded that he was lathing hollow aluminum rings of various dimensions, and while they could speculate the rings were packed with C-4 and machined to fit the bombs' noses, that would be as far as they would get.

Only three people in the world knew the secret. And one of them is dead. That leaves two—himself and the co-pilot on the ill-fated mission.

Though the conversation had taken place over forty years ago, it as clear to him as if it happened yesterday. "They lost contact with the aircraft somewhere over New Jersey," the weapons control officer at Westover Air Force Base had informed Jamal over the phone. His name was Victor Obinson, Colonel Victor Obinson. By chance, Jamal had noticed his obit a couple years ago in the *Inquirer*. In the early days before Oak Ridge was fully staffed and funded, engineers often interfaced with their military counterparts at SAC bases. Though they had never met, they had spoken on the phone many times in the three years Obinson was stationed at Westover.

"The official word is that it went down offshore," Obinson went on to tell Jamal. "But for my money that's a smokescreen. I don't think anyone really knows for sure. Now security is clamped down so tight chances are you'll never hear about the incident again."

"So you need a replacement Mk-15 mod 0?" Jamal asked. In emergencies, weapons were often flown directly from Oak Ridge.

"Yes, with a nuclear capsule."

"The capsule also was lost? It was loaded into the bomb?"

The weapons control officer uttered the words Jamal would never forget. "We're lucky the damn thing didn't go off. Wherever the hell it is, let's just hope it rusts away quickly."

For almost forty years, the fact that the lost bomb was fully armed stayed buried under layers of evasion and confidentiality so even the top Pentagon officials aren't aware of the threat it poses. When Mehran had found Collyer's website and had alerted them to the opportunity, Jamal hadn't imagined there would be a connection between the location of Mehran's lost bombs and the one his associate had told him about so many years ago.

But Collyer has found the location of the weapon—the same one—the bomb with the nuclear capsule. Even if he learns the truth about the bomb from the pilot it will be too late to do anything about it. The Americans' horrible secret is no longer hidden away in the mud somewhere. Mehran is going to find it.

Jamal smiles as he sits looking out at the Jeddah skyline.

And when he does, what a shock it will be.

41

[KALORAMA, D.C., MONDAY MORNING]

Jimmick stands over the side of the bed gently shaking his wife's shoulder as he buttons his shirt. "Cassie, I need to ask you a question."

His wife opens one eye. Seeing the lights on in the bedroom, her husband half dressed with an unsettled expression on his face, she bolts upright. "What's going on?"

"Tell me everything you know about dahlias," Jimmick says to her as he quickly folds down his collar and buttons his cuffs. She's propped up, groggily rubbing her eyes, squinting at the clock on the bedside table.

"Dahlias? Are you out of your mind? It's not even six o'clock in the morning."

Jimmick tightens his tie. "Take me to school on the damn things, and don't leave out a detail. I made some coffee for you," Jimmick points at the mug on her bedside table.

Rathon had woken him up at 5:30 to tell him the news. The lab was halfway through the analysis of the swimmer's hard drive. "It's raw data, needs to be thoroughly analyzed," Rathon explained on the secure line. "I just glanced through it but one thing jumped out at me. Kid logged on to a couple websites five and six times a day. And you'd never guess what he was looking at."

Porn was Jimmick's instinctive reaction. But he was as surprised as Rathon was when he heard the answer.

"Flowers."

"You're shitting me."

"Dahlias, to be exact."

"How did you find it?"

"Stroke of luck—I tripped over it." Rathon didn't mention all the spadework he'd done to get into the website, logging on the first site, following the link to the second, then spending over an hour on its innocuous-looking homepage clicking on every square millimeter until a window popped open. He used a password-generating program FBI computer experts had written to come up with the magic combination of letters and numbers to unlock the file. Recently developed to bust child molesters on the web, the program ginned up random combinations until a series hit paydirt.

Inside Rathon had found a string of posts, all kinds of talk about flowers—dahlias specifically. The last post in the string said, *Meet with Cindy as soon as possible. She has a prize dahlia she wants to dig up.*

"Jesus," Jimmick said as Rathon read the intercepts to him over the phone. "I'm no cryptoanalyst but that sounds pretty damn ominous." That's when he decided to wake up his wife.

Hiked up on one elbow and rubbing the sleep out of her eyes, Cassie takes a sip of coffee. "I can't believe you're up at the break of day quizzing me about flowers."

"You're the big garden clubber. While I finish getting dressed, give me everything from A to Z."

"Why dahlias?"

"Sorry, that's as much as I can tell you."

Cassie sighs and takes a second sip. "Okay—dahlias are perennials, very colorful, lots of varieties. Some are as big as dinner plates. But unlike most bulbs like tulips that you leave in the ground over the winter, in this part of the country you need to dig dahlias up before the first frost."

"Sometime in November?"

"Often earlier—and store them so they will bloom again in the spring."

"So if you had a prize dahlia, you wouldn't dig it up now?"

"We've had at least three frosts already. It would be dead as a doornail."

"So someone who's talking about digging up a prize dahlia in December—"

Cassie completes the thought, "—doesn't know anything about flowers."

"Thanks, that's what I needed to know," Jimmick says, leaning down and giving his wife a kiss on the cheek, the phrase *she has a prize dahlia she wants to dig up ringing in his ears.*

As she listens to her husband dashing downstairs and out the door, Cassie reaches up to flick off the lights wondering how much more she can take. Friday her husband woke her at two in the morning and she was up again at some ungodly hour making him a fried egg sandwich after he was out most of the night. Last night he left at three. And now it's five something and she's fielding questions about flowers. The clock radio reads 5:43. As her head sinks back into the pillow, her eyes wide open, Cassie Jimmick stares blankly up at the cream-colored ceiling wondering what in the world is going down.

It's still dark as Jimmick tells the driver to pull up on the 10th Street side of the Hoover Building. Rathon steps out of the shadows at the corner of E wearing a topcoat and hat. He turns and quickly checks up and down the block.

Jimmick pays the driver and climbs out. "You certain no one else knows about this?" he asks as the cab drives off.

"If they did, I wouldn't have been able to get it out of the lab."

"Where is it?"

Rathon turns and nods around the corner at a row of leafless trees bordering the sidewalk. "I stuck it between the branches of the fifth one down. I didn't want anyone to see me handing it to you. Better go grab it before some overzealous security guard decides there's a bomb in it."

Jimmick is tempted to say, *There might be,* but he thinks better of it. "I can't thank you enough."

"I've got to go," Rathon says, looking over his shoulder. One thing to be seen surreptitiously meeting with a cabinet member at six in the morning, another to be giving him confidential FBI information.

"I'll let you know what happens."

"Hope I don't read it in the paper first. Good luck."

"Thanks," Jimmick says, turning the corner and heading down the block. He checks up and down the street before snatching the package out from between the limbs and tucking it under his arm. He quickly starts down E Street thinking he'll cut back over to Pennsylvania Avenue and grab another cab once he's sure no one is following him.

He remembers an espresso joint around here somewhere. As much as he could use a triple cappuccino, he knows he can't take the time. He's got to get his butt out to Langley. When he called Straub to tell him about the website Rathon had ferreted out, Straub had told him to get out to CIA headquarters as fast as possible, telling Jimmick he'd arrange for a CIA bird to fly him down to The Farm.

"And read me those posts the minute you get your hands on them," Straub told him before he hung up.

Listening to Jimmick on a speakerphone at Peary, Straub sits at a table with a team of CIA analysts gathered around.

"Digging up dahlias takes patience," Jimmick reads from the FBI file he's juggling in the back of the cab. "Often they are not where you remember you planted them. So gently and carefully digging up the entire area is necessary to find the missing tubers."

"What was the time on that post?"

""Yesterday afternoon, 3:54."

"The same time Howie was out on the bay looking for the bomb."

"Listen to this: 'Time and forbearance are critical qualities to dahlia seekers. Once your dahlias are brought to light and secured in a safe place, they will provide you with lasting delight in the upcoming season.'"

"If that isn't code for finding a lost nuke, I don't know what it is. Get down here and let's get to work on it."

"See you in twenty minutes."

"One more thing—"

"Yes, Winn."

"Transfer Warren. Make him believe the mission is winding down and you need him somewhere else."

"Actually I do."

"Good, get him the hell out of there."

"Vector Eleven got to him?"

"A crewman told Howie on the QT that Warren ordered him to shut a valve down. There was no mechanical malfunction. Warren scuttled the damn boat himself."

"Why would he do that?"

"So Vector Eleven could flush out the terrorists and ride in for the rescue."

"You're convinced this is the way it was supposed to go down?"

"I heard it from a good source."

"Who's that?"

Straub pauses to heighten the drama before he drops the bomb. "The president of the United States."

No answer on the other end of the line for a long while.

Then Straub says, "Pick up a *Washington Post* and read all about it."

Jimmick jumps out of the cab at the next paper box and is back in a flash in the backseat, a copy of that morning's *Washington Post* opened in front of him.

He can hardly believe his eyes.

42

[Camp Peary, outside of Williamsburg, Monday morning]

"Mr. Straub, it's your wife, she insists on talking to you."

Straub gives his aide a pained expression as if to ask, *Why in the hell can't you screen my calls? The last person I need to talk to is Barbara.*

"Sorry, sir," the aide shrugs. As hard as his aide had tried, Barbara Straub wasn't taking no for an answer. The woman was known for her short fuse. When he asked her to leave a message she practically blew out his eardrums.

Winn gets up, excusing himself. His team is minutes away from breaking the code. For the first time they will have a window on the terrorists' activities. He is on the verge of feeling elated—until he hears his wife's voice on the other end of the line. From her tone, he instantly knows what the call is about. Their daughter's been having marriage problems.

"Sandy swallowed a fistful of sleeping pills last night after a knock-down drag-out with Harold," she tells him.

"Is she okay?"

"They pumped her stomach in time."

"Where is she now?"

"Georgetown Hospital."

"What are the docs saying?"

"They are discharging her this afternoon but she's an emotional basket case. I'm afraid that deadbeat husband of hers has driven her off the deep end."

"Let's get her over the physical part then we'll deal with him."

Barbara launches into a tirade, she hasn't had any sleep and is coming unglued. Doesn't help that he's been keeping crazy hours. It takes Winn ten minutes to scrape her off the ceiling.

It isn't surprising given Barbara's emotional state that she demands that Winn come home immediately and when he demurs—claiming that he's in the midst of a crisis—she screams, "What could be more important than your daughter's welfare? You selfish son of a bitch!" and slams the phone down.

He's heading back into the operations room wondering how long it will take to repair the domestic damage when a second call comes in. It's Abner Dickson. He sounds flustered, almost panicky, his voice an octave higher than normal.

Straub holds the phone away from his ear as Dickson raves, "You sent me out with bogus information, Straub, the White House is coming down on me like a ton of bricks. They say there's no bomb, no terrorists, it was all a CIA plot to undercut the Pentagon."

"What the hell are you talking about? I read in the *Post* that the president gave Kessel a chewing-out at the dinner last night."

"That was yesterday, now they've turned the tables. And they are pointing the finger at you."

"Last night the president was patting me on the back."

"Things change fast in this town. Now you're on his shitlist and the whole White House staff is gunning for me."

"What do they want?"

Dickson sighs, "My job and your ass. They'd bring charges if they could. Bunch of pissed-off people. You'd better keep your head down."

"Give me two days, Abner."

"And then what?"

"I'll make you a hero. CIA is going to save the day and you will get the credit."

"Why should I believe you?"

"Trust me, Abner, this is going to bring the Pentagon down. And your name will be written in history."

Dickson has a vain streak a mile wide. Two more sentences and the conversation is over. Straub says a quick goodbye and hangs up, thinking, *I might have bought two days but I'll be lucky if I get a couple hours. When they turn the heat up on Dickson, the boy's going to melt fast.*

He picks up his cell phone to make two calls, the last ones he'll make on his CIA mobile.

After an initial testy exchange at the state dinner, Charlie Kessel was able to take the president aside and reassure him that the nation was never at risk. Kessel maintained it was inter-agency politics run amuck and promised a full briefing the next morning. When the president seemed unconvinced, Kessel leaned close and whispered, "No nuke and no terrorists—what does that tell you, Mr. President? Someone's crying wolf, that's all."

"I'll see you tomorrow morning, Charlie," the president said, shifting his attention to the NATO ambassador waiting to get his ear.

Twelve hours later, sitting in front of the president's huge oak desk, Kessel holds back until the stewards shuffle out with the coffee service before putting the last nail in the coffin. "I'm not saying Dickson was complicitous, Mr. President. Only that Straub and DHS sold him a bill of goods. Convinced him there was imminent danger and spooked him so he pushed the panic button."

"He had no hard evidence there were terrorists involved?"

"As you know, we get bits and pieces of information about terrorist activity on a regular basis. But there's been no consistent pattern."

"So no reason to be waving a red flag?"

"It's a case of Dickson losing his nerve. He should have pushed back at Straub and Jimmick, demanded more proof—instead he caved."

"Always knew he was in over his head. Who would you suggest to replace him?"

"There are a number of excellent candidates in my department. I'll get some resumes over by the end of the day." He doesn't know if General Whitey Hatkin would even consider taking the CIA job. But someone like Hatkin would insure the military's position as kingpin of intelligence.

"What should we do with Jimmick?" Kessel wants to tell him he should clean house over at DHS while he's at it. But no point in pushing his case too far, Kessel thinks. *If events keep playing out the way they are, the boss will come to that conclusion on his own.*

"Your call, Mr. President."

"And Straub and this whistleblower character—what's his name?"

"Collyer, Howard Collyer."

"We need to do something about them so this doesn't happen again."

"They scrubbed the search, we think they've given up."

"But they are a couple of loose cannons, we don't need people like that wandering around Washington. Do something about them."

"Yes, Mr. President." Kessel smiles confidently while thinking, *Easier said than done.*

Five minutes after Warren's SUV abruptly sped out of the boatyard, kicking up dust and chirping its tires as it roared off down the main road, seven stocky Coast Guard noncoms, armed and all business, come bursting into the office where Sharon, Howie and Risstup are having coffee. "We have orders to move you immediately, please come with us!" the lead guy announces, pointing to the Hummers pulled up in front of the building.

"Can you tell us where we're going?" Howie asks, as they herd him out the door.

"Sorry, sir, we need to get a move on," the officer snaps back at him. Howie helps Risstup out onto the landing, thinking back at the sound of his friend's voice in the brief phone call twenty minutes earlier, clipped and edgy, definitely out of character.

Winn had only told him two things. *This is the last time we'll use this cell.* And, *we're going to move you soon.* Howie was about to ask where when the line went dead.

These guys aren't wasting any time, Howie thinks as the men hustle them into the lead SUV, the rest of the group piling into remaining Hummers. The vehicle containing Risstup, Howie and Sharon tears out of the yard, the other SUVs following, heading down the narrow road leading into Fairhaven. Riding up on the bumper of a car poking along ahead of them, the driver leans on the horn until the car pulls over. The convoy speeds past, careening down the winding country road. Sharon bumps up against Howie as the truck swerves around a corner. Off to his left, Howie can see the bay through the trees. *We are heading south. Warren took off to the north. Probably headed back to base. Hope that's the last I see of him.*

"Do you have any idea of what's going on?" Sharon asks him.

"I'd say they are taking us to a more secure location."

"I bet that's what they tell people on their way to Guantanamo."

"Winn didn't have time to talk."

"Well, maybe I'll just ask."

"Go right ahead."

Sharon leans forward and says into the front seat, "Can you tell me where we're headed? I think we have a right to know."

The Coast Guardsman riding shotgun turns slowly, glares at her and says, "You'll see when we get there, ma'am."

Sharon slumps back in her seat, snorts and turns to stare out the window at the passing scenery.

Straub is relieved when he sees the line of Hummers wheeling into the lot of the St. Inigoes Coast Guard Station. After his conversation with Dickson, he hustled Jimmick out of the control room and they rushed out to the chopper that Jimmick had taken down from Langley. Straub was relieved when the helicopter lifted off and he watched the wooded terrain of Camp Peary dropping away beneath him.

En route to the station, Winn updated Jimmick on developments over the past six hours. Kessel must have convinced the president that Dickson was operating on flawed intelligence. What the president and the Pentagon are going to do now is anyone's guess. But it made sense to keep their heads down until they can figure out their next move.

Jimmick knew the perfect place, a Coast Guard rescue station on the northern shore of the Potomac less than an hour's drive from Fairhaven. He quickly made arrangements with the senior chief in charge, an enlisted man named Andersen, and in fifteen minutes they were landing in a field down the street.

A small concrete block building set back from the water, with two patrol boats moored on the inlet, it's a real hole in the wall, Straub decided as the chief showed them around the station—small office, radio room, head and galley—low profile and out in the sticks—just what he needed.

A half hour later, the convoy pulled up in front of the building.

"Hard-core crew, looks like Delta Force," he says to Jimmick as they watch the men in blue uniforms scrambling around helping their passengers out of the vehicles.

"What did you expect—Sea Scouts?" Jimmick reacts. Looking out the window at the three coming up the walk, he asks, "So the tall one's Collyer?"

"Yes, that's Howie and the other guy's the pilot."

"Who's the woman?"

"The nurse from the VA hospital."

"She's been tagging along this whole time?"

"This lady doesn't tag along. Wait until you meet her."

Straub watches out the window as the group approaches. He hasn't seen Howie since Friday at Tysons. *Looks fine but still is in need of a shave.*

Winn, Jimmick and Andersen stand to greet the new arrivals as they come in the front door. Straub gets a big hug and wide smile from Howie.

"Sure glad to see you, buddy," Howie says.

"Been a rough couple days, I know. I'd like to have you meet Lucien Jimmick, Secretary of Homeland Security," Straub says, introducing everyone. "Lucien has the Coast Guard in his department, so we're his guests. And this is Chief Andersen, he's our host."

Sharon shakes hands with Winn. "Thanks for the exciting ride."

"We didn't have any choice but to get you out of there fast."

"You want to tell us what's going on? I'm tired of being the only bump on a log around here."

"Certainly, please sit down," Straub says, pulling out a chair from a good-sized table. "I'll explain it all."

"Finally," she huffs.

Straub, Jimmick, Howie and Sharon take their places at the table, Risstup sits off to the side.

Howie starts off, "Time to get out of Dodge, huh?"

"It's getting hot up there, for sure," Straub says. "For a while we were on a roll. We had the president's ear. But the blowback on this has already begun. Kessel's turning the situation to his advantage. First thing he did was to pull the rug on Dickson. Told the president it's Langley's last gasp, a desperate attempt to save its ass."

"I bet I don't last the week," Jimmick adds.

"How did it all go to shit so fast?" Howie asks.

"The Secretary of Defense trumps the director of the CIA. All he has to do is tell the president a bigger lie."

"Is there any good news?" Sharon asks.

"As a matter of fact, yes," Jimmick says. "We had a metallurgist and a mechanical engineer inspect a bomb factory we found in Philly. Their best guess is that they were machining hollow stainless steel rings there. The engineer described them as hollow doughnuts—"

"No doubt packed with C-4," Howie adds.

"Most likely."

"How big?" Howie asks.

"Size of a large life preserver. Diameter of three to four feet."

Howie pauses before he says, "We're in more trouble than I thought."

"Why do you say that?"

"The nukes deployed at the time Risstup's plane went down were designed with the TNT charge at the top. Imagine a cylinder with a tip shaped like the nose of a bullet. The TNT was packed around the atomic charge inside that point."

"So what does the doughnut shape have to do with it?"

"The continuing question about these lost nukes is whether the TNT has been degraded to the point it's no longer explosive. That's what the Pentagon's position has been since they lost the damn things."

"I still don't get it."

"The engineer designed the ring as a primer for the TNT. The suicide diver slips it over the top of the nuke so it completely encircles the TNT. When the C-4 goes off, it's like a booster, evenly distributing the explosive charge of the C-4 around the TNT so no matter what condition it is in, detonation is guaranteed. It's absolutely brilliant."

"What if the nuke is upside down?'

"The nuke from Risstup's plane was a Mk-15. It was dropped with three parachutes so in all likelihood it would have gone into the water tail first. If it's down there, chances are it's upright."

"So that's what the swimmer was doing in the pool, practicing handling heavy objects under water?"

"Right, and in the tank he rehearsed placing the doughnut on the nose of the bomb."

"Doesn't he have to set off the C-4 somehow?"

"That's the easy part."

"Under water?"

Straub jumps in, "Done every day in routine underwater demolitions work. Small battery gives off an electrical charge and the C-4 is history. If this nuclear engineer designed a sophisticated booster, it would be like falling off a log for him to figure out how to ignite the C-4."

"How long do you figure it would take the suicide diver to put the ring on the bomb?" Jimmick asks.

"Only a matter of seconds, the swim coach at Rutgers clocked him at ten miles an hour," Straub answers. "That's why we have to flush him out. Since they have a foolproof way to detonate a nuke, they can take the technology and apply it anywhere. The hundreds of bombs lying around in bays, lakes and rivers all over Russia, Europe and the U.S. that we hoped were harmless, now every one is a possible threat. Just like the Jersey bomb, if they can find it chances are they can set it off."

"There's another aspect to consider," Howie adds. "Major Risstup confirmed that this Mk-15 has a nuclear capsule. It's like a firing pin. No safeties to keep it from going off. Slip that ring over the nose of the nuke and instantly you've got hundreds of times the devastation of the bombs we dropped on Japan."

"How much time do we have?"

"Since Warren was reassigned and we scrammed, they probably think we've given up the search. I'd say maybe a day or two if we're lucky."

"That's all we're going to need," Howie says.

"Why do you say that?" Straub asks. He's taken aback by Howie's sudden change in attitude. Before he went out on the Bay, he had been skittish and tense. Straub even wondered whether his friend would hold up. But now he's showing a new side, composed and confident. Straub wonders, *What does he know that we don't?*

"Anything new about the suicide diver?" Howie asks.

Jimmick answers, "The FBI cooked his computer, discovered a website the terrorists are using to communicate."

"And—?"

"We cracked the code a couple hours ago. We can tell their every move. They just have to make one."

"Is there a PC around here I can use?" Howie stands. Straub's brow furrows. *Now what kind of plan is Howie hatching?*

Straub points to Andersen, "I'm sure the chief will let you use his. You want to tell me what you're thinking?"

"First, I have to get on that computer."

El-Khadr stands looking over his meteorologist's shoulder console as the expert outlines the situation. Having watched the storm for the past twelve hours, El-Khadr likes what he sees, a front creeping up the coast, a large green mass now hovering over North Carolina with the potential to turn into a full-fledged system that will shift the prevailing winds.

Between the months of October and April, he knows conditions can occur spawning violent weather with eighty-mile-an-hour winds, heavy rain, thunder and lightning. El-Khadr rode out a Northeaster one fall when he lived in Baltimore. Shingles flew, cars were pummeled with hail while the rain blew sideways for hours.

The meteorologist points out the second component of the storm pattern, a cold front dropping down from Canada. "While the storm with all the moisture from the Gulf is coming up," he explains, "and the cold front is dropping down toward it, a major collision is possible. Though some systems slide out to sea, once in a while they work their way up the coast and wreak havoc."

"What's your guess on this one?"

"Highly unpredictable. Still too early to tell, but I don't see enough energy in the warm front to go up against it."

"If the storm heads out over the Atlantic, what direction will the wind rotation be?" El-Khadr asks.

His meteorologist's answer makes him smile. It might not turn out to be the perfect storm, but it will do. Instead of the mushroom cloud heading out to sea, it will be swept inland.

Pressure has been coming down from the mountains above Pakistan, the messages becoming more and more insistent. *All eyes are upon you. Seize the moment, strike when the iron is hot,* the posts read. If he had more evidence that the spot where Collyer's boat stopped was the site of the bomb, he wouldn't hesitate to pull the trigger. Everything is ready. Mehran already has the coordinates and is prepared to strike. Yet the storm leaves El-Khadr little choice. He cannot miss the opportunity to have the winds spread Mehran's gift far and wide, scattering deadly radiation as far west as the Ohio Valley, as far north as New York and New England.

"Send a post to Mehran. Tell him he must be patient. We are waiting for the helping hand of Allah to make dahlias bloom all over the Eastern Seaboard."

Straub, Jimmick and Howie sit in front of the PC reading through the posts on Jeffri's Garden. Sharon stands behind them, alternately horrified and spellbound by the wealth of information and detail in the messages over the past ten days. What she's reading confirms everything that Howie's been telling her.

Not only have the terrorists been shadowing every move they made, from Pittsburgh to Baltimore, they have prepared for every eventuality—deep water recovery or shallow water detonation—and seem to have teams everywhere ready to perform their mission.

All of a sudden a new post pops up.

"This is real time—exactly what they are saying to the suicide diver," Straub explains. "He's probably reading it right now."

You must be patient. We are waiting for the helping hand of Allah to make dahlias bloom all over the Eastern Seaboard.

"Dahlias are bombs?" Sharon asks.

"H-bombs, right," Jimmick confirms.

"You don't have to be a codebreaker to know what they are talking about," Howie says as they sit staring at the screen. "They are waiting for the weather to explode the bomb. Look—"

Howie clicks on a NOAA weather site displaying radar and satellite pictures of the Atlantic Coast and points to the front coming up the coast. "That's what they mean by dahlias blooming all over the Eastern Seaboard. Instead of the prevailing winds taking the radiation out to sea, this storm will sweep it inland and spread it everywhere across the northeast U.S."

Straub says, "They must be certain the bomb's where your boat stopped yesterday."

"If they aren't, they soon will be," Howie says, jumping up from his chair and turning to Jimmick. "Mr. Secretary, can you arrange for Chief Andersen to take me for a cruise?"

"It's his call. What do you say, Chief?"

The chief turns from the window overlooking the inlet in front of the station. "It's starting to get pretty nasty out there, sir."

Howie's on his feet, heading for the rack of foul-weather gear as he says, "Not half as nasty as it will be if we don't finish this guy off."

Mehran can feel the wind picking up, rattling the doors on the boathouse and whipping up the bay. He hears waves breaking on the pilings outside. Retracting the canvas floor, even inside the boathouse the water is stirred up and sloshing around. He checks the readings on his instruments, the winds are up to twelve knots from the southwest. The temperature is steady at 47° but the barometer is sinking fast. *The weather system is approaching, and so is my time.*

He picks up his cell phone and clicks on Jeffri's Garden. Since Saturday afternoon, he has been logging on every hour anticipating the signal. Catching a few winks, looking at the website again, off and on for almost eighty hours. He has double and triple-checked everything. The collar has been carefully loaded into the rack, gas tank filled to the brim, batteries fully charged, his tanks at the recommended PSI, the coordinates logged into his GPS. The posts advise him to be patient. So he sits quietly in his makeshift loft reading the Koran, listening to the gulls squawking overhead and the waves noisily slapping the boathouse walls.

Mehran turns to the wetsuit that he has carefully laid out on the towel next to him. Other mujahid go to their maker wearing ceremonial scarves and headcloths painstakingly woven by their wives or mothers. He smoothes out the wrinkles on his suit, straightening the straps and lining up the buckles, arranging the sleek rubber garment as neatly as he can, thinking, *Not only will my wetsuit enable me to accomplish my mission, it will also be what I will be wearing when I first meet Allah.*

As they slam through the heavy chop toward their destination, Howie clutches the piece of paper with the GPS coordinates on it deep in the pocket of his storm coat.

"Can you tell me where we're headed?" Andersen yells at him.

The increasing winds are whipping the water up into confused peaks, some three, some five feet. Despite Andersen's best efforts to keep the craft steady, it careens up and down the face of the waves, veering from port to starboard and back again. Howie crouches down behind the windshield to keep the flying spray out of his face, gripping the handrails tightly as the bow bangs up and down in the water.

"A location just off Holland Point," he shouts back at the chief.

"Sir, can you tell me what's there?"

"It's what's *not there* that's important."

"I'm afraid I don't understand."

"You don't have to, Chief, just skipper us to these coordinates," Howie says, taking the slip of paper out of his pocket and handing it to Andersen.

"Aye, aye, sir," he says as he keys the figures into his GPS monitor.

Whatever Warren's motivation was for stopping the boat, it is playing to their advantage. From the posts, he can tell the terrorists have decided that's where the bomb is. Now all Howie has to do is reinforce the location by dropping a buoy, wait for the winds to work themselves into a frenzy, then pray like hell they take the bait.

El-Khadr was relieved when Naguib rushed into his office and told him the news. He hurried into the control room and watched the boat that had earlier pulled out of the mouth of the Potomac. While the thickening weather obscured its progress, through breaks in the clouds El-Khadr could see the craft gradually swing to port and head north into the upper reaches of the Chesapeake. He had not seen any action from Collyer since yesterday when he completed the search and did not know what to make of it. *Is Collyer waiting for recovery equipment to begin salvaging the bomb?* he wondered. *When the weather calms down is he planning to dive the location and check its condition?*

So El-Khadr watched with mounting interest as the boat sailed up the bay, steering north-northeast in the general direction of the same spot where Collyer had stopped the day before.

One hour passes, the boat is halfway to the location. More people gather around the large screen on the wall showing the satellite feed, staring as the tiny object creeps northward.

El-Khadr quickly checks the weather. As his meteorologist predicted, this storm is starting to veer east, taking a right turn and heading out across the bay into the Atlantic. If the winds hold he will be in good shape. The minutes tick by. The control room is silent as everyone's eyes follow the boat's course.

El-Khadr sees the boat reduce speed. Clouds cover it for a long minute, then clear. His pulse jumps as the craft slows and pulls to a complete stop. He lets out an uncharacteristic whoop when he sees the readout of the GPS coordinates. Collyer has returned to the same location.

"He dropped a radio buoy. He has marked the spot," a man sitting at a screen reports to him.

"Double check the coordinates, it is time to give Mehran the order!" he shouts, turning and peglegging as fast as he can back to Naguib's station.

From the second he felt the winds die down, Howie knew he had set the perfect trap. Not only had he again marked the spot, but the weather was cooperating. If they are going to strike, they have only a narrow window of opportunity.

"Look," Andersen says, pointing up at the swirling clouds passing over them. "It's pushing the front out to sea. In a matter of hours, the bay will be back to being flat as glass."

Howie grabs the handset, "Get those Jayhawks airborne," he yells at Straub over the radio.

"We haven't seen any posts on the website," Straub responds.

"We can't afford to wait. The message could come at any time. You have to get in the air now. He could come out of nowhere," Howie shouts. "Get going!"

Friday, Jimmick had ordered three Jayhawks, the Coast Guard's version of the Black Hawk, positioned just inland from Herring Bay, parked in a field out of sight behind a line of cedars. The three white helos with their orange stripes sit prepared to take off at a moment's notice. Specially equipped with Hellfires, 7.62 caliber machine guns and .50 caliber Robar sniper rifles designed to blow the engines out of drug-running boats, they can be out over the bay in seconds ready to deal with anything.

Howie's relieved to hear Winn's voice saying, "They are starting their engines."

"Patch us into the pilot's frequency," he tells Winn. "I want to hear what's going on."

Howie has Andersen throttle back when the boat is a safe distance from where they dropped the buoy and they sit rocking up and down on the waves. Howie's scanning the coastline looking for any craft coming toward them.

"We're airborne, sir," Howie can hear one of the helo pilots reporting to Jimmick.

"Stand off a half mile from shore. Hang tight, we'll be talking to you," he hears Jimmick order the pilots. Straub had told Howie that he and Jimmick had run operations together in Florida, remembering that Winn had boasted, "You ought to see the two of us in command mode, we're right out of the movies."

"No posts, Howie, nothing's coming across the screen."

Howie can tell Winn's exasperated. If the Pentagon is watching, with their AWACS radar, even if they are not visible on satellite, they can easily pick up on the three blips hovering over Maryland farm country. A half hour later Vector Eleven would be swarming all over them. Howie creeps his binocs across the coastline.

"Still nothing, Howie, I'm going to set the helos back down."

"No, Winn, wait a minute."

"I'll give you thirty seconds. If anyone at the Building picks up these birds they'll be on us like flies to shit."

"Just give it a little more time, Winn."

Howie's counting to himself, *23, 24, 25, 26, 27*—when he hears the magic words, "Wait a minute, we have a post. *Time to dig up dahlias.*"

The second Mehran sees the words on the screen, he tosses the phone aside, scrambles into his wetsuit, hustles down the stairs, vaults on deck and slides into the cockpit. Flipping the switch to open the doors, he hits the button to lower the Donzi. As the doors crank open, the bay is revealed, the chop heavy but the visibility workable. Once in the water, Mehran knows that he can accomplish the mission blindfolded. He clicks on his GPS. The coordinates he entered earlier will take him to the precise spot.

As the Donzi settles into the water, Mehran turns the key and the engines rumble to life. The doors open fully, folding up into the roof and leaving the Chesapeake spread out before him.

He shoves the throttles forward and blasts out with its engines thundering. Above the roaring Donzi and windswept water, he's the only one who can hear the blood-curdling shriek that he leaves hanging in the air behind him.

Allahu akbar!

Straub shouts, "Who's on the target? Who is on the target? Has anyone picked it up?" He barks out the coordinates again to the Coast Guard helicopters. "Is anyone seeing it? C'mon, guys, give me some help here. I need it fast."

Howie's sweeping the coast, all of a sudden he can make out the pinpoint profile of a boat silhouetted against the shoreline. "Check out the object coming off Holland Point at ninety degrees," Howie yells into the handset.

Static, then a click and the sound of an unfamiliar voice buzzes over the radio, "This is Lieutenant Waite in Helo Three. I have the target." Waite's circling his Jayhawk over the fastboat banging through the chop a hundred yards below him. "I'm perched right off his stern. I don't think he has a visual on us yet. Standing by for orders." Waite is low enough to see a man in a wetsuit standing at the wheel of the speedboat crashing hell bent for leather across the bay.

Jimmick lets out a sigh of relief, "Okay, Lieutenant Waite. I want to make sure the target notices you. Come around on his bow and fly up his nostrils. Let him know you're the boss and he's going exactly where you tell him."

Even though they are directly overhead, Mehran can't hear the throbbing sound of the helo's engines over the roar of his own and the slamming of the Donzi's hull as he pounds across the bay. All his attention is focused on his GPS screen, *six-tenths of a mile, five-tenths, four-tenths, three, two,* until he reaches his target.

Waite sweeps his Jayhawk wide, swinging around the boat and

dropping down to pull up fifty feet off its bow and twenty feet in the air, the helo's rotor wash splashing over the deck and frothing up the waves, forcing the driver to shield his face with his arms from the spray flying at him from all sides.

Mehran doesn't see the source of the spray until the helicopter settles down in front of him. A gigantic orange-and-white insect hovering over the water twenty feet overhead with its turbines whining, its bulbous fuselage suspended off his bow, rotors slashing the air overhead, he's staring right into the dark barrels of its machine guns and two banks of missiles.

Mehran jams the throttles wide open and races into the nose of the chopper, daring the pilot to take him out.

Waite gooses his twin GE turbines, backing off the onrushing Donzi but still holding position. "I'm right in his face, sir," Waite reports. "But this boy's on a mission. He's not stopping at anything."

"Put a volley into his stern, take out his engines," Jimmick orders.

"Aye, aye, sir." Waite quickly darts back alongside the boat and lines up the stern in the crosshairs of his sniper rifle. Squeezing off three quick shots, he watches as the slugs stitch across the boat's butt. Waite smiles as the sleek, glassed tail shatters. *Donzis aren't engineered to take a bunch of .50 cal slugs in the ass,* the Coast Guard lieutenant thinks as he watches flames blaze up from the back of the boat followed by a soaring cloud of black smoke.

Waite hangs off twenty feet to his starboard, fifty feet in the air, keeping an eye on the boat's skipper.

"Wherever he was headed, he's not going there anymore. Our target's dead in the water," Waite reports as he hovers over the crippled Donzi.

Mehran senses his stern settling under the waves. He turns the key, flicking it back and forth frantically. *No power. Nothing.* He feels acrid smoke billowing around him, the flames from the back surging forward, licking up into the air. Reaching around and feeling for the collar, he grabs it out of the rack, making sure the remote is clipped to his wetsuit.

The helicopter hangs above him, its rotor wash fanning the flames. *If I can just get into the water,* he thinks as he lifts the heavy collar and slips it over his head.

"Keep an eye on him, Waite," Jimmick orders, "we don't want him getting out of the damn boat. Take him out if you have to."

"I'm starting to lose him now." Waite slants his helo so the rotors sweep the swirling gray clouds off the cockpit.

"You can't let him get into the fucking water! If he gets in the water we're goners," Jimmick screams. "Take him out! Take him the hell out!"

Waite drops down to not more than ten feet above the blazing Donzi and scans the cabin area, looking for any sign of the diver.

"Do you see him? Do you have him?" Jimmick bellows.

"He must have slipped overboard."

"Lieutenant Waite, do you see a stainless ring anywhere on the boat?"

"No, sir."

"How about a set of monofins, big flippers?"

"Negative, sir. But his tanks are on board so he's not going far. I'll blow him away the second he surfaces."

Waite hears the radio go silent. No one on the other end is saying a thing.

At that instant, Straub, Jimmick and Howie are sharing a single thought. *Have we let the unimaginable happen?* Right this second is a suicide diver streaking somewhere underneath the waves with a collar packed with C-4 to slip over the nose of a nuke and detonate in a millisecond?

"Howie, is it possible they know where the bomb is?" Straub screams over the radio. "Howie? Howie? Are you there?"

Howie hears his friend's frantic voice. "I don't know, I don't know, I'm trying to figure out what could have gone wrong." Howie was certain he had found the bomb, sailed right over another location five miles away when he was in the workboat. No one else had seen it, Sharon was feeding seagulls, Waite was down below. Scribbling down the coordinates, he had tucked the piece of paper in his pocket. Howie Collyer's secret.

But was he wrong? Had he read the magnetometer incorrectly? Has he been the victim of a cruel joke? Thinking he was laying a trap for them while all along he was leading them to the nuke?

"He's in the goddamn water, Howie. If the nuke's down there it's only a matter of minutes."

"Is there anything we can do?" Jimmick asks.

"Pray," is the only thing Winston Straub can think of saying.

The control room has fallen silent as thirty pairs of eyes search the monitors hoping for a sign. Groans of shock and dismay went up from the group when they saw the first explosion but El-Khadr screamed for them to shut up.

"Much too small to be the collar exploding, Mehran can still be in the water going for the bomb!" he shouts, waving his arms for them to be still. Through the clouds over the bay, he can see tiny dots circling the smoke from Mehran's boat. *The Americans are all over him but if they are lucky and Allah is watching, Mehran could be bearing down on the bomb.*

Twenty feet below the surface, Mehran silently glides toward his rendezvous, the collar tucked in tight to his body, his powerful legs silently and gracefully sweeping the monofin up and down as they race him through the water. He quickly checks the GPS readout on his wrist receiver. *Less than forty yards remaining.* His body is behaving beautifully, just as it was trained, his lungs not yet screaming for air, his mind clear and focused on the prize ahead.

He ducks his head so the water at the bottom of his mask sloshes up and clears the glass. Though the water is murky, through the gloomy haze faint outlines of an object come into focus. Long and cylindrical, it sits askew in the sand, as if it had settled in at an angle. He struggles to keep his heart rate under control.

"Lieutenant Waite, do you see him? Do you see anything?" Jimmick shouts into his handset.

"No, sir. Nothing yet," Waite reports as he circles a hundred feet off the water, the two other helos on his port and starboard. "How long can this character stay under water? It's been seven minutes already. He can't last much longer."

Neither can I, Straub thinks, checking his wristwatch again.

Everyone stands motionless in the control room in Indonesia. Eyes riveted on the monitors overhead, staring at the satellite feed showing clouds drifting over the bay, every once in a while parting to reveal the drama going on hundreds of miles below. Each person praying that

Mehran at any moment will sight the steel nose cone and gently slide the collar down. When it clicks into place it will change the world forever.

At first he thinks barnacles have grown over the bomb. His fingers scratch at the rough surface, seeking metal, knowing that the collar has to have contact. He has seconds of air left, he takes his knife and gashes at the strange material but it billows into a cloud. He stabs at it again but he is running out of air. His chest is beginning to cramp, the muscles around his lungs vainly grabbing for oxygen. One more slash with his knife reveals the reality. It is bark he has been scraping at—tree bark. Flotsam off some barge, stuck in the sand at an odd angle.

Mehran's training tells him that in five seconds he will black out, the collar will drift down to the bottom and his body will slowly ascend. Breaking the surface, it will bob helplessly on the waves, a perfect target for the American helicopters.

I will not let that happen. They will pay, at least in a small way. He kicks quickly to the surface, slipping his body inside the ring. If he plans it right, his first breath of air will be his last and he will go to greet Allah having taken an enemy helicopter along with him. He pushes upward, the steel bird hanging high above the water. Taking the remote in his hand, he puts his finger on the trigger as his head breaks the surface.

"I have him," Waite shouts over the radio. "He's surfacing off to my port, fifty yards ahead. He's got a life preserver and he's waving at us like he wants to be rescued."

Howie's mind stumbles over the helo pilot's words. He yells to Jimmick and Straub, "Tell him that's a goddamn bomb, not a life preserver. Get him the hell away from there!"

Jimmick immediately responds, yelling into his radio, "Lieutenant Waite, get your ass out of there pronto, do you understand? He's going to blow himself sky high."

Mehran's hand clenches the detonator, he says a silent prayer and presses the button.

Waite swings the Jayhawk up and away just as a sharp, rattling explosion booms over the water and a second later a three-hundred-foot orange fireball spurts up from the spot where the swimmer used to be.

"Thanks for the heads up, guys," Waite says to the crowd back in the boathouse as he hovers above the water watching the greasy column of fire and smoke blaze up into the swirling gray sky. "You sure were right about that life preserver."

In the instant before the collar exploded and the terrorist went to Allah, Howie Collyer's life had flashed in front of his eyes. He would be held responsible for alerting the terrorists to the bomb's existence and for leading them to it. His only consolation would be that, having been less than a mile away, he would be instantly vaporized.

"You okay, sir? Andersen asks him as the two stand at the helm watching the smoke coil into the sky.

"Let's get back to the station," Collyer tells him, barely able to get the words out.

El-Khadr cannot believe his eyes. He watched with horror as the blip on the screen chased Mehran across the bay, hung over him for what seemed like an hour, and then there was a cloud of smoke. For a split second, El-Khadr thought he was seeing the blossoming of a nuclear detonation. But when he saw the explosion fizzle and the blip start back toward shore, he knew the worst had happened.

A pall of gloom blankets the room. The images persist on the glowing screens overhead and the computer consoles throughout the room drone on but everyone in control knows the mission is over. Heads slowly swivel toward him.

El-Khadr stares at them blankly. There is nothing to say. He turns and slowly walks toward the door.

Naguib is at his console. El-Khadr's eyes are on the floor as he shuffles into his room. His leader is stooped and bent over, his wooden leg trailing behind as he crosses in front of him, no longer making the crisp rat-tat-tat, instead making a plaintive, scratching sound as it drags along the floor.

El-Khadr closes the door behind him. He stands leaning against it, staring vacantly into his office. It is over for him. There is nothing more he can do. When they hear the news in the mountains, maybe they will decide to go back to the plan to infiltrate Oak Ridge or Los Alamos. Perhaps they will choose a nuclear power plant.

But two things he is certain of. They will never go back to the lost bombs. The Great Satan has been awakened to the threat they present. And whatever operation the group chooses in the future, he is certain they will assign a new leader.

He shambles behind his desk, slowly opens a drawer and takes out a key. Inserting it into the lock on a credenza behind him, he leans down, opens the door and takes out a remote control with a black toggle switch and a chrome antenna. Three years ago, before his people had moved in, he had carefully placed the ten plastic charges at key points around the perimeter and five incendiary charges up the center line so that when he lifts the toggle and presses the red button, the interior will explode upward and the walls will collapse inward, the intense firestorm broiling everyone inside to a crisp.

As he slides the toggle forward and pushes the button, El-Khadr knows one thing for certain—his last operation will be a total success.

The hallways smell different is an expression Pentagon insiders use to describe times of momentous change in the Building.

The saying could not have been more apt or fitting as the two grim-faced generals stride quickly down the E ring corridor toward the SecDef's office. People pause to watch since you don't see two- and three-star generals quick timing through the hallways.

Whitey Hatkin had never heard Kessel sound so livid. If it was true that a Coast Guard helo had taken out a terrorist racing to detonate a nuke in the upper part of the Chesapeake Bay, he and Watt would pay for it with their careers.

And that's if they were lucky. Court martials were a possibility and could even have them facing time in Leavenworth.

Both are fully aware of what awaits them in the SecDef's office. Kessel is going into damage control. And the first thing he would do is offer up the heads of a couple flag officers.

Their worst suspicions are confirmed when they round the corner and see four armed MPs standing outside the entrance to the Secretary of Defense's suite.

43

[St. Inigoes Coast Guard Station, Monday noon]

Despite the front surging out to sea, it was still blustery on the Chesapeake, *blowing like stink* as sailors like to say, so Howie didn't expect a welcoming committee at the dock to greet him.

But he does look forward to triumphant smiles and celebration when he opens the front door. Instead, he sees long faces, gloomy looks, everyone sitting silently.

"Someone want to tell me what's going on?"

Straub slowly gets up and turns to face him. "Risstup collapsed. Sharon is at the hospital with him."

"What's the best guess?"

"Cerebral hemorrhage. One minute he was with us, the next he was pitched face first on the table with his eyes rolled up into his head. Still had his vital signs but nothing much else. I'm sorry, Howie."

"To get this far and then—"

"It's a tragedy. And I don't mean just for him." Straub gets up and walks to a window, staring out at the neatly tended front yard of the station.

"What do you mean?"

"We don't have a leg to stand on any longer."

"I don't get it."

"Look, we took care of a terrorist and we'll get credit for that, but with Risstup gone we don't have any evidence there ever was a bomb."

Hearing a car pulling up, Howie quickly walks to the window and looks out. Sharon slowly climbs out of a sedan marked with a Coast Guard insignia. She has a handkerchief in her hand, her eyes are red. She dabs at her cheeks.

Howie starts for the door, opens it, then stops and without looking back into the room, says, "Yes, we do."

"What are you talking about?" Straub asks.

"Get me in to see the president," is all Howie says before he hurries out to meet Sharon. As she comes down the walk, she lets out a wail and collapses into Howie's open arms.

44

[The White House, Tuesday afternoon]

"The president wants me to convey his appreciation for uncovering the terrorist plot. Without the help of experienced and dedicated people like you, we would not be winning the war on terror," the president's chief of staff says, leaning over his desk and smiling at the group standing in front of him.

"Cut the crap, Donalson," Howie sneers. "We didn't come here to get a pat on the back from his flunky, we came to see the president."

"The president deeply regrets that he could not fit you in. But as you can understand, he has a crowded schedule these days."

"Have it your way," Howie nods. He slowly gets up and walks to the door as if he's going to leave. He turns back with his hand on the doorknob, saying over his shoulder, "Then he can read about it in *The New York Times*."

Reuven Donalson looks like just he pulled his finger out of a light socket. "I beg your pardon," he sputters.

Howie walks back toward Donalson. "I pitched the story of these lost nukes to the *Times* two years ago. Back then they didn't want to touch it. But now they might be interested."

Donalson is deferential to the point of being insulting. "You'll have to help me understand, Mr. Collyer. Has anything changed?"

Howie looks him in the eye, "I know where a hydrogen bomb is."

Donalson smiles dismissively, "Mr. Collyer, I'm afraid that's old news."

"Really? How about if I show you a picture?" Howie slips a manila folder out of coat pocket.

Donalson's eyes bug out, his gaze riveted on the yellow envelope held in Howie's hand. "You don't have photographs—" he stammers.

"Full color. Sure candidates for a Pulitzer," he says, holding the envelope out to Donalson. He reaches for it tentatively. Just as his hand touches it, Howie snatches it back.

"On second thought, I think we should wait for the president," Howie says, slipping the folder back into his pocket. "These photographs might be for his eyes only. Now would you get him?"

"Just a minute, please," Donalson says, suddenly displaying a new attitude.

Howie smiles at Straub and Sharon as the president's chief of staff scurries out.

"Amazing what a good photograph can do," Howie says to Winn. Though the water was cloudy, there was no mistaking the contours of the twelve-foot-long object jutting out of the floor of the bay. And any expert could confirm that the photograph was of a Mk-15 mod 0.

Chief Andersen is an expert scuba diver. It had taken longer to sail up to Herring Bay and back than to locate the bomb and snap the photos. The first time he surfaced, Andersen shook his head and said in amazement, "Dammit if there isn't a bomb down there. I wouldn't have ever believed it unless I'd seen it for myself."

When he first saw the telltale signature on the Coast Guard workboat's magnetometer, Howie had not been able to believe it either. Not in the area it was supposed to be, it was a good two miles from where he'd charted its location. Fortunately he was at the helm when the boat passed over it, twenty minutes before Warren sabotaged the water line. Fortunately Winn had prepped him to ignore it. So except for Howie, no one else knew its location. The GPS coordinates had stayed tucked away—until he needed them.

"As the saying goes, a picture is worth a thousand words," Straub says.

All turn at the sound of a door opening. "Ms. Thorsen, Mr. Straub, Mr. Collyer," Donalson announces. "The president will see you now."

45

[Arlington National Cemetery, Friday]

Despite the presence of the President of the United States, a host of dignitaries, and the din of the horde of photographers and reporters hovering behind the barricades, the ceremony is quiet and dignified. The morning is sunny but cold, the leafless trees swaying overhead in the light breeze and the endless rows of white gravestones adding to the somber atmosphere.

A cousin named Caroline was the only living Risstup able to travel. Caroline Risstup couldn't stop talking about the flight on Air Force One from San Diego to Andrews. "It's so roomy and comfortable. The food is a far cry from airline food. Rice pudding is my favorite. And it's so nice of the president to fly me home," the blue-haired octogenarian would prattle on to anyone who would listen.

Howie's entire family came up from Charlottesville, Sylvie, Grace, Bridey and Donald, baby Jasmine of course and Jock and Richie, Howie's two irrepressible grandsons. Due to the boys' fascination with the caisson and riderless horse, the resplendent royal and navy uniforms of the U.S Army Ceremonial band and guns carried by the honor guard, they are on their best behavior and not a peep's been heard from them.

Sharon declined the president's offer to fly her sister and brother in from Hawaii, telling him, "Thank you, but no one knew Major Risstup except for myself."

The president had bent over backward to make sure Risstup received every honor and courtesy possible. He granted an exception so he could be honored with a caparisoned horse with one boot facing to the rear, a venerated tradition reserved for higher ranks. Back pay and the funds accumulated in his pension fund would be awarded to his cousin

Caroline, a presidential citation would be placed in his permanent record and a Silver Star was pinned on the uniform he was to be buried in.

While the chaplain performs the service, Howie scans the faces solemnly gazing down at the flag-draped coffin. Though everyone is reflective and respectful, looking behind their expressions Howie can easily read other emotions. The color had come back into Sylvie's face and she looked glamorous in the new suit she had purchased for the occasion. She couldn't stop gushing about how proud she was of Howie. Which after the past two weeks was music to Howie's ears.

Next to Sylvie stood Winston Straub, the newly appointed deputy director of the CIA. Though he was wearing an understated dark blue suit and a muted tie, Winn looked like he'd swallowed a canary. And he might as well have.

While Abner Dickson had received accolades from the president for spearheading an undercover operation against terrorists and had been lionized in the press and media, the understanding was he would step aside at the beginning of the year citing health problems and the president would name his new deputy to succeed him.

Winn Straub had received Langan's word that civilian control over intelligence would be restored and the Pentagon's role would be dramatically reduced. Kessel had already been fired, unceremoniously escorted from his suite of offices by the president's chief of staff, and rumors around the Beltway were that the other shoe was going to drop—DIA and NSA would soon be transferred to CIA. Winn's wife Barbara stands at his side, looking snootier than ever having discovered that as a result of her husband's recent heroic exploits, they were even more in demand on the Washington social scene.

Lucien Jimmick and his wife Cassie stand at the foot of the grave, reserved but gratified smiles on their faces. The president had been generous to DHS, promising Jimmick increased funding for the Coast Guard, instant access to the Oval Office and a right-out-of-the-box Gulfstream so his wife wouldn't miss her garden club meetings in Miami. The president offered Lucien the plane along with a bunch of other goodies for staying on for another two years.

President Langan had been endlessly accommodating for good reason—his own self-interest. The last thing he wanted was for his administration to go down in history as having nearly allowed terrorists to detonate a bomb thirty miles from the Capitol. So with a few revisions, the story of how a few brave Americans conducted an undercover operation with the support of CIA and DHS to disrupt a terrorist plot involving nuclear weapons was released at an elaborate press conference the day before.

President Langan pinned Medals of Freedom on the lapels of Winn Straub, Lucien Jimmick, Abner Dickson, Sharon Thorsen and Howie Collyer and praised them to the skies for their bravery and devotion to their country.

Of course, the story the president told had undergone extensive edits—there had never actually been a live nuke in the Chesapeake—the sanitized version was that a dud had been planted to deceive the terrorists. No point in unnecessarily alarming the nation. But as the president stated in his press conference, the incident dramatized the threat that weapons posed and he proposed mounting an international effort to locate and recover all bombs lost by the nuclear powers over the past forty years.

Sharon winces at the honor guard's rifle volley resounding across the rolling fields of Arlington. Howie smiles, catching her eye. She's planning to do graduate work in nursing and is hoping to get into a program at UVa. Sylvie's given her a standing invitation for dinner so at least Howie will get to see her once in a while.

As the mournful sound of taps echoes around the cemetery, the tears again start to stream down Sharon's cheeks. So many times she'd talked about looking forward to filling in the rest of the blanks in Mark Risstup's memory, promised to take him back to Arcata, locate any old Air Force buddies who might still be alive, find out how he finally made it to Pittsburgh. Now that was not to be. Sharon's not the only one crying. Howie's eyes are brimming too.

As they slowly fold the flag and the officer in command presents it to Risstup's cousin, Howie thinks back to his second meeting in the Oval Office. He went in expecting he would have to fall on his sword. But he was delighted to hear that ridding the nation and world of the threat of unrecovered nukes had become the president's priority. "You gave us a huge wake-up call, Mr. Collyer, a warning that no one in this administration is going to ignore." And when the president asked him what a grateful nation could do for him, Howie shrugged and said, "Frankly, Mr. President, I'd just like a little peace and quiet."

At the end of the ceremony, the president takes the time to walk around and shake hands and say a quick word to the attendees before the Secret Service whisks him off, leaving the mob of reporters swarming around the remaining dignitaries.

Howie's able to avoid the crush, hustling Sylvie and Sharon over the grass to their waiting limousine while Jimmick, Dickson and Straub stand in front of the crowd of reporters fielding questions.

"I'm going to take the two smartest and most beautiful women in the world to the fanciest restaurant in Georgetown and we're going to enjoy a lavish lunch," Howie had announced as they drove into Arlington before the service. Both were tickled and eagerly accepted. Though invited, the rest of the family was eager to get back to Charlottesville. As he helps the ladies into the backseat, just about to lean down to climb in behind them, he's surprised to hear a voice calling his name.

"Mr. Collyer! Mr. Collyer!" He looks down the roadway and sees a familiar face jogging toward him waving. An up-and-coming investigative reporter, Jason Foote was recently named Washington bureau chief of the *Times.* Howie smiles, thinking, *Two weeks ago, this boy wouldn't have given me the time of day. Now he's salivating to get an interview.*

"Mr. Collyer, I'd like to talk to you if you have a minute," he says, rushing up to the open door.

"I'm sorry, it's not really a good time, Mr. Foote."

"I've heard you were the point person on foiling the terrorist plot."

"Where in the world did you get that?"

"Word is you were the mastermind."

Howie shakes his head and says, "Hate to disappoint you but I only played a minor role." He nods in the direction of the three men, Straub, Jimmick and Dickson, who are facing the cameras. "Those guys deserve all the credit."

"I want to hear your point of view on the nuclear weapons recovery operation. I'd like to do an in-depth interview with you soon."

"Be glad to."

"When's a good time?"

"Let's say next December."

"But that's a year from now—"

"I've got a lot of bushhogging to do down on the farm, all kinds of stuff I've neglected. See you next year, Mr. Foote," Howie says, quickly ducking into his car and pulling the door shut.

Jason Foote watches the sleek black limousine slowly pulling down the roadway toward the exit to Arlington National, wending its way through the rolling fields of stark white gravestones. He has a nose for a story. And he senses one here. Way beyond the barebones version the president is peddling in the press—a whistleblower, a VA nurse, an elderly B-52 pilot, a lost H-bomb, Collyer's best buddy who's a top dog at CIA, interagency rivalry, al Qaeda—all the ingredients of a great tale begin to come together in the reporter's mind.

As the limo tops a rise in the distance and disappears over the hill, Jason Foote decides, *It could be juicy, real juicy, might even be a book in it.*

THE END